A SHOP GIRL GETS THE VOTE

1911, Bath. Banished from her ancestral home, passionate suffrage campaigner Esther Stanbury works as a window dresser in Pennington's Department Store. She has hopes for women's progression and will do anything to help secure the vote.

Owner of the prestigious Phoenix Hotel, Lawrence Culford has what most would view as a successful life. But Lawrence is harbouring shame, resentment and an anger that threatens his future happiness.

When Esther and Lawrence meet, their mutual understanding of life's challenges unites them, and they are drawn to the possibility of a love that neither thought existed.

With the Coronation of King-Emperor George V looming, the atmosphere in Bath is building to fever pitch, as is the suffragists' determination to secure the vote. Will Esther's rebellious nature lead her to ruin or can Esther and Lawrence overcome their pasts?

SPECIAL MESSAGE TO READERS

THE ULVERSCROFT FOUNDATION
(registered UK charity number 264873)
was established in 1972 to provide funds for research, diagnosis and treatment of eye diseases. Examples of major projects funded by the Ulverscroft Foundation are:-

- The Children's Eye Unit at Moorfelds Eye Hospital, London
- The Ulverscroft Children's Eye Unit at Great Ormond Street Hospital for Sick Children
- Funding research into eye diseases and treatment at the Department of Ophthalmology, University of Leicester
- The Ulverscroft Vision Research Group, Institute of Child Health
- Operating theatres at the Western Ophthalmic Hospital, London
- The Chair of Ophthalmology at the Royal Australian College of Ophthalmologists

You can help further the work of the Foundation by making a donation or leaving a legacy. Every contribution is gratefully received. If you would like to help support the Foundation or require further information, please contact:

THE ULVERSCROFT FOUNDATION
The Green, Bradgate Road, Anstey
Leicester LE7 7FU, England
Tel: (0116) 236 4325

website: www.ulverscroft-foundation.org.uk

RACHEL BRIMBLE

---◆---

A SHOP GIRL GETS THE VOTE

Complete and Unabridged

MAGNA
Leicester

First published in Great Britain in 2019 by
Aria
An imprint of Head of Zeus Ltd
London

First Ulverscroft Edition
published 2021
by arrangement with
Head of Zeus Ltd
London

*A catalogue record for this book is available
from the British Library.*

ISBN 978–0–7505–4894–6

Published by
Ulverscroft Limited
Anstey, Leicestershire

Printed and bound in Great Britain by
TJ Books Ltd., Padstow, Cornwall

This book is printed on acid-free paper

I am dedicating *A Shop Girl Gets the Vote* to my fabulous father who I recently lost after a long battle with a rare form of dementia.

He was a truly wonderful man who was so proud of my writing and everything I have achieved since I set out on my career in 2007.

You are loved so very much, Dad – enjoy your peace now your suffering is finally over. I love you, Becca xx

1

City of Bath – 1911

In a small post office situated in one of the many back alleys that wound like a spider's web throughout Bath's city centre, Esther Stanbury feigned interest in a rotary stand of greeting cards. Furrowing her brow as her impatience grew, she snuck another look at the customer talking to her friend and fellow member of the Women's Suffrage Society, Louise Marlow. Would the grey-haired, bespectacled woman ever leave?

'That's right, Mrs Baldwin. The post office will be running a normal service regardless of the rumours to the contrary. The Coronation will not affect the postal service for more than a day, I assure you.' Louise smiled, deftly steering Mrs Baldwin towards the shop door and pulling it open, causing the bell above it to tinkle. 'There's no need to worry. Your sister will receive her birthday present in ample time.'

Mrs Baldwin shook her head, her expression etched with anxiety. 'But if Margery receives it even a day late, she will —'

'You have my word.' Louise gently gripped the older woman's elbow and firmly, but comfortingly, deposited Mrs Baldwin onto the cobbled street outside. 'All will be well.'

With a swift wave, Louise closed the door and returned to Esther's side. 'That woman will send me to an early grave, I swear.'

Esther laughed. 'I thought she'd never leave.'

'Now . . . ' Louise walked behind the counter and leaned her hands on the dark wood. 'What can I get for you?'

'Could I have some stamps and three small envelopes, please? I have so much correspondence to sort out for Aunt Mary. I really must get on with it this evening.'

'And how is your aunt?'

Esther sighed. 'The usual. Moody, miserable and moaning.'

Louise smiled. 'And is she all that's bothering you? You seemed so agitated at the last Society meeting.'

'I was, but, unfortunately, I really don't have time to talk about it now.' She glanced at the clock on the wall behind Louise. 'I must get to work.'

'Two minutes, Esther. I don't like to see you unhappy.'

Esther sighed and slumped her shoulders. 'I'm just becoming more and more exasperated that our efforts to obtain the vote remain fruitless. Our peaceful campaigning doesn't seem to be getting us anywhere. I can't help but wonder whether the suffragettes' militant action isn't only the correct path but the right way forward, if women are ever to be heard.'

Louise frowned, concern shadowing her dark brown eyes. 'We *are* getting somewhere. We have more and more women joining the Society and last week's petition was attended by double the number of spectators than we've ever had before. You must keep faith that we'll triumph.'

'And I'm trying.' Esther stepped away from the counter, sliding the rolled and bound poster designs she'd worked on the night before beneath her arm. 'I'm just so frustrated.'

2

'We all are, but we'll see this through.' Louise tilted her head towards Esther's posters. 'Make the final touches as we've discussed, and we'll present them to the others at the next meeting. We'll see victory, Esther. I know we will.'

Esther stared at her friend as doubt wound through her, but Louise was right. Losing faith would do no good at all. They had to stay positive and committed. Only time and dedication could change the status quo. 'You're right. Belief is key.' With a firm nod, Esther turned to the door. 'I'll see you soon.'

Leaving the post office, she walked through the alleyway and along the street until she reached Milsom Street. As Esther walked, heedless to the rows of shops either side of her, a gust of the May wind jolted her from her preoccupation and Esther slapped her hand to her hat. 'Ooh!'

A little boy beside her giggled, his hand grasped in his mother's as they passed by. Esther laughed and tipped him a wink, the brief exchange dousing a little of her mental frustration. Quickening her pace, she strode towards Pennington's, Bath's premier department store and her treasured place of work.

At least she had the love of her occupation to hold close. She had to count her blessings. Had to believe that being banished by her father from her childhood home, because of her involvement in the Cause, no longer affected her. She had been, and would always remain, staunchly determined to continue the suffrage work her mother had involved Esther in since a young age.

When her mother had passed, Esther's father had mistakenly believed his daughter would give up the fight.

How very wrong he had been.

Now, thanks to the poison Esther's stepmother had slowly dripped into her father's ear, Esther found herself living away from her familial home in the Cotswolds and, instead, in the centre of Bath with her aunt. Although Aunt Mary certainly sided with her brother and his new wife about Esther's activities, at least she had somewhere to stay and was now more active than ever as a member of a bigger and more determined suffragist group.

She hurried along the street, passing stalls selling flowers, fruit and vegetables, as she made her way through the slowly increasing crowds. Inhaling the scents of horses and petrol as carriages and shiny, new motorcars swept by, Esther took little notice of the goings-on around her, her mind so full of thoughts and distraction.

There had to be more the Society could do. Anticipation her fellow campaigners might support her new poster designs, not to mention other strategies she'd put forward, gave Esther a much-needed injection of hope, but it still wasn't enough. Again and again, they acknowledged her creative talent. Had even commented that her position as head window dresser at Pennington's could serve them well in the fight. But there had to be more she could do.

Nerves leapt in Esther's stomach as she battled her guilt over the growing temptation to leave the suffragist group and join the suffragettes. The differences between peaceful campaigning versus militant meant publicity for the Cause was becoming feverish. Her allegiance to the Society, and her fellow campaigners' approval of her enrolment, meant she had finally found her true place in the world. That she was

4

valued and needed. But she could not allow their lack of progress to assuage the fire that burned deep inside of her.

The familiar heat of possibility inched into her veins and Esther stood a little taller as the mammoth shadow of Pennington's Department Store touched the tips of her booted toes. She neared the building, the mid-morning sun teasing her senses with the promise of summer.

Esther breathed deep and stared at Pennington's façade. Painted entirely white, with two tall columns flanking the gilded double doors, Bath's finest department store stretched to five storeys and encompassed everything a consumer could wish for.

From hats and gloves, to jewellery, toys and perfume, Pennington's was a store that inspired and influenced. A promised land where people from every walk of life came to shop, take lunch and socialise.

Straightening the lapels of her uniform jacket, Esther hoped her appearance wasn't below par. For over a year, Pennington's had prided itself on its new staff uniforms and the unity of everyone who worked there. As head of a small team of four women and three men, Esther liked to think the pride Elizabeth Pennington had in the dressers' department was justified.

Esther stepped forward . . . only to stop again.

A man stood in front of one of the store windows with a little girl and, judging by the scowl on the girl's face and the exasperation on the man's, father and daughter were in the throes of debate.

'But, Daddy, I want the cricket set. Please!'

'Why don't I buy you the doll? And, if you don't like it, we can change it for the cricket set another day.'

'But —'

'Dolls are for girls, Rose. Cricket sets for boys.'

Esther narrowed her eyes as she approached them and the young boy, standing a little to the side, who she assumed to be the man's son. The little boy bounced a ball against a paddle, seemingly oblivious to the redness of his father's and sister's combative faces. The man held his daughter's hand while pointing towards one of Pennington's huge picture windows. The colourful and flamboyant toy display beyond had been erected by Esther and her team just a few days before. She stopped beside them, clutching her handbag in tightened fingers. Rightly or wrongly, she could not walk away from the gentleman's clear fault in the argument. 'Excuse me?'

The man straightened, and Esther resisted the urge to step back. He towered over her by at least six inches, his broad shoulders only accentuating his physical dominance over her petite five feet four inches and, some might say, too slender frame.

Forcing a smile, she pushed down her irritation, all too aware she represented Pennington's and rudeness to a potential customer was always to be avoided. 'I couldn't help overhearing your words to your daughter.'

His bright blue gaze bored into hers. 'And?'

'And I don't believe it's anyone's place to say what another person should prefer, whether adult or child, male or female.'

He arched an eyebrow, the exasperation in his eyes softening to amusement, which only hitched Esther's temper higher. Her smile faltered as she struggled to maintain a semblance of pleasantness.

6

'I see.' He slid his hand onto his daughter's shoulder, her hair shining in a sheet of glossy brown down her back. Esther noted it was the exact same colour as her father's, which peeked from beneath the edges of his hat. 'Rose is something of a conundrum. Yesterday, dolls were her favourite thing in the whole world, today it's cricket. As for Nathanial here ...' He touched the little boy's head. 'Yesterday he was convinced the sky was always only blue. Whereas today, it's blue *and* grey.'

Esther lifted her chin. 'That is neither here nor there. If your children —'

'Are you a mother, Mrs ...?'

She almost corrected his presumption of her marital status but quickly snapped her mouth closed. He had no need to know her title or name. He had no need to know anything about her. 'I'm not, but I know the importance of choice as well as anyone.'

'Yet how would you understand a confrontation between parent and child when you have merely caught the briefest of moments in what has been an argument lasting ...' He pulled a gold pocket watch from his waistcoat. 'Fifteen minutes.'

Esther held his frustratingly calm gaze and fought to muster her wavering confidence. His impertinent question regarding her maternal status had thrown her from the subject, but he was right to question her. What *did* she really know of children? Of parenting?

Heat crept into her cheeks, but she stood firm as she turned her attention to his daughter rather than her imperviously forthright father. 'Do I find myself standing in front of a keen cricketer?' Esther beamed at the little girl who grinned back. 'Could you be the first young lady to join the men at the Oval?'

7

The little girl giggled as she sidled closer to her father, her head bobbing up and down.

Esther laughed before addressing the little boy. 'And I agree, the sky is most definitely blue and grey.'

The boy flashed an impish grin and Esther straightened, glancing at their father. Her smile vanished at the intense way the gentleman studied her.

She cleared her throat. 'Your children are delightful, sir. I would just like certain people to see that it's important every human being, no matter how young, is allowed the liberty of choice.'

His gaze lingered on hers until he blinked and looked along the street as though bored by her conversation. 'I see.'

Esther glared at his profile before remembering his children watched her. She forced a tight smile. 'I can't imagine your wife would approve of you encouraging such a division in your children.'

He stilled, before facing her, his blue eyes wholly darker than they'd been before. 'My wife?'

'Yes, sir. Your wife. Is it not enough that women are forced to fight for a position in the world without — '

'We're discussing a doll and cricket set. Hardly an argument for or against women's suffrage.' Two spots of angry colour now darkened his cheeks. 'That's what you're referring to, correct?'

Esther swallowed and glanced at his children before tilting her chin at their father. 'Not in this instance.'

He raised his eyebrows. 'No?'

'No.'

'That's just as well.' He glanced along the street. 'As an active suffragist supporter myself, I really wouldn't appreciate you casting aspersions without knowing me.'

Surprised, she lowered her tense shoulders. 'You support the Cause?'

He faced her. 'I do and have for many months.'

Her heart quickened, and she turned away from his penetrating gaze. So, he was one of the men supporting the women in their fight, that did not mean he could hoodwink his daughter into convention.

'Well, as pleased as I am to hear that, sir, we clearly have a long way to go with regards to gender equality. The Cause is just one aspect of women's rights that needs to change. Wouldn't you agree?'

'Indeed, I would. I imagine the fight to close the avenue between the sexes will be an ongoing one for many years to come.'

'Exactly.' She looked at the young girl and smiled. 'Do you think we've persuaded your father you should have the cricket set?'

His daughter shook her head, but her eyes shone with mischief. 'Daddy is stubborn.'

Trying not to laugh, Esther nodded. 'Yes, I believe he is.'

The gentleman coughed.

Esther faced him, disconcerted by the unexpected softness that had replaced the defiance in his eyes. 'Well, it seems you have found a friend in Rose, if nothing else.'

'Yes, I think you could be right.' She smiled at his daughter, delighting in her happy gaze, before she turned to the little boy. 'And I have in you, too, I hope?'

He nodded, his smile impossibly enchanting.

Their father cleared his throat. 'But, new friends or not, that doesn't mean I'll weaken in my decision about what to buy them.'

Of all the obstinate . . . She pointed to the window. 'This display was purposely designed to amalgamate children's interests and tastes. Do you see nothing is segregated? Nothing clearly marked as boys' toys versus girls?'

His gaze momentarily dropped to her mouth in such intense study further heat flared in her cheeks. The man had an unnerving way of examining a person. As though he could look at her and see something beyond what she presented to him. It was annoying. *Supremely* annoying.

He slowly turned to the window. 'That is the dresser's intention?'

'Absolutely.'

'And you can be quite certain of that because . . . '

'Because, sir, I am her. My motivation behind this design was to show it's neither here nor there which gender chooses to play with which toy. Why not allow children to be children regardless of whether they are male or female?' Esther's pride swelled. 'And with that thought, I will bid you good day.' She smiled at his children in turn. 'It was lovely to meet you all. Goodbye.'

Esther marched past the family towards Pennington's open double doors. That told him. The way he'd looked at her! Almost as if she entertained him. Well, maybe next time, he'd think twice before declaring what was, or wasn't, a suitable toy or pastime for his children. It was attitudes like his that held back progress; that scuppered the Cause's efforts time and time again.

Taking a deep breath to calm herself, Esther walked through Pennington's doors and into the glittering, brightly lit atrium. The mammoth space burst with activity, customers strolling arm in arm around the glistening counters and dressed mannequins standing on platforms dotted throughout. Wide-brimmed hats and tailored suits provided a seemingly endless flow of colour. At Pennington's, dancers and actors, gentry and businessmen shared the same space with middle-class housewives, labourers or nannies with prams. The sight of such equality never failed to brighten Esther's most sombre mood.

When Elizabeth's father, Edward Pennington, had finally seen sense and passed the store's reins to his daughter, Elizabeth had quickly and decisively implemented changes that meant the demographic of Pennington's shoppers instantly modernised from being shamefully elitist to encompassing people from every walk of life. The struggle Elizabeth had gone through to be valued and respected by her father had bordered on painful, but she'd succeeded in her endeavours, despite the odds stacked against her.

She'd utilised every ounce of her passion and drive to do all she could to help female workers labour towards an equal footing with men. To encourage and inspire belief in the department heads and their staff that the stark differences between men and women was a thing of the past at Pennington's.

Working alongside her new husband, Joseph Carter, Elizabeth retained her maiden name for her professional life only. As her friend, Esther knew only too well how much Elizabeth relished being Mrs Carter. Not as a sign of inferiority or bondage to her husband but as a proud public acknowledgement to a man she loved and respected. Someone who had been far below her social standing when they'd met and fallen in love, but despite the obstacles, Elizabeth and Joseph had fought her father in order to spend their lives together. Her love for her husband was tangible whenever Esther was near them, whether in the workplace or socially. They were a formidable team, and one Esther felt honoured to work with.

Esther lifted her gaze to the sunlight that flowed through the glass dome, casting pink, blue and green in every direction, prismed by the huge chandeliers hung throughout the seemingly endless store. She smelt the soft scent of perfume mixed with the sweetness emanating from the numerous bouquets of flowers standing in vases on marble plinths and breathed deep, as love for her job and the people she worked with hastened her steps and demolished her temper.

Esther weaved through the throng towards the stairs leading to her department in the store's basement. She was thankful Elizabeth had agreed she could start work a little later this morning. The ten-hour days she'd worked for the last month to get the toy window display finished as well as adding bits and pieces to the store's plans for the upcoming Coronation had finally taken their toll and — added to the constant and growing demands of her aging aunt — Esther's focus had woefully drifted. Something she'd never allowed to happen before and was determined to rectify. Her constant need to prove herself had become an obsession.

She inhaled. An obsession she feared she'd never satisfy.

Her father's rejection of her and her ensuing need to feel worthy of her mother's belief in her had meant Esther worked hard, often forgoing fun in a bid to succeed in her work for the Cause and here at Pennington's.

12

Her desperate need to feel valued and wanted sometimes hung over her like a heavy cloud, and she had absolutely no idea what, or who, would make that change. All she knew, with the utmost certainty, was that she'd never give up until she'd succeeded.

2

Lawrence narrowed his gaze as he continued to stare at the doors through which the blonde, exceptionally beautiful young woman had disappeared. Rose and Nathanial chattered and giggled around his legs, seeming to have forgotten about her. If only the same thing could be said of Lawrence.

He pressed his lips together as annoyance gathered inside him. He had not liked being beaten to the final word on such a conversation. What had possessed her to show such clear disdain towards a complete stranger?

Yet, it was incredibly difficult to dismiss such a strong, beautiful, clearly intelligent woman who'd smiled so softly at his children. Every part of him wanted to go after her. Finish the conversation on his terms, rather than hers.

He glanced at Rose and Nathanial as they chased one another in circles about him on the bustling street, heedless to the crowds separating around them as they shopped, hurried to work or elsewhere. Lawrence inhaled a deep breath as rare indecision badgered him.

It was a fine day and he should forget the woman and take his children to the park. It was Saturday, after all. It was his personal rule that he never worked at the weekend, unless there was an unavoidable crisis at The Phoenix, the prestigious hotel he owned, situated in the very centre of town. Lawrence was more than content to leave the running of his premises in the hands of his capable staff from Friday evening to Monday morning.

Over and over, Rose and Nathanial had asked him if they could feed the ducks, followed by eating an ice cream on Victoria Park's immense grassland. They had only stopped outside Pennington's to momentarily look at the window display that had so mesmerised his children. Then, before he knew it, their day had been derailed by a complete stranger.

'Daddy?'

'Hmm.' He dragged his gaze from Pennington's doors and looked at Rose. 'What is it, darling?'

'Can we have the cricket set? Please.' His daughter stared up at him with heart-rendingly beautiful blue eyes, her hands clasped together in pleading. 'Nathanial and I will be the best behaved we've ever, ever, ever been. I promise.'

Lawrence fought back his smile, his resolve broken by one look into her eyes, so similar to her mother's. 'So, you'd rather we went shopping than the park?'

'Yes!' Rose enthused.

'Yes!' Nathanial chorused.

Lawrence shook his head, his smile breaking as Rose and Nathanial clasped hands and leapt up and down. 'Fine. Shopping it is.'

His children whooped with delight, and Lawrence grasped their hands as he led them into the store, secretly pleased by this unexpected change of plan. Pennington's atrium was lit in all its glory, people walking back and forth as Lawrence searched over their heads for a sight of only one female. She'd said she was responsible for the store window so the chances of seeing a dresser on the shop floor were slim, but still . . .

He tightened his fingers around his children's hands. 'Right. The toy department, I think.'

As they headed for the lift, Lawrence's mind filled with ponderings of his passed wife whom he had shamefully not thought of for many months. Abigail had died four years before, during Nathanial's long and painful birth. A tragedy that resulted in an untimely end to her life and, in turn, hers and Lawrence's arranged marriage. Throughout their brief time together, he and Abigail had tried to make one another happy, to find more than a semblance of joy within the entrapment in which they'd played willing marital and financial pawns.

Although he never came to love her as he'd hoped, Abigail had been a wonderful mother, beautiful, both inside and out, and Rose grew more and more like her every year. Intelligent and caring, his wife had taken interest in their staff, both in and out of their home, as well as being an active charity worker and support to Lawrence in his work. Theirs might not have been a love connection, but there was every possibility their lives would have gone along well enough had Abigail not died.

Her death had ripped through the heart of their family life and Lawrence counted himself immensely lucky they had such dedicated and loyal staff that he'd been able to rely on to help raise the children these past four years.

The experience of their marriage and Abigail's horrible and wasteful death had diluted any serious intention Lawrence had towards women ever since. Except he couldn't completely eradicate his belief that his children deserved and relied on him to find a new mother for them one day. A mother he loved.

16

Someone else to unconditionally love them. The closest Rose and Nathanial had to a mother figure came in the form of their nanny, Helen, who adored everything about them . . . cared for them as if the children were her own. But that was where her service ended.

Lawrence's relationship with Helen, his butler, Charles, and Mrs Jackson the cook was one of employer and employees. Nothing more, nothing less. They were a team who silently looked out for each other and worked together for the good of the children. When Lawrence would actively begin to seek a woman to take Abigail's place as his wife and the children's mother was anyone's guess. Including his own.

Burying his melancholy, Lawrence rode the lift with Rose and Nathanial, smiling at the young male attendant, who they learned was named Henry. The young man's kind face and wide smile had quickly won them over, especially when he'd allowed Rose and Nathanial to take turns pressing the buttons as people entered and alighted the extravagant gold and red velveted lift.

They stopped on the third floor and Lawrence took Rose and Nathanial's hands again as they stepped out. 'Thank you, Henry. These two will want to come back again tomorrow after your generosity.'

'Not a problem, sir. Enjoy your day, children.'

The lift doors had barely brushed closed before Rose and Nathanial whipped their hands from Lawrence's and raced along the carpeted landing towards the marble pillars outside Pennington's toy department. Lawrence followed them and scanned the space for a glimpse of the woman who'd accosted him outside.

He glanced at the abundance of games, toys and

dolls stretched out before him. Shelves and tables were fit to bursting with every conceivable distraction for children from the very young to early adolescence.

What was he doing here? Why was he even remotely concerned about speaking with such an audacious female?

Well, for one, her eyes were the brightest, prettiest shade of hazel he'd ever seen, her hair thick and blonde, pinned beneath a hat she wore with panache and style. Then there was her mouth. Bowed-lipped and painted the softest pink. And finally, the passion in her tone, the lift of her determined chin and the challenge in her gaze.

Everything about her had aroused his interest.

Lawrence pulled back his shoulders. And he would prove to her that he was equally au fait with the rights of males and females as she appeared to be and then depart the store with his pride intact. Not give her another thought. Why should he leave her to her clearly mistaken assumptions about him? He had every right to defend himself and set the record straight.

He looked around the department again, an unnerving disappointment she was nowhere to be seen nagging him.

Rubbing his hand over the back of his neck, Lawrence slowly strolled around, his gaze flitting back and forth to Rose and Nathanial as they picked up and replaced toy after toy.

A few months ago, nothing had looked quite as spectacular in Pennington's as it did nowadays. Rumours and gossip had indicated a change in management this past year was responsible for the renewed, more jovial atmosphere and Lawrence couldn't help but acknowledge the improvements were all for the better.

18

'Daddy, Daddy!'

He snapped his gaze to Rose as she and Nathanial each held up a cricket set wrapped in dark green netting. Despite the window dresser's impression of him, he'd had every intention of buying the set all along. It was her presumptions that had riled him enough to quarrel with her. Now he'd have the immense pleasure in showing the woman the cricket set Rose and Nathanial had chosen.

Wandering towards them, Lawrence shook his head. 'We don't need two.

Pick one and you can share it.'

Their smiles dissolved as they looked at one another with determination burning in their blue eyes, their mouths pinched with disappointment.

Stifling his smile, Lawrence continued on his slow walk, picking up puzzles and balls, not really seeing any of the things he touched. His attention wandered towards the exit. Would she be in the ladies' department? He had absolutely no idea where a department store dresser would work.

'Might I help you, sir?'

He turned and smiled at the young shop girl who'd approached him. 'My children are just bickering over a cricket set. I'm fine, thank you.'

'Can I interest you in anything else today? We have a new supply of toys just over there in the corner. All of which are featured in our window displays. If you'd like to —'

'The window displays . . . ' Lawrence coughed, and smoothed his tie. 'I think I might have met one of your dressers earlier. She quite impressed me.'

The girl smiled. 'Was she blonde? Pretty?'

'Yes, that's her.'

'Well, Esther impresses everyone. She's fabulously talented. And kind.' She laughed. 'Everything really. Oh, and funny when she comes out with us in the evening. Which isn't as often as we'd like.'

'Esther? That's her name?' He'd fought not to sound overly-interested but feared his voice betrayed him.

'Yes, sir. Esther Stanbury.'

Lawrence nodded, trying hard to ignore an inexplicable triumph that reverberated through him. 'I'd like to speak with her. Would you be able to point me in the right direction?'

'I'm sorry, sir, but she works in a department out of bounds to the public. Although you might find her in the ladies' department. She spends a lot of time there discussing future displays with the head of the department and Miss Pennington.'

'Fabulous. Then I'll — ' A tug to his jacket sleeve made Lawrence dip his gaze to Rose and Nathanial standing beside him. 'Aha, we've chosen, have we?'

They nodded in unison, their eyes bright with happiness once more.

He took the cricket set and held it out to the shop girl. 'Just this for now, please.'

'Of course.' She smiled at the children. 'Why don't you follow me and I'll wrap your gift for you?'

Lawrence slowly followed the shop assistant and his two overexcited children, impatient to get to the ladies' department. He wanted to show Miss Stanbury . . . He stilled. Was she a Miss? She hadn't corrected his addressing her as Mrs and he hadn't thought to check her hand for a wedding or engagement ring. Well, married or not, he refused to leave their exchange unfinished.

He was a successful hotelier with plenty of money

in his pocket, a lovely home on The Circus and two beautiful children. Since when did he lose face in a confrontation? Never, that's when.

Walking to the counter, Lawrence paid for the cricket set and Rose and Nathanial hurried from the department ahead of him. He strode to catch up with them and placed a hand on each of their shoulders, steering them towards the grand staircase that wound from the bottom floor to the top.

'Let's take the stairs to the second floor. I want to see if we can show your cricket set to the lady we spoke to outside.'

The children walked beside him, Rose tightly clutching the cricket set. Never had Lawrence been so grateful for their obvious disinterest. He was beginning to feel decidedly, uncomfortably, idiotic pursuing Esther Stanbury this way.

But as soon as he stepped into the ladies' department, his gaze was drawn to her despite the number of shop girls and female customers wandering around

She had her back to him, talking to a red-haired woman dressed in an expensively tailored suit and heels higher than he saw most women wear. She was stunning, there could be no argument about that, but it was Esther who drew his eye. The two women leaned side by side over a broad sheet of paper, talking in earnest as Miss — or Mrs — Stanbury pointed with the nib of a pencil to different spots on the sheet.

Purposefully harnessing his previous irritation with her, he gripped his children's shoulders and halted them a few feet behind the women. He cleared his throat. 'Excuse me. Miss Stanbury?'

She started and turned, her eyes immediately widening. 'Mr . . .'

'Culford. Lawrence Culford.' He slipped his hands from Rose and Nathanial's shoulders and came forward, his hand outstretched and all too aware that, once again, she hadn't corrected him about her title, which meant he was still none the wiser. 'I'm glad to have found you.'

Her fingers barely grazed his before she pulled her hand away, her cheeks darkening as she glanced towards her red-haired colleague and back again. 'Can I help you with something?'

'I think you can, yes.'

Another glance at her colleague. 'Oh?'

The woman held out her hand. 'Elizabeth Pennington, sir. It's a pleasure to meet you.'

'And you.' He turned to Rose, gesturing her forward with a wave. 'Show Miss Stanbury your present, Rose.'

His beautiful daughter beamed as she held the cricket set aloft, Nathanial standing tall and proud beside her. 'Daddy bought me the cricket set.'

Miss Stanbury looked from Rose and Nathanial to Lawrence and back again, her face lighting with a smile. 'Well, look at that. I'm so glad your father saw sense in the end.' She met Lawrence's gaze over their heads, her eyes glittering with victory. 'That's wonderful.'

He stared at her, his smile fixed and his heart pounding with frustration. Did the woman not see how condescending she sounded? 'Wonderful or not. I thought it important you know I am not the tyrant you clearly consider me.' Dragging his gaze from hers, Lawrence looked at his children. 'Come, Rose. Nathanial. Let's leave the nice lady to her work.' He took their hands before looking at Esther once more.

22

'It was . . . *interesting* meeting you.'

Her gaze shadowed as she glared, her smile too bright to be sincere. 'I hardly thought you a tyrant, Mr Culford.'

'Good, then the matter is settled.' Even though the matter felt strangely less settled than it had before.

He turned towards the department exit and didn't look back . . . regardless of the almost overwhelming urge to do so.

The woman had infuriated him, bewildered him and left him feeling she'd ended the conversation on her terms once again. Damnation!

3

Esther turned back to her latest sketch, fingering the brooch at her throat with slightly trembling fingers. Why on earth had Lawrence Culford sought her out? She'd barely given the man a second thought since she entered the store. Yet, clearly, he'd thought of her. Why? She neither wanted, nor needed, a man's attention.

Lawrence Culford might have two of the most delightful children she'd ever met. And, yes, he might have a certain something that appealed to her sensibilities. That *jumbled* her sensibilities, but he was still an ill-mannered fool.

It was of no consequence how much she missed being part of a complete family with a mother and father. It was of no consequence that she missed her parents every day since her mother's death and her father's estrangement. She could not allow this man's strange need to seek her out and laud his decision to buy the cricket set for his children to shake her new independence. Self-reliance was the only way forward in this newly emerging world.

She had her colleagues, she had friends both here in the city and at home in the Cotswolds. What did it matter that she no longer kicked up her heels at parties and gatherings as often as she once had? She still laughed and joked from time to time . . . still found joy in the company of those she worked with. So, she no longer had her beautiful, caring, passionate mother to confide and whisper with. But she had others she was coming to care for and slowly reaching out the hand of friendship.

Especially Louise and the woman standing next to her.

Remembering Elizabeth beside her and feeling decidedly discomfited, Esther smoothed her skirt and lightly patted her hair, steadfastly avoiding Elizabeth's gaze as it burned into Esther's temple.

'Esther?'

She turned, an automatic smile slipping into place as she snatched her hand from her hair. 'Yes?'

Elizabeth raised her eyebrows, her gaze amused. 'Do you know who that man is?'

'No, and neither do I want to. Clearly Mr Culford had no care for the fact I'm working when he chose to interrupt us. Just another indication of his character.' Esther looked pointedly at her latest design determined Elizabeth not be concerned by Mr Culford or his ability to unsettle her professional aptitude. 'So, what you'd like for me to do is — '

'Esther Stanbury, look at me.'

Briefly squeezing her eyes shut, Esther opened them again and faced her employer and friend. 'Yes?'

'That man is Lawrence Culford, the owner of The Phoenix hotel. A man who sadly lost his wife a few years ago. In childbirth, I believe.'

Esther's heart twisted in sympathy. 'He's a widower?' She glanced towards the entrance, hating that she'd been so short with him and that she'd referred to his wife when they'd been outside. 'I didn't realise.'

'And I'm sure you also didn't realise quite how wealthy he is or how he's admired around town.' Elizabeth followed Esther's gaze towards the entrance of

25

the ladies' department. 'Or that he is quite the mystery. Although, by reputation, kind, handsome and unassuming, he's also someone who is rarely seen at social occasions.'

Elizabeth's hushed tone ignited Esther's curiosity even as she tried to quell it. 'Well, if he's a father raising his children alone *and* running a hotel, I would assume he wouldn't have time to be social.'

'Hmm, maybe.' Elizabeth put her hand on her hip and narrowed her eyes. 'But I can't help wondering why he has you so flustered.'

'I'm not flustered,' Esther retorted a little too quickly. 'I'm just . . . busy.'

'The man is as handsome as they come and has two beautiful children, and you say you're not flustered? I was flustered, and I happen to be deeply in love with Joseph. Lawrence Culford has a presence, I think. How does he know you? And what is the significance of the cricket set?'

Esther waved her hand dismissively. 'Oh, it was something and nothing. I ran into them looking into Pennington's window and overheard him say cricket sets are for boys, dolls for girls. We had a short conversation and that was it.'

Elizabeth arched an eyebrow. 'And you expect me to believe your exchange was no more than that?'

Knowing when she was beaten, Esther slowly laid down her pencil and folded her arms. 'Fine. I might have confronted him more than I conversed.'

Elizabeth's smile immediately dissolved, concern sparking in her dark green eyes. 'Confronted him? A customer? Esther, you know you have to hold your tongue —'

'Oh, trust me, I did.' Feeling like a chicken puffing

26

her feathers, Esther battled to keep her righteous anger in place. 'The man is an ignoramus.'

'Is that so?'

'Yes. He . . . ' She pushed a stray curl back from her cheek, culpability uncomfortably pressing down on her. 'I wanted him to understand that girls shouldn't be limited by the toys they're given, and do you know what he had the audacity to say to me?'

Elizabeth glanced towards the department exit, clearly unhappy. 'Were you rude to him?'

'I . . . Well, no. Of course not.'

'Esther . . . '

Her heart quickened, and Esther grimaced. 'No. I was merely . . . firm.'

Elizabeth studied her, her canny gaze boring into Esther's before her shoulders relaxed and she shook her head, making her deep red curls softly sway. 'You shouldn't push your views on our customers. Our job is to ensure they come inside and spend their money. Having said that, it seems Mr Culford concurred with your opinions enough that he gave into them and sought you out to tell you of his transformation. You clearly snagged his interest.' She gave a knowing smile. 'I suspect in more ways than one.'

Heat warmed Esther's cheeks. 'Don't be silly. The man is nothing more than a father trying to push his viewpoint onto his young daughter. If he came to tell me about his purchase, it's because he wanted the last word. Nothing more, nothing less.'

'Hmm.' Elizabeth turned back to the design sheet. 'I'm not convinced, but let us get back to work.'

Esther released a shaky breath. Crisis averted. At least, the crisis that Elizabeth might push her for more information about her exchange with Mr Culford. As for the crisis going on inside of her? That was a different matter altogether. He was widowed, possibly raising his children alone. Did he presume her to be a game target for his attention?

Or was she being presumptuous?

Annoyance stirred, Esther forced her concentration to Elizabeth as she spoke.

'We need to expand on housewares in the west window, I think. If we include another set of dining — '

Esther's mind wandered once more. As much as she wanted — needed — to think badly of Lawrence Culford, she somehow couldn't align him with anything entirely bad-tempered. In fact, his rising to her challenge, of acquiescing to buy little Rose the cricket set and then seeking Esther out spoke of a man who was willing to admit he could have been wrong. Of a man willing to apologise, even if he hadn't quite managed to utter the word.

Which meant there was every chance she had misjudged him.

The cut of his clothes, his upper-class tone and impeccably dressed children indicated a man of money and status. One who'd almost certainly received an expensive education and was more than conversant with the ways of the world. A man not a million miles from her father.

Yet, the two of them were beyond compare. Mr Culford had said he supported the Cause.

Had he recognised her from a demonstration or rally? Seen her petitioning on the street? Maybe it was that which had led him to seek further contact with her? Could he be a possible ally to the Society?

Deep curiosity whispered through her as she tried

to listen to Elizabeth.

'So, moving on to your design for the forthcoming Coronation . . . '

Esther frowned. But she hadn't seen him at the local suffragists' meetings, nor at any public petitions. Yet, why would he lie about being a suffrage supporter if he wasn't? There seemed no reason why he would so vehemently tell her of his involvement unless he truly cared about it.

Which made him even harder to dismiss from her thoughts.

' — and, to be frank, I really think the standard is slipping, Esther.'

Jolted from her thoughts, she turned to Elizabeth. 'I'm sorry?'

'This design isn't up to your usual excellence. I hate to say it, but I'm a little disappointed.'

Dread and shame twisted inside Esther as familiar fingers of insecurity crept along her spine. Elizabeth had never said such a thing about her work before. Her position at Pennington's was as vital to Esther's heart and mind as the Cause.

Swallowing against the sudden dryness in her throat, Esther frowned. 'What is it that disappoints you?'

'I think it lacks your usual sparkle. Your flair. Pennington's windows are, of course, yours and your team's doing, but it's your designs I rely upon to astound people, to entice them inside. It's your skill that makes people desperate to purchase that hat, that purse, that toy, that necklace. Design ideas for the Coronation need to be bigger, brighter and more spellbinding than anything you've done before. This is a once-in-a-lifetime opportunity.' She paused.

'How many Coronations do we get to celebrate? The city is already simmering with anticipation. Can you imagine how that will grow and swell as the day comes ever closer?' Elizabeth stepped back and splayed her fingers on her hips, her eyes bright with excitement. 'Milsom Street will be filled with well-wishers, balloons and banners. We need those people to stop at *our* windows, be inspired by *our* wares and congratulations to King George V.' She slumped as her brow furrowed. 'I worry you haven't got the passion for the store you once had.' Concern clouded Elizabeth's eyes and her voice softened. 'Unless, of course, it isn't the store bothering you, but something else entirely?'

Although Elizabeth's excitement had gone some way to reigniting Esther's anticipation for the upcoming Coronation, words and explanations about her father, her demanding Aunt Mary and the pressures of performing well for the Society flailed on her tongue. How was she to confess her hardships to Elizabeth? They were friends, but it was imperative she maintained professionalism whilst they were at the store.

Esther looked to the design, battling the stinging in her eyes. 'I'll do better. I promise.'

Elizabeth gently touched Esther's arm. 'Esther, please tell me what's worrying you. Is it the suffrage movement? I imagine things at the Society continue to escalate with every passing week.'

Esther slumped her shoulders. 'I have been more and more wrapped up in the Society. Clearly, that has been detrimental to my work here. I'm sorry, Elizabeth.'

'Don't apologise for something as important as the vote.' Elizabeth touched her hand to Esther's arm. 'I wish I could do more than support you by listening and suggesting things, but if I'm seen as any more active — '

'It could affect the store. I know, but I am determined to make a difference. Do something to enable a breakthrough. Do you not read in the papers the lengths some women are going to in London?' Passion sped Esther's heart, her need to do something more burning deep inside. Although Elizabeth supported the Cause and did as much as she could, the movement was not as crucial to her. 'There are more arrests, more force feeding, but these women do not falter nor step down. It's been two years since Prime Minister Asquith came under attack in Birmingham and two years since Winston Churchill was assaulted in Bristol, yet nothing has changed.'

'What are you saying?' Concern clouded Elizabeth's gaze and she lowered her voice. 'Please tell me you are not considering joining the women in militancy?'

'I don't know. All I do know is I feel I'm failing to take up the mantle that my mother left behind. She prepared me for this path. She took me to rallies, explained militant and peaceful action. Made me read the newspapers with her. I have a passion for the vote like nothing else, but my work here.' Esther's heart picked up speed. 'I sometimes feel I am letting myself and my mother down so badly.' She reached past Elizabeth and started to roll up the large sheet of paper, regretful she had said so much. 'I'll work on this tonight and have something better for you in the morning.'

'Esther, please look at me.'

She lifted her eyes to Elizabeth's.

Her friend's gaze was astute and steady. 'I care

about you. You do know that, don't you?'

'Of course.'

'Whatever your efforts for the Cause, you *are* making a difference and your mother would be so proud of you. We will win this fight. We have to.' Elizabeth continued to consider her awhile longer before she lifted her hands in surrender. 'I'll leave you to see what else you can come up with. Why don't you take until the end of the week? That will still give us plenty of time to get things organised.'

'I'll start straight away.'

Before Elizabeth could say anything else, Esther took the rolled design sheet from the counter and hurried from the department. How could she have allowed even the slightest doubt and lack of confidence to appear in Elizabeth's mind? Without her work to distract her, Esther would be back in the dark hopelessness she fought against daily.

Her work at the store and the Society should buoy her, but sometimes a horrible inferiority surfaced, as though her father's anger and resentment would forever hold her in its grasp. She had to find the strength to see through what had drawn her to Bath. Her desire to be in a city, in the thick of the fight, had become so vital to her integrity, she had not fought for her right to stay at home but walked away. Her head held high. Albeit, her heart broken.

She would never be what her father wished her to be. A woman who was happy to stay at home and do her husband's bidding. A woman so different to who her mother had been when they first married. Her mother had changed over the years, Esther knew that. She had told her as much. And Esther was so grateful she had. If her mother hadn't been inspired

32

and impassioned by female progression and exposed Esther to an alternative existence, there was no saying what her life might have looked like today.

She had to cling to her blessings. Her talent. A wonderful job. The Cause. Things she would not give up, *couldn't* give up. Not for anyone.

Pushing open the door to the design department, Esther glanced at her colleagues as they worked side by side. These people were her team — her achievement — and she would protect them with everything she had. As much as she loved her work for the Cause, she also loved her role at Pennington's and needed to ensure her concentration on her job never faltered.

Lawrence Culford flashed in her mind and she quickly pushed away the image of his handsome face. Thinking about an interesting, outspoken man with an attentiveness to the fight would do no good for her survival. No good at all.

She had to focus on creating a bigger and better window for the Coronation. Astound Elizabeth and, in turn, the hundreds of people who would line the streets on the twenty-second of June. Just three short weeks from now, Great Britain would have a new King-Emperor and maybe George V would be the new figurehead of hope the women of this country had been waiting for. She wished for that more than anything.

4

Lawrence hit the cricket ball with controlled force towards Rose where she stood in front of the stumps on the green outside his townhouse, situated in the famous Circus. Pride swelled inside him as his children ran to retrieve the ball. He'd provided them with a lovely home and enough food to fill their bellies. Enough warmth that they should never feel the chill in their home as he had within the cold corridors of his family's manor house in Oxfordshire.

Yet, time and again, his fierce determination to protect his children's happiness felt threatened. As though at any moment, his father would rise from the grave to beat him again, his mother looking on, her eyes alight with malicious satisfaction as this time they left him for dead and assumed guardianship of Rose and Nathanial.

He stabbed the bat into the grass and looked around the circle of houses and the people gathered on the green for the impromptu cricket game. The sun shone high in the sky and the first shimmers of hazy heat warmed his raised face. Yet it had no hope of melting the ice around his heart.

Once heir to the Culford estate, Lawrence's father had raised his son with an iron hand, determined Lawrence would know hardship as James Culford had. How disappointed Lawrence's parents must have been when they realised their son was neither boy nor man with a drop of superiority, cruelty or abuse in his nature.

Lawrence glared ahead. Those particular family traits had bypassed him and his eldest sister, Cornelia, and, instead, showed signs of manifesting in their snobbish, money-hungry younger sister, Harriet.

Yet, because she was female, their parents were adamant Harriet would not inherit.

So, Lawrence was dealt every ounce of James' and Ophelia's frustration and disappointment.

No matter the mask he wore in front of the children, his staff, colleagues or friends, the fact remained, Lawrence was damaged. Damaged and afraid. So very afraid that beneath his carefully maintained veneer, he feared he could one day be provoked and reveal a deeply buried anger, proving all too clearly he had bad Culford blood running through his veins.

How was he to be everything Rose and Nathanial needed when such bitter, hateful thoughts about his childhood and parents marred his mind and blackened his soul? Would he ever fully breathe while his mother was still living with Harriet and continually dripping venom into his sister's ear?

He had fantastic neighbours, glorious friends, two beautiful children and more money than he could ever need — his money. Not Culford money, but money earned through his arduous work, investment savvy and a burning need to get away from a mother and father he resented to the very soles of his feet.

Although lonely and desperate for something . . . someone . . . to show him real love was possible, Lawrence was scared to fall in love, find comfort in a lover's arms. What if his masquerade were to slip, and that woman learned of his weakness and cowardly obedience as a child . . . as a young man?

Yet something had to change before he fell so far

into his discontented abyss that he lost all hope of ever climbing out again. If he were to ever stop believing himself a better man than his parents' cruelty had made him, he would give up and lose everything. He had to find a way to destroy that man. Pulverise him. For his sake, but most importantly, for his children's sake.

Sickness churned deep in his stomach.

He'd gone on to marry a woman of his parents' choosing. A woman he didn't love, yet sired children with her so they both might find a modicum of happiness in the eyes and comfort of their babies. A man who'd kept his promise of marriage yet ensured the shame of who he'd once been remained hidden. Its reality continued to twist in his blood, making him burn with rage and frustration behind his closed bedroom door.

His only course was to live his life for Rose and Nathanial. Maybe an inauthentic life in some ways, but one where his children only knew their father to be happy, smiling and playing. But how could he deny his children the potential to be loved and nurtured by a female touch he could never give them?

At the sound of footsteps, Lawrence turned. Nodding at Charles, his butler and confidante of the last six years, Lawrence's bogus smile slipped easily into place. 'Ah, you come bearing refreshments. Good man. Rose? Nathanial? Come and have a drink.'

Rose threw the ball to one of the neighbours' children and raced towards Lawrence, Nathanial doing his best to keep up with her on his short, four-year-old legs. They each took a glass of milk and biscuit from Charles' tray, his butler pulling his face into an almost impossible expression that sent the children

36

into fits of giggles.

Lawrence grinned. 'Go and take your treats to the bench under the tree. You look hot and bothered.'

The children walked away slowly, carefully balancing their drinks and biscuits as Lawrence took a glass of lemonade from the tray.

'They're enjoying themselves, I think. It's nice to see so many of us out here using the green. It felt like a very long winter.'

A young woman walked past them, hand in hand with a toddling boy, and glanced at Lawrence from beneath lowered lashes.

Esther Stanbury immediately leapt into Lawrence's mind. She was the antithesis of the woman who smiled at him so shyly, yet Esther continued to poke and prod at his memory.

He looked at Charles. 'I met someone yesterday. A woman.'

'Oh?' His butler's grey eyes widened in surprise, his eyebrows almost brushing the edges of his black hair. 'And?'

'And she intrigued me.' Lawrence admitted, adding a shrug in the hope the gesture might deflect the depth of his interest considering how often Esther Stanbury had entered his thoughts in the last twenty-four hours. 'I should've been infuriated by her, but I'm man enough to admit it's not infuriation I'm feeling whenever I think about her.'

'Then what are you feeling?'

He took a deep breath, surprised and confused by his sudden need to share his meeting Esther with Charles. Although Lawrence encouraged a much more personal relationship between himself and his staff than his parents would ever have considered,

37

his candour did not bode well for maintaining his carefully tended control. 'Nervous.'

Charles raised his eyebrows. 'Nervous? I'm surprised by that. You have never struck me as nervous about any situation.'

'And far too curious.'

'I see.' Charles looked across at the children. 'And what did this woman do that *should* have infuriated you?'

'It's difficult to say. Her whole demeanour was of a nature I've not come across before. Not even with the suffragists. It's as though Miss Stanbury is willing to fight for what she believes is right, even if she has to stand alone. She's . . . quite remarkable.'

Charles smiled and pulled back his wide shoulders. 'Well, that is interesting. Will you be seeing her again?'

Lawrence sighed, indecision warring with sanity inside him. 'To do so would undoubtedly be foolish . . .'

'But?'

'I can't help thinking I'd come to enjoy her company. In a friendship way, of course. Romance is the furthest thing from my mind,' he insisted.

'Of course.' Charles laid the tray on the grass and crossed his arms, his gaze on their neighbours as they walked or ran across the grass. 'But there doesn't appear to be anything wrong with this young woman?'

'On the contrary.' Lawrence flashed a genuine smile. 'She's beautiful. Clearly intelligent, if not a little too opinionated. Passionate, most definitely fond of children and, for some reason I'm yet to identify, has well and truly captured my attention.'

'May I ask the lady's name?'

'Esther. Esther Stanbury.' Lawrence frowned. He'd

38

actually savoured her name on his tongue and he didn't doubt she'd taste as softly sweet as the lingering scent of her perfume which incessantly clung to his nostrils. Where on earth were such thoughts coming from? 'She's a working woman. A woman my mother would undoubtedly disapprove of.'

'I think your mother's approval, one way or another, no longer matters to you, so why not ask this lady to dinner? She can only refuse, and then you'll know for certain if your meeting with her was nothing more than an encounter that momentarily threw you off balance.' Charles raised his eyebrows again. 'Because that is how you're feeling, isn't it?'

'Off balance.' Lawrence nodded, ridiculously grateful his butler had named the absurdity currently threatening his self-preservation. 'Indeed.'

Rose and Nathanial approached them, wearing matching milk moustaches complete with biscuit crumb sprinkles. Lawrence stepped forward, his momentary lapse in attention to them quashed. They mattered more than anything. His children had to come first. His own wants — his own desires — could not overshadow what mattered most: his children's happiness and raising them in a loving and secure environment.

The strange and inexplicable urge to get to know Esther Stanbury was of no consequence. She wasn't the right woman for him to pursue, even if such a miracle were to ever arise. How would such an independent woman with views and strong opinions, however just and right, ever be happy staying at home and helping raise another woman's children?

Because that was the kind of spouse he should want for Rose and Nathanial. Only a woman who wanted

39

to be with them would suffice. His children deserved that singular commitment and unfailing devotion. They needed to know they were loved above all else.

He had to be careful. Had to maintain his willpower. To make a mistake could affect Rose and Nathanial in ways from which they may never recover.

An arranged marriage, even a marriage of convenience, would eventually fail and he would not re-expose his children to the heartache he'd slowly managed to pull them out of when they'd lost Abigail. A truly loving and obedient woman who'd been nothing more to his parents than another person in their plans to continue their self-made lineage and increase the family wealth.

His chest tightened as isolation gripped him and Lawrence quickly swiped his hand over his face, the scuff of his jaw rasping against his palm.

Forcing a smile, he wiggled his eyebrows at the children as he passed his empty glass to Charles. 'Right, who's ready for our next innings?'

They squealed and laughed as Lawrence gave an almighty roar and grappled them into his arms. He ran across the grass bouncing and jolting the most precious gifts Abigail could ever have given him in her too-short life.

5

Esther clutched her wooden clipboard to her chest and squinted against the sunshine glinting off one of Pennington's display windows, silently admonishing herself for not coming up to her usual standard with the Coronation display plans. Elizabeth was right; Esther's mind wasn't on her work as it should be. Worse, the effects could have been made public.

She had to pull something out of the bag that would not merely impress Elizabeth but astound her. Anything less presented the risk of Esther missing out on the opportunity to lead the arrangement of the Coronation window. She could not allow that to happen. Her position at Pennington's was the basis of her independence, her income and source of her growing self-esteem. Her work had become essential to her drive and confidence to push forwards, take risks and maintain complete ownership of her life as her beloved mother had encouraged her to do.

She watched Amelia Wakefield as she worked behind the glass, carrying out Esther's instructions to rearrange the ornaments and merchandise atop an oak dresser. At twenty-two, the girl was barely three years younger than Esther, but Amelia held no less conviction to advance her position at the store.

Although lucky to have such a vibrant woman on her team, Amelia also served as a reminder there would always be another woman, another person, wanting as much from life as Esther wanted. She was also mindful her work for the Cause made it important that she

41

encouraged other women as much as she did herself to do more and *be* more.

If she faltered in her new way of thinking, the long-reaching fingers of self-doubt she suffered when she'd started living with her aunt would creep back in and crush every ounce of the confidence she'd so painstakingly erected.

Esther crossed her arms tightly as her thoughts filled with her stepmother, Viola. A woman so completely different to Esther's mother that her very presence was an insult to Katherine Stanbury's memory.

As much of a social climber as Esther's Aunt Mary, Viola had done nothing short of pursue Esther's father, entrapping and enchanting him until he believed this was the type of woman — so different to his first wife and daughter — he wanted to look after him in his advancing years. A woman who held more importance in her looks, clothes and social circle than interest in women's rights or liberation.

In just three short years, Viola had borne Esther's father two strapping sons in quick succession and convinced him that Esther's similarities to her mother and her drive for women's suffrage was the cause of his despair. All too soon, with Viola's bidding, Esther's father had presented his daughter with an ultimatum if she was to stay under his roof: give up the Cause or move in with his sister in Bath.

Esther had chosen the latter . . . even if it pained her to leave her darling little half-brothers, Peter and Benedict. Of course, moving in with her aunt had presented new demands. Including Aunt Mary asking questions about Esther's future intentions and other things she had no wish to explain or share.

When tears threatened, Esther quickly swiped at

42

her eyes. None of her pain and loss mattered any more. At least, not when Viola continued to make her presence known by constantly coming to Bath and staying in the best hotels on the pretence of visiting Aunt Mary while avoiding Esther, at all costs. As long as Aunt Mary fed Viola information about Esther's life that her stepmother could digest, rewrite and report back to her father, the venomous woman was happy. To say it was easy living with Aunt Mary would be a complete mistruth, but her living situation now was still preferable to putting up with Viola and her father's constant disapproval.

A knock on the store window startled Esther from her preoccupation. Amelia smiled and stood back from the dresser, swiping a lock of brown hair from her brow before stretching her hand over the scene, asking for Esther's approval. Forcing her concentration to work, Esther smiled and gave a curt nod, indicating her endorsement to the changes before pointing to a mahogany dining table and chairs to the side of the window. Her colleague immediately set about pulling out the chairs and shifting one end of the table so that it stood at a better angle, allowing passers-by to view the elegant porcelain dinner set, silver candelabra, pink tapered candles and matching napkins that decorated the table's surface.

Satisfied, Esther jotted a few notes onto the paper attached to her clipboard before lifting her pencil and tapping it against her teeth. The parlour design still needed more. She wanted it to reflect the new lifestyle changes happening all over the country. Scribbling a rough outline of the new cribs and baby blankets that had arrived in store the day before, Esther was convinced she could combine homeware with infant merchandise. Two departments receiving a much-needed boost could be merged into one.

Waving to Amelia and two other members of her team, Esther indicated she was gratified and they could return to the basement department. She wandered along the front of the mammoth store until she came to its largest window. Narrowing her eyes, she considered its size and possibility, before flipping over several sheets on her clipboard to the sketches and notes she'd made at home the previous evening.

It wasn't so much the content she'd decided on for the Coronation window that caused a niggling dissatisfaction, but the colours. More gold and scarlet were needed. More navy and white to make the window shine with the pomp and pageantry of the occasion. The soon-to-be King-Emperor was handsome, regal and devoted to his wife. A naval man with rigid shoulders and lifted chin. A man not to be ignored.

Power. Prestige.

Excitement churned deep in Esther's stomach as familiar innovation and creativity swept through her pencil and onto the page.

And what of his queen, the beautiful but austere Mary of Teck?

A popular princess who would undoubtedly be an equally popular queen. An attentive mother to her children and patron to the London Needlework Guild, Queen Mary liked embroidery and constantly accompanied her husband on royal duties. Important values the British public admired and enjoyed of their leading family.

Esther smiled. Patronage. Loyalty. Love and devotion. Things that could easily be added to Pennington's Coronation display in one form or another.

A sudden and strange sense of someone watching her clouded Esther's concentration and she slowly turned.

Her heart skipped a beat as Lawrence Culford crossed the street towards her, his gaze on hers, seemingly oblivious to the passing horse and carriage that separated them for a brief second. He was alone. No children to act as a barrier or distraction should he look at her for too long with his deep blue eyes.

Eyes that were maddeningly memorable.

She swallowed against the sudden dryness in her throat. What was he doing here? Was it coincidence? Pennington's was at the very heart of Bath's premier shopping street, after all.

Or could he be looking for her? The sentiment sent a shiver through her which she wasn't certain derived from pleasure or alarm.

Turning to the window, she quickly feigned intense interest in her notes, hating the slight tremor in her pencil.

'Miss Stanbury?'

She briefly closed her eyes against the warming effect of his deep, rich voice before turning, her smile in place. This man should not have such control of her faculties.

She turned. 'Mr Culford. No children today?'

'Alas, Nathanial is taking a trip to the park with his nanny, and Rose is at school.'

'So, you find yourself in town. Might I ask, for business or pleasure?'

'Business. I'm a hotelier.'

'Yes, I know.'

'You know?'

Heat pinched her cheeks for so willingly admitting

she'd learned more about him than he'd previously offered. 'Yes, Elizabeth . . . Miss Pennington knew of you when she saw you the other day.'

He drew his gaze over her hair and face. 'I see.'

'Yes. I'll leave you to carry on. I'm sure you're just as busy as I am.'

But Mr Culford continued unperturbed. 'You'll be pleased to know we spent the entire weekend playing cricket. Rose will be forever grateful to you for your insistence I purchase the set for her.'

A traitorous smile pulled at her lips. His eyes shone with fondness for his daughter, which she found incredibly sweet. 'I'm glad she's enjoying it. You're clearly a very loving father.'

'Loving and manipulated.' He laughed. 'But I don't mind as long as they're happy and appreciate the blessings they have. Many children have to make do with a rubber ball and a plank of wood. I ensure Rose and Nathanial know the way most of the children in this city are forced to live.'

Esther relaxed her shoulders, warming to him. 'I'm glad. I imagine it's hard to teach children who have a loving home, food on the table and games to play with that there is an entirely different world not far from their door.'

'Did you grow up in the city?' he asked.

A little taken aback that he'd so quickly moved to the personal, Esther hesitated but conceded answering his question could do no harm. 'No. I grew up in the Cotswolds but moved here about two years ago.'

'Then that's another thing we have in common.'

She frowned. 'Another? I wasn't aware there was a first.'

46

His eyes gleamed with that infernal spark of amusement. 'But, of course.'

Pulling back her shoulders, Esther regarded him with suspicion. 'Which is?'

'The Cause, of course.'

She exhaled. 'Oh, yes. Of course. You never told me your role in the fight. Are you a campaigner?'

'More of a supporter. I help as and when I can.'

'I see.' Although a little disappointed he didn't play a more active role, Esther nodded, pleased he was at least on the women's side. 'Well, we could most definitely use more men behind us.' She glanced towards Pennington's doors, unusually perturbed that she was at work and couldn't continue their conversation further. 'I'm afraid I really must get back to work, Mr Culford.' She stepped back. 'If you'll excuse me . . .'

As she turned, he gently clutched her elbow. 'Miss Stanbury, I . . .'

Her heart raced at the contact and when she looked into his eyes, she saw what could only be described as over-interest. What did he want with her? Worse, why was he having such an alien effect on her? No one had ever made her feel such confusion or interest.

She eased her arm from his grasp, the indecision in his gaze rousing her self-protection. 'Why are you here?'

He closed his eyes and swiped his hand over his face before opening them again. 'That is a question I am scrambling to answer myself.' He lifted his shoulders. 'In all honesty, I don't know, but I do know it feels right to be here. Talking. With you.'

Time stood still as their gazes locked and Esther's body heated under the sudden sombreness of his gaze. He smiled so often, his eyes lighting with amusement and humour, yet both had now disappeared as he considered her.

And, in that moment, she had no idea which of the two sides of him she preferred.

★ ★ ★

What is wrong with you, man? Why say that to her? She'll think you a predator.

Lawrence shook his head and huffed a laugh. 'Sorry, you must think me — '

'A little mad and entirely disconcerting?' Esther Stanbury's hazel eyes glistened with a hint of amusement. 'Does that about sum you up, do you think?'

Relieved by her humour, Lawrence took off his hat and pushed the hair from his brow. 'Can I try again?'

'With what?'

He swallowed as her quiet beauty and delicately flushed cheeks caused a protectiveness in him that was insane considering the feistiness beneath her sedate outer layer. She was beautiful, seemed so wise and kind, and the effect those attributes had on him were, quite frankly, terrifying.

'Mr Culford?' She raised her eyebrows, her eyes almost golden in the sunlight. 'I need to get back inside. I'm quite certain you have business to attend to also?'

Lawrence quickly put on his hat and nodded. 'Yes, I do. Of course, but . . . '

He wanted to ask her to dinner, but the question flailed on his tongue. If she agreed and he spent more time with her, what would become of it? She was clearly ambitious and wanted to make her mark on the world. Something he would usually wholeheartedly

48

applaud, but he also accepted such a woman would never fit into his life when he had the children to think of.

She frowned. 'Mr Culford?'

Clearing his throat, he stalled for time and forced a smile. 'Can I ask you a question? Were you responsible for the window designs that caused such an uproar last year? The suggestion of female empowerment and having the mannequins wearing military-inspired dress to symbolise the battle they are fighting was quite a statement. I thought it ingenious.'

Pride immediately brightened her eyes and her shoulders relaxed. 'I was, yes.'

'They were most impressive. Served their purpose with your exact intention and provocation. Very clever. Your employers must think your interest in women's rights a progressive one, if they agreed to such a bold statement all those months ago.'

'Elizabeth Pennington and Joseph Carter are very forward-thinking.'

'Joseph Carter?'

'Elizabeth's husband and co-manager. She is known by the name Pennington at the store only. Her married name is Elizabeth Carter and, yes, they wholeheartedly support equal rights and opportunities for everyone. Regardless of gender, financial background, colour or creed.' Her brow furrowed. 'Elizabeth is someone I admire very much and I'm very fortunate to be able to call her my friend as well as employer. She's ambitious, hard-working and always caring and attentive to others. Just because I believe . . . ' She halted and briefly closed her eyes before opening them again and softly smiling. 'I apologise. Once I start to talk about women and our place in society, it's like opening a floodgate.'

He shook his head, not wanting her to halt. Seeing her so passionate and alive with focus only served to enhance his interest and attraction. 'On the contrary. I'd like to hear more from you. It's something I have a great interest in, too. It was my keen interest in the continuing newspaper coverage of the suffrage campaign that led me to adding my support. I'm sympathetic to the Cause and have wondered how I can do more, but everything seems to be constantly hindered by government barriers.'

Her gaze grew intense on his as though assessing his sincerity. 'Yes, it's frustrating. The barriers are there and no matter the petitions, letters to governors and others, we don't seem to be getting any closer to our goal.' She stared into the distance before facing him once more. 'The suffragettes are taking more and more radical action. For many months, I've thought their tactics unnecessary, but as time goes on . . .'

Lawrence stilled as concern whispered through him. 'You're considering jumping sides?'

'Well, yes, but —'

'The suffragettes' actions are escalating. Do you really want to become involved? There were further reports of bombings and violent petitions in the papers last week. These occurrences are happening more and more.'

She pulled back her shoulders, her gaze darkening with clear defensiveness. 'What I decide to do or not do is not your concern. I really must bid you good day, Mr Culford.'

Turning on her heel, she walked towards Pennington's open double doors.

Inwardly cursing, Lawrence let her go.

Her vexation had been tangible, and although he had no right to steer her in any direction, the notion of her getting caught up in anything violent worried him.

Once she'd disappeared from his view, Lawrence slowly walked away from Pennington's, his feet moving of their own accord along Milsom Street towards The Phoenix, his hotel on Queens Square.

How could he have been so foolish to assert any sort of opinion on Miss Stanbury? He should have told her of his widowhood. For all he knew, she could assume him married. A man without morals or mindfulness.

He continued to walk, his head bowed and mentally kicking himself for behaving like a fool.

6

Esther leaned over Louise's shoulder and pointed to her latest slogan design. 'The lioness could easily become a recognisable symbol of the group. A new image that will pertain to the Society right here in Bath.'

Louise frowned and placed her hands on her slender hips. 'I'm not so sure a lioness portrays what we are.'

Esther straightened, her passion for the Cause driving her excitement. 'A lioness is the hunter, the provider of food and sustenance to her young. The one the lion depends upon to nourish their family, their pride, so they might thrive and strengthen. Isn't that everything we want for our fellow women, our families and children?'

Murmurs of agreement sounded from the sixteen women seated in the back room of the post office Louise ran with her husband, Wyatt. If Esther secured the backing of the others for a new campaign, it would bring their section of the suffragist movement far more respect than they had managed to achieve in the city thus far.

Lawrence Culford's concern when she'd mentioned the suffragettes had harangued her conscience all day. She had never been an advocate for violence and, despite her impatience for the group to move forward, Lawrence's obvious concern had made her realise it was too soon to resort to something she could come to regret.

For she already regretted snapping at him the way she had.

Since when had she become so embroiled in her quest for the vote that she retorted to genuine alarm with harshness? That was something that reminded her far too much of her stepmother. And Lawrence had been alarmed. Despite barely knowing him, Esther seemed to sense his emotions more quickly and more assuredly than she'd like.

She forced her attention back to the here and now as she strolled around the table. The women turned in their chairs and she caught the eyes of each as she walked. 'We need to launch ourselves as a force to be respected. To watch. A group that women can access and join. At the moment, who knows where we meet? Who knows how to speak with us?'

'But it has to be that way for our safety.' Louise lifted Esther's sketch. 'These are good, but parading our group in such a way will mean we become that much more of a target for the authorities. Not to mention the press. Our meetings are held in secret for a reason. They state in the papers that enforced feeding of suffragette campaigners is at an all-time high. Sooner or later, someone is going to die. For the time being, I am not prepared to expose myself, or any of you, to such risk.' Louise looked at Esther and her eyes clearly indicated the silent end of her sentence. *But that may well change in time . . .*

Esther nodded. 'I agree, but we do need more members to join the fight. We need more men like your husband.'

Part of her mentioned men as a secret atonement to Lawrence and everything he clearly stood for. She didn't doubt his involvement in the Cause . . . even if she did doubt if his interest in her was entirely about her work for the Society. Whatever the man wanted from her, her trust and respect for him, if she were to ever see him again, would have to be earned.

She pulled back her shoulders. 'My mother worked tirelessly for the Cause and involved me as soon as I was old enough. I have listened for half of my life to the frustrations and wants of so many women. I will not stop for me and I will not stop for my mother.'

Murmurings sounded around the room.

Esther straightened her spine as fire burned hot inside of her.

Since her father had banished her, she'd supported herself even while her aunt continued to receive payouts from her father. She didn't need or want his money. He no longer wished to have his daughter living with him but continued to send monetary compensation. No doubt as a way to soothe his conscience for betraying the trust and care Esther's mother would have expected of him when she died. Aunt Mary rarely disclosed her feelings about Esther's work or, indeed, her estrangement from her father. Which, more often than not, left Esther feeling that her living with her aunt was as fragile a situation as it had been when she'd been at home with her father.

How was she to explain to the women of the Society the effects on her should she fail to achieve all she set out to do when so many of them had security, money, families and soft places to fall?

Determined that her ideas would be seriously considered, Esther pushed forward, despite the groans and scuffles that resounded around the room, threatening her confidence. Louise's husband supported their campaign, even if his help was reluctantly welcomed by some members. It sometimes felt as though she and Louise would never make certain women seated in the room believe that men were not the enemy but extra bodies that could help them succeed in their endeavours.

Frustrated but not ready to give up, Esther strode back to her empty seat and picked up the poster she'd designed, holding it aloft. 'If we paste this to as many billboards and buildings as possible, we will garner further support from both men and women. Here I have joined the lioness with the lion, thus demonstrating that human beings, regardless of their gender, can work together. Just because the government fights us at every corner, there are plenty of men who encourage and support our right to vote.'

'Is that so?' Cecilia Reed, a staunch woman in her mid-thirties, sniffed.

She often cited herself above Louise, who was the group's elected leader. There was something about Cecilia that Esther didn't entirely trust. Her negativity and questioning sometimes poked at her intuition that Cecilia's agenda for the group was far from their goals of suffrage and unity.

Esther mustered every ounce of bravado she had and crossed her arms. 'Do you have something to add, Cecilia?'

'I do. Perhaps you would like to name these so-called male supporters? I am yet to find a single man who comes to more than one petition before he disappears again. The last campaign we held, the only man there, along with his infernal scribbling, was the journalist, Robert Sharp. We all know he only writes what serves to brighten his name in the public's opinion. What man actually wants to give us one iota of real

55

empowerment?' She glanced around the table, her cheeks flushed. 'I know my husband doesn't. And, in my experience, most husbands believe the same.'

Esther held Cecilia's gaze, her mind filling with Lawrence and his admiration of her window design and his keen attentiveness in everything she'd had to say about women's progression. Did she really know him well enough to voice his name as a supporter? It suddenly felt incredibly unfortunate that she did not.

She cleared her throat. 'I know of a few men, for your information.'

'Really?' Cecilia raised her eyebrows, torment glinting in her dark brown eyes. 'Care to name them?'

Despite the goading Cecilia seemed intent on pursuing, Esther shook her head. 'It isn't my place to name anyone who shows support unless they wish it. Only people willing to publicly show their commitment and who are fully aware of the challenges they're exposing themselves to should be named. Anything else is immoral and controlling. Don't you think?'

Murmurs of 'hear, hear' and 'absolutely' sounded around the room.

Cecilia threw a final glare at Esther before she leaned back and crossed her arms under her ample bosom.

Triumphant, Esther turned to Louise, who smiled as she rose to her feet. 'On that note, I'm calling tonight's meeting to a close. Please each take one of Esther's posters and pamphlet designs to consider for our demonstration next week. I'd really appreciate your opinions on deciding if we go forward with these new messages. Is Esther right? Should we focus on enrolling more women *and* men into the Bath chapter? It's highly probable in doing so, it will better

56

serve us in getting councillors to speak for us in Parliament. We'll meet again two nights from now and, if we're all in agreement, Wyatt will ensure we have enough copies of Esther's designs to distribute before the demonstration. Good evening, ladies.'

Pleased that Louise had shown some support for the new slogans, Esther stood back as the other members filed from the room, noticing that only Cecilia pointedly ignored the samples and continued, empty-handed, from the room. Shaking her head, Esther resolutely pushed away the infernal self-doubt that stubbornly resurfaced upon a rejection — regardless of the majority support.

As she gathered the remaining posters and pamphlets, Esther's mind wandered once more to Lawrence and their abrupt parting. Her misgivings about him were warning enough that any further contact would be a mistake, so why did she keep thinking of him?

It was because of his interest in the Cause. Because she'd looked into his eyes and saw that he cared what she had to say, what she felt. An understanding she desperately wanted.

Esther pushed her designs into her leather portfolio, whipping the zip closed.

Her father's harsh words had been enough to last a lifetime. Without her mother's guidance, support and protection, self-reliance was her only defence against a loss that burned like an unhealed wound across her heart. She could not falter. The Cause had been in her life since she was barely ten years old and always would be until women all over the country secured the right to vote.

'Esther?'

She started and turned.

Louise stood on the other side of the table, her blue eyes concerned, and her brow furrowed. 'You know not to take Cecilia too seriously. She'll be onboard with the designs soon enough.'

'Oh yes, I know.'

'Then why are you so glum? Are you worried about something else we discussed tonight?'

'No, not at all.' Esther forced a smile. The last thing she wanted was for Louise to think her passion for the Cause wavered. Having Elizabeth doubt her was hard enough. 'My mind has turned to other things. Nothing to do with the Society.'

Louise gathered the pens scattered atop the table. 'Anything I might be able to help you with?'

Deciding it would do no harm to confide in Louise, Esther exhaled. Louise was a good and trusted friend. One who neither gossiped nor judged. 'It's bothering me that I was rather rude to a gentleman today.'

'Rude?' Louise's eyebrows rose. 'Why?'

'Because I thought he overstepped the mark with his care for me. I was wrong.'

'I see. Then apologise and I'm quite sure the matter will be forgotten.'

'How can I apologise when there's every chance I'll never see him again?'

'In that case, the matter is surely settled?'

Esther sighed, feeling strangely regretful at the notion of not seeing Lawrence Culford again. She would've liked to have learned more of his thoughts about the Cause, if nothing else. 'I suppose you're right.'

'Whatever you said to this gentleman, I'm sure it's forgotten.'

'Maybe.'

58

Louise sat in one of the chairs at the table. 'You look so worried. I didn't mean to make light of the situation. If you really feel you want to apologise, then you should seek him out. Where did you meet him?'

'At the store.'

'At Pennington's? Then I'm certain he'll be back sooner or later.'

Esther's heart quickened. 'But what will I say to him? He's a father, a widower, with no underhand intentions, I'm sure, but he makes me inexplicably uneasy.'

'Well, that is interesting. You've never struck me as a woman whose control can be shaken by anyone.'

Affronted, Esther immediately straightened, her cheeks burning. 'He doesn't shake me.'

Louise smiled knowingly. 'Are you sure?'

Words stuck in Esther's throat.

Standing, Louise lifted her shoulders. 'Whenever you happen upon him again, give him your apology and be done with it. After all, this was nothing more than a chance meeting between you . . . wasn't it?'

Esther's stomach knotted as Lawrence's handsome, smiling face appeared in her mind. 'Absolutely.'

Uncertainty coiled in Esther's stomach. How could she apologise to Lawrence Culford and not risk her disturbing interest in him deepening? If he forgave her, then what? Did she ask him more about himself? His work? His support of the Society?

Abruptly, she walked to the coat stand by the door.

She pulled on her shawl. 'I'll see you at the next meeting. You take care and pass on my regards to Wyatt, won't you?'

'Of course. See you soon.'

Esther walked from the room, down the stairs and

out of the back door into the street.

As she made her way along the alleyway, Esther breathed deeply, faltering in her steps as she reached the embankment running alongside the River Avon. The stench of water and waste infused her nostrils as she stared over the high wall and into the swirling, moonlit water, her loneliness surging through her on an unwanted wave.

For some reason, Lawrence Culford was the first man to well and truly catch her attention. Admittedly, she was very fond of Elizabeth's new husband, Joseph Carter, whose talent and vision inspired Esther daily at the store, but whatever she felt was unfathomably personal with Lawrence. There was a quiet vulnerability to him despite his big smile and glittering eyes that so appealed to her.

Even the way he constantly reached out to touch his children as though checking they were still beside him had softened her to his assertions. He seemed complex, a contradiction and his face continued to badger her.

She pushed away from the wall and continued a slow walk to her aunt's house, neither relishing the prospect of another evening playing cards in front of the hearth or closing the front door on another day where Esther felt possible achievement had been missed.

Maybe she should seek out Lawrence's address in the ledgers at the store? Or would he think her a little insane if she were to arrive unannounced on his doorstep? Yet if she sought him out at his hotel, she'd be disturbing his work time which also felt intrusive. No, a quick visit to his home where less people would have cause to see her was the safer option.

A slow smile curved her lips and her stomach dipped with reckless abandon as she walked a little faster towards her aunt's house.

7

Lawrence contemplated the blooming snapdragon and delphiniums in the borders edging his garden and marvelled at how Helen, his maid-cum-nanny, so willingly volunteered to tend the garden on top of everything else she did for his family. He relied on her so much, it became increasingly difficult to know how to reward her. He was in awe of her multitude of skills, calmness, humour and care around the children and wasn't entirely sure how he, or indeed Rose and Nathanial, would cope if she were ever to leave their household.

She was a young woman who deserved a life outside of his needs, but the longer he continued to raise the children alone, the longer he would rely on Helen's help. It wasn't right or fair.

Occasionally, Cornelia would come to visit and help out. Never his mother and never Harriet. He would, of course, welcome his youngest sister at any time. As for his mother . . . he wanted her nowhere near his children, despite his guilt that Rose and Nathanial would never have a relationship with their paternal grandmother. It was a sacrifice Lawrence was prepared to make if it meant his mother's vindictiveness never tainted the children's lives as it had his.

As for Abigail's parents, they spent most of their time travelling the globe. Abigail had been an only child and, after her death, Rose and Nathanial's grandmama and papa had shown interest in their upbringing for many months . . . That interest soon waned as time went on and now Lawrence relied on them for nothing. Although he occasionally missed the company of his in-laws, he had no want of people who were not fully committed to Rose and Nathanial. Not that the sentiment alleviated his remorse that the children only had him and the staff as constant figures in their young lives.

He wandered along the narrow stone path that zigzagged from the rear door of the house to the gate at the bottom of the garden.

'Ah, there you are, sir.'

Lawrence blinked and turned. 'Yes, Charles. What is it?'

'You have a lady visitor, sir. Miss Esther Stanbury.'

Surprised, Lawrence stilled. 'Here? Now?'

'Yes, sir. She's in the drawing room.' Charles looked solemn enough but the amused glint in his eyes would have been visible from the moon. 'As I couldn't find you straight away, I didn't think it proper to leave the lady waiting on the doorstep.'

Startled and unsure what to say or do, Lawrence nodded. 'Right. I see. I'll be right there.'

Charles retreated, but Lawrence couldn't move.

For the love of God, man. Pull yourself together before the woman thinks you are a man of twenty-two rather than thirty-two.

Lawrence pulled back his shoulders and walked towards the open back door of the house. Foreboding whispered through him. Why on earth was Esther here? Nothing but further trouble could have possibly brought her to his home considering the manner they'd parted outside Pennington's. He had no idea how she'd learned of his address. Surely, anything she had to say to him could have been said in a letter.

Unless the conversation held a sensitivity, she did not want to risk others reading.

The first noise to reach him when he walked along the hallway and up the stairs was his children's laughter. Lawrence halted, his heart missing a beat. They sounded so happy. So relaxed. Their laughter seeped into his soul, making him want to bottle it so he could listen to it over and over again.

Rose screeched, her giggles reverberating from the open drawing room door. Was it Esther making his daughter laugh in such a way? Warmth ran through him at the possibility and his reservations about why she was there abruptly vanished.

Taking a deep breath, Lawrence stepped into the room . . . and stopped.

Esther sat on the rug in front of the fire along with Helen and the children. The area was strewn with wooden soldiers and horses, a forgotten, half-finished jigsaw puzzle, pencils and paper. Yet, it wasn't the playthings the children touched and watched, but Esther.

She sat with her shoulders relaxed as Rose stood behind her, playing with the pins in Esther's hair, securing strand after strand into the most god-awful mess. He shifted his study to Esther and smiled.

She made google-eyes at Nathanial, sticking her tongue out of the side of her mouth and playfully flinching every time Rose inserted a pin.

His children's eyes were alight with joy, their smiles wide. Even Helen held her stomach as she shuddered with suppressed laughter.

Reluctant to interrupt the moment but knowing he must, Lawrence stepped into the room. 'Miss Stanbury. This is a surprise.'

She snapped her head around, her cheeks immediately flushing a deep red. 'Mr Culford. We . . . were . . . '

Helen stood. 'Having the most marvellous time, are we not, children?'

'Look, Daddy.' Rose gently placed her hands on either side of Esther's head and eased her around so Rose could show off her handiwork. 'Miss Stanbury let me play with her hair. Doesn't she look pretty?'

'Very.' Lawrence locked his gaze on Esther's, his body humming with the strength of his undeniable attraction to this woman who had somehow managed to break through his barriers to enchant him . . . and seemingly his children, too. 'Do you mind if I have a few minutes alone with Miss Stanbury? I think she's come to speak with me about something important.'

When Rose's face dropped in disappointment, Lawrence felt a jolt of guilt even as his daughter dutifully nodded and stood back. Slowly, Esther rose to her feet, her eyes resolutely fixed to her skirt as she smoothed and fussed with it. Helen took the children's hands and, as she passed him, she slowed and raised her eyebrows, her gaze sparkling with teasing.

Lawrence widened his eyes in warning, even as he struggled to suppress his smile. 'Could you ask Mrs Jackson for some tea, please?'

'Of course.' Helen grinned, before leading the children from the room and quietly closing the door.

Facing Esther, Lawrence pointed towards the ivory-upholstered settee. 'Won't you take a seat? It's not very often I find my guests sitting on the floor.'

'Oh.' Clearly flustered, she quickly stood, her hands fluttering about her skirts. I — '

'But to hear my children laughing like that, makes me forever grateful to you that you let them play that way.'

She blushed and sat on the settee, glancing at her lap before meeting his eyes once more, her smile unusually shy. 'I'm not sure who enjoyed our play more. Them or me.' She lifted her hands to her hair, carefully plucking out Rose's haphazardly placed pins. 'I must look a frightful mess. I apologise.'

'Not at all.' Lawrence admired her long, blonde hair as it cascaded over her shoulders. He slowly sat beside her, forcing his gaze to the fireplace to stop from frightening her with his study. 'Was there something you wanted to speak to me about? Only . . . ' He faced her. 'I'm not entirely sure why you're here. Not that I mind in the slightest.'

She pulled her hair to one side before gathering it and twisting it onto the back of her head, then deftly plucked the pins from her mouth and secured it neatly in place. With her hair miraculously close to perfection, she laid her hands in her lap and met his gaze. 'I'm here because I owe you an apology. The way I spoke to you yesterday has bothered me ever since. You were merely being kind, worrying about my welfare should I join the suffragettes. My defensiveness was unnecessary, and, for that, I apologise.'

Lawrence smiled, somewhat surprised given her previous defiance, but wholly pleasured that her morality led her to offer an apology. 'You're forgiven. As I hope you'll forgive me for even implying you shouldn't do whatever you feel compelled to do. I had no right to assert myself that way.' She dropped her shoulders and rose to her feet. 'Then let us put the matter behind us. It's nice that we can part in a much better manner this time.'

A jolt of unexpected panic shot through him. 'You're

leaving?'

'Well, yes. I — '

'Please, I've ordered tea, which will undoubtedly come with some delicious cake. Trust me, you do not want to miss the chance to sample Mrs Jackson's baking.' He stood. He couldn't let her go. Not yet. 'Besides, there's something I'd like to discuss with you.'

'Oh?' Her gaze turned cautious as she slowly lowered to the settee, her hands gripping the brim of her burgundy hat so tightly, her knuckles showed white.

Lawrence returned to his seat beside her and drew in a slow breath. There were no two ways about it, Esther Stanbury was a woman with an unfathomable power to pull him backwards, forwards and sideways with a few carefully placed words. A woman who unwittingly hitched his heart whenever he looked into her eyes, so rich a hazel, they shone green one minute and the softest brown and gold the next. Could he really be this attracted to her in such a short space of time?

'You're staring, Mr Culford.'

Lawrence blinked, his cheeks warming. 'Sorry . . . '

The door opened and Mrs Jackson, his housekeeper and cook, entered carrying a laden tea tray complete with the Victoria sponge he'd been confident would be forthcoming.

'Ah, thank you, Mrs Jackson.' Lawrence smiled, grateful for his cook's interruption after Esther had caught him staring. 'Might I introduce you to Miss Esther Stanbury? She works as a window dresser at Pennington's.'

'How do you do, Miss?' Mrs Jackson flashed her kindly smile and laid the tray on a low table in front

67

of them, gave a curt nod and quickly left, closing the door behind her.

'Mrs Jackson is one of the best cooks in Bath, I swear.' Lawrence shook his head and laughed. 'Believe me when I say, she likes you already.'

She smiled. 'How can you possibly know that?'

'Because she's worked in this house for as long as I've lived here, which will be five years in November. Abigail employed Mrs Jackson almost as soon as we could afford a cook and they became very close. She picks and chooses how to greet my guests and I rely on her instincts absolutely. She smiled at you, which means you have her approval.'

'I'm glad.' Her gaze softened. 'Abigail was your wife?'

'Yes, she died during childbirth with Nathanial.'

She dipped her head. 'I'm so sorry.'

'Thank you.' Lawrence looked to the tea tray and busied himself stirring the pot. 'She is missed by all of us. The children most of all.'

'I'm sure she is. Rose and Nathanial are a true credit to you. I'm sure Abigail looks down on all of you with immense pride.'

Moved by her comments and care, he poured the tea and offered her cup, keen to move the conversation to safer, less personal, territory. 'So, how did you come by my address?'

Esther took the cup and glanced at him from under her lashes. 'I looked up your name and address in the toy department ledger.' She lifted her eyes, her cheeks lightly pinked. 'It was very forward of me, I know, but I so wanted to apologise.'

'And I'm glad you did.' Their eyes met for a moment before she looked towards the window.

Lawrence stared at her, suddenly a little nervous about the question urgently dancing on his tongue. 'Would you consider taking dinner with me, Esther? Can I call you Esther?'

She turned, her eyes wide with surprise. 'Dinner?'

'Yes, to further discuss the Cause. There will be nothing improper about you dining with me,' he said, a little too quickly if only to reassure himself as much as her. A dinner to discuss a mutual interest was his only motivation for his invitation. There was absolutely nothing more to it. 'I want to assure you of that. And, please, call me Lawrence.'

She softly smiled. 'Lawrence.'

He swallowed. She'd almost whispered his name and the sound had felt entirely seductive. 'So, what do you think? Would you take dinner with me?'

She regarded him for a long moment before she inhaled. 'All right. Why not?'

★ ★ ★

With her heart thundering with astonishment that she'd accepted his invitation of dinner, Esther looked to the marble fireplace. She stared at the vase in the centre of the hearth filled with pink, white and lilac blooms, desperate to change the subject. 'I can't help thinking your priorities must be vastly different to mine.'

'Oh?'

She turned as unwanted loneliness pressed down on her. His home was so warm and inviting. Seemingly full of love. The atmosphere so different to what she'd become accustomed to in recent years with her father and stepmother . . . maybe even latterly with

69

Aunt Mary. 'You have a beautiful home, staff and two wonderful children. I have no idea how you manage work and a family.'

'With difficulty sometimes, I must admit.' He sipped his tea and leaned back, the cup and saucer in his hand. 'But with Helen's help, Charles' and Mrs Jackson's, we manage well enough. My work life can sometimes be a different story.'

'How so?'

'Well, I try not to work at the weekends, unless it's absolutely unavoidable, but The Phoenix is a busy and popular hotel. For which I'm grateful, of course, but with success comes responsibility and I employ a lot of people as well as trying to be seen by as many guests as possible. Occasionally, those employees and guests can try a man's patience.' He smiled wryly. 'I've been known to lose my temper. Never overly so, but still . . . it's not ideal when you're trying to run a place designed to make people feel relaxed and comfortable.'

Pleased that he would be so open with her, Esther smiled in a bid to encourage his sharing . . . however misplaced and dangerous her interest. 'And how do *you* relax?'

He blinked as though no one had ever asked such a question of him. 'Well, I . . . '

'Play with the children?' She teased, hoping he realised she was interested rather than judging him in any way. 'I'm guessing that's the best relaxation any father could wish for.'

He lowered his shoulders and laughed. 'Yes, I suppose it is.' The faint sound of the children squabbling filtered through the ceiling, but neither he nor Esther glanced upwards. He raised his eyebrows and laughed.

70

'Most of the time.'

Their eyes locked and, just for a moment, Esther could believe they were alone. Entirely alone . . . and it was unnerving how little the notion scared her.

She blinked and put her cup and saucer on the table. 'I should go.'

Lawrence immediately followed suit. 'But you've not had any cake.'

'It's fine. I really must get home.' She placed her hat on her head, taking two pins from the moss-green cushion beside her and pushing them into place. 'Thank you so much for the tea.'

'You're welcome.'

She stood and walked to an elegant bureau where she'd laid her purse earlier in order to play with Rose and Nathanial. 'Where and when would you like to meet for dinner?'

'How about two nights from now? I'm really very keen to help with the Cause.'

The sincerity in his eyes was clear and Esther nodded, suddenly entirely certain Lawrence Culford's motives for their dinner were genuine. The fact her own wish to see him again had slightly blurred lines was neither here nor there. 'And I would very much like that, too.'

'I've previously supported the Cause by speaking with some influential people and offering funding, but I want to do more. I've an avid interest in local politics and our environment. You can check into my charitable work or, better still, see the fundraising events and auctions hosted at my hotel. I am not speaking empty words. I firmly believe it is right and just that women are granted the vote.'

'I'm glad.'

He smiled. 'Excellent. If you give me your address —'

'Why don't I meet you at The Orchard?' She interrupted, not wanting Lawrence anywhere near Aunt Mary's house so that she might report his presence back to her father and Viola. 'Shall we say seven o'clock?'

'Perfect. I really think you're going to be quite a challenge for me, you know.'

'Yes, I think I might well be.' She flashed him a smile, her stomach knotting with the hint of flirtation in his voice. She slowly walked to the door and pulled it open. 'I'll see myself out. Goodbye for now.'

'Goodbye, Esther.'

She closed the drawing room door and released a slow breath, thankful that the corridor was empty. She walked downstairs, casting a single disappointed glance upwards when she reached the bottom. She would have so liked to have said goodbye to the children. It wasn't until she was outside, along the short pathway of the house and safely around the corner that she could fully breathe again.

8

Lawrence leaned back from his desk and steepled his fingers beneath his chin as he stared at The Phoenix's manager, William Moorebrook. 'And has the band who decided to hold a party in one of their rooms last night been dealt with?'

'Yes, sir. Their singer, who I gather is in charge of the band, has agreed that the damages to the curtains and the bed coverings will be paid for upon their departure tomorrow.'

'Good. We cannot have that kind of thing going on in the hotel, William. I want to know immediately if there is any further confrontation when they check out.'

'Yes, sir.'

Lawrence pulled himself forward and reached for some papers beside him. 'If there's nothing else, I need to get on — '

'Well, there is one more thing.'

'Oh.' Lawrence leaned back again. 'Go on.'

William cleared his throat, looking uncharacteristically awkward.

Lawrence frowned. 'William?'

His manager coughed. 'It's been brought to my attention by Mrs Lewis that several of the chambermaids have been frequenting The Cavendish Club for several weeks now, sir.'

'The head of Housekeeping told you this?'

'Yes, sir.'

The Cavendish club was well-known throughout

73

Bath as a place of abundant drink, frivolity and new, slightly outrageous bands, not unlike the motley crew who'd taken advantage of The Phoenix's hospitality. That said, it didn't matter to Lawrence where his staff chose to spend their free time, and nor should it concern Mrs Lewis or William. 'And why should that concern me?'

'It seems three women in your employment were rather inebriated the other night and caused such a ruckus, they were ejected from the premises.'

'Ejected?'

'Yes, sir. Apparently, one of them had fallen onto a group of wealthy bankers, soaking one or two of them with her spilled glass of alcohol and, instead of apologising, the chambermaid retaliated with verbal abuse.'

'I see.' Now that sort of behaviour was most definitely a concern when he had the Phoenix's reputation to uphold. 'Were they arrested?'

'No, sir. This time they were lucky and only received a warning from the club's manager, but I really think we need to step in and speak with them.' William shook his head, his disapproval clear in his tightened lips. 'It's the Phoenix's duty as their employer to keep an eye on them. One, it will not be good for the hotel's reputation to have our employees falling about in a less than acceptable establishment and, two, Mrs Lewis is worried for their safety, sir. It has come to her attention that these particular women are taking it upon themselves to go out alone at night. Often seeking the company of wealthy men. Men they neither know nor should be so easily trusting. They are getting the reputation of being . . . ' Faint colour darkened William's cheeks. 'Free with themselves, sir.'

74

His deputy's discomfort should have been comical but, considering the gravity and potential danger of the situation, Lawrence felt anything but amused. 'I see. And Mrs Lewis thinks they're leaving themselves open to assault? Is that it?'

'Yes, sir.'

Protectiveness rose inside Lawrence and he nodded. 'Then I agree we need to get involved. I'll speak to them myself. What are their names?'

William handed a sheet of paper across the desk from the sheaf on his lap. 'I've taken the liberty of writing down their names, their length of service and performance records, sir. I thought you might want to speak with them and thought it best you were informed before you do so.'

'Good.' Lawrence scanned the names. 'Anna Baker, Victoria Griffiths and Ruth Parker. I have never known Mrs Lewis to have an issue with any of them before.' Lawrence looked up. 'She'll know these women a lot better than me.'

'I agree, but as she's raised concerns for their safety, I really think it must be dealt with by you.'

'Agreed. If anything should happen to one of these maids, I'd never forgive myself.'

'Indeed, sir. These girls are young. Barely into their late teens.'

Lawrence stared at his deputy who had the reputation of being fair but firm. A man with a cool head, whatever the crisis. The depth of worry in William's eyes was unprecedented. Lawrence frowned. 'Is there more to this than you're telling me, William?'

'No. I'm a father, sir. That's all.'

Nodding, Lawrence looked again at the names. Parenthood and what William implied lay deep and dangerous within himself, too. If these women were in jeopardy, it was just as much Lawrence's duty to keep them safe as their kin's.

'Leave it with me. I will speak to them later today.'

'Thank you, sir.'

William stood and dipped his head before walking from Lawrence's office, softly closing the door behind him.

Lawrence picked up the sheet of paper William had given him and leaned back in his chair. There had been genuine fear in his deputy's eyes and manner and Lawrence couldn't help but feel there had been more than the normal amount of apprehension in William's reaction. Was one, or all, of these women involved in something more perilous than high spirits and over-indulgence? Either way, Lawrence would get to the bottom of their behaviour and do all he could to help them.

9

Esther closed her tired eyes and fought the headache building at her temples. She sat at her aunt's dining room table working on an idea of Elizabeth's to feature a new display in the jewellery department, but every scratch of Esther's pencil seemed to propel her one step back rather than forwards.

However, for once, she could not blame her distraction on the Cause. Instead, it was Lawrence Culford who stole her concentration.

Opening her eyes, she stood and walked to a sideboard where she kept her files and documents pertaining to the Society. She removed a ledger and took it to the table, opening the pages at a list of the delegates in the Bath chapter. They still remained woefully low. Would such a meagre number of dedicated members hold the attention of a man used to dealing with hundreds of wealthy hotel guests? He'd already said he had influential associates, possibly friends, too.

Hopelessness that the group would never make a difference threatened. They had to invent a way to entice new supporters and members. Women all over the country were risking their lives . . . and the lives of others. The entire campaign had the potential to spiral out of control and lives could be lost if the government remained steadfast in their decision to exclude women from the vote.

Maybe Lawrence could canvas support and enrol other men to the Cause? Publicise the fight in his hotel?

Esther exhaled. She could not get ahead of herself. She suspected the interest in Lawrence's eyes whenever he looked at her had not been purely professional. But what could she really say or think when her own attraction continued to build, the more she learned about him?

'Ah, you're still working, I see.'

Esther turned as her aunt entered the room. 'I am, but I've moved from Pennington's work to the Cause.'

Her aunt shook her head, setting her grey curls trembling, her expression settling into a scowl. 'I might have agreed to take you into my home when my brother ordered you away, Esther, but that does not mean I disagree with his disapproval of your involvement in what will undoubtedly become an ever-increasing and dangerously volatile fight. Why do you not give up this nonsense? Your mother died with this campaign in her weakened heart and I am convinced that was the cause of her death. The government are unlikely to change their minds about the vote anytime soon.'

Annoyed, Esther closed the ledger and returned it to the sideboard, firmly closing the door. 'If the women involved give up hope, then there will be no chance at all of us winning. I will fight on for however long it takes.'

'Hmm, to the detriment of my well-being as well as your own, no doubt.'

'How can you say that?' Esther gathered her pencils and papers from the table. 'I look after you to the best of my ability, do I not? I pay towards your rent and put food on the table. I do all I can to ensure my staying here doesn't influence — '

'Doesn't influence what exactly? I cook a large amount of your meals, occasionally press your clothes and even sometimes shine your shoes.' Her aunt visibly bristled as she sat at the table. 'As your stepmother often says, do not fool yourself into thinking I need you, Esther. From where I'm sitting, it is much more the other way around.'

Esther glared, hating every time Aunt Mary said anything to infer her loyalty lie with Esther's stepmother rather than Esther, herself. Didn't she see how Viola was trying to manipulate her? Drive a wedge between Esther and her aunt? Sometimes, Esther began to hope Aunt Mary genuinely cared for her, only to have that hope quashed whenever she spoke of Viola. 'And by that I assume you have been talking to Viola today?'

'I have. She telephoned to see how I am and I told her I was entirely exhausted.'

Exasperated, Esther lowered herself into a seat opposite. 'If you do not wish to do things for me, then please, don't feel you have to. I see us as a unit, Aunt. Viola is trying to exert her control even from father's home in the Cotswolds. She has Papa under her thumb, do not let her do the same to you.'

'Under her thumb? Don't talk nonsense.' Her aunt snapped. 'She is a lovely woman with only your and my best interests at heart. If you choose not to see that, then — '

'Then it may be for the best that we do not discuss my stepmother. Speak to her and have her visit, if you must, but I have no desire to see her or hear of her opinions.'

Silence descended, and Esther was just about to speak when her aunt got there first.

'I care for you and you are running yourself into the ground for nothing. When was the last time you went for afternoon tea with a friend? Had even a passing interest in a gentleman? Good Lord, Esther, do you want to end up as I am? Alone and dependent on her niece's company?'

The hitch in her aunt's voice stilled Esther. This was a woman Esther considered unshakeable, a force to be reckoned with. Concerned, she reached across the table for her aunt's hand. 'Is something wrong, Aunt Mary?'

'Of course not.' She snatched her hand from Esther's, her gaze angry. 'I am merely saying it is un-ladylike, unnatural even, that you should work all day and then think nothing of standing on the street shouting at passers-by like a newspaper boy.' She stood, her cheeks red. 'My brother was not wrong when he sent you to me. I will see you married, Esther. For that, you should be grateful.'

'See me married?' Esther's concern vanished under the weight of her aunt's presumptions. 'What if I do not wish to marry? Maybe I'm happier alone.'

Her aunt gave an inelegant sniff. 'For the time being, possibly, but you are young. This independent charade of yours will soon crack as time goes on.'

Incensed, Esther stood, her body trembling. 'Well, for your information, I have a dinner arranged with a gentleman tomorrow evening.'

Her aunt's gaze lit with triumph. 'Aha. So, you do possess a heart and wanting beneath your stiff exterior.'

Hurt by her aunt's words, Esther flinched. 'How can you think me without heart when I do all I can to ensure your comfort and well-being?'

'In exchange for a home.'

Cursing the telephone call from Viola that had provoked yet another unmitigated attack from her aunt, Esther glared. 'That is not true.'

Her aunt gave a dismissive wave of her hand. 'It does not matter. Tell me, who is this gentleman you are dining with?'

Esther shook her head. There was not a chance on earth that she would reveal Lawrence's name. Mary Stanbury was the social climber to end all social climbers and Esther didn't doubt for a moment her aunt would recognise his name as owner of one of Bath's most prestigious hotels. Until she was certain of just how long, and on what foundation, their relationship would last, Esther would breathe nothing about Lawrence to anyone. 'There is no need for you to know who he is. He is a kind man whom I like very much, but we are nothing more than associates.'

'Associates? Does he work at Pennington's?' She pushed.

'No. He's an associate of the Cause.' Esther said the words with defiance, knowing any links with the Cause would put an end to her aunt's interest.

'The Cause? Oh, for heaven's sake, Esther.' Her aunt stood, before marching to the door. 'Will you never learn?'

Esther glared at the doorway as her aunt disappeared into the hallway. Sometimes she couldn't help but wonder if her aunt cared for her at all. Her constant questions, judgement and disparagement barely differed from her father's. Yet, his sister had taken Esther in, had told her she had a home for as long as she needed it. Why would her aunt do that if she did not love her?

She had to believe it was only fear for Esther's future that drove Aunt Mary to be harsh from time to time. If she and Aunt Mary became estranged too, Viola would have succeeded in ostracising Esther from yet another family member. She would not allow that to happen.

Striding from the dining room with her plans, Esther walked upstairs to her bedroom. Tomorrow she would see Lawrence. Maybe a meal and conversation with a man who interested her would be just what she needed to keep the insecurities about her life at bay.

Walking to her wardrobe, she pulled out a long, satin dress, then another, then another — all clothes she had brought from home when she'd relied on her father's wealth to feed and clothe her. The more she examined her clothes, the more her old life felt in touching distance and she pushed the notion deep down inside where it couldn't hurt her.

She must focus on the here and now. Who she was today.

But nerves tumbled through her as she considered her dinner with Lawrence. Was she mad going through with this? Lawrence was wealthy, refined and a wonderfully caring father. She lived with her aunt, going from pay packet to pay packet with no idea what her future held.

She moved to the mirror and critically assessed her face and hair. Could it really be that his only interest in her was the Cause? Was she a fool to think she detected something deeper in the way he watched and spoke with her?

Esther closed her eyes.

When would she ever believe she was wanted and valued?

10

Lawrence glanced at the huge, ornate white clock hanging above The Orchard's entrance. Even though it was barely a minute past seven, his foot tapped against the parquet flooring. Nerves poked and prodded at him, but no matter how hard he tried to relax, repose felt an unachievable task until Esther arrived . . . *If* she arrived.

He reached for his water, shaking his head as a suited waiter approached holding a wine list. The young man dipped his head and retreated.

The alien feeling of being out of control made Lawrence sit a little straighter in his seat. Finely decorated in shades of pale cream and blue, tables laid with shining tableware and glinting crystal, intricate cornices and marble statues giving an ambience of serenity, the restaurant's interior should have held a calming quality. Yet nothing but self-reproach that he had orchestrated time with Esther tormented him. His motivations did not lie with what was best for his children. Nor did they entirely lie with the Cause. A whole lot of reasoning came down to his own desires. His own pleasure. He liked Esther. A lot. In fact, his emotions ran worryingly wild.

An hour before, he'd walked the foyer and dining room of The Phoenix purely for something to do. He should have utilised the time to think what he would say to Esther about the Cause, but he couldn't consider anything but his concern that she wouldn't arrive at all.

He would do his best tonight to entice her wonderful smile, evoke the glorious softening he'd seen in her eyes whenever she was with the children. He'd only seen her dressed in her Pennington's uniform, the green skirt and jacket cinched tight with a wide black belt that accentuated every inch of her delicate figure.

She was stunning.

But he also understood her occasional need for walls.

Whether for self-preservation or caution.

Knew all too well how vital they were to a person's sanity and mental liberty.

How could he expect Esther to trust him on little more than a few fleeting meetings? A few minutes of conversation? Such expectation was entirely unfair when he continued to fear the disclosure of his own buried secrets.

He reached for his water glass, his other hand fisted beneath the table. Time and again, he battled the need to yell out loud about all that had happened to him. The way he'd been raised, the physical and psychological effects of the abuse he'd endured and how it continued to haunt him —

The entrance doors opened, and the attendant stepped forward.

Esther.

Relief she'd come flooded through him and Lawrence cursed the kick in his chest. The way he immediately rose to his feet and approached her indicated every inch of his impatience.

She smiled at the maître d' as he took her coat, her gaze flitting behind him towards the main restaurant. Lawrence slowed, wanting to watch her for a moment without her noticing him. She wore a pink dress that fell to her ankles, the silk satin material flowing over every curve, and the neckline low, yet decently so, accentuated by a single string of pearls. Her hair was piled high on her head, a pink feather pinned amongst the blonde tresses. Simple, yet breathtaking.

Desire stirred in his groin, and Lawrence breathed deep, berating the way his body betrayed him. He wanted so much for her to think him a thoughtful man. Capable and strong. Carnal attraction was far below what she evoked in him and he wanted to ensure she perceived as much.

This was a woman who deserved his full attention about an issue that mattered to her — mattered to him — and if he was to impress Esther enough to secure another dinner, a picnic, ride or walk, he had to show her his interest in her went beyond desire.

He studied her again. She carried herself with elegance and grace. So much so he wondered if she'd been tutored in deportment and etiquette.

Were her family moneyed? He could only guess so considering her poise and the clear quality and beauty of her gown. She spoke so eloquently, was hugely intelligent and clearly well-educated. Everything about her spoke of upper-middle class.

Yet, she worked in a store, albeit as a dresser with a creative flair that was entirely unique. Curiosity about her background and her life once more stirred in him, indicating just how much better he wanted to get to know her.

The maître d' leaned close to her and she said something, before he nodded and turned.

Lawrence's gaze immediately locked with hers.

Her smile faltered as her study quickly travelled

over him from head to toe, before she met his eyes, her shoulders slightly higher than when she'd spoken with the maître d'.

She walked towards him, the maître d' ahead of her. 'Mr Culford, Miss Stanbury has arrived. Can I return you to your table?'

Lawrence barely heard the man as he brushed past him to take Esther's arm. As he touched her, she lifted her gaze, a glimpse of happiness in her eyes before she looked ahead. Relieved she didn't think him forward or obtuse for touching her, Lawrence stood a little taller.

As they walked, men turned or glanced towards Esther, their eyes darkening with interest. Lawrence pulled back his shoulders, proud that it was him escorting her tonight. Hopefully, for another night, should the evening go well.

They reached their table and the maître d' held Esther's chair as she gracefully sat. Lawrence took his seat, unable to look away from her. She looked astounding, but he suspected she hadn't noticed a single gentleman admiring her. Her focus travelled over their surroundings, towards the chandeliers, to the right and left at their fellow diners, before she looked at the opulent white crockery and glittering glasses adorning the table.

'Can I ask Richard to bring the wine list, Mr Culford?'

Lawrence dragged his gaze to the maître d'. 'Wonderful, thank you.'

The maître d' nodded at Lawrence and then Esther before moving away.

Esther met his eyes as she released a shaky breath. 'It has been quite a while since I've been in a place like this.'

Concerned that she might not like the surroundings or regretted her suggestion they dine at The Orchard, Lawrence frowned. 'You don't like the restaurant? We can always go somewhere else, if you'd prefer?'

'Oh, no. It's lovely. But it's also rich. Fancy. My tastes are a lot simpler than my family's.' Her cheeks lightly flushed. 'I think I might have suggested this particular restaurant to impress you that I knew of it.'

'You've been here with your family?' Had he been right in his deduction that she came from a wealthy family? If so, he prayed to God her childhood had been happier than his own.

'A few times, but that was many years ago.' She sighed, wistfully. 'The Orchard was one of my mother's favourite places to eat in the city.'

Hating the sudden sadness in her voice, Lawrence leaned closer. 'Was?'

The skin at her neck shifted as she swallowed. 'My mother died a few years ago. Influenza.'

He moved to touch her hand where it lay on the table but hesitated and reached for his glass instead. To touch her could be too much, too soon. His heart went out to her that the death of her mother should still so deeply affect her. 'I'm so sorry.'

She smiled softly. 'So am I. She was a wonderful woman and I miss her every day.' Her eyes brightened with pride. 'She was everything to me. It was her that introduced me to women's struggles and rights, the importance of gaining the vote. She was beautiful, inspirational and a wonderful mother.'

Lawrence stared in quiet contemplation. What would it feel like to have been raised by such a woman? He swallowed. Happy for Esther beyond belief that

87

she'd known such love and security but also saddened that it had been taken from her, he fought to find the words that might offer her comfort. 'Now it makes complete sense how you came to be such a wonderful person, too.'

Her cheeks tinged with pink. 'Thank you. I grew up happy, but in adulthood things changed and now I'm estranged from my father because of the Cause.'

Lawrence raised his eyebrows. 'But your mother fought for the vote and you followed in her footsteps. Surely your father has been surrounded by the issue for many years?'

'Yes.' She sighed. 'And tolerating my mother's passions was enough. When I followed in her footsteps, it was too much. He wasn't prepared 'to go through all that again', as he put it.'

'Then it's his loss.' Tension rippled through him that their lives weren't worlds apart after all. How could her father not appreciate such a beautiful, passionate and caring daughter? 'He should be extremely proud of you.'

She smiled even though a semblance of sadness shadowed her gaze. 'Thank you.'

The waiter approached and handed Lawrence the wine list. He immediately passed it to Esther.

'Why don't you choose?'

She raised her eyebrows in surprise before she smiled and took the leather-bound menu.

Once the wine, their appetisers and main courses had been ordered, Lawrence clasped his hands on top of the table. 'So, tell me more about your work.'

She sipped her water. 'For the Cause or Pennington's?'

All of it. I want to know everything about you. 'Either.

88

Both.'

'Well, Pennington's is a wonderful place and I thank God every day that Elizabeth gave me a position there.'

'Ah, Elizabeth Pennington. I should've guessed she was the daughter of Edward Pennington.'

'You know him?'

'I know *of* him. I've heard he isn't the most amicable of men. Is that true? I assume you knew him when he ran the store?'

'I did but have learned a lot more about him as Elizabeth and I have grown closer. It seems that his old-fashioned views on society and commerce have lessened somewhat, but that might well be because he's happy travelling the globe with his new fiancée.'

'Fiancée?' The man had to be at least sixty years old.

'Yes. Annabelle Heimann. She's absolutely lovely, glamorous and kind. Elizabeth could fall at her feet for keeping her father away from the store, I'm sure.'

Lawrence laughed. 'Well, I've never actually spoken to him, but the changes Pennington's have made since he handed over the reins are remarkable.'

Satisfaction burned in her eyes. 'I'll be sure to pass on your compliments to Elizabeth.'

'And you're happier there now?'

'Much. As is everyone else who works there, I suspect. Edward Pennington was not a man crusading for equal rights or opportunity, believe me. He'd much prefer for rich and poor, young and old, male and female, to be put in little boxes where he could decide who he allowed to do what.'

Lawrence smiled, his fondness of her escalating. He could listen to her all night. She burst with passion and care. 'You started work there as a window dresser?'

'Oh, no.' She laughed. 'I was a shop girl for at least a year before I grew brave enough to one day voice my opinions to Elizabeth about the windows. She was instantly interested in what I had to say, and we got along so well.' She took another sip of water. 'I was lucky. I desperately needed a job and consider myself even more fortunate I have one I love.'

The waiter came to the table with their wine and appetisers, and Lawrence watched Esther as she smiled at the waiter and placed her napkin across her lap. She had shared some of her history with him, but details of his own remained buried. Maybe he could at least share a little about Abigail and his sisters this evening.

The waiter retreated and Esther picked up her spoon. 'Hmm, this soup is delicious.'

'Good.' Lawrence dipped his spoon into his bowl. 'Your visit to the house caused Mrs Jackson to ask a few questions, you know.'

She laughed. 'I'm not surprised. Your cook struck me as a formidable woman from your summary of her.'

'She is. Even though my marriage to Abigail was arranged and we made no secret of that, Mrs Jackson reads a lot of romance novels and she liked to look at Abigail and me as a hero and heroine, bound together on a path of eternal bliss. As much as we cared for each other, we also respected each other's roles in the house, work and with Rose. We were a good team.'

She carefully watched him, concern shadowing her eyes. 'And you miss her?'

'Yes. Yes, I do. It wasn't right that she died so young.' Lawrence shook his head. 'The children will suffer

90

the most over time from her death.'

'I've no idea how you've managed without her these past years.'

'With the help of my amazing staff and the occasional visits from my sister, Cornelia.'

Esther's hazel eyes brightened with interest. 'You have a sister?'

'Two. Cornelia, the eldest, and Harriet, the youngest.'

'And you're the elder brother.'

'I am.'

They ate in silence for a moment before Esther spoke again, her brow furrowed. 'You said occasional visits. Do you not see your sisters very often? I have two half-siblings, Peter and Benedict. I'd like to think we'll one day see each other more often than we do now. Especially if one or all of us have children.'

Pleased that she mentioned one day having children, Lawrence smiled. 'Cornelia has two boys, Alfred and Francis. When she visits, the house is loud, messy and filled with laughter. Just the way it should be. As for Harriet? She's on a very different path than motherhood and family life.'

'Oh?'

'Money. It's all about money with Harriet.' He cleared his throat and decided to shift the conversation to safer ground, lest she ask about his and his sisters' upbringing. 'Enough from me, let's discuss your work for the Cause. Tell me what you'd like me to help with.'

'Why don't you tell me what you'd like to do to help? It interests me to gain a man's perspective on a fight that is widely considered a woman's struggle. The more male support we have, the more the government is likely to take notice. There's only so many steps we can take to make these people realise women matter, too.'

'Unfortunately, I fear you're right.' Lawrence put down his spoon and picked up his wine. 'I don't doubt your passion and insight is shared by thousands of women across the country and the Government are regrettably short-sighted. Something must be done. I'd love to offer you the use of The Phoenix in your endeavours. We welcome a large scope of people, from businessmen, to foreign visitors, to families travelling through the south-west. Visitors from all over the country, all over Europe, want to see our famous Georgian spa town. The city is an attraction. Men and women alike come to see the Roman Baths, Royal Crescent, The Pump Room . . . even where Jane Austen lived for a few years. Bath is a tourist attraction, which can only be to the Cause's benefit. Why not capitalise on the passing trade? Why not gain their interest in the hope they'll add their voices to the fight? Maybe some will even leave the city with a mind to starting their own group of campaigners.'

Her eyes were alight with interest. 'You want to host an event at the hotel? Well, it's definitely an interesting idea, but what about you?'

Lawrence hovered his spoon at his mouth as caution whispered through him. 'Me?'

'Yes. What can *you* bring to the Cause? The hotel is something you own, it isn't you. I want to know what sparked your interest in the Suffrage Bill. Why it speaks to you personally? Once I know that, then I'll know what makes you tick, so to speak.'

Uneasy, he was struck dumb and slowly lowered his spoon. Except for Cornelia, never before had anyone wanted to know who he really was inside. Never before had anyone not taken him and his actions at face value and not accepted what he said and did as anything but his truth. Esther was different. Intelligent. Astute. Canny . . . and he should be wary. Very wary. If he failed to maintain the stronghold on the face he presented to the world and allow his attraction to this woman to tilt the balance of his self-control, their relationship could end in his utter humiliation.

'Lawrence? Have I said something wrong?'

His automatic smile slipped into place. 'Not at all.' He took another sip of his soup, thankful that it went some way to easing the sudden dryness in his throat. 'My interest in the Cause started when I heard some women who work for me discussing it at the hotel. I stopped. Asked questions. These women were mature, competent, intelligent and hard-working. It is wrong that they haven't a hand in our country's decision-making. On top of that, I have Rose and I want her to grow up in a world where she has a voice.'

There. He'd kept his explanations truthful, if not entirely all-encompassing. His other reasons, his more personal reasons, would remain hidden. Esther did not need to know how hard he had fought, the pain he'd had to overcome to speak his mind. She didn't need to know how complicit his parents had been in their treatment of him, and the kind of boy and man Lawrence had been for the first two and half decades of his life.

He acted with cowardice, but what choice did he have if he wanted Esther to remain interested in him? If she were to learn how he'd grown up and the scars he carried on his skin and deep inside, she wouldn't look at him with attentiveness but pity.

'I like that very much.' She smiled and laid down her spoon. 'You want change. For Rose, your staff. Maybe even a new wife one day.'

He stilled. 'A new wife?'

Her cheeks reddened and she quickly reached for her wine. 'I apologise. I shouldn't presume you'll want to marry again.' She took a drink and returned her glass to the table. 'After all, marriage is the last thing I want.'

The last thing? Did she not see a husband in her future? She'd mentioned children. Didn't she want a family? After the way she'd been with Rose and Nathanial, Lawrence could all too easily — too unnervingly — imagine her embracing motherhood.

He picked up his wine and leaned back, feigning repose. 'Tell me what you need me to do.'

11

Esther gripped her knife and fork as her appetite for food was replaced with an appetite for Lawrence's understanding. 'The Cause is about more than the vote. It's about . . . ' She searched the restaurant, her gaze falling on one woman after another. She faced him, enthusiasm rolling through her. 'It's about liberation. Having women embrace the belief they are equally as capable, equally as powerful, as the men with whom they share their lives.'

'Hmm.' His eyes glazed a little as though a thought had struck him and then he frowned. 'Yesterday, I had to speak with three of the hotel's chambermaids about their recent behaviour away from the hotel.'

Confused by the change in subject, Esther raised her eyebrows. 'And their behaviour had something to do with what I just said?'

'Yes and no.' He picked up his water and drank, before slowly lowering the glass to the table. 'My manager was disturbed that they were asked to leave a club recently for overexuberance fuelled by drink and youth. I was immediately concerned but wanted to hear their side of the story. They explained they were doing little more than what men do all the time. They asked why they shouldn't have some innocent fun in their leisure time, too? Why it's frowned upon for them to go out unchaperoned when men are free to come and go as they please.'

Esther smiled. 'Exactly. These women seem admirably spirited.'

'Oh, they are. And by the end of my time talking with them, a reprimand from me had felt entirely unjustified. I asked them to show a little discretion and sent them on their way. I'm wondering now if they could be the perfect candidates to set to work on any suffrage campaigning we might plan from the hotel.'

'That's a wonderful idea.' Esther eagerly sat forward. 'Are these women fairly young?'

'Eighteen or nineteen.'

'Then they will be perfect. Women as young as eighteen sometimes feel the fight is not theirs as they cannot see how a vote will ever be given to them. Whereas I think the younger the women involved, the better. They are our future, after all.'

His beautiful blue eyes remained intense on hers. 'Are you widely open with your work?'

'What do you mean?'

He lifted his shoulders. 'Do you demonstrate? Talk publicly about your dreams and desires for women?'

'Of course.' Esther studied him. The lowered tone of his voice and the seriousness of his expression indicated a shift in his demeanour. She couldn't help but worry her slipped reference to his remarrying had in some way offended him. She cleared her throat. 'Why would you think otherwise?'

'Oh, I don't. I can imagine you're as forthright with anyone else as you are with me.'

So, she had annoyed him. Her confidence wavered and she took a sip of her water. 'I try to be, but it's not always easy. There are more suffragists groups throughout the south-west than there are suffragettes. As a suffragist, I aim to help with peaceful campaigning, but, as I said to you before, I'm finding doing so increasingly difficult. I appreciate your concern for my welfare, but, if the future should require it, I'll do whatever is necessary for women to be heard, and I'm sure others in our group will, too. This isn't a battle, Lawrence, it's a war. If we must take up arms to prove victorious, so be it.'

He stared at her before giving a curt nod and picking up his knife and fork. 'Then I'll do all I can in the hope you aren't forced into militant action.'

The softer tone of his voice spoke of his care. Of intimacy.

Esther looked to her food and speared a small piece of potato. She could not encourage his care. She needed his support and help, but not his care. That would mean they had traversed the line between associates and friends. She wasn't sure that either of them should step over that line. At least, not yet.

'And I thank you, but you barely know me. The Cause and what it means to you should be your only interest.' She lifted her eyes to his. 'What do you have in mind to contribute?'

'I've hosted fundraising events for many different causes as well as helping to fund the *Votes For Women* newspaper. I'm also a member of the Men's League for Women's suffrage, an active role . . . but a peaceful one.'

Esther could only stare at him. To happen upon a man in the street admonishing his daughter for wanting a cricket set and making such a snap judgement of his character was shaming.

She shook her head. 'I misjudged you very badly indeed, didn't I?'

He smiled. 'You did.'

'I'm sorry, Lawrence. Truly. I sometimes allow my

passions to run away with me. My father considered that to the detriment of my character, whereas I'd like to think it a virtue, but that doesn't mean our meeting hasn't made me realise the folly of quick and mistaken judgement.'

He ran his gaze over her face, lingering a moment on her mouth. 'I would hate to see you change in any way. There are many men out there who, like me, believe it will only be a positive step forward for women to have the vote. Let's try to achieve that without causing harm to anyone or anything.'

Esther ate another bite of lamb. How could she think less of him for his care? Think less of him for believing there would be a peaceful breakthrough. But how was she, Lawrence or the Society supposed to achieve such a thing? Still she failed to come up with an intervention that would lead to success. As one of the leading group members, many of the women looked not only to Louise for guidance and inspiration, but Esther, too. Yet, as more and more time passed, she felt herself failing them.

Would the government eventually agree to the women's demands through speech only? She couldn't believe it to be true.

She laid down her fork and picked up her water glass. 'Women have resourcefulness, courage and endurance to match that of any man. Do men not resort to war eventually? Battle lines will be drawn, Lawrence, no matter how much you or I might not want that.' She inhaled and slowly released a breath, suddenly wanting him to understand how much she had already revolted against. How she'd learned to stand tall and strong alone. Frustration seeped into Lawrence's expression and unease whispered through her, causing her defences to rise. 'Why are you looking at me that way? Have I said something you don't like? Something to make you think asking me to dinner is the very last thing you should've done?'

'You misread me. What you see is genuine concern. Concern for you. To the life I believe you cherish.'

Her heart thundered, as she fought not to squirm under his scrutiny. Why did she suddenly feel as though he could see inside her heart and mind? What was wrong with her? Why had she told him — a relative stranger — so much of her history? Of her parents? He had clearly guessed that her passions were everything to her. Something she hadn't even shared with Louise or Elizabeth.

Esther swallowed. Because no one else had ever looked into her eyes and immediately known how she truly felt, rather than the outside façade of independence and determination.

He continued to study her; the chatter, clinking of glasses and cutlery seeming to increase in volume, only adding to her sudden claustrophobia.

At last, he lowered his shoulders and looked to his plate. 'Let us put our heads together and come up with a new avenue to explore. A new strategy to action. Then I can decide what funding I'm willing to donate.'

Money. Why was he turning the conversation to money? Did he think she wanted him to join forces with her because he was wealthy? Indignation swept through her. 'You think I don't have money of my own?'

'I didn't say — '

'I have possibilities of my own making. It's not money I am looking for from you, it's belief.' She cursed the prick of tears behind her eyes. 'In me. In women. In Rose.'

His jaw tightened. 'I've already told you Rose is in my thoughts with this. You have my belief. How can you think otherwise when I've already told you of my prior commitment to the Cause before we met?' He glanced past her shoulder as though not wanting to look at her. 'If we're to work together, you have to stop presuming anything about me or my children.'

Frustration lowered her voice as she stared at his profile. 'I'm not presuming anything. By whatever means, I intend to make a change in this world. Shake the authorities out of their ignorance and better the country. But the moment I mention Rose, a little girl who will one day be a woman of my age, you become angry. Why?'

He turned his gaze to hers, his cheeks mottled. 'Is it really necessary I explain myself? You're clearly already a good judge of my character.'

Esther's heart thundered. Were they really arguing in so public a place? Yet, instead of leaving, she leaned closer, adrenaline flowing through her on a dangerous wave.

'Could it be you're angered because, deep inside, you don't really want anything more for Rose than for her to be dependent on you, to love you forever and never doubt your word or your motivation? That, in her eyes, you are forever her saviour, teacher and controller. Maybe you're a member of the League to soothe your own foibles. To make yourself acceptable to your female hotel guests and staff as much as the men. Could you be straddling two sides of the argument in an effort to keep everyone happy? If yes, then your part in the fight is merely superficial.'

'Super — ' His eyes flashed with fury. 'I have never controlled Rose or Nathanial in any way other than fatherly and with love. I believe in the vote. I believe in women. How can you even think to say such things to me?'

She'd pushed him too far. She had no right to paint him the same colour as her father. Yet he'd provoked her shame, her fear for other girls who loved their fathers with the depth she loved hers. It wasn't right for a daughter to rely solely on a man who could one day let her down and send her into exile when her opinions differed with his.

She stood and dropped her napkin onto the table, her hands shaking. 'I should leave.'

'Do you not like me challenging you?'

Insult struck her, and no matter how much she felt the right thing to do was to go, she could not when such anger burned in his eyes.

She slowly lowered to her seat and took a hefty gulp of her wine. 'I don't want to argue with you, but you must understand how hard it is to be reliant on a man when he could let you down.' Her words tumbled out of her despite wanting to bring their dispute to an end. 'One who might have a life planned for you that you want no part of.'

'I would never do that to Rose.'

She looked deep into his eyes, her heart stumbling to witness such sincerity in him. She lowered her voice. 'You can't be certain of that. I've been forced to see that no father can. No matter how much he might have loved his daughter when she was growing up.'

'Loved? I'll *always* love Rose.'

Esther closed her eyes, fighting her tears as the love her father had once had for her slammed into

101

her heart, splintering another crack across its surface. She opened her eyes. 'Well, my father stopped loving me a long time ago.' With that, she stood. 'I'm leaving, Lawrence. I'm sorry.'

12

Lawrence stared after her.

By God, did he not understand parental pain more than most? Did he not understand how fathers and mothers could give birth to their children and when they grew into individuals with their own minds, scruples, dreams and desires, they could be tossed aside, or else pummelled into submission? Hadn't his hatred towards his parents been drawn by not just the way they treated him, but how they had stood side by side in their actions. Equally to blame and equally ambitious.

'Damnation.'

He lifted his hand and nodded to a nearby waiter that he wished to pay his bill.

As he waited, he drummed his fingers on the table-top, his foot rapidly tapping against the expensive flooring, each minute like an hour. When the waiter reappeared, Lawrence scribbled his signature across the bill and leapt to his feet. He had to catch up with Esther.

Self-disgust twisted inside him. No one on earth could understand the desire to want more for the next generation. The cruelty inflicted on him in the name of making him a man had ensured he would never disparage or deny Rose and Nathanial the paths they chose for themselves.

Instead of listening to Esther, doing his utmost to understand her frustration, he'd turned her words into knives with which to stab at his own insecurities, his own fears that he might harbour the genetic traits of her father that could one day bubble to the surface, spill over and hurt everyone in their path.

He stalked towards the entrance. Her coat. Had she picked up her coat? Rain battered the windows and ran in rivulets down the glass, the evening sky heavy and dark. It was pouring, and Esther might as well have been wearing a satin sheath for all the protection her beautiful dress would provide. He stepped in front of the maître d', ignoring the grumbled protests from the gentleman beside him.

'Did Miss Stanbury take her coat? An umbrella?'

'She's left the restaurant?' The maître d' looked behind him towards their empty table. He faced Lawrence. 'Well, no, sir. I didn't notice that she — '

'Then could you please retrieve her coat for me? I must find her before she is half-drowned.' Self-admonishment pressed down on him. It was his fault he pushed her away; his fault she'd fled into the night unprotected.

'Of course.' The maître d' grimaced at the fuming customer beside Lawrence. 'Please, sir. Just one moment.' He walked to the cloakroom at the side of the restaurant and spoke quietly with the young girl checking and hanging coats. Moments later, he came back with Esther's coat.

'Thank you.' Lawrence took the coat and turned to the gentleman beside him. 'My apologies, sir.'

Before the man could respond, Lawrence dashed to the door and ducked outside into the rain. He could've sworn there had been tears in Esther's eyes before she'd fled the restaurant — and she *had* fled. Her rushed steps so very different from the confident, graceful walk he'd watched the handful of times she'd

104

left his side before.

This evening her gait had been flustered, upset and its cause lay entirely with him.

Scanning the busy street, Lawrence breathed in the scent of expensive perfume mixed with hair cream as dressed-up couples passed him arm in arm. The feeling of the upcoming Coronation seemed to be everywhere, from the banner stretched across the street to the chatter and laughter filtering from restaurant and store windows. A day of celebration. A day of new beginnings. Only time would tell if those beginnings would change this city and country for the better.

As he hurried along the stone-flagged pavement, a small boy stopped in his path, his cupped hands outstretched. 'A penny for a hot roll, sir?'

Lawrence reached into his pocket and put two pennies in the boy's hand. 'Here. Get two.'

'Thank you, sir.' The boy's eyes widened as he flitted his gaze from Lawrence to the coins and back again.

'You're welcome.' Smiling, Lawrence touched his hat, nodded at the boy and continued along the street looking for Esther.

On and on he walked, passing more and more poor, malnourished adults and children vying for charity from the wealthy who strolled back and forth. The differences between the rich and poor in Bath was abhorrent. Something had to be done to change the vast chasm between the privileged and the starving. It was neither fair nor right that some died from hunger while others grew obese.

He drew to a stop.

Esther stood under the awning of a latticed-windowed shop, her dress darker pink in places where the rain had soaked through. Staring at the wares inside, she seemed oblivious to the falling rain.

Slowly, he approached, uncertainty and self-judgement in every step. How did he speak with her, apologise for his behaviour without sharing any of his familial history?

Lawrence closed the distance, the street suddenly feeling strangely empty of people and transport. The ground shone beneath his feet, the lamps reflected in the puddles and the rain drenching his hair and the shoulders of his suit jacket.

Esther turned, and he halted as her eyes met his across the few yards that separated them. Her beautiful face was a mask of sadness. Her eyes almost pleading with him as he came closer. Once he was under the awning, she looked into his eyes, seemingly searching for something. A quip lingered on his tongue. To say something to make her laugh. Even the urge to replicate the funny face she'd pulled for Nathanial suddenly felt plausible compared to the blankness he was certain his face showed. What did he do now?

He shook out her coat and held it open.

She lowered her focus to his mouth, her expression inscrutable.

Stepping closer, she leaned into him, her gaze locked on his lips. His hands itched to touch her, to pull her into his embrace and kiss away her sorrow. She lifted her eyes to his and an unimaginable hunger burned in her gaze, her mouth dropping slightly open. Lawrence's heart beat a little faster as he stepped closer still.

He wrapped her coat around her and released his held breath . . . and then took an impulsive leap that could so easily end in disaster. He lowered his mouth

106

to hers.

She sighed softly before clasping her arms about his waist. He pressed his body closer to hers, wrapping her more firmly into his warmth.

She tasted like rainwater and the softest, sweetest perfume. He breathed in the floral scent of her skin, marvelled at the softness of her lips. This wasn't the time to think, to contemplate or even panic. He eased his tongue tentatively against hers, and she shuddered gently in his arms as she raised onto her toes to deepen the kiss. Every part of him burned with a desire that had never been ignited before. His erection strained, his heart thundered, and his mind filled with only her.

The rest of the world ceased to exist.

He could've stayed in their kiss forever . . .

A salty wetness slipped onto his mouth.

Tears. *Her* tears.

He eased back, glistening drops ran slowly over her cheeks and he lifted his hands, thumbed away her sadness. 'I'm so sorry.'

Her eyes were glazed as though she'd been as lost in their shared moment as he had been.

She blinked, and her eyes widened before she stepped back. 'I . . . shouldn't have let you kiss — '

'Yes. Yes, you should.' He opened the coat, so she could put her arms into the sleeves. 'And I hope, in time, you will again.'

She shook her head, her eyes lowered revealing a vulnerability he hadn't seen in her before. 'But our argument — '

'Is forgotten.' How could she even begin to come to a different conclusion when his mind and heart was now filled with nothing but their kiss?

Her distress showed in her beautiful eyes, her brow

furrowed. 'How can our words be so easily dismissed when they became so heated?'

'Because they can. I meant it when I said I want to help with your endeavours. If you don't want my financial help then, maybe, I could come to your next demonstration to understand more fully what you do and how I can help?'

She tipped her head back to meet his gaze, her eyes lingering on his as she considered. Finally, she exhaled. 'Not a protest. Not yet.'

Hope spread. *Not yet.* Did this mean she wanted to see him again. 'But another time?'

'Yes.' She dipped her gaze to the pavement before meeting his eyes once more. 'Why don't you come to the store tomorrow evening? With Rose?'

'Pennington's?'

'Yes. A lady author is coming in. She's written a book about her rise from widowhood and how she was left a small bakery by her husband. Despite the odds stacked against her, she went on to open a second shop and, now, a third. She seems very inspiring. A woman forging forward. I think you'd enjoy listening to her speak.'

'And you think Rose would, too.'

Mischief sparkled in her eyes as she smiled. 'Absolutely.'

'Then tomorrow night it is.' Satisfaction and joy swept through him. Whatever she'd suggested, he would have agreed as long as he saw her again.

He buttoned her coat and brushed a damp curl from her cheek, hoping upon hope she did not disappear from his life as quickly as she'd appeared. He wanted so much to get to know her, to share a little of her life even if he could never share it all. 'Will you

108

allow me to hire a cab? I'd like to ensure you get home safely.'

'You don't need to . . . ' She stopped, her shoulders dropping as she softly smiled. 'Yes. I'd like that very much.'

'Good. I'll go along the street and find one. I'll not be more than a few minutes.'

He turned and jogged along the street, happiness and pride filling his chest in a great heave, pushing the air from his lungs. He had to find a way to gain Esther's trust. Because, right now, she needed him . . . and he needed her.

13

Esther stood with her back to the mahogany book-shelves lining Pennington's book department and scanned the area around her. She and her team had transformed the space for this evening's event and she felt as proud of them as she had for the live manne-quin shows they had held last year.

A small platform had been erected at the back of the room, with rows of gold-painted chairs, uphol-stered in sapphire blue velvet, lined up in front of it. Her department had excelled in the manufacturing of a wooden backdrop, painted to look like the façade of a small bakery. Grace Hadley, widow, now baker extraordinaire, would surely love the setting and everything Esther and her team had achieved.

Everything looked spectacular, which meant the cause of Esther's persistent nerves could only be the worry of whether Lawrence would come and if lovely Rose would accompany him.

Lovely Rose? Esther sighed. She could not look at Lawrence's daughter that way. Neither should she constantly ponder Nathanial's cheeky loveliness. Why had this beautiful family appeared so unexpectedly in her life? Of course, she'd like to think that one day she would fall in love and grow to trust her lover enough that marriage, a home and children lay on her horizon. But, for now, her work and commitment to the Cause superseded any intimate desires she might have.

Yet, if or when love and a family appeared, she would model her parenting on her mother and use her father's later attitude as a reminder that lives change, her children would change and with that should come parental understanding, patience and the ability to listen rather than merely judge and discard.

Esther inhaled a shaky breath. Her commitment to the women's movement provided safety from further heartbreak. If she allowed herself to muse about the kiss she'd shared with Lawrence, to daydream about a handsome, kind and intelligent man, then the distraction would most certainly destroy all her hard work. The passion that had emanated from him in that moment had taken her breath away, making her itch to explore the mystery within the portrait he unwittingly painted of a possible future.

She'd once thought of children constantly. Wondering how and when she'd meet the man she would marry. When and how many children they would have. 'An incurable romantic' her father had often smiled at her. Incurable, and then ridiculous, as her involvement in the Cause gathered momentum and ferocity.

Pulling back her shoulders, Esther shook off her regret and forced her mind to the evening ahead just as the soft scent of Elizabeth's signature perfume drifted into her nostrils.

Esther turned. 'What do you think?'

Her friend and employer stood beside her and narrowed her eyes, surveying the room. 'It looks wonderful. Congratulations.'

'Don't congratulate me until we know the evening to be a success.' Esther smiled, glad of Elizabeth's approval. From this day forward, she would not allow another drop of doubt in her ability to worry Elizabeth.

'How can it not? I'm expecting plenty of people

here tonight, not just on the impetus to hear Mrs Hadley speak but also to see if we'll reveal any titbits of what we have planned for the Coronation.'

'You are really excited about the Coronation.' Esther grinned. 'I've never seen you so full of animated energy.'

'I could say quite the same of you. You've had much more vitality and verve today when I've spotted you around the store. It pleases me that we're approaching this with renewed creativity.'

Esther's stomach knotted. Her vitality and verve had not come just from the anticipation of the upcoming Coronation. She glanced at Elizabeth as she stared ahead. Should she tell her about kissing Lawrence? Her and Elizabeth's friendship grew ever deeper and suddenly Esther really wanted to share news of her recent tryst.

She lightly coughed. 'I've something to tell you.'

'Oh?' Elizabeth turned, her eyes immediately filled with concern. 'About the Coronation?'

'No, about me.'

Elizabeth's gaze lit with avid interest as she smiled. 'Well, judging by the way your eyes are sparkling, I'm guessing this is of a personal nature?'

'Very.' Esther looked about her and took Elizabeth's elbow, urging her away from the hubbub going on around them. 'Lawrence Culford and I shared a meal at The Orchard . . . a meal that ended in a kiss.' Her traitorous smile broke, no doubt revealing every inch of her happiness.

'Oh, Esther, that's fabulous!' Elizabeth grinned before she seemed to think again. 'Isn't it?'

'Yes, of course, it is. Even if I'm not entirely sure where things will go from here. I'm not even sure I want to pursue a relationship right now, but Lawrence . . . he makes me feel that maybe, just maybe, he would not stand in the way of my work or campaigning. He's . . . a good man.'

'Then stop questioning your time together and enjoy it.' Elizabeth clutched Esther's hand and squeezed. 'Falling in love does not have to spell disaster for a woman, you know. This is your life. Your destiny. Don't turn away from something that could be wonderful.' She smiled. 'I knew there was something about Mr Culford I liked.'

Esther laughed and, as they turned, she fumbled to change the subject. Entirely unsure of her feelings for Lawrence, she wasn't ready for them to talk at length about him. Standing back, she admired Elizabeth's clothing. The dress she wore was a deep emerald green, enhancing her eyes to perfection, the neck low-cut and beaded. 'You look beautiful. Is that dress one of Joseph's?'

'It is indeed.' Elizabeth executed a semi-curtsey. 'My husband's talents continue to grow and astound me. If only he could find every happiness in his work as I do.'

'Joseph is unhappy? I never would have believed it. He's been at the store for well over a year now and his glove designs are a major success. Not to mention his innovation and influence over other departments and Pennington's marketing. Joseph has established himself as your partner, personally and professionally. Surely he sees that?'

'Oh, he does, but it's not his work causing him unhappiness.' Sadness darkened Elizabeth's eyes. 'But I can't talk about this here.'

'But you do want to talk about it?'

'Unfortunately, I think I must. I'm no longer convinced I can carry this burden alone and still be as supportive to Joseph as I want to be.' She looked left and right and lowered her voice. 'Joseph is carrying a pain so deep, I'm afraid he'll one day do something irreparable to heal it. And whatever that might be, he'll still never get over what happened.'

Esther touched her hand to Elizabeth's. 'Is there anything I can do to help?'

Elizabeth sighed. 'Not at the moment, but there might come a day when Joseph and I need your help outside of the store.'

'Can you not tell me what it is? I hate to think of you and Joseph suffering.'

Elizabeth's eyes turned glassy with unshed tears. 'I will tell you, but not yet. It's not my secret to share, but I hold hope that Joseph will come to see he can't fix his trauma alone. Or even with my help. We need to enrol other people. Share ideas and skills. I fear we'll never move on with our lives, start making plans for our personal futures, until Joseph finds peace.' She shook her head and looked across the department and then stopped, a flush darkening her cheeks at whatever, or whomever, had caught her eye. 'Speak of the devil.'

Esther followed Elizabeth's gaze to Joseph Carter as he directed a member of staff to realign the backboard banner displaying a picture of Grace's book as well as her photograph.

She glanced at Elizabeth. 'If only all men could support women as Joseph does.'

'The ones who don't aren't worth our time.' Elizabeth faced her, her momentary expression of love replaced with businesslike sobriety. 'You and I know to hold back women these days is a grave mistake, and one Pennington's will not be making under any circumstances.'

Previously, Elizabeth had made it clear that Pennington's could not be seen to be supporting one women's society over another. Could it be that the increased ferocity and uproar surrounding the Cause had ignited a deeper connection to women's progression than Elizabeth might have previously felt? Esther glanced at her friend. To have Elizabeth's agreement to promote the Bath Society chapter at Pennington's would be a real advantage.

She gently touched her friend's arm. 'Lawrence has offered to do something at The Phoenix in support of the Society. Holding an event right in the centre of the city would help the Bath group so much. I wonder . . . '

Elizabeth frowned. 'Yes?'

'I wonder if maybe Pennington's could help in some way, too? A sale maybe, with the proceeds going to help the Cause? Not new items, of course, but items that have been languishing in the stores from previous seasons.'

Elizabeth tilted her head to the side, her gaze showing her consideration. 'I've stayed away from the movement in case we ostracised certain women, but as the fight grows in momentum, I no longer want my opinions and support hidden.' She nodded and glanced towards Joseph again. 'Once the Coronation is over, I'll speak to Joseph about the vote and see if he has any ideas of how we can show support without pushing our views too harshly.'

'Anything you can do to help would be so appreciated. Thank you.'

'And, on that note, let's get to work. There are

people queuing outside the department and Grace is waiting in my office. I think it's time to begin our evening, don't you?'

'Absolutely. Good luck.'

'Luck has no place in Pennington's, Esther. It's action that counts.'

As Elizabeth walked away, Esther's mind mulled over her friend's words. Action. Didn't everything come down to that? Whatever happened next between her and Lawrence, whether personally or professionally, their kiss couldn't be retracted. Maybe she'd been foolish to reciprocate his advances so passionately, but to do so was all she'd wanted in that moment. Today, however, she had to remain stalwart. If she allowed Lawrence, Rose and Nathanial to come anywhere near her heart, what then? To weaken would surely mean another heartbreak. She couldn't — wouldn't — expose herself to that risk.

The tapping of shoes against the department's floorboards and murmured voices broke Esther from her thoughts. She stepped back as the audience filed into the room. As expected, the crowd was predominantly female, but it pleased her to see a good number of men, too.

She wandered to the back as the attendees were seated. Grace's grand entrance would follow, along with a brief introduction from Elizabeth.

The crowd thinned and so did Esther's hope that Lawrence would attend.

Ignoring the kick of disappointment in her heart, she focused on Grace Hadley as she entered the department ahead of Elizabeth. Tall, with copper-brown hair styled beneath a beribboned, burgundy hat exactly the same shade as her stylish ankle-length

116

skirt and jacket, the bakery owner looked the epitome of female chic and success.

Grace took to the platform, standing to the side and smiling at the audience as Elizabeth stepped to the small podium in the centre.

'Ladies and gentlemen, it is my absolute pleasure to welcome you here this evening to what promises to be a wonderful and inspirational talk. Let me start by telling you a little of Grace Hadley's journey after the loss of her husband, the coping mechanisms she employed to struggle from her grief and, of course, her ensuing business success.

'Grace fell in love with Ernest Hadley when they were barely nineteen years old. She . . . '

Whispered voices turned Esther's head to the department entrance and, at the sight of Lawrence and Rose, Elizabeth's voice faded into the background.

Esther's heart lifted, and her smile bloomed as Lawrence walked farther into the room, tipping her a wink as he steered Rose towards two seats a couple of rows from the back. Once seated, Rose turned and waved at Esther. She lifted her hand, fondness for the little girl twisting inside her.

What could she do but fight the terrifying pull towards this family? She had to protect herself. She had to . . .

'Ladies and gentlemen, I give you Mrs Grace Hadley.'

Esther dragged her gaze from the back of Lawrence's head and gave Mrs Hadley her full attention. Tonight was about inspiration. For both her and Rose. Maybe the little girl was too young to fully understand what she might learn, but maybe, one day, a nugget of Mrs Hadley's wisdom would develop and make Rose shine brighter than she ever thought possible.

That was what Esther wanted for Lawrence's daughter and every other woman and girl present. A fair chance. An equal crack of the whip. Why couldn't the government see women were as important and valuable to the success of the country as men were?

Grace Hadley smiled at the audience and gripped the sides of the podium. 'When my husband died, I thought my life over. Not only was he kind and considerate, but he also fervently believed in me. He gave me self-confidence, courage and support. I'm not even sure he was aware of how rare a man he was. A man I lost far, far too early.

'My grief was debilitating. I couldn't eat or sleep. I could barely get out of bed. All I wanted to do was lie under the blankets and blame God for all he had taken from me. A future with the man I loved . . . children. Alas, it was not to be.'

Esther's heart saddened for Mrs Hadley, her remembered grief clearly etched on her beautiful face, her eyes glassy under the department lights. Here was a woman who had known real heartbreak. The loss of the man she had loved with her entire being, and it was deep fear that Esther might love and lose one day that held her back from seeking a partner, a man to have beside her through good times and bad. Would that ever change?

She looked towards Lawrence.

He softly studied her and her cheeks warmed. The way he looked at her inferred he was equally moved by Mrs Hadley's sadness. Esther looked away. He, too, was widowed. Had he and his wife once shared the same love that Grace Hadley spoke of?

Shamed by the jolt of jealousy that shot through

her, Esther walked to stand behind a pillar that blocked Lawrence's sight of her but gave her full view of Mrs Hadley. A familiar sense of unworthiness knotted Esther's stomach. If Lawrence understood Grace Hadley's words and sorrow, then, he too, must have known deep and meaningful love with his wife.

She would never be enough to compete with such a ghost. Would never be enough to be with a man who bore such longing for a person he'd lost. If she listened to her body and how it so treacherously reacted to Lawrence, her attraction to him would only end badly.

She could not forgo everything she had built. Somehow, she had to find the strength to fight the temptation of Lawrence's gaze and quash the yearning to see him again . . . to see his children again. The emotions he'd evoked in her proved her capable of feeling. Something she had doubted for so very long. Her meeting him had been worth that, at least.

Esther ran her gaze over the assembled audience and then caught the eye of the one woman in the whole of Bath she had absolutely no wish to encounter and would never have an ounce of affinity with.

Viola Stanbury.

Her stepmother.

14

Lawrence applauded along with everyone else as Grace Hadley finished her talk. Anyone who'd clawed their way out of despair had his admiration and respect. The most important lesson he'd learned from his father's physical, and his mother's mental, cruelty was that everyone had a history. Everyone had parts to their lives no one else knew of or had the right to judge. Grace Hadley had found the courage to tell her story and reveal her emotional scars to anyone who wished to listen.

If only he could be that brave . . .

A smartly dressed man walked onto the platform and the audience quieted as he approached the podium. Whoever this man was, he held a unique authority, his stature tall and commanding. Was this Joseph Carter? The man recently married to Pennington's heiress and whom Esther had spoken of so fondly?

The man opened his arms, his smile wide. 'Ladies and gentlemen, my name is Joseph Carter and, as co-manager of Pennington's, I cannot thank you enough for being here tonight to hear Mrs Hadley speak. I am continually impressed with the strength of women in a world that is often seen as a male paradise. I'm married to the strongest, most influential and caring woman I know, and because of her and her experiences, I know there are other women who are capable of so much more than they've been given the chance to demonstrate. Please join me in a final round of applause for Mrs Hadley before she moves into the corridor to sign the copies of her book I suspect you're dying to get your hands on.'

Joseph Carter winked and a ripple of laughter filled the room. Lawrence smiled. Pennington's co-manager certainly had an unarguable charisma that Lawrence imagined went a big way to improving the store's profits.

Grace Hadley stepped forward and accepted a kiss to her cheek from Mr Carter and the room burst into applause. Lawrence clapped as he scanned the room looking for Esther just as he had for much of the evening.

She was nowhere to be seen.

He turned to Rose, her eyes glazed, and her brow furrowed as she stared at the now empty platform. Lawrence silently vowed to do all he could to ensure she became the woman she wanted to be. Whatever course Rose wished her life to follow, he would do his utmost to empower her with whatever she needed to succeed. Esther was right. It wasn't enough to love and protect his children. If he didn't do all he could to ensure Rose and Nathanial reached for the stars, he, their father, would be little more than their warden. The man who clipped their wings.

He slipped his arm around his daughter's slender shoulders. 'Are you all right, darling?'

'That lady was sad. Then happy.'

Lawrence smiled. 'She was. Quite a lady, wasn't she?'

'Yes. I like that she bakes cakes in her own shops. Not one, not two, but three.' Her frown deepened as concern flashed in her eyes. 'Will she find a new husband one day?'

Startled by such an unexpected question, Lawrence's throat tightened with disquiet for his daughter's

121

musings. 'I don't know. Do you think she should?'

'She doesn't have babies, so there's no one to need a daddy, and . . . ' She looked to her dress and plucked at the skirt. 'I'm only sometimes sad I don't have a mummy. Maybe the lady can be happy on her own.'

Lawrence's heart lurched. 'Do you want me to marry again someday?'

Rose shrugged, her mouth pulled into a tight line as though stopping herself from elaborating further. He pulled her close and kissed her hair, inhaling his daughter's soft sweetness. His children had been his life ever since Abigail had passed and he couldn't help feeling he failed them by remaining unmarried. The first woman who had thoroughly moved him to feel again was Esther, but she was proudly independent, and he did not imagine she'd ever wish to be stepmother to his children . . . no matter her clear fondness for them.

He scanned the room again to no avail and turned to Rose. 'Would you like me to buy a book, so you can say hello to the nice lady?'

Her eyes lit with eagerness and she smiled. 'Can we?'

'Of course. We'll sit here a while longer and let the queue go down a little, then we'll move next door.'

Rose nodded and leaned into him, the stiffness in her body once again soft.

How and when he would ever be able to fill the gaping hole Abigail's death had left in Rose and Nathanial's lives, he had no idea, but it was time he tried. No matter how much he feared a woman — a spouse — discovering his childhood trauma and the fears it had left behind, it was selfish to continue life as a widower when his children deserved the love of a woman who adored them. They deserved kindness and laughter in their lives. Yet, the thought of introducing a woman to his children filled Lawrence with dread when, from his upbringing to the lack of intimate connection between him and Abigail, he knew all too well how difficult some relationships could be.

When he and Abigail were first married and lived at Culford Manor, his father's rural estate, Lawrence had worked ten- to twelve-hour days. In the mornings, he would visit four or five of their many tenants. The afternoons were spent checking and working on various land jobs that needed his attention. In the evenings, he'd often wander to the pub to share a tankard or two with the locals, often returning late at night when Abigail had already retired.

They had married when he'd been twenty-four, and Abigail had fallen pregnant with Rose shortly afterwards. Although he and Abigail had never truly loved one another, their delight in the prospect of parenthood had filled them both with joy. Joy that had garnered a mutual respect, understanding and care that hadn't been there when they'd agreed to marry as per their families' wishes.

He and Abigail had gone along well enough and most probably would have continued to do so, if not for his final break from his family home. That fateful day had meant he and Abigail only had each other for company rather than the buffers of his parents and youngest sister, who had always treated Abigail with an amicability they'd rarely bestowed on Lawrence.

On that explosive day in April 1904, Lawrence's rage towards his father had finally erupted, leading to him leaving the estate with his pregnant wife, determined to start a new life in Bath. With only his accumulated savings behind them, his and Abigail's new beginning had been frugal but comfortable. The reason he'd saved, he realised afterwards, was because he'd always known he would leave his family home sooner than either of his parents wanted.

The hardest part of that life-changing day was the knowledge that, in that moment, he couldn't take Cornelia and Harriet with him, too. Yet, he had vowed to never abandon them. Always be close by, reachable and accessible. To this day, he'd kept that promise . . . even if his relationship with Harriet wasn't quite the one he'd hoped for.

Although love never fully blossomed between them, he and Abigail built a good life with Rose serving to bring them closer. Abigail had been content as a mother and soon they could afford to employ Mrs Jackson, followed by Helen and Charles. By the time he'd acquired The Phoenix and Abigail became pregnant again, Lawrence was convinced their marriage would last.

Then Abigail had died a few months later, leaving him with the final precious gift of Nathanial.

Pressing another kiss to Rose's hair, Lawrence searched the room again for Esther.

Next time, he'd only marry for love. Not for status, family or wealth. Esther had made him see how much he'd let pass by without concern or desire for more. Even though he'd barely known her any time at all, he longed for her company. He wanted to look into her eyes, see her smile, hear her laugh. His perplexity about these yearnings made him all the more determined to get to know her and uncover why she had caused such an interest for him.

Physically, she'd made him come alive. Mentally,

he sought her knowledge and wisdom. Emotionally — he swallowed — he had no idea what he felt, except for an exhilarating mix of the unknown and absolute certainty.

'Daddy?'

He blinked from his reverie and looked at Rose as she eased away from him.

She smiled, her eyes bright and happy once more. 'Could we find Esther?

I want to show her my dress.'

'Don't you want to meet Mrs Hadley?'

She shook her head. 'I want to see Esther instead.'

Smiling at Rose's way of leaping from one decision to the next, he took her hand, pleased she'd provided an excuse to seek out Esther 'Then let's go and find her.'

They walked from the department and Lawrence scanned the corridor for Esther's blonde hair and pretty face. Around and around they walked,

Rose's fingers intertwined with his as she smothered her yawns with her other hand.

'She doesn't seem to be here, sweetheart.' He lifted Rose onto his hip. 'She's probably had a long day and left already.'

'I should be tired, too.' Her eyes danced with mischief. 'But I'm not. Not even a little bit.'

Lawrence smoothed his daughter's hair from her face. 'I think you could be a little tired.'

She curtly shook her head, her blue eyes darkening with wilfulness.

Smiling, Lawrence tilted his head towards the grand staircase. 'Come on then. Let's have a final look around before we go home.'

She dropped her head onto his shoulder and he

headed for the stairs. Judging by the fabulous transformation in the book department, he suspected Esther had worked non-stop for the last few days. But, whether exhausted or not, she'd found the time to change from her usual uniform for this evening's event and, if her aim had been to remain unnoticed when she'd moved behind a pillar during Mrs Hadley's talk, Esther had failed.

Dressed in a smart red and grey checked skirt and jacket, the lace of the blouse beneath ruffled at the neck and peeking from beneath the cuffs, she'd looked phenomenal. Her grey hat was larger than he'd seen her wear before and extraordinarily arresting against her thick, blonde hair. He didn't doubt the ensemble had been acquired within Pennington's and she looked splendidly glamourous, yet businesslike.

Entirely Esther.

And finally Lawrence spotted her. Even though the room was full of elegantly dressed, sophisticated women, Esther stood out in the crowd. His heart stuttered. She was so damn beautiful.

'There's Esther, Daddy.' Rose grinned. 'Let's surprise her.'

Lawrence smiled and was about to approach her, when he abruptly stopped.

'Just a minute, darling.'

Esther appeared to be amid an altercation with a woman in her mid-thirties, maybe a little younger. It was difficult to be certain. Although her dark, brown hair, long neck and slender figure encased in a smart, navy-blue dress should bring the woman attention, the tilt of her decidedly pointed chin and clearly enforced smile made her immensely unattractive.

Lawrence flicked his gaze to Esther and wariness

skittered through him. He'd never seen such an expression of distaste on her face, or even imagined her capable of looking at anyone that way. His concern rose along with a hefty dose of protectiveness. Who was this woman? And why was she causing such venom in Esther's eyes?

He slowly walked forwards and stopped again, unsure if he should intervene.

Rose touched his shoulder. 'Who is that lady with Esther, Daddy? She doesn't look very nice and Esther looks sad.'

'It's all right, sweetheart.' Lawrence stroked her cheek. 'Let's just wait here until Esther's finished speaking with the lady, shall we?'

'Why are you even here?' Esther's voice was low and her cheeks red as she jabbed her finger towards the lift. 'Just leave, Viola. You know as well as I do that you've no interest in a woman who has truly loved someone. Who has made her way independently in the world. You are clearly here to cause me trouble.'

The woman's laugh was laced with spite. 'Can't your stepmother take an interest in your place of work? Your aunt suggested I came to see what you're up to this evening.'

'Aunt Mary didn't want to come, too?'

Lawrence frowned. He wasn't sure if he detected disbelief or hurt in Esther's tone.

The woman sighed. 'No, she seems to have little interest in whatever it is you do here. I'm in town with my sister for a few days and paid a visit to Mary earlier but told her Constance and I were busy this evening. I had no intention of entering the store until I heard your name mentioned outside. It seems you're causing quite the anticipation with what you will do

127

with the windows for the Coronation. Can't a proud stepmother stop by to see her stepdaughter?'

Esther crossed her arms, her eyes narrowed with clear suspicion. 'And where is Constance now?'

'Oh, she's gone ahead to the restaurant. She has no vested interest in you, of course.'

'Just go, Viola. You have no care for me either. Go home to my father and your own children. Leave me alone.'

Lawrence pulled back his shoulders as the anger in Esther's tone ignited his fury. How dare this woman speak to Esther this way. The urge to step forward and confront her stepmother pulsed through him but, just then, she shot a sneer at Esther, pushed her purse under her arm and marched towards the lift.

Lawrence looked at Esther, care and concern rising inside him. She dropped her shoulders and tipped back her head, her eyes tightly closed.

He would have given anything to take her in his arms and comfort her. He could not leave her in such a state of distress. He had to speak with her.

'Esther has finished talking, Daddy. Can we see her now?'

'Yes. Yes, we can.' He stepped closer, only to stop again when Elizabeth Pennington approached and slid her arm around Esther's shoulders.

'Are you all right?'

Esther shook her head, her gaze firmly on the lift. 'I'm fine.'

'But —'

'Elizabeth, really. I'm perfectly all right, but I'd really like to leave for the day, if I may?'

'Of course, but who was that wom —'

Esther whirled away and hurried along the corridor,

disappearing into another department. Elizabeth Pennington stared after her, her hands planted on her hips and her brow furrowed.

Lawrence hitched Rose tighter into his embrace and inhaled a long breath.

He had to be certain Esther was all right. He couldn't leave without at least speaking with her. 'Come on, darling. Let's see if we can cheer Esther up, shall we?'

15

Esther slowly descended Pennington's grand staircase, her demeanour a little more under control now she'd collected her purse from the design department and could leave the store for the day.

Instead of walking the high road the moment Viola appeared, Esther had panicked and seen red. Malicious satisfaction had gleamed in her stepmother's eyes, illustrating that she'd clearly been intent on goading Esther, heedless to the hordes of customers hurrying around the bustling corridor.

Damnation. Why didn't I just smile? Been so pleasant Viola would've had no choice but to go back and tell Father how happy I am. Instead, I . . .

'Esther?'

Lawrence and Rose stood at the bottom of the staircase, his face etched with concern, whereas Rose beamed with delight despite the tiredness that showed in the way her arms limply lay around her father's shoulders. A wave of anxiety rolled through Esther. Why had Lawrence chosen to seek her now when she felt so horribly vulnerable? Worse, why did he have to look so handsome and Rose so adorable?

Esther forced a wide smile. 'Well, hello. Did you enjoy listening to Mrs Hadley, Rose?'

'Yes, but . . . ' Her face dropped. 'I worried for her because her husband died.'

'Yes, he did.' Esther tried to keep her focus on the little girl despite the heat of Lawrence's stare at her temple. It was patently obvious it was her deep care for her father that had triggered Rose's disquiet. 'But she's doing very well, regardless. Don't you think?'

Rose nodded and stared around the opulent, sparkling atrium that was Pennington's pride and joy. Esther watched her, her heart filling with affection.

Dragging her gaze from Rose's pretty brown hair, Esther turned to Lawrence. His dark blue gaze made a slow, contemplative study of her face, his brow creased. 'Are you all right?'

Her smile faltered. 'Of course. Why wouldn't I be?'

'I saw you.' His voice lowered as he glanced at Rose who continued to look about them. He faced Esther again. 'Overheard you. With your stepmother.'

Her cheeks heated as she swallowed. What on earth must he think of her?

'I see.' Esther glanced at Rose just as she turned. She stared at Esther, her gaze curious. She'd obviously detected the care in her father's voice. Clearing her throat, Esther faced Lawrence. 'Viola and I will never be the best of friends. I tend to make myself scarce whenever she visits my aunt. To have Viola appear unannounced at the store, especially when I've put so much into this evening, was typical of her.'

He looked towards the store's double doors, his jaw tight, and then faced her and, as if remembering himself, he smiled. 'We are going to have some hot chocolate. Would you like to join us?'

'Please, Esther.' Rose, her tiredness vanishing, bobbed up and down in Lawrence's arms. 'Daddy lets me have chocolate sprinkles on top, too.'

The pressure that bore down on Esther was shaming. To go with him and Rose now would be a mistake. Esther wanted him to continue to like her and enjoy her company. If she showed her anger and resentment towards her meddling stepmother, there was every chance Lawrence could turn away from her.

She gently touched Rose's shoulder. 'I'm sorry, darling, but I must get back to my aunt and spend some time with her before she goes to bed.'

Disappointment flickered in the little girl's eyes, the exact same shade of startling blue as her father's. 'But another time?'

Just as Esther's resolve began to buckle, the tip-tapping of approaching heels served as the perfect distraction.

Turning, relief lowered Esther's tense shoulders as Elizabeth and Joseph, looking every inch the handsome couple they were, walked closer. Esther quickly stepped forwards. 'Elizabeth. Joseph. Do you need me for something?' *Please*...

Joseph looked from Esther to Lawrence and extended his hand. 'Joseph Carter, sir. It's nice to finally meet you. My wife told me she saw you in the store a while ago.'

Esther stood immobile, her heart beating hard as Lawrence slipped his hand into Joseph's, his expression relaxed and friendly. 'She did, and I'm glad to make your acquaintance also. This is my daughter, Rose.'

Joseph beamed, his gaze soft as he studied Rose. 'Well, hel — '

'Hello again, Rose.' Elizabeth's eyes lit as she whipped in front of Joseph and smiled with pleasure as she gently touched Rose's cheek. 'Would you like to see the new rocking horse we have in the toy department? Children have been riding him all week.'

'Yes, please! Can I, Daddy?'

Esther looked at Lawrence. His gaze sought hers,

132

rather than Rose's. He nodded. 'Of course.' He carefully lowered Rose to the marble floor and she immediately slipped her hand into Elizabeth's. Lawrence nodded, his focus still on Esther. 'I'll wait right here for you.'

Although desperate to escape, Esther watched helplessly as Elizabeth walked away with Rose.

'So, Elizabeth tells me you own The Phoenix, Mr Culford.' Joseph stared after his wife, his gaze full of desire before he blinked and faced Lawrence. 'It seems an impressive establishment. I come from a background of lesser means and couldn't afford to step inside your hotel until recently. I must rectify that as soon as I can.'

'It would be a pleasure to have you dine in the restaurant or take afternoon tea with Mrs Carter. Whatever you'd like, my staff will be at your service.'

'Then I'll arrange something sooner rather than later. I think I'll hasten my father to join us. He most certainly enjoys the finer things in life since his retirement. You might well know him. Robert Carter of Carter & Sons.'

Esther silently watched the exchange in bemusement. Nerves jumbled in her stomach and she couldn't stop fidgeting. She had no idea why she was so perturbed by Joseph and Lawrence meeting. Maybe it was the fear that Joseph might assume she and Lawrence were an item, whereas Elizabeth would never assume such a thing.

'Anyway,' Joseph held his hand out to Lawrence again. 'It was nice to meet you and I hope to see you again soon.' He nodded at Esther. 'Wonderful job tonight, Esther. See you in the morning.'

Esther watched Joseph walked away, more than a

little concerned by his strained expression and the distraction in his eyes. Was his uncharacteristic agitation caused by whatever problem Elizabeth had alluded to? She must speak further with Elizabeth and offer her help again.

She faced Lawrence.

His gaze softened. 'Are you all right?'

The worry in his eyes was her undoing and guilt slithered through her. Was he beginning to care for her as she was him? Although their feelings for one another could be detrimental to everything she was striving to do, his kiss remained branded on her lips. If she yielded to the emotions he caused in her, how could they make their relationship work when he had the children to consider and she had her work?

She sighed. 'I'm quite all right. Truly. There's no need to be concerned.'

'There's every need; I care about you.' He studied her. 'We kissed, Esther.' His voice lowered. 'Whether or not you regret that, I, do not. In fact, I wish for it to happen again. Please, don't shut me out without at least getting to know me better.'

Words failed her as she looked into his eyes. Soft admiration mixed with pleading, which only served to weaken her defences. Why did she find him so irresistible? She raised her eyebrows. 'You are very fond of your own charm, you know.'

He smiled. 'I merely wish to improve the end of your day after what was clearly an unwanted visitor.'

She glanced towards Pennington's doors, the weight and sadness of her estrangement from her father pressing down on her. 'My stepmother has no interest in my life other than making sure I don't grace the family threshold ever again. I'm sure she'll see fit to

134

leave me alone for a while.'

'Good, then join us for chocolate and to hell with her.'

The vehemence in his voice sparked the temptation to do as he suggested, elevating the deep-seated rebellion she'd grasped whenever she found herself trapped in a moment of vulnerability. She exhaled a shaky breath. 'Come and sit with me.'

Esther led him to a circular seating area in the centre of the atrium, a huge palm tree in the middle. The store hummed with conversation, interspersed with bursts of laughter from the remaining guests who had attended tonight's event. Every colour and scent filled the space as people slowly descended the grand staircase and strolled through the atrium, temptations in the numerous glass counters stationed throughout the mammoth space catching their eyes.

She and Lawrence were far from alone, yet, when she met his eyes, it was as though no other person existed. Was this what the beginnings of romance felt like? If it was, what was she to do? Her unwillingness to fully open her heart and risk its complete destruction meant it would be unfair to them both to pursue anything deeper.

Esther exhaled. 'There's something you should know.'

His steady gaze bored into hers. 'What?'

She drew in a shaky breath, slowly released it. 'I'm starting to like you, very much, but I'll not risk my heart, or my head, when I have so much important work to do.'

'Esther —'

'When I left home, I thought I'd live an often-solitary life except for the company the Cause brought me.' Although it was rude to interrupt him, she could not allow him to appease her. 'Yet, now, I have several male and female associates I both respect and admire. But with you . . . ' She shook her head, fell into his deep blue gaze, her heart thundering with loss and regret. 'I fear being with you at some point in the future could mean I'll be tempted to abandon a little of my independence. I won't do that. I can't. If I became involved in your life and my desires were curbed, I would flee. Away from you. Away from Rose and Nathanial. You should not be seeking a woman like me. I'm damaged, Lawrence. You need to stay away from me.'

'Aren't we all damaged in some way or another?' Something she couldn't decipher flickered in his gaze, before his jaw tightened and he shook his head. 'The Cause is equally important to me. I want to do all I can to contribute to a more balanced world for my children.'

She stared at him, a whisper of recognition rippling through her when she saw the hope in his eyes. Slumping, she softly smiled. 'I look at you and see a man who has not only made his way in the world but has loved and lost and still pushes forward. I don't have that strength. I'm sorry.'

'You think me strong?' His gaze burned with an intensity she hadn't seen before. 'Then work with me, Esther. Let us do something together that will make a difference to you *and* the Cause. I still want to help you, even if I can't be with you in a way I think we should explore.'

The longer she looked at him, the more desire and protection pulled her in a hundred different directions.

She looked across the atrium at two young lovers arm in arm at the jewellery counter, another couple looking at the wedding display and mannequins. Would marriage ever be possible for a woman determined to make her mark outside of domesticity?

She faced Lawrence. 'My father's treatment of me hurt deeply. It made me see the world as it really is, rather than through the eyes of a young girl looking for love and happiness.'

He took her hand. 'You are racing ahead. Let's just focus on working for the Cause for the time being. Let me show you around my hotel and how we help so many worthy causes. Let me come to a demonstration and meet the women you work with.' He curled his fingers tighter around hers. 'Let me in just a little.'

The softness of his voice poked at her fragile heart. What if he could do good for the Cause and rejecting his help meant she'd only thought of her own suffering rather than the injustice all women suffered?

She briefly closed her eyes and then opened them again, her shoulders slumping. 'If I was to come to your hotel, you must promise me you'll respect my wishes and we concentrate on the Cause rather than us.'

'You'll come?' His smile was like a sunbeam lighting his handsome face. 'When?'

'Promise me, Lawrence.'

'Must I? Can we not just get to know one another without conditions?' His beautiful eyes gleamed with a happiness she found difficult to resist.

She shook her head and smiled. 'You are insufferable.'

'I am and I'm quite happy that's what you like about me.' He grinned. 'When is your next day off?'

'Wednesday. Why?'

'Come to The Phoenix and I'll ensure my diary is cleared for the afternoon.'

She stared at him, momentary uncertainty rising once more. No, she should see his hotel. Accept his support and help. She smiled. 'All right. That would be wonderful.'

'Daddy! Daddy!'

They both jumped and immediately leapt to their feet as Rose came running through the foyer ahead of Elizabeth.

'Look, Miss Pennington gave me a teddy bear. To keep for ever and ever.'

Elizabeth glanced at Esther's hand still in Lawrence's and Esther quickly snatched it away, keeping her gaze resolutely locked with Elizabeth's.

Lawrence bent to pick up his daughter and swung her into his arms and Elizabeth raised her eyebrows at Esther, questions burning in her dark green gaze.

Esther quickly looked to Lawrence and Rose.

He smiled, his eyes filled with happiness. 'Right, I think it best I get Rose home to bed.'

'But I'm *still* not tired, Daddy.'

They all laughed and a little of Esther's tension caused by Elizabeth's relentless scrutiny lessened. 'Well, I'm most certainly tired so maybe I'll be in bed before you.'

Rose giggled, and Esther turned to Lawrence.

He winked. 'I'll see you soon.' He turned to Elizabeth. 'Goodnight, Miss Pennington and thank you for Rose's teddy bear.'

Elizabeth turned her gentle gaze to Rose. 'You're welcome. Goodnight, lovely Rose.'

'Goodnight, Miss Pennington. Thank you for my

bear, I'll love him forever.'

With a final wave, Lawrence walked towards the doors with Rose in his arms, her head dropped to his shoulder.

'Well, I see you haven't run away from whatever it is between you and Mr Culford.' Elizabeth's smile widened. 'And before you say anything, I'm glad.'

Esther sighed. 'And I'm terrified. But I like him, Elizabeth. I really do.'

Her friend slipped her arm around Esther's waist and squeezed. 'Then enjoy the journey, sweetheart. Life isn't always happy or easy. Take these moments of joyful uncertainty and let them play out. Life is a mystery until everything seems blatantly clear.'

Elizabeth walked away, leaving Esther standing alone in the atrium. *But what if 'the clear' became something a person doesn't want to see?*

16

Two days had passed when Lawrence wandered towards the Abbey, swiping at his lapels and straightening his hat, agitated and grumpy. After being trapped in meeting after meeting at his hotel, the sun's bright warmth was welcome against his face.

The newspaper beneath his arm was full of stories covering the life of the soon-to-be crowned King George V. From his service in the Royal Navy, to his seemingly close, united relationship with his wife, to his parenting of their six children, and all manner of other patriotic pomp and ceremony. Across Bath, people were decorating the outside of their homes with paraphernalia, lamps and bunting being added to Victoria Park's trees and railings.

Lawrence's shoulders relaxed as a trio of children dressed in clothes held together by sewn patches and twine about their waists raced past him, their grubby fingers clasping Union Jack flags and coloured ribbons. Lord only knew where they'd found them, but it warmed his heart to see that even the children and parents with next to nothing were joining in with the building excitement for the event.

People jostled and nudged him as he strode past the Pump Rooms and came into the courtyard at the side of the Abbey. The noises, shouts and jeers of the crowd rose as he walked across the cobbled stones and deeper into the fray.

He strained his neck to see over the heads and shoulders of the men and women in front of him.

An array of black and white placards glinted in the sun, the women holding them wearing expressions of dogged determination.

Votes for Women! Support Women's Suffrage! United We Stand!

The non-aggressive, unified undertone of the demonstration confirmed this group to be suffragists and Lawrence pushed forwards, elbowing his way through the throng towards the front in the hope that he might, by chance, happen upon Esther. Narrowing his eyes, he scanned the women standing on boxes and those around them handing out pamphlets and papers.

Today was Wednesday and Esther's day off. Even though they were scheduled to meet that afternoon at The Phoenix, Lawrence would enjoy seeing her campaigning without her knowing. She intrigued and fascinated him beyond measure. To see her working would be wonderful.

'Votes for women!' they cried, the assembled crowd either cheering or scoffing the women's appeals.

He could not see Esther amongst them and, although disappointed, he wouldn't waste the chance to learn more about her work and passion.

The women pointedly jutted their chins, ignoring the negative slews tossed like discarded crumbs at their feet, standing tall and proud, their dress both respectable and flattering. These weren't females looking for favours or pity, only for the chance to be heard and recruit support, and he could not wait to discuss his idea of a fundraising luncheon and auction with Esther later. He'd run the idea past William Moorebrook yesterday and his manager had visibly paled, instantly citing at least five reasons why supporting the suffragists or the suffragettes could have an adverse effect on the hotel. Each reason had been about prosperity, snobbery and elitism. None of which had swayed Lawrence in his decision to help Esther and her associates in any way he could. He was decided and being here now only reconfirmed his conviction. These women were fighting for what was right, not only for themselves, but for girls like Rose, too . . .

A man — clearly the worse for drink — lurched towards the women and Lawrence braced to step in. But, far from being deterred, one of the women came forward and gripped his collar. None too gently, she frogmarched the drunkard to the side of the open space, much to the amusement and cheers of the onlookers.

Lawrence smiled. The suffragists might be non-militant but, clearly, they were far from placid in their endeavours.

Strong. Determined. Passionate.

All things he associated with Esther and what he wished to witness in Rose as she grew older.

Despite the heckling, the women stood united, not caring nor wasting their energy on the pressure and ignorance around them. Forging forward with what they wanted, regardless of the supposed rules and regulations of a good proportion of the nation. They were an example to everyone, including him.

Lawrence turned and slowly shouldered his way back through the crowd. He'd lacked fortitude and determination in his formative years. Maybe even, at times, during his enforced marriage to Abigail. He hadn't resisted, but fallen into the marriage pre-ordained by his parents and Abigail's — Abigail, herself, pleading with him to keep the betrothal that was arranged before either of them had reached adolescence. Not that their union was any fault of Abigail's. The blame lay heavy on his shoulders, caused by his inability to stand up to his parents.

These women campaigners, some younger than Lawrence, showed no such weakness.

He'd been vacillating, whereas he should've been strong.

He'd been afraid, whereas he should've been courageous.

Esther had shifted his mindset. Shifted his heart. Her beauty was astounding, but it was her spirit he was falling in love with.

He stopped.

Could love really grip a person that quickly, that suddenly, and be so wholly affecting? Surely, such an instinctive comprehension of a person was impossible? Just because he was physically attracted to her, just because her kiss still lingered in his memory, that did not equate to lasting love.

Lawrence swiped his hand over his face, gripped his folded newspaper and marched through the crowds with more fervour.

A familiar figure ahead snagged his attention.

Charles, Lawrence's butler and friend, stood in front of a pie seller's wagon.

Tipping his hat to the vendor, Charles carried his purchase to a nearby bench. Opening his wrapped package, he quickly sank his teeth into the pie, its steam billowing from the crust.

Lawrence's mouth watered as he walked closer, the smell of grease mixing with a delicate perfume as people of every age and class hurried through the centre on market day. He passed a couple of stalls, one selling handkerchiefs and colourful scarves, the other sporting an array of nails, screws, hammers and saws.

Charles seemed happy to sit amid the chaos and Lawrence was happy to join him. He approached the pie seller. 'One of your finest pies, please, sir.'

The vendor pushed up his half-rim glasses, his salt-and-pepper hair pointing in a hundred different directions like a haphazard haystack. 'Coming right up, sir.' He took a pie and wrapped it in paper, twirling the ends with a flourish. 'That will be one fine penny, young man.'

Lawrence handed over the money, adding an extra penny for the man's compliment. 'Thank you gladly, sir.'

'Much obliged to you.'

Lawrence touched the brim of his hat and walked to the bench. 'Enjoying the day's sunshine, Charles?'

His butler started before his face broke into a sheepish smile. 'I thought I'd stretch my legs through lunch rather than taking food in the kitchen. Mrs Jackson is on the warpath because yesterday's delivery was short, and neither myself nor Helen checked it. Even though I don't necessarily deem the kitchen our responsibility.'

Lawrence bit into his pie, savouring its rich meat and flavoursome juices. 'Well, these are such fine pies, I'm sure we'll cope with lessened rations tonight.'

They ate in silence for a few moments, each watching the people as they passed by. Lawrence's eye was drawn to every black and white Pennington's box or bag that came into view as he wondered what Esther was doing for lunch on such a sunny afternoon. When futile imaginings of a picnic in Victoria Park, the sun

144

glinting on her golden hair and her eyes soft on his came into his mind, he forced his thoughts to the demonstration he'd seen by the Abbey.

It was right and just that he publicly declared his support for the Cause if he wanted Rose to grow up knowing she could achieve anything she desired. It no longer felt enough to host the occasional fundraiser or be a member of the Men's League. He wanted to be seen by the people, rally support and appeal to members of Parliament alongside the women campaigners. As much as these women toiled for a breakthrough, there remained an inherent possibility it would only be a man's voice that would be heard by the government. Until that changed, Lawrence refused to stand by and not do anything.

'Did you see the demonstration by the Abbey, Charles?' Lawrence lowered his pie. 'I really feel the Men's League should be doing something similar. Show our support more publicly than we are now.'

'I agree. I spent several minutes watching the women earlier and the disapproving looks on some of the spectators' faces — male and female — was downright ridiculous. What is so threatening about women casting a ballot?'

'Exactly.'

Lawrence watched a flower girl standing at a stall a small distance away, her hair somewhat matted to her small head and her cheeks streaked with grime as she held out a bunch of lavender to a woman dressed almost as grandly as Britain's new Queen Mary. Unfortunately, this *grand lady* lifted her nose to the air as though smelling something distasteful and walked on by, proving herself nothing like the Queen at all.

He smiled when the flower seller poked out her

tongue behind the woman's back.

'Just because a person is born one sex over another, does that mean they shouldn't have a voice? I think not.' He took another bite of his pie, his mood sombre.

'Have you discussed your support with Miss Stanbury? She struck me as the type of woman who'd be involved.'

Surprised that Charles should mention Esther, Lawrence nodded at the realisation his staff had undoubtedly been discussing Esther. After all, she was the first woman since Abigail to play so openly with his children. He suspected the speculation amongst his staff was rife . . . which he could hardly be annoyed about as his own speculation about Esther was so very frequent and distracting.

He cleared his throat. 'Miss Stanbury is deeply involved with the Cause. So involved, in fact, I worry she'll come to feel she has no alternative than to join the suffragettes and volunteer herself to more militant action.'

Charles lifted his eyebrows. 'Surely not.'

'Her passion is palpable, Charles, even if it is under control at the moment. She has a want for free speech that I'm convinced is born from being unable to speak in other areas of her life. She has a fire in her eyes that's as intriguing as it is sometimes concerning.' Lawrence's mind wandered to the evening he'd seen Esther speaking with her stepmother. He would do anything not to see such anger in Esther's eyes again.

His butler shook his head. 'Something has to change. This is nineteen-eleven, not seventeen-eleven.'

Lawrence put the final crust edge of his pie into his

mouth, his mind wandering to more personal concerns. 'Do you think the children are saddened that they no longer have a mother? I suspect they think about Abigail more than I've realised.'

'What's brought this on, if I might ask?'

Lawrence blew a heavy breath. 'My concern for them deepens each year they grow older. We managed when Abigail passed. Helen effortlessly coped with Nathanial as a baby and Rose was always so good and happy in your company as well as mine.'

'But?'

'They're growing up, Charles. Rose doesn't seem as happy any more. I took her to Pennington's to listen to a lady speak about her bakery business. Rose was in awe of her success, but she was also saddened that the woman was a widow. It made me wonder what she thinks of me being alone, of her and Nathanial not having a mother figure. My mother doesn't take any interest in them and, as much as Helen and Cornelia love them, the children are not their responsibility.'

Charles' eyes widened. 'So, you're saying you want to marry again?'

'Yes, I think I do.'

'Well, well.'

Lawrence stilled. Was he being foolish sharing so much with Charles? 'You think it a bad idea?'

'Not at all.'

'Then what?'

Charles lifted his shoulders. 'Just ensure you love this woman with all your heart and be certain she loves you and the children with all of hers. Anything less and Rose and Nathanial might never recover.'

The vehemence in Charles' words showed his deep

love of Lawrence's children and a humbleness whispered through him. He never would have managed the happiness Rose and Nathanial enjoy without Charles', Helen's and even the stalwart Mrs Jackson's care for them, too.

Charles cleared his throat. 'Miss Stanbury seemed awfully taken with them when she dropped by the other night. It is her you're thinking of, isn't it?'

Ignoring the question, Lawrence inhaled. 'She's not the type to stay at home mothering children. I imagine she'd be even less keen to mother another woman's children.'

'Do you know that for certain?'

'No, but —'

'Then you shouldn't make such a huge presumption. Why not ask her?'

Lawrence stared. 'To marry me?'

Charles laughed. 'No. How she feels about motherhood.'

'Oh. I see. Of course.' Looking across the market, Lawrence exhaled. 'She's a special lady, Charles, but unlikely to ever be *my* special lady.'

'And you're giving up on her just like that?'

'What choice do I have? I must respect her wishes. If I was to continue to pursue her romantically, I fear she'd wrap me up in a sack and toss me in the River Avon. She's not the type to suffer fools. Believe me.'

'But you will be seeing her again?'

'Yes, later today. I plan to help her suffrage society by hosting something at the hotel in aid of the Cause and she appears interested. We'll be discussing it anon.'

'Good, because from where I'm sitting, that young lady is going places. If you wish to court her, it might help to show her how much her work means to you. If you succeed in convincing her of your sincerity, she just might be yours, come the end.'

Lawrence screwed the paper pie bag into a ball as he considered Charles' words. He was right. He needed to prove to Esther he respected her. Liked her. The falling in love part could be ignored. For now.

17

For the very first time, Esther walked up the stone steps in front of The Phoenix and under the long black awning that covered the hotel's patrons from the unpredictable British weather. She stepped into the lobby and halted, absorbing the sights and sounds around her. From the sumptuous sapphire blue carpet beneath her feet, to the matching velvet drapes edging each of the many windows, her first impression of The Phoenix was one full of welcome. As if it whispered, 'take a seat', 'stay awhile'. It was so classically beautiful, it took Esther's breath away.

People walked back and forth around her as she continued to stare. Women in smart suits with long, flowing skirts, or dresses with pearl buttons at their throats. Every gentleman was suited, their ties perfectly tied and their shoes polished to a high sheen.

Since Pennington's had started to welcome every class of person to shop there, Esther had become slowly removed from the difference between the rich and the poor. The sights inside The Phoenix brought the reality sharply back.

She should feel affronted, but she was amazed.

She should feel annoyed, but she was in awe.

Forcing herself forward, she looked left and right before deciding to head towards two beautiful opaque double doors that stood open revealing a sumptuous lounge beyond. She nodded hello as men, women and children walked past her and was almost at the entrance when a familiar musky cologne enveloped her.

'You're here.'

Lawrence stood so close behind her, had leaned so near to her ear, that his soft breath lifted the wisps of hair at her nape.

She smiled, turning around and taking a small step back. She looked into his deep blue eyes and her stomach tightened. 'I am.'

He smiled back. 'I'm a very happy man. Come, let me show you around.'

Taking her hand and placing it in the crook of his elbow, he led her inside the lounge. Struggling to focus on her surroundings rather than the way Lawrence looked at her ... so easily touched her, Esther pointedly looked about her. The walls were panelled in shiny dark wood, the floor a slightly lighter shade and highly polished. There was an array of tables and chairs set across the left, allowing for families or couples to relax with drinks and appetisers. On the right were huge leather sofas, wing-backed chairs and low tables where people could peruse a book or newspaper while enjoying an afternoon aperitif or tea.

As it was after lunch but too soon for tea, there were only a few people wandering around or looking out of the windows towards the recreational space beyond.

Lawrence turned, his gaze gentle. 'What do you think so far?'

The soft, intimate tone of his voice pulled at her as she smiled. 'It's lovely, Lawrence. Truly.'

'Well, as much as I wish we had time to give you a complete tour, unfortunately, I have a meeting in a couple of hours that I couldn't get out of.' His apology showed in his eyes and he exhaled. 'Such is business, I suppose. But I promise you a full tour many times

151

over before whatever date we decide for the event. In the meantime, let's go to my office.'

He guided her from the lounge into the lobby, past the reception and along a corridor. Closed doors lined one side with various name plaques on the doors. One for Head of Housekeeping, another for Assistant Manager, another for Manager, until, at last, Lawrence stopped at a door at the far end of the corridor and pushed it open.

Esther entered the modest space that was so utterly Lawrence. A large desk stood at the far end of the room, the afternoon's sunlight bathing it in an amber glow. Two lamps were set at either side, their dark green and gold shades perfectly masculine and professional. She looked to her left towards a stone fireplace with a huge portrait of Lawrence, Rose and Nathanial hung above it.

No Abigail. She swallowed the unexpected sadness that welled in her throat.

'I commissioned that last year. I thought it would be nice to show the children we're still a family even though Abigail has gone.'

'It's beautiful.'

He gently touched her elbow. 'Why don't we sit over here in the seating area? Would you like coffee? Tea?'

'No, I'm fine, thank you.' Esther walked across the plush carpet towards a settee and two armchairs situated in front of the window. She carefully placed her purse on the floor and sat. 'I am completely overwhelmed by the hotel, this office. It's wonderful.'

'Thank you. I certainly like it and so do my staff and guests.'

She smiled at the humour in his voice, loving that he was seemingly so unaware of just how successful,

152

handsome and attractive he must be to a hundred and one women. Including herself.

'So . . . ' He walked to his desk and picked up a brown folder before returning and sitting on the settee beside her. 'I've drawn up some preliminary plans, but you're the expert as far as the Society and the Cause is concerned, so I'm more than happy to be led by you.'

Taking the folder, Esther flipped through the pages. He suggested holding an auction in the hotel's ballroom, which she was yet to see. They would set out chairs and use the stage for the auctioneer and showing the lots that included overnight stays at The Phoenix as well as horse and carriage tours of the city. The guests would range from business people, the gentry to visiting middle-class families that Lawrence clearly knew well. He'd also outlined two months of publicising the event through posters, pamphlets and advertisements in shops, music halls and theatres throughout the city.

Excitement bubbled inside her. There was no way the Society could achieve Lawrence's ambitious plans without his help and input. Slowly, she lowered the papers to her lap. 'Are you sure about this? It seems an awfully large amount of work. Can you really spare the time?'

'I'll *make* time. I want to do this, Esther. I want to make a difference to the Cause. It's not enough for me to stand in the background any more. I also want this for you.'

She ran her gaze over his handsome face, his dark hair and perfectly trimmed moustache and short beard. Her heart stumbled at the look of hope and determination burning in his eyes. He was sincere,

153

genuine and she was deeply grateful.

Smiling, she nodded. 'Then I would love to work on this with you once the Coronation is over and I've spoken to the other members of the Society. We can't go forward with these plans until the women have taken a vote and we're all in agreement. Considering the extent of what you're proposing, and more ideas that myself and the group might come up with, we'll need all the help we can get.'

'I agree, which is why I was going to ask if you are happy for me to enlist further help. Do you remember those three chambermaids I spoke of?'

She nodded.

'Well, I mentioned the auction to them and asked if they would like a hand in helping. As promotion. They are thrilled and, fingers crossed, I'm hoping the auction and the Cause will prove a big enough distraction that there will be no more repeats of them being ejected from any clubs in town.'

Esther laughed. 'Busy hands?'

'Exactly.'

She looked again to the notes, excitement bubbling inside her 'Why don't we aim for three months from now for the auction? If we host it in September and it goes well, we could then think about a ball in time for Christmas.' She grinned. 'A ball in your hotel would be fantastic and appeal to so many people.'

'You're right. Who doesn't like a ball at Christmastime? I'm sure we'll sell all the tickets we decide upon.'

She closed the folder and handed it back to him, grateful for all he had planned to help her. How wrong she'd been about him when they'd first met. It had been a mistake she'd never make again.

He raised his hand. 'That's for you. I have a copy,

too. Show it to the Society ladies, take some minutes or notes and then we can reconvene and come up with a definitive plan after the Coronation. Now, I'm going to insist you stay for afternoon tea, even if it is a little early. You cannot have your first time in The Phoenix without taking tea.'

Smiling, she raised her hands in surrender. 'Then I'll have to stay.'

He tipped her a wink and walked to the door, pausing with his hand on the knob. 'I'll be right back.'

Once the door closed behind him, Esther collapsed back on the settee, unable to wipe away her smile. He was making it harder and harder to fight the feelings rising and swelling inside her. Every time she was with him, spoke to him, laughed with him, her heart fell a little deeper.

She wanted to work with Lawrence, spend time with him, whilst forging a path to aid the Cause and all the women of the country. She couldn't help but believe that, side by side, she and Lawrence would be a formidable team. Of course, whether or not she could keep her personal feelings for him from mixing with the professional was a different matter.

18

The following week in Pennington's basement department, Esther stood back from her latest window
design and surveyed the sketch with a critical eye as
her staff chattered and worked around her. The proposed design was good. Very good. In fact, she was
more than a little embarrassed that it had taken Elizabeth pointing out Esther's failings to make her realise
her previous work had been woefully below par.

Laying down her pencil, Esther walked into the
store cupboard and breathed deep, enjoying the comfort of knowing her work was something she excelled
at, that she could successfully execute time and again.
Something that held the power to make her happy.

Running her hand over the bolts of material and
netting, she considered which props would work best
when displayed with Homeware's latest pots and
pans. The domesticity in front of her turned her mind
once again to Lawrence and his children.

The depth of her growing fondness for them was
frightening. Made her accept just how easily a person
could be seduced by the notion of familial bliss.

She had yet to come across proof that such a thing
truly existed.

Her heart and soul were so deeply embedded in her
work at the store and at the Society, she worried that
she might disappoint his children in the future. Love
seemed to come with unspecified parameters, rules and
expectations that were little more than chains preventing a person from reaching their true potential. How

could she promise to be all she could for him, Rose and Nathanial when she wasn't entirely sure she'd ever manage to be all she was meant to be herself?

The anger in her father's gaze and the livid disapproval in his expression had cut to her core when she'd thought he loved her mother and, although never active, respected her fight for the vote. But the day he'd ejected Esther from his home, with Viola gleefully looking on, it was as though he could not bear to look at his daughter and his cruel, dismissive words still rang in Esther's ears, perpetually clawing at her heart.

'You are little more than a harlot. Parading yourself around the streets and drawing attention from anyone who cares to look at you. A disgrace is what you are. A complete disgrace to me and your poor stepmother. I want you out and never come back.'

Tears burned behind her eyes and Esther dug her fingers into the cushion beside her. Her mother had died from influenza years before and her father had barely grieved his wife of twenty years before marrying the much-younger Viola and moving her into their home. Within months of Esther and Viola living in strained coexistence, her stepmother had fallen pregnant with Benedict, quickly followed by little Peter. Esther had found herself the older sister to two young boys who each took a piece of her heart when they'd been born so innocently into a household that felt strained and unhomely.

Until she'd met Lawrence, Esther was of the absolute conviction that a man could not survive more than a few weeks alone. Now, he'd shaken that belief and it terrified her. How was she to deny the admiration and respect she had for Lawrence's dedication and love of his children?

Pulling a bolt of crimson satin from one of the many wooden cubbyholes lining the storeroom, Esther carried it into the main area of the department, determined to focus on her work. She placed the material next to her design and searched the room for Amelia. She spotted her at the far end of the room sorting through the various garments hanging on a brass rack.

Approaching her young assistant, Esther stopped at Amelia's side and flipped through the jacket and skirt combinations in a variety of pale pinks, blues and ivory. 'These are excellent selections, Amelia. Just the right colours to promote the new summer collections. Well done.'

'Thank you.' Amelia smiled briefly before she turned to the rack. 'I wasn't sure about the hats and shoes. Did you want something traditional? Only, I thought Miss Pennington might like the idea of promoting lines that didn't sell very well through the spring. Mr Carter's designs and the materials he used for the spring collection could easily be worn and enjoyed through July and, possibly, August. It's just an idea. If you think — '

'I think that's an excellent idea.' Esther gently laid her hand on Amelia's shoulder. 'Don't ever hold back with your suggestions. If Miss Pennington thought for one minute I wasn't encouraging my team's innovation, she'd send me out the door. Pennington's is all about progression, excitement and new opportunities. I think a last attempt at pushing the older merchandise would be welcomed by Miss Pennington *and* Mr Carter.'

Amelia's shoulders lowered and she smiled. 'Shall I head up to the ladies' and men's departments now

158

and discuss with the heads which lines haven't sold as well as we'd hoped?'

'Absolutely. I need to go outside, so why don't we walk out together?'

As they left the department, Esther stole a glance at Amelia. Every now and then, she became momentarily threatened by Amelia's enthusiasm and talent. Esther's insecurities were shaming and had absolutely nothing to do with Amelia or her work. She was an ally rather than competition. A fellow woman doing her utmost to forge forwards in what was still very much a man's world. In fact, Amelia was just the sort of young woman the Society needed to recruit. Quiet, yet hardworking and ambitious, she would suit the suffragists perfectly.

Esther halted at the bottom of the grand staircase. 'Can I ask you a question, Amelia?'

Amelia turned on the bottom step. 'Of course.'

'Have you any interest in the women's suffrage bill?'

'Well, yes. Yes, I have. The pictures in the newspapers never fail to snag my attention whenever I see them.'

'But you have no wish to be part of the fight?'

'I agree with what the women are trying to do, but . . . ' Amelia frowned and came down the step to stand closer to Esther. She lowered her voice. 'Some of the things these women are doing look incredibly dangerous. They say arrests are happening all the time.'

Esther gently took Amelia's elbow and moved her out of earshot of the nearby customers. 'That's the suffragettes as opposed to suffragists. The suffragettes' actions are born out of frustration. One that I understand but not fully share. At least, not at the moment.

There are still plenty of other avenues to explore. The real danger most certainly sits with women too afraid or those who do not care to do anything at all to help us win this battle. I try to keep quiet about my participation while I'm at work, but I'm part of the suffragists society.' She gently squeezed Amelia's elbow. 'I'd love for you to join us. I have made some wonderful friends, as well as learning so much more about the women in our community. Would joining be something you'd consider?'

Amelia's eyes widened, and her cheeks flushed. 'But suffragist or not, aren't you afraid of the authorities?'

'We've had no reason to be.' Esther inhaled. 'Of course, that could change if we're forced to increase the ferocity of our campaigning.'

Amelia's gaze turned hopeful, the colour in her cheeks darkening. 'You really think I could help?'

'Of course. You do fabulous work here at the store. Why not further your skills for the greater good? With your organisational support and optimistic attitude, you'd be a real asset. Our group is low on women of our age and we need to encourage others to join and do everything they can. If women of all ages unite, how can the government continue to ignore such a universal petition? I'll be working side by side with you every step of the way.'

Amelia smiled. 'All right, why not? I'd love to.'

'Marvellous. I'll give you all the details of tonight's meeting later.' She squeezed Amelia's elbow again. 'You won't regret coming along, I promise.'

With a nod, Amelia walked up the stairs and, smiling, Esther headed for Pennington's gilded front doors. Walking outside into the day's bright sunshine,

160

she strode along the pavement until she reached the empty window waiting for her next display. It was the smallest of Pennington's three windows, but she would still ensure it was as eye-catching as possible.

Esther scribbled some notes, looking from the window to her clipboard. Studying the window again, she tapped her pencil against her bottom lip. The reflection acted like a mirror and when she saw Lawrence approaching from behind her, her heart stuttered.

She turned around. 'Lawrence, this is a surprise.'

He stepped closer. 'You looked so engrossed, I was afraid to break your concentration.' He glanced at the window. 'What are you considering?'

'What I hope will be a fabulous display of men and women's clothing. Rose inspired me, actually.'

His eyes brightened with clear pride. 'She did?'

'Yes,' Esther smiled, all too aware of just how difficult it was of late to stop thinking about Lawrence's children. 'I'm going to display summer sports. Both for those who play and those who spectate. I don't think Pennington's has had a window entirely dedicated to outdoor pursuits before. I hope Miss Pennington will love the idea.'

'I'll be sure to tell Rose of her contribution.'

Esther swallowed. He really had the most penetrating way of looking at her. It shouldn't have been considered anything but polite, but her physical reaction to him, the quickened beat of her heart and the heat low in her stomach, proved the opposite. She quickly looked to her notes, hoping her desire hadn't shown in her eyes. 'So, are you here to shop for something?'

'No.'

'Oh.' She met his soft gaze. Then — '

'I'd like to invite you to dinner at my home tomorrow night,' he said quickly. 'If you are free, that is.'

She froze. 'Your home?'

'Yes, just a chance for us to catch up and discuss what I've started moving forward with for the fundraiser.'

Esther's heart picked up speed. Was his invitation only about the auction and ball? Or could she dare to imagine his interest in her began to lean towards the personal, too? Her wish that it did was uncomfortably strong. She forced a smile. 'Well, in that case, how can I say no? What time should I arrive?'

His blue eyes lit with satisfaction. 'Shall we say seven?'

'Perfect.'

His gaze lingered on hers a moment longer and just as Esther thought he might kiss her on the street, right in front of Pennington's, he comically doffed his hat. 'Until tomorrow evening, Miss Stanbury.'

Esther's heart beat fast, her smile absurdly wide as he marched across the street, the epitome of masculine confidence.

She sighed. How on earth was she to resist him, should he attempt to kiss her again? Did she even want to?

19

Lawrence pushed his hand through his hair and hastily smoothed it again as he surveyed the food set out on the kitchen table. A small bribe of a meal and the theatre had convinced Mrs Jackson to allow him free use of her domain for the night. He'd waved her, Helen, Charles and the children off at the door half an hour before.

He glanced at his watch. Esther was due any moment. He'd offered to send her a carriage, which she'd abruptly refused, saying a carriage was an unnecessary extravagance and she'd be more than happy to walk.

He studied the food again and tried to turn his thoughts away from any danger that might befall Esther as she walked alone through Bath's streets. When Abigail died, he'd made it his business to have weekly meetings with Mrs Jackson, Charles and Helen just as his wife had. To ensure himself fully aware about the running of the house, the meals they'd eat and the weekly outgoings.

Upon leaving Culford Manor, he could only afford two rented rooms for him and Abigail in a house run by a kindly and widowed housewife. The woman had adored Abigail and was fond of Lawrence. By the time Rose arrived, he'd saved enough money working in various kitchens as an aid to the chefs, eventually learning to cook well enough himself that he'd started to look beyond the kitchens and imagine owning a hotel of his own one day.

A small loan from the bank a year later, and he'd purchased a small bed and breakfast when he was just twenty-seven. Wise investment, frugal spending and a whole lot of ambition had meant within five years he had a thriving hotel and enough money for his family and staff to be comfortable for the foreseeable future.

Hence why The Phoenix, one of the Bath's most exclusive establishments, was his pride and joy. The hotel was entirely his, bought, kept and paid for without a single penny from his parents

He stood back and planted his fists on his hips.

The simple meal of soup, followed by cheese and potato pie and ice cream for dessert should be more than passable. Yet nerves continued to harangue him. He could only pray everything tasted as good as the wholesome smells permeating the kitchen.

Whipping Charles' apron from his waist, Lawrence tossed it onto a chair and walked upstairs, along the entrance hall and into the dining room. Narrowing his eyes, he critically assessed the table and room decoration.

White crockery, rimmed with a delicate rose design, and silver cutlery shone beneath the lit wall sconces and tapered candles on the table. Red napkins perfectly matched the carnations in the centre arrangement and the wine had been decanted.

Everything looked the best it could be, and he thanked God he'd accepted the privilege of a woman's touch to the room, courtesy of Helen. Where he'd be without the children's nanny, he had no idea. In the morning, he would consider increasing his loyal staff's wages. Helen, Charles and even Mrs Jackson had gone above and beyond their usual duties the moment Abigail had lost her life.

He fought the memory of her terrible screams during a labour that had gone on for hours. The midwife and then the doctor were called, but still Abigail lost her battle. When the ensuing haemorrhage took her life, the staff who'd loved her were devastated. Lawrence had been thrown into a state of stunned shock. He'd cared for Abigail deeply, even if he hadn't loved her as a husband should.

His sad memories were halted by a knock at the front door.

He momentarily stilled, before rushing downstairs and into the hallway.

The silhouette of a woman's hat showed through the glass in the door. The image so still and petite, it could only be Esther who seemed to hold herself in a constant state of unshakeable poise . . . aside from that one meeting with her stepmother. A meeting that continued to bother him, no matter how hard he tried to put it behind him as Esther had appeared to have done.

Relief she'd arrived flooded through him, dispelling his anguish, even though she might be angry when she realised his subterfuge of ensuring the staff and children were absent for the night. He would make it clear she was free to leave if she so wished. He just wanted some time alone with her. Just him and her. No staff. No children. No customers or colleagues.

Taking a deep breath, Lawrence strode to the door and pulled it open.

Esther flinched as though startled before her face lit with a smile and she huffed a laugh.

'Sorry, I expected your butler or Helen to answer the door. You're clearly a very modern employer.'

He smiled. 'Won't you come in?'

She brushed past him into the house, the soft floral scent of her perfume infusing his nostrils. She wore a pale blue dress that brought out hints of sapphire in her hazel eyes, her hat the same shade of blue bore a single white feather.

She looked beautiful and he wondered, again, if her dress was another she'd salvaged from her previous life in the Cotswolds.

He closed the door and smoothed the lapels of his dinner jacket. 'Would you like a drink before we eat?'

'A glass of wine would be nice.'

He waved her towards the dining room, nerves rolling through him. He needed to tell her they were alone, rather than have her draw the conclusion. If he was immediately honest, she'd then have the choice to leave. He prayed she wouldn't.

Once they were in the dining room, Lawrence cleared his throat. 'I've sent the staff out with the children for the evening. I thought it would be nice for us to have some time alone. Is that all right?'

The skin at her neck shifted as she swallowed, her glorious eyes wide. 'We're alone?'

He nodded.

'But what if someone saw them leave followed by my arrival?'

He gently touched her hand. 'Could we not let what others think concern us tonight?'

She glanced towards the door. 'Unfortunately, whether rightly or wrongly, a woman's reputation still remains everyone's concern.'

He could hardly argue with the ridiculous, anti-quated truth of her words. 'If I've made a mistake, I'm sorry.'

She glanced towards the open door a second time.

166

'Isn't Mrs Jackson here, at least?'

'No. I prepared this evening's dinner myself.'

Her eyebrows lifted as an amused smile pulled at the corners of her pretty lips. 'You cook?'

'A little. It's nothing fancy and I'm praying it's edible, but yes, I cook.'

Her gaze softened, and her shoulders relaxed. 'Then you've put me in rather a difficult position. How can I leave when you've gone to such trouble?'

Relieved beyond measure, Lawrence smiled. 'You'll stay?'

'Yes.' Her eyes glinted with teasing. 'You're forgiven. This time.' She walked to the window and stared towards the green beyond. 'This street is so pretty.'

'It is. When Abigail and I came to Bath, she fell in love with the Circus. She wanted to live and raise our children here. So, I promised her I'd one day earn enough money to buy any house she wanted.' He exhaled a shaky breath as he walked to the drinks cabinet, finding it easier to talk about Abigail without Esther looking at him so intently. 'Unfortunately, she died before we could afford to move here, but I kept my promise to her, anyway.'

The rustle of her dress sounded through the silence and, instinctively, Lawrence sensed she'd sat at the table. It suddenly mattered more than anything that she was comfortable and relaxed in his home. That she was comfortable and relaxed being alone with him.

Glasses filled, he stoppered the decanter, picked up their glasses and turned.

She sat at the table, her gaze soft on his. 'You really didn't have to go to all this trouble. I'm not even sure what to say.'

'Then say nothing. All I want you to do is enjoy this

evening.'

He passed her a glass of wine and then walked to the window, unable to look into her beautiful eyes and stop the words of admiration that danced on his tongue. Dusk was falling and the recreational area opposite the house was bathed in golden light. It was a beautiful evening. He would insist on escorting Esther home later.

Taking a sip of his wine, he returned to the table and put down his glass. 'I'll serve the soup and then we can talk.' He met her gaze. 'I'm so glad you came.'

'Did you think I wouldn't?'

'I've jumped from certainty you would, to absolute conviction you wouldn't.' He huffed a laugh. 'The one thing you manage to do is keep me on my toes.'

She grinned, her gaze delighted. 'Then my intention is working.'

The flirtation in her voice and the happiness in her eyes sent him from the room like a man who'd won the biggest prize at the county fair. He pulled back his shoulders, barely resisting the urge to puff out his chest as he entered the kitchen.

It had felt good to tell Esther of Abigail's wish to live in the Circus and that he'd eventually granted it. Albeit, she wasn't here to see the house, come the end. He hoped it showed Esther he kept his promises. That no matter what the world might throw at him, he found a way through in the end. Hopefully, that would instil confidence in her that he'd be right beside her with the Cause and any other time she might call on him for help.

Ladling the soup from the pot on the stove into two bowls, Lawrence carefully wiped the edges with a cloth before carrying them into the dining room.

As he entered, he noticed a slight tremor in Esther's hand as she lowered her glass to the table. Maybe she wasn't quite as relaxed as he assumed, after all.

Uneasy, he forced a smile. 'Soup is served, madam.'

20

Esther laid down her knife and fork, her stomach fit to bursting and her tongue tingling from the rich, delicious taste of Lawrence's home-made cheese and potato pie. 'I can't possibly eat another bite. I am absolutely stuffed.'

His blue eyes twinkled in the candlelight. 'I'm glad. You look happy.'

'I am.' Esther swallowed, wondering again whether his intentions inviting her this evening were entirely about the Cause. Or was it also about them? She warmed with a flicker of hope that it was. 'I should be angry that you arranged to be alone with me like this, but, in all honesty, I'm so pleased you wish to help me with ideas for the Society that I find myself perfectly relaxed.'

His gaze lingered on hers and something shifted between them. A subtle non-verbal confirmation that they both knew tonight was not entirely about the Cause.

How was she to deny how attracted she was to him? How much his words about his wife and what he'd achieved in such a short amount of time to ensure Abigail's happiness affected Esther's longing for stability and love.

She picked up her wine and sipped. Was she playing with fire being here?

Lowering her glass, she forced her gaze to his. 'Why don't you share your thoughts about the fundraiser?'

The intensity she found so appealing came into his

eyes and trepidation for being reckless with him again burned inside her.

He must think her so young and inexperienced with the ways of flirtation. He was a man of the world. A father. Did he know what he was becoming to her? That he made her feel her father's betrayal hadn't entirely destroyed her capability to feel . . . to love and be loved?

'Well . . . ' He pushed his plate to the side, picked up his glass and leaned back. 'Even though we've decided to hold the fundraiser after the Coronation, the celebrations will certainly carry on in one form or another for weeks afterwards. What do you think about tying the fundraiser and the monarchy together? Demonstrate a new King and a new beginning. Women being at the forefront of that beginning. Women from all walks of life standing side by side with men at the elections.'

'That's a wonderful idea. Such a thing is bound to evoke unity and inspiration. I imagine the Coronation will mark a new start for many people looking for better, brighter futures. It's ingenious, Lawrence. Truly.'

'But I can't take credit for it. It was the three chambermaids from the hotel. Anna, Victoria and Ruth have shone with this new opportunity. They have so much more to offer than, to my shame, I realised.'

She smiled. 'Then you are learning what Miss Pennington learned a long time ago: there is always untapped talent and ambition in everyone. It's just a case of giving people the opportunity to show it.'

'Exactly, and all three of them are enjoying planning this fundraiser more than I ever could have imagined. I am more than happy to leave the initial planning to them and then we can come on board after the

171

Coronation to add any changes or tweaks. That way, the ball is rolling, at least.'

'I trust you to implement whatever you think best at this stage. I'm sure these women will be delighted to be left to their own creativity for a few weeks.'

'Something else also occurred to me. Whether we like it or not, it's the people in the upper echelons of society who have the most influence with the powers that be. These are the people who can get their feet into government offices, speak to Members of Parliament and fund ongoing campaigning. We need as many influential people at the fundraiser as possible.'

'Maybe, but doesn't it leave a bad taste in your mouth if we have to resort to flattering these people for the regard their positions and wealth might bring us?'

'Not at all, and it mustn't you, either. The women's suffrage campaign is a fight. A battle. We must use every piece of armoury. Every tactic. But most of all I want you to use *me*.'

A dangerous flutter took flight in her stomach. The notion of using him suddenly bore connotations that were unforgiveable. Maybe even sinful. 'Thank you.'

An unfathomable look came over his face and his expression sobered. 'When you look at me, what do you see?'

Her mind raced. Wasn't that the ultimate question? Didn't everyone want to know how they were perceived? The importance of that first vital impression? Everything about Lawrence and his children had struck her the moment she'd met them and even now, weeks later, they continued to linger in her heart and mind.

'Esther?'

What did it matter if she admitted her feelings? They were alone and adults. Maybe he needed her to expose a little of who she was in order to tempt him to do the same. 'I see a man I am growing to like very much. A man who is devoted to his children. Most of all, I see a man who inspires me and makes me want to be more than I am. But . . . '

'But?'

'I'm confused by my constant thoughts of you. Confused by what I feel when you touch me. My inner compass is off-centre for the first time in forever and the fault lies entirely at your feet.'

The muted sounds of passing voices and horses on the cobblestones outside the window quietly filtered into the room.

He slowly stood, and Esther's pulse beat loud in her ears. If he should touch her now . . .

Stopping in front of her, he offered her his hand. Every part of her screamed to refuse his silent invitation, to turn away from his penetrating gaze and gain the time to realign her equilibrium. Instead, she slipped her hand into his and he gently pulled her to her feet.

His gaze moved from her eyes to linger softly at her mouth. The hunger in the stark blue of his eyes caused a spark of sexual tension to permeate the air. Insecurity battled with her desire to have him take her in his arms and kiss her again. Yet, shouldn't she be sure of who he was before they progressed any further? Who was to say he would come to be no different than her father? A man equally capable of loving her, and then hurting her.

'Come and sit with me in the drawing room.'

Releasing a slow breath, Esther followed him from

the room and up the stairs. Dragging her gaze from his back, she flitted her eyes over the portraits lining the staircase. One after the other was of Rose and Nathanial at different ages, another of Lawrence at a desk either at home or work.

They reached the landing and Esther's heart kicked as she stared into the soft, pretty gaze of a woman around the age of twenty-two. She had the most astonishing mane of curled blonde hair, elegantly dressed and cradling a swaddled babe in her arms.

'That's Abigail. My wife.'

She turned to the quiet sound of Lawrence's voice. He watched her intently, his expression unreadable. Esther glanced at Abigail's picture again and slowly nodded. 'She's lovely.'

'Yes. She was. I commissioned that painting after Rose was born. It was an extravagance we could not truthfully afford, but, with Abigail now gone, it was worth every penny. This picture is important to me, but especially important to the children.' He offered her his hand. 'Come through.'

Esther glanced at the image one more time, her heart twisting with sadness for Lawrence, Rose and Nathanial. She imagined the Culford family would have made quite the picture had they been granted the opportunity.

She entered the semi-darkness of the drawing room. Shadows from the jewel-coloured lamps played across floral walls, the ornate sideboard and stone fireplace. The dried flowers and foliage in the hearth were enormous, set in a white porcelain jug. Knick-knacks and framed pictures scattered the tops of the sideboard and small side tables adjacent to an ivory upholstered settee and armchairs set in front of the fireplace.

All was in perfect order as opposed to the glorious childhood chaos that had surrounded her when she'd played so happily with Rose and Nathanial on her last visit. The absence of the children echoed in the stillness, fuelling her temptation to flee.

No. She would not run. She could be here with Lawrence like this. To whom did she have to answer to but herself? And maybe Abigail.

She followed Lawrence to the settee and sat, only releasing her held breath when he took the seat beside her, her hand still held in his. He circled the back of her hand with his thumb.

'There are things you don't know about me, Esther. Serious things. If we are to move forward with our relationship, I owe you my honesty about everything, but I need a little more time. Do you want me as I want you? Do you think you could come to care for me past friendship?'

Nodding, her pulse leapt and jumped. She could not deny how she wanted him to become an intimate part her life. Wanted him in ways that had absolutely nothing to do with her work or the Cause. 'Yes, I think I could.'

'When I'm with you . . . ' He briefly closed his eyes and opened them again. His gaze blazed with sincerity and conviction. 'I feel a connection with you. As though we've experienced the same pain. That we have the same sense of the world turning while we try to understand the right direction to take. Your spirit and determination echo inside of me. I love spending time with you.'

Her heart swelled with misplaced pride that he would so openly admit his feelings for her, but that could not lessen her natural state of caution. 'And I'm

175

flattered but, still, you must tell me what it is you need to be honest about. You're a father. You have a warm, loving home, so very different to my own. My father turned his back on me on the constant suggestions of a stepmother I despise. My trust has been broken and my heart betrayed by the people I should've been able to rely upon the most. I will not expose myself to risk again, so I need your honesty, Lawrence, or our future together can never exist.'

His gaze travelled over her face. 'Please, Esther, just give me a little more time.'

His sadness seemed too sincere to be deceitful. Too deep to be beguiling.

And suddenly she was too weak to resist him. Too afraid of never meeting another man so handsome, gentle and caring. Could she not control the path they took? Hold onto a big piece of her heart and lock it away so he might never cause her irreparable harm? Wasn't her fear of being disappointed, hurt and banished again strong enough to restrain at least a modicum of emotional attachment even if she couldn't forsake her body and mind?

She stared into his eyes, her body drawn to him. He looked so exposed and vulnerable. She cupped her hand to his jaw. His eyes immediately darkened with a dangerous heat that brought a low hum of want high between her legs.

Leaning slowly forward, she hesitated, her study dropping to his mouth.

And then he kissed her.

Fervently, passionately, his hands moving to her waist.

Esther eased closer as craving caught and ensnared her, melting away her fears and making her want him with every part of her. She squeezed her eyes tightly closed, praying this moment of owning her yearnings, of acting on her desires for the very first time, did not shock or deter him. Whenever she was with him, she longed to be uninhibited and free, no matter how unwise.

His mouth moved from hers to kiss her jaw and Esther leaned her head back. Hot kisses trailed along her neck to the sensitive spot below her ear and liberation rushed through her body, annihilating her conscience and strengthening her need to feel worthy and wholly desirable. Merit every ounce of this man's undivided attention.

★ ★ ★

Blood burned hot and urgent through Lawrence's groin, his fingers brushing the neckline of Esther's dress as he moved his knuckles across the soft skin above her breasts. It had been months since such lust had shrouded him and, when it had, it had risen from an innate need for unattached sexual gratification. Sex with a woman with the same need of liberation. A woman who might help him forget his loneliness, to avoid another night of feeling he had no one . . . *was* no one. A woman with whom he could spend a few hours without discourse into his innermost feelings, fears or failings.

Now, for the first time in his life, he understood why sex was sometimes referred to as making love. Of adoring, of wanting to watch a woman succumb to the pleasures of her body, to yearn and crave for more.

Yet, no matter how much he wanted to witness

Esther's satisfaction, he also wanted her to know the real him. To know everything about him. He was in awe of her candour and desperately wanted to share his self-loathing, but to do so now would take from the pleasure he could give her as her inhibitions fell away and she surrendered to the possibilities of intimate human touch.

'Esther.' He whispered her name against her neck and moved lower to kiss the skin his fingers had explored moments before. 'You are so beautiful.'

He eased back and looked into her eyes, dark with wanting and arousal, her cheeks flushed pink. How could he not have contemplated what she would be like in the throes of lovemaking? Everything about her, everything she did, revealed the concealed passion of the woman beneath. She voiced her opinions without censure. Why on earth wouldn't she enjoy unbridled fervency? Passion epitomised Esther in one beautiful, erotic package.

But he would not take her now — no matter how much he might want to — instead, he'd show her what she did to him. What she made him feel. *How* she made him feel.

Releasing her, he locked his gaze on hers and loosened his tie, unbuttoned the top few fasteners on his shirt. Her study dropped to his partially exposed chest as he ran his hand over the skirt of her dress and she slowly relaxed, her knees dropping open a little wider.

He leaned forward and kissed her, gently easing his tongue to the warmth of hers. She met his passion and Lawrence gripped the hem of her skirt. He gently eased it higher and waited.

Opening his eyes, his heart pounded as he studied her gaze to ensure she wanted him to continue.

Her eyes were clouded with hunger, her plea evident and confirmed. She reached for his hand and guided it beneath her skirt to the naked skin of her inner thigh. His erection strained as he fought against every instinct to take her, devour her and love her as she deserved.

He had no idea if she was a virgin, but he would bestow care regardless.

Inching his hand higher, he smoothed his fingers over every centimetre of her exposed flesh until he tentatively slipped his fingers into her drawers. Satisfaction warmed him and heightened his pleasure to discover wetness. He gently rubbed her, probing a cautious finger at her entrance. To touch her like this was an honour he'd neither forget nor waste. Her eyes drifted closed as she sank her teeth into her bottom lip.

Her softly whispered groan urged his exploration deeper.

She lifted her hand to her breast and cupped it, her nails digging into the silk of her dress.

He caressed her with precision and intention. Her breathing turned from quiet whispers to harried breaths as he increased the pressure, moved his fingers faster over her core. She writhed against him, her eyes squeezing more tightly closed.

Was this how they could be together? Would a mere touch of one another ignite a powerful, silent possession that no one else on earth could evoke? Their fathers had changed them, destroyed their trust, yet together they could break free and embrace everything they should've known themselves capable of their entire lives.

She stilled . . .

Lawrence stared at her beautiful face, his desire for her showing in the perspiration beaded on his skin and the stiffness behind the confines of his trousers. She came undone and tightened around him as she gripped his shoulders, her mouth dropping open, her cheeks and neck flushing with colour.

This could not be the only time he saw her this way.

He wanted her in his bed, in his home and in his life. If he had to let her go . . . No, he couldn't think that way. She was meant to be with him. He ran his fingers over the side of her long neck. 'Esther, you are like no one else I have ever met.'

'As are you.'

He eased away and turned her in his arms so her back was against his chest. He smoothed the hair from her brow and kissed her crown. 'You've made me see in the shortest time how the things that happened to me sculpted me into the man I am today. I want to be entirely myself for Rose and Nathanial. For me. And for you.'

21

Esther closed her eyes as Lawrence continued to gently touch her hair, but, no matter how comforting the feeling, tears welled behind her closed lids. Shame enveloped her that she'd allowed him to touch her so intimately. He would now know how weak she really was, how much she yearned for a man's respect and love. Her carefully erected armour had been torn away in his arms, at his touch, and soon he would realise her no stronger than any other woman he might have had this way.

She needed to leave. Go. Before he said anything more to make her want him . . . make her love him.

Easing from his arms, she drew forth every ounce of her strength and stood. Smoothing her hair and skirts, she despised that her fingers trembled with weakness. 'I really need to go. Thank you so much for such a lovely evening.'

'Esther, wait.' He scrambled to his feet, his gaze concerned.

She turned away from the horrible disappointment in his eyes. 'I have to get back to my aunt. I'm sorry.'

'But — '

She hurried from the room and down the stairs, the portraits beside her seeming to stare in judgement. Their faces no longer smiling but twisted with disapproval. Swiftly entering the dining room, her heart raced, and her body shook, but Esther kept her chin high as she claimed her purse from one of the chairs around the table. The heavy guilt pressing down on her could not deter her from leaving. She had to re-establish power over her emotions. Lock them down and keep everything safely inside, lest her life be pulled apart as it had before.

When she looked up, Lawrence stood at the door, his face a mask of stone. 'Why are you leaving?'

No anger or accusation resounded in his voice. Worse, his question was little more than polite enquiry. Was he distancing himself now he knew her to be wanton? Or was he enforcing space for the same sense of self- preservation?

She walked slowly towards him, forcing her gaze to remain steady on his. 'The meal was wonderful, as were your company and caresses, but I have to work in the morning. Not to mention my aunt will soon be fretting about where I am.'

'Did you not tell her you were dining with me tonight?' She shook her head.

'Why not?'

The reasons for her secrecy were entrenched in survival. If she'd uttered a word about this evening's assignation, her aunt would have reported back to Viola and she, in turn, would have told her father. Esther wanted them to know nothing of her life. Not about her work at Pennington's, her work for the Cause and, certainly, not anything that might pertain to her heart.

Her father could visit her at any time, but he did not. If he deigned to visit her now, all he would do is bestow disparagement on her work and life. Worse, he could confront her at Pennington's, humiliate her in front of her colleagues and associates. She missed him more than she'd ever admit, but, in the same breath, she wanted her father far, far away so she'd never see the angry displeasure in his eyes again.

She pulled back her shoulders. 'My relationship with my family is steeped in poison. I've not shared anything with them since I left home. It's better that way. My stepmother will do anything she can to destroy whatever gives me an ounce of pleasure. Would revel in telling my father anything to blacken me further. He had an ideal for me. A plan. One that did not include work and causes but homemaking and children. I refused to conform to his expectations and he'll never accept who I am.'

'I see. And homemaking and children will never be on your agenda? In your future?' His gaze softened. 'Do you see that to live a life entirely alone is an impossible aspiration? Everyone has people in their lives. Even you.'

Her mentioning children would have undoubtedly drawn his mind to Rose and Nathanial. Maybe now he'd surmise they could never be linked romantically. No matter their attraction. His children and their happiness were everything to him. Just another aspect of him she was falling in love with.

She swallowed past the lump in her throat. 'I have a few friends and associates at the store and Society. I don't need anyone else.'

Regret flashed in his eyes. 'No one personal to you? What about your aunt?'

Hating the concern in his gaze, Esther lifted her chin against the pain in her heart. 'She is a reluctant companion. A person my father elected to take me in so that he could not be seen publicly as expelling me. So that he might not be embarrassed if I am seen without a chaperone.'

'But your aunt feels differently?'

183

'She's never denied me any choices I've made. Although I'm not certain if that's because she's waiting for me to make a mistake. What does it matter? Why should I care for their opinion? I decided a long time ago that the only way forward for me was to make the life *I* want. My mother . . .' Her voice cracked. 'My mother would have been proud of me. That's all I need.'

His jaw tightened, frustration showing in his dark blue eyes. 'And that means never loving someone else? Never trusting anyone?'

The loneliness that struck her was sharp and sudden, and she crossed her arms. 'What other way is there for a woman to be happy? If she shows weakness, there will always be someone ready to manipulate it.'

He shook his head and paced a few steps before stopping again. 'At least your reluctance to allow *me* to court you isn't a singular revolution. Clearly, you intend the same defence of family, friends, colleagues and associates.'

His tone was laced with iciness and Esther's irritation flared. 'I am not unhappy living this way, Lawrence. I like that my destiny is my own.'

She moved to brush past him and he gently gripped her elbow, halting her. 'I asked you here tonight because I admire your conviction. I want to be with you. Get to know you.'

She eased her arm from his grasp. 'Life doesn't have hard and fast rules that people aren't allowed to test or stretch. When my mother died, my father wanted me to accept everything he said and did without argument. If I couldn't do that for him, a man who meant the world to me, how can you expect me to do the same for someone I've only known a matter of weeks?

I enjoy your company, but I am not, and never will be, a possession who will talk and act on your will rather than my own.'

'I'm not asking that you — '

'You, too, are a chameleon of sorts, so how can you judge me?'

'A chame — '

'Yes, Lawrence. A chameleon. Didn't you admit you want me, Rose and Nathanial to know the real you? Then, have you not been hiding who you are from me since the day we met?' She pulled back her shoulders. 'And with that thought, I bid you goodnight.'

She strode past him and down the stairs to the front door. Without looking back, she pulled it open and hurried along the short pathway onto the street. Tears pricked her eyes and her lips trembled, but she refused to cry. Right now, she was little more than a cheap harlot. A woman so desperate for love and affection, she'd let Lawrence touch and satisfy her.

Did he know her to be a virgin? Most likely, he thought her shamefully experienced. The truth was, she was a woman who dreamed of lovemaking, who knew herself capable of enjoying the bedroom. Never before had it embarrassed her that she explored and knew her body.

Until now.

Her actions and words had turned Lawrence away from her, the same as they had her father. Once again, she'd purposefully defied compromise and now stood alone.

And that was the way it would always be if protecting her heart remained her staunch priority. Her self-worth came from her work, not the advent of a lover. Her recognition came from her input to the

Cause, acting as an advocate of women and their future.

She inhaled a strengthening breath and stepped up her pace, determination raging through her and diluting the infernal sadness that swirled painfully around her heart. It had been a mistake to think Lawrence had her interests in his thoughts. It seemed he only considered the victory of making her weak so that he might mould her in the same way her father had hoped he could.

Well, she would be nobody's puppet. At least now, Lawrence knew who *she* really was. Whereas, she had no idea who Lawrence Culford might, or might not, be at all.

22

Lawrence stared ahead as Rose and Nathanial hopped and jumped along Victoria Park's cobbled walkway, his mind on his troubled feelings despite the brightness of a beautiful Sunday afternoon. Helen strolled beside him. Her quiet demeanour should have added to the peacefulness of the day, yet his mind and emotions were in turmoil, the full trees and the flowering beds mocking his inner feelings of withering and wilting.

He hadn't felt such a failure since Abigail had lain dying and he'd been unable to do anything to save her. Since his departing altercation with Esther over a week before, an unease had gripped him that he could not shake off, no matter how much he turned to work, the fundraiser or his children.

For years, work, Rose and Nathanial had been his saviours. His parents' treatment of him should have destroyed any hope of him learning to love and trust, but how was he to convince Esther he wanted her in every way? That he would never come between her and her work?

Self-disgust twisted inside him.

No matter how much he told himself the scars of his father's belt, the confining of Lawrence in a darkened cupboard for hours, sometimes an entire night, until he agreed to whatever demand his father wanted, had been buried and forgotten, Esther had clearly heard every ounce of his weakness in his words.

Why on earth would a woman so strong and determined want a man like him? She deserved a lover who

187

stood tall and proud beside her. Not one who continued to linger on his harsh childhood.

'Mr Culford? Is something the matter, sir?'

Helen's voice broke his thoughts and Lawrence turned, his smile appearing as easily as it always did. 'Not at all. Why do you ask?'

'I asked if you have plans this evening, but you were miles away.'

'A night's reading is as far as my plans are likely to stretch tonight.' He turned to the pond glistening and sparkling beneath the warm sunshine. 'I've worked hard this week and it seems a similar week lies ahead of me, so a quiet night will be welcomed.'

'I see.'

Lawrence glanced at her. Her tone indicated Helen was far from satisfied with his reply. He frowned. 'Is that not what you expected me to say?'

Her cheeks flushed and she grimaced. 'Forgive me if I am speaking out of turn, sir, but you've not been yourself since your dinner with Miss Stanbury. I'm a little worried about you. As is Charles.'

Lawrence inhaled a long breath as they strolled further along the path, people passing by arm in arm and children skipping and running. 'Miss Stanbury is an acquaintance. There's no need for your or Charles' concern. I'm quite all right.'

'So, you'll be seeing Miss Stanbury again? She seemed awfully taken with Rose and Nathanial. Plus, when you returned with Rose after the book signing at Pennington's, she couldn't stop telling me how nice she found Miss Stanbury. Do you know she told me she wanted to work in Pennington's, too, when she was old enough?'

Amusement and warmth spread through him as

Lawrence looked at Rose as she hopped ahead of them, hand in hand with her brother. 'She said that?'

Helen nodded and smiled. 'She said Miss Stanbury and Miss Pennington were happy, and she wants to be happy, too.'

Lawrence studied his daughter and guilt pressed down on him, his smile dissolving. Whenever her little brother looked at her, Rose smiled and then it slowly evaporated whenever Nathanial looked away. Was Rose wearing the same self-serving mask as her father?

He swallowed the lump that lodged painfully in his throat. 'She surmised Pennington's is where people find happiness?'

'It's not a naïve assumption.' Helen laughed. 'I know I'm happy whenever I'm there.'

He faced her. 'Do you go to Pennington's often? Had you seen Miss Stanbury before she came to the house?'

'I don't think so.' Helen frowned. 'But both myself and Charles like her very much, sir. Mrs Jackson, too. It seems a shame that you won't step out together again.'

'We haven't stepped out at all,' Lawrence said quickly, not wanting Helen or anyone else at the house contemplating a future that was non-existent. The children stopped beside the duck pond, Nathanial giggling as he flapped his arms to his side and waddled up and down. 'I'm organising a fundraiser at the hotel for Miss Stanbury's suffragist group. So, although I'm likely to see her again, it will be business only.'

Regret whispered inside him.

He'd lectured and challenged Esther on her choice

to live a life alone, yet he was living the same lonely way. All the money and success in the world would not take the look of subdued longing from Rose's face, only love, laughter and care could do that. He'd once felt he and his staff provided all the care and stability Rose and Nathanial needed, but the older his children became, the more guidance they needed. How could he show them the meaning of true happiness when he had no idea of it himself?

He faced Helen. 'I know your questions are born out of concern, but, truly, Miss Stanbury is unlikely to become a feature in my life. Maybe that will remain something I regret, but that's the way it seems things will be.'

She nodded, her eyes soft with a sympathy he neither wanted nor deserved. Glancing towards the children, she sighed. 'I only worry for you, sir. I hate the thought that you might never find a sweetheart. Someone to love Rose and Nathanial. They deserve that.' She turned. 'As do you.'

He forced a smile. 'And so do you. I like to imagine you falling in love one day. Having a family of your own.'

Helen's pretty blue eyes twinkled with mischief. 'I already have a special someone.'

Surprised that Helen had never mentioned a man in her life before, Lawrence raised his eyebrows. 'You do?'

She blushed. 'There are some things a girl likes to keep to herself, sir.'

'Of course. Well, I am very pleased. I hope he treats you in the manner you deserve.' He feigned a glare. 'If he doesn't, he'll have me to answer to.'

She laughed. 'He treats me very well.'

'Good. And on another note, I'll be increasing your, Charles' and Mrs Jackson's wages with immediate effect.'

'But, sir, you're already very generous — '

'Helen, I would have been lost without all three of you for many years. You have all gone above and beyond what is expected of you without protest, argument or question. Your service is vital to me and I want to pay you accordingly.'

She dipped her head as she smiled. 'Well, thank you, sir. I'm sure Charles and Mrs Jackson will be as delighted as I am.'

The children moved on from the pond and Lawrence and Helen fell into step behind them. As they walked, he scanned the park and the women walking back and forth: nannies with prams and young women in groups. Now he'd met Esther, every other woman faded into insignificance. He neither acknowledged their beauty, nor their possible suitability.

He had to rid himself of his scars. Had to stop his duplicity of not being entirely himself. He didn't like the idea of his staff worrying about him, or from what, or where, his moroseness originated.

How would he ever be happy unless he shed his humiliation and began to believe his shame didn't show in the cracks of his carefully maintained façade? So, he hadn't turned out to be the robust, strict, iron-handed heir his parents felt was needed to maintain his father's fortune and estate. They tried their best to beat those virtues into him in an effort to secure a hardened, immovable Culford line and they'd failed.

He couldn't give a damn.

'It's nearing teatime, sir. Shall we head home?'

He blinked and turned to Helen. 'Absolutely.'

191

She called the children and Rose and Nathanial came running into their nanny's open arms. When Helen had spoken of her beau, her eyes had shone with love and excitement. There was every possibility the children could soon lose the only woman they had who truly cared for them. He had to move on for their sakes', if not for his own.

It was time to face his past and bury it once and for all.

23

Esther sat in front of Elizabeth's desk on the fifth floor of Pennington's, the early-June sunshine streaming through the windows, bathing the feminine, but businesslike office in bright warmth.

Esther sighed as she looked towards the window. 'It's such a beautiful day. Summer will soon be upon us.'

Elizabeth smiled and smoothed the collar of her navy silk blouse, her pale coral-painted nails glinting in the sunlight. 'As will the Coronation, which is less than two weeks away.'

'And the excitement is palpable on the streets. The city is looking more and more cheerful as banners and flags are erected outside shops, stores and on the trams. I know Bath's procession will not be anything like the real thing in London, but it's going to be so lovely to see clowns and acrobats, the brass band and other wonderful sights go by the store. Do you know the exact route?'

Elizabeth shook her head. 'Only that the procession will definitely be coming along Milsom Street as it's one of the busiest shopping streets in the city. The only thing I am quite sure of is the organisers would not have thought it suitable to take the procession anywhere near the river and the poor people living there.' She sighed. 'It saddens me to think of the small children who are unable to come further into the city missing out on such a parade.'

Esther sighed as regret wound tight inside her.

'There's only so much any of us can do for the poor and needy.'

Silence lingered for a moment before Elizabeth spoke again. 'So, we are nearly ready to start on the window?'

Concerned about the air of sadness surrounding her friend, Esther longed to ask her again about Joseph, but the timing wasn't right when they were at work. She leaned forward in her seat. 'We are more than ready.'

'Judging by your sketches and plans, the window will be a triumph. If you begin work next week, will that give you enough time to be ready to reveal the display on the morning of the Coronation? I'd like to get ahead with our promotion efforts. We need to ensure we have appropriate merchandise displayed inside the store but leave the grand reveal of the main window to the actual Coronation day.'

'Agreed. I think we should pay special attention to jewellery and accessories. The more sparkle and shine people see around the Coronation, the more they'll want to buy.' Lifting her notebook from her lap, Esther scanned her notes. 'I also thought it would be good to push homewares that include the new dinner sets and glassware we've recently acquired. They have a wonderful regal style to them. What do you think?'

'I agree.' Elizabeth smiled. 'I'm so pleased you're focused on your work again. I was genuinely concerned you might be losing interest in Pennington's and contemplating moving on.'

'From Pennington's?' Esther's heart gave a little blip. 'Never. I love it here.'

'I'm relieved to hear it, but you have been so uncharacteristically distracted these past few weeks.

Is everything all right at home? The last thing I want is to pry, but I hope you know I'll help if I can.'

Esther swallowed. She'd barely stopped thinking about Lawrence and their growing intimacy . . . and now, their separation. Had her sorrow been etched on her face for everyone to see? She lifted her shoulders. 'Everything is absolutely fine.'

Elizabeth studied her before propping her elbows on top of her desk. 'Good, because you're an important part of Pennington's continuing success. Not to mention the person I rely on to make decisions as far as branding and promotion is concerned. But we spend time together away from here, too. Socially. I'd like to think you'd talk to me, if you needed to.'

Although heartened by her friend's warmth and support, Esther was still reluctant to share her worries with Elizabeth when she clearly had enough concerns of her own. 'I will, if and when I need to. I promise.'

'Good. Then why don't we arrange a night out together after the Coronation? We could both do with a treat considering all our hard work.'

Esther smiled. 'That's a fabulous idea. And there's no need for you to be worried about me. I'm fine. Honestly.' Esther held her friend's gaze, praying her eyes did not reflect the sadness she'd been fighting since walking away from Lawrence. 'The distractions I had are settled now. There's absolutely nothing for you to be worried about.'

Nonetheless, concern shadowed Elizabeth's gaze. 'And the distractions had nothing to do with the recent visit from your stepmother?'

Heat leapt into Esther's cheeks, fuelled more by anger at Viola than embarrassment. 'She and I have never seen eye to eye. I have no idea why she came to Grace Hadley's talk. My stepmother is hardly an advocate for women's progression. She comes into Bath to visit her sister and has taken to striking up a friendship with my aunt. A friendship in which she can drill Aunt Mary to find out what I'm up to.'

'I see. Then it is as I thought.'

'What is?'

'That your distraction must be caused by the very charming, very attractive, Mr Culford.' Elizabeth grinned, her green gaze alight with teasing. 'Am I right?'

Esther closed her eyes. Lying to Elizabeth was futile.

She opened her eyes and sighed. 'Mr Culford was a momentary disruption, nothing more. We've gone our separate ways as far as anything personal is concerned.'

'Is that what you want?'

Esther hesitated, the ache in her chest deepening. 'That's neither here nor there.'

'Why not?'

'Because . . .' Esther inhaled a shaky breath. 'He would only come to be wrong for me.'

'Why? He seemed courteous and attentive and his daughter clearly adores him.'

Esther slumped her shoulders. 'And I could, too. That's the problem. I just can't go down that path, Elizabeth. I won't.'

'Esther . . .' Elizabeth stood and walked around the desk. She sat in the chair beside Esther and took her hand. 'What is so bad that you can't spend some time with this man? Has he upset you?'

'No. It's me.'

Elizabeth raised her eyebrows. 'You've upset *him*?'

'Undoubtedly.' Esther slowly drew her hand from

196

Elizabeth's. 'But the problem remains with me. It has nothing to do with Lawrence. Or any man who might want to get close to me. Distance is something I purposely impose. I have to if I am to remain stalwart in my work for the Cause. I've already lost all contact with my father over my passions. Why risk loving and losing someone else?'

'Esther, you can't live that way. Your work is as important to you as it was your mother, but she would not want you to forsake the chance of love for the vote or anything else. You're kind, hard-working and extraordinarily talented.' Elizabeth's gaze softened. 'Anyone would love to be a part of your life.'

Esther shook her head, sadness bearing down on her. 'Maybe for a while, but not forever.'

'You're as deserving as anyone else of finding some-one who — '

'I won't be happy until I've made the life I want.' Fervour for the Cause and the dream she shared with her mother rose hot and urgent. 'I can't imagine any man wanting to love a woman who is — '

'Passionate? Believes in women's rights and progression? Who wants to make positive changes in this world?' Elizabeth's cheeks darkened and she abruptly stood. She stalked behind her desk and sat, her green eyes blazing with determination. 'Your father is no different than mine. You know the difficulties I faced with him last year and look at me now. I'm married to the man I love and we're running Pennington's together. If I'd bowed down to my father and adhered to his every word, do you think either of those things would've happened? You must fight the negativity and doubt your father has put inside of you, Esther. You *have to.*'

197

A modicum of hope simmered deep inside her as Esther considered the woman Elizabeth was today compared to the frustrated, caged, parentally-limited daughter she'd been a year before.

'My father is now travelling the world, Esther. Enjoying his life with a woman to whom he has fully opened his heart. He's proposed marriage. Could you have ever imagined such a thing a year ago? People change. Lives alter. Don't let the past cause a terrible effect on your future.'

Esther shook her head as her infernal self-doubt emerged once more. 'That is much easier said than done. I'm trying to live my best life in every way I know.'

'Are you?'

Esther lifted her chin. If Elizabeth didn't understand the reasons why she worked so hard, who else would? 'Yes.'

'I'm sorry, but you're not. If your father is still affecting the way you live, the choices you make, he's winning. Your stepmother, too. Until you believe you deserve the life you want, the *love* you want, you're not fighting hard enough. Speak with your father. Tell him what he's done to you and what he continues to do. Confronting my father, defending my rightful place here and with Joseph changed the way I perceive everything. I was prepared to sacrifice all I had for the way I wanted to live. Are you? Only then will you realise your true potential. In everything.'

Esther's heart picked up speed. It was a speech similar to those she'd given to rally her associates in the Society. To invoke others to join. Yet, wasn't she ignoring her own spirit and desires?

Self-hatred and fear knotted her stomach. The

thought of seeing her father again, let alone speaking with him, terrified her. Made her feel like his controlled daughter instead of the independent, self-sufficient woman she constantly tried to convince herself she had become.

'I can't see him. I'm too angry, too weak. He'll see that. Worse, so will my stepmother.'

'Then, for the time being, spend more time with Mr Culford and really embrace how you feel when you are with him. Does he excite you? Inspire you? Make you wonder what your life could be like with him?'

He does. So much.

Memories of the way she'd acted when she'd been alone with Lawrence rose in Esther's mind in a way that was as thrilling as it was shameful. She met Elizabeth's knowing gaze and softly smiled. 'Maybe.'

Elizabeth grinned. 'Excellent. Then call on him. Tonight.'

'What?'

'I mean it. You know as well as I that if women want something in this world, we have to go out and take it.' Elizabeth pulled some papers towards her. 'Now, back to work. You have a busy night ahead.'

Esther stood and, with a final shake of her head in Elizabeth's direction, strode across the plush cream carpet to the door, wondering what on earth had just happened. Whatever it was, her heart felt more hopeful than it had all week, her steps lighter.

Should she really call on Lawrence? Was Elizabeth right and it was conceivable that every woman could have all they wanted? Whether yes or no, Esther breathed deep, didn't she owe it to herself to at least explore the possibility?

24

Lawrence strode through the wood-panelled lobby of the Phoenix Hotel and tried his best to bask in his triumphs. Situated in Queen's Square, each of the sixty rooms was decorated to the highest standard, using both classic and modern themes, giving guests a choice of ambience during their stay.

The lobby bustled with activity as people smiled and laughed, read newspapers in the wing-backed chairs or drank coffee at the small tables in front of the floor-to-ceiling windows with a view to the tree-lined square beyond. Lawrence looked to his right towards the open double doors leading to the lounge, pleased to see guests milling back and forth as they chatted amicably with each other or his staff.

His achievements were marked in every polished table, every inch of the deep blue carpet and every crystal droplet of the hotel's many chandeliers. In terms of success, he'd surpassed many a man before him and had much to be proud of, but still he longed to live authentically, truthfully.

He was fair and trusted amongst his staff, liked and admired by his peers and loved by his children. But who truly knew him? Who knew he struggled to control a burning resentment that simmered beneath the surface of his personality? Or the way hatred burned like an inferno deep in his heart, scalding any hope of him being truly happy?

Before Esther, he'd handled his weaknesses. Dealt with his emotions when the darkness fell. But Esther's

200

determination to see through the goals that mattered to her made him want to push forth and become a man free of his past . . . a man free.

He had to see her again . . . couldn't *not* see her.

The way she'd left his house had meant he'd managed little sleep for days. The soft, floral scent of her continued to wash over him at the most inopportune moments. The quiet, yet confident tone of her voice seeping into his mind, causing an odd tightness in his chest time and again. And her body . . . Arousal whispered through him and Lawrence quickly shut down his carnal thoughts.

Esther had confessed her fierce independence came from her father's banishment, but he had yet to tell her how his father's cruelty meant he hid behind smiles and affability rather than face the anger and resentment writhing like poison inside of him. He had to step up. Had to confess his truth to her. To do anything less felt like an opportunity to heal would be lost. No one had ever made him feel that way. Wasn't that omen enough that Esther was special?

He walked through the lobby and outside onto the stone steps at the hotel's entrance. The clatter of the passing carriages, shouts of paperboys and calls from the street vendors mixed in his ears and Lawrence breathed deep. There was no doubt the city was where he belonged. The smog, the noise and chaos acted like an engine to his soul. It was the reason he'd come to Bath for a fresh start.

The city served as an antithesis to the elitism and privilege he'd known amongst the people who visited his home during his childhood. The moneyed came to Bath during the Season, but there were also reminders of life's discrimination and inequality that he'd been kept from in the country. The rich mixed with the poor, the lucky with the unlucky, the literate with the illiterate.

There was much to do, change and improve, but, because of his deepening attraction to Esther, the women's suffrage bill had become the most pressing.

She wanted so much from life, and most of it could be seen in her designs and ideals for a better future. He was progressive in his thinking, a non-traditionalist in many ways. They could make something good together. He was certain of it.

The only aspect that bit savagely at his surety was Rose and Nathanial.

His protection of them, his need for their happiness meant only a woman who came to love them as he did could ever truly be his wife. Esther was already so fond of his children. She made them laugh, dream and think as he'd never known them to before. Especially Rose. But Esther had walked away from him. Left, and not made any attempt to contact him again as far as he knew. If he pursued and won her heart, would she flee again someday?

Either way, he had to speak with her again.

Today. Now.

Decision made, Lawrence strode down the hotel's steps, intent on finding her at Pennington's . . . only to draw to an abrupt halt.

The carriage that pulled to a stop at the kerb belonged to his eldest sister, Cornelia. He glanced along the street, torn between seeing Esther and greeting the beloved sister he hadn't seen in weeks. He and Cornelia occasionally telephoned, but to see her in the flesh was a rarity he couldn't renounce.

Burying his desire to see Esther for the time being,

he planted on a smile.

Cornelia emerged from the carriage. When her eyes met his, her pretty face lit with happiness. 'Lawrence! Oh, my goodness, it's so lovely to see you.'

The epitome of elegance, his eldest sister rushed towards him on a soft cloud of perfume, her grey suit and wide-brimmed, dusky-pink hat unrumpled by what must have been a tiring journey from her home in Oxfordshire.

Lawrence gathered her in his arms, heedless to the people having to part around them. He closed his eyes and squeezed her tightly. 'What are you doing here?'

She pulled back, her blue eyes shining. 'I needed to see you. Are you happy I'm here?'

'Of course.' Lawrence laughed and peered over her head towards the carriage. 'Aren't the children with you? David?'

She turned. 'Children, come out and say hello to your uncle Lawrence.' His nephews clambered from the carriage and came to Cornelia's side, each having grown by a good half foot since Lawrence had last seen them. It was truly wonderful to have them visit and looking so well. 'Look at you both. How are you?'

'Well, thank you, Uncle Lawrence.' Alfred, the eldest, grinned before tipping his head back to look at the covered walkway leading to the hotel's entrance. 'You have a super hotel, Uncle.'

'Thank you.' Lawrence turned to Francis who, at only six, did not yet have his brother's confidence. 'How are you, young man? Looking after your mama?'

Francis nodded with a shy smile and slipped his hand into Cornelia's.

Embracing their visit, Lawrence stepped back and held out his hand towards the hotel. 'Why don't we go inside for some tea? We have a new chef from London. His cakes are like none you'll ever have tasted.'

The boys swept ahead of them and Lawrence offered Cornelia his arm as they slowly walked.

'Those boys look more and more like David every day. Same hair. Same colour eyes. How is David, by the way?'

'Oh, you know David. Everything is always absolutely fine with *him*.'

Lawrence glanced at her. The irony dripping from her words was little short of acidic. 'Is everything all right between you?'

'Everything is grand. Can't a sister see her brother without there being a problem or prior invitation?'

Lawrence noted the high colour in her cheeks and the way she stared resolutely ahead. He gently gripped her elbow and drew her to a stop on the entrance steps. 'What's wrong?'

'Nothing. Don't be silly. I'm here for a while, if you'll have me. I'm hoping to stay in one of your fabulous rooms for a few nights.'

Lawrence frowned. *A few nights?* 'Without David?'

'Yes, without David. He's busy with work.' She eased her arm from his grasp and stepped towards the doors being held open by one of his staff. Cornelia glanced over her shoulder. 'You of all people should understand that.'

Concerned, Lawrence followed her inside. He'd leave interrogating Cornelia further until later. Maybe she was just tired.

She stood in the centre of the vast lobby, her gaze scanning the area all around her. A soft smile played at her lips that didn't quite reach her eyes and Lawrence's disquiet deepened.

Something was definitely wrong, but he'd give her space. At least for the time being. He forced a smile. 'I'll ensure you and the boys are given the best room available. It's good that you arrived today rather than in a few days' time as I'm not sure where I could have put you. Every suite has been pre-booked and most rooms, too. For the Coronation, you see.'

'Oh. Yes, of course.' Her brow furrowed, and her gaze shadowed. 'I was hoping to stay through the Coronation. Will that be all right?'

He raised his eyebrows, his concern deepening. 'But that's over a week away.'

She lifted her shoulders as though weeks away from her husband and home were of no consequence. 'I know.'

'Then you must stay with me at the house. You'll be much more relaxed there.' Lawrence stared into her worried eyes, her face paler than it had been a few moments before. 'Cornelia, if something's wrong, why don't you te —'

'Are you quite certain you have time to take tea with us?' Her gaze darted about the lobby, her shoulders lowering when she spotted her children staring through the window ahead of them. 'I appreciate you must be busy. If you have more pressing things to do, we can always dine together later.'

Thoughts of Esther seeped into his mind and Lawrence quickly pushed them away, knowing full well whatever had brought Cornelia to the city, and was making her look so unusually anxious, had to take priority for now. 'Nothing that can't wait.'

'Are you sure?'

'Absolutely.'

Lawrence squeezed her hand and she called to

Alfred and Francis. They walked into the dining room and Lawrence guided them to an empty table in the far corner. As soon as Cornelia was seated, the boys ran to the windows and stared into the street once more, their fascination with the city showing in their wide eyes and infectious smiles.

The pale green walls shone beneath the crystal chandeliers and the pure white crockery glistened amid the low hum of conversation, interspersed with bouts of laughter. The Phoenix's dining room offered 'home away from home' comfort with a touch of luxury. Immense pride filled him each time he had the opportunity to share its opulence with his sister and nephews.

'This room is absolutely resplendent,' Cornelia sighed as she unpinned her hat and laid it on the chair beside her, her dark brown hair gleaming. 'It's been too long since I last came here. I think I'll let you entirely spoil me.'

'And doing so will be my pleasure.' He sat beside her and glanced around for a waiter. He caught Frederick's gaze and gestured him to the table, before turning to Cornelia. 'Shall I order full tea? Are you hungry?'

'No, but the boys are constantly, so full tea will be perfect.'

Lawrence studied her. She had lost weight in the weeks since he'd seen her, and her complexion had lost its usual lustre. He turned to Frederick as he came to stand at the table. 'Full tea for two, please, Frederick, and smaller servings for my two nephews.'

'Of course, sir. Which tea would you like served?'

'Earl Grey.' He glanced at Cornelia. 'Unless, your taste has changed?'

'Grey is perfect.' She smiled at Frederick. 'Thank

you.'

The young waiter nodded, his gaze lingering on Cornelia even as she dropped her gaze to her purse and fumbled inside. Pride bloomed in Lawrence's chest. With their beautiful, long dark hair, bright blue eyes and exceptionally feminine figures, Cornelia and his younger sister, Harriet, were outstandingly attractive. Even if Cornelia was oblivious to her allure and Harriet positively basked in it and used it to her every advantage.

He looked at Frederick. 'That will be all for now. Thank you.'

'Yes, sir.'

As Frederick retreated, Lawrence leaned his arms on the table. 'So, why don't you share with me why you're here? It's no good telling me everything is fine. I know you better than that.'

Her gaze lingered on his, indecision warring in her eyes before she turned to the boys. They still stood at the window engrossed in whatever sights had caught their undivided attention. She drew in a shaky breath and turned. 'David's planning to leave me, Lawrence. Go with his mistress and I have no intention of stopping him. His affair has gone on long enough despite him lying to me that it was over. It never was and never will be. So he's left me with no choice but to move home to Mama . . .' Her eyes glazed with tears.

Words caught in Lawrence's throat as a torrent of emotions assailed him.

Anger at David, worry for Cornelia and the boys. 'David's leaving you?'

'Yes.'

'But I don't understand. I thought you were happy together.'

'No, and we haven't been for a long time.'

'Have you spoken to the children about this?'

'No, and they know nothing of Sophie Hughes, either.'

'That's his lover's name?' Lawrence frowned. 'She sounds familiar.'

'She should. She lives just outside of Bath on an estate near Colerne. I'm quite sure she will have stayed at your hotel while visiting the city.'

Lawrence's mind reeled with Cornelia's news and how the name Sophie Hughes was familiar to him. Then it struck him. 'Isn't her father Baron Hughes of Middleton Park? I believe he's stayed here several times with his family.'

'The one and only. The not-so-honourable Sophie Hughes has been sleeping with my husband for a number of years and now David's decided he wishes to marry her. She was quite happy to continue to be the lover of a married man and risk her reputation, but apparently the Baron has said enough is enough and David is to divorce me and marry her, or else they go their separate ways. Clearly, David, being the social leech he is, cannot wait to marry into a wealthy and landed family.'

Lawrence curled his napkin in his fist. 'The man is a cretin. Pure and simple.'

'I agree. Which is why I'm here with you. I will visit Mama and assess the state of her health, but I refuse to return to Culford and all it entails permanently. Neither will I continue to live in Oxfordshire amid gossip and spite that could reach the children.'

Lawrence stilled. 'Mother is ill?'

'Yes. Gravely so. Harriet telephoned a while ago but with everything happening with David . . . ' She shook her head. 'We need to visit the Manor and see what we can do to help Mama and Harriet. You will come with me, won't you?'

Dread unfurled in Lawrence's stomach. 'I have no wish to see her. You know this.' Pushing his ailing mother to the back of his mind for the time being, Lawrence focused on Cornelia's welfare and uncertain future. 'So, you plan to live in Bath?'

'Yes.' Her jaw tightened. 'If David so desperately wishes for his freedom, then he can pay for it by buying a home for me and the children as well as providing us with a fair income.'

'And if the fair income is not enough to see you are comfortable? Has Mother given you any of your inheritance over the years?'

She smiled wryly. 'Of course not. Why would she when David is so much wealthier than I will ever be? It's of no matter. If David resists my demands, then I'll work.' She smiled, the excited anticipation in her eyes taking Lawrence by surprise. 'Papa never let any of us exist without occupation, after all. He was terribly hard on you, but he kept Harriet and myself busy, too. There is little chance of me wilting from daily work.'

'You've given this thought, haven't you?'

'I have. I didn't come here without a plan. You can be assured of that.'

'Then I'm incredibly proud of you.' Lawrence smiled, pleased with his sister's optimism but still a quiet dread of what her future might hold whispered through him. Whatever happened next for her and his nephews, he would be there for them every step of the way. 'Would you like me to find you a position at the hotel?'

She shook her head. 'Not unless it comes that I can't find a position myself. If you're happy for us to be here awhile longer, I'd like to seek something alone for now.'

'Very well, and you can stay as long as you wish. Although, I think it would be good for me to speak with David on your behalf.' Lawrence frowned as he considered the best way forward as far as his brother-in-law's deceit and Cornelia's happiness were concerned. 'Is there any chance at all you'd want him back? I presume if he came crawling back on his hands and knees, begging for your forgiveness, you might consider giving him a second chance?'

'Presumption is a very dangerous thing, Lawrence.' Cornelia said, her gaze averted. 'David and I are over. I'll never want him back regardless of him begging or anything else.'

Although pleased by Cornelia's standing, the potential effects any public condemnation or stigma about divorce could have on his once happy sister worried him. 'Your marriage might have been arranged by Mother, but I've witnessed real warmth between you and David over the years. Has his affair really destroyed everything you ever felt for him?'

Irritation darkened her blue eyes. 'Are you saying you think I should take him back, should he ask?'

The mere thought of David wrangling his way back into Cornelia's life irked Lawrence more than he dared to admit. He was entirely incensed by David's treatment of his sister and nephews and he needed Cornelia to believe that. 'Of course not.'

'Then why do I feel you're questioning my decision?'

'I'm just concerned for you and the children, should

any gossip surround your divorce. That doesn't mean I think you're not strong enough to deal with it.'

'Good. Because I am, and I will. I learned to live with David's infidelity a long time ago. It's because he walked away from the children so easily that I have no wish to see him again. Perhaps there was some warmth between us for a time, but, as for passion, there was none. I'm not sure there ever was. Why would I want to continue the way we were now he's clearly shown to whom his loyalty and love resides? If you or I pressure David to return home and he concedes, he'll not come back out of love or care for me or the boys, he'll come out of duty. Or guilt. Why would I want him back knowing that? I'm sure I'll be perfectly fine in time. Mama is a bigger concern right now.'

Lawrence stared. Whatever she said, a deep pain burned in Cornelia's eyes and he didn't doubt her suffering was more about David than care for their mother. His sisters might have had a fractionally better relationship with their parents than he'd had, but he could hardly claim Cornelia, or even Harriet, who had practically grown into his mother, adored them. He leaned back. 'What's wrong with Mother?'

'You really should know, Lawrence. It wouldn't hurt for you to at least write or telephone her every now and then, even if you can't bring yourself to see her. Time has passed, Father's gone and now Mama is ill. It's time to bury the past.'

'I've nothing to say to her.' Lawrence looked about the restaurant, tightness gripping his chest. 'There's too much anger and hostility.' He looked at her. 'On both sides.'

'Then you must find a way to lessen it.' Cornelia's shoulders slumped, her pretty eyes pleading with

211

him. 'The doctor has said it's a complication with her lungs. He's not entirely certain but fears it may be terminal. You must come home. Even if it's just for a short while. It's not fair for either of us to leave Harriet to manage Mama alone.'

Coldness inched into his blood. He had no idea what he felt or thought about his mother's suffering. It had been three years since he'd returned to Culford and stood beside his mother at his father's funeral. The thought of stepping inside the Manor again brought the bitter taste of nausea to his throat. 'Let me think about it. Mother has not sought to speak with me at all these past years and, as far I know, hasn't been concerned by our lack of contact.'

'That doesn't mean she wouldn't want to see you now. She could be dying, Lawrence.'

Pressure bore down on him. How could he leave his sisters to deal with their mother alone? 'I can't think about this now. You need to give me some time.'

Her eyes clouded with concern before she nodded. 'As you wish.'

'Thank you. But what about you? You said David has been carrying on behind your back for a number of years. How many specifically?' Fury swirled inside of him. He'd thought he could trust his brother-in-law to look after his sister and nephews. A man Lawrence had happily watched stand by Cornelia on their wedding day, the boys' christenings . . . 'Cornelia?'

She looked at the children and swiped her fingers beneath her eyes, leaving a faint smudge on her linen gloves. 'Three years. Possibly four.' She turned. 'He loves her, Lawrence. There's not an awful lot I can do about that.'

'Bastard.' He spat the word from between clenched

teeth as he grappled not to get out of his chair and leap into a carriage to hunt David down. 'It's senseless for me to ask how you are, but how are you managing? Why didn't you contact me? I would've been there for you in a shot. You know that. Does Mother know?'

Cornelia shook her head. 'I can't tell her. Not yet. You know how she'll react and I need to be stronger than I am right now to face her criticism and blame.' She briefly closed her eyes and, when she opened them, another tear rolled over her cheek. She glanced at the boys and quickly wiped it away. 'I'll be back on my feet in no time. It will take more than David's betrayal and desertion to break me.'

'But — '

'David married as you did, Lawrence. On his mother's orders. Unfortunately for me, I fell in love with David, but those feelings were never reciprocated. No matter how good a wife I tried to be, how much I cared for him and the children, it was never enough.' She looked at her sons. 'Boys, come and sit down. Your tea will be here shortly.'

As Cornelia busied herself moving cutlery and condiments, Lawrence studied her. She needed him more than she had in months. He would track David down and when he found him . . . there would be hell to pay. As for seeing his mother? That was a different matter entirely.

25

Esther pushed her key into the lock of her aunt's house and stopped, her fingers tightly clutching the brass. She closed her eyes and mustered the strength to get through another night filled with disappointed glances and disparaging words. Despite Elizabeth's coaxing for Esther to call on Lawrence, the day had been frantic when a little boy got loose of his mother and decided it would be fun to rearrange as many mannequins' hats and jewellery as possible before one of the security watchmen scooped him up.

Kicking and screaming, the boy had been carried throughout the atrium until a member of staff finally located his mother, only for her to promptly lay the blame on Pennington's. Esther had quite happily taken her to Joseph's office. The man was famed for his charm and charisma . . . even in the most ridiculous of situations.

After having to go around the store and undo the mess the young boy had made, Esther was dead on her feet. But she would do her utmost to see Lawrence tomorrow. Elizabeth was right. It was up to Esther to forge the life she wanted. Not bury her feelings and not run away.

She inhaled a long breath and pushed open the door. She walked into the hallway and removed her hat, placing it on a small side table before unbuttoning her coat. 'I'm home, Aunt Mary. Would you like a cup of tea?'

'If I wanted tea, I would've made it myself. Why on

214

earth are you home so late?'

Rolling her eyes, Esther counted to ten as she took the same number of steps towards the parlour. She stepped into the room and met her aunt's steely gaze from where she sat in front of the fireplace, her knitting on her lap.

Esther sighed. 'I'm really busy organising things for the Coronation display. I'll most likely be home later than usual every night for the remainder of the week, I'm afraid.'

'And what do you suggest I do as I sit here alone night after night?' She picked up her knitting, her brow furrowed as she studied the stitches. 'You know full well Veronica leaves the house at six o'clock every evening, regardless if I need her to stay.'

Convinced her aunt's maid left on time every evening in desperation to be away from her employer, Esther held every sympathy for the girl. 'I'm sure she has plans most evenings and you were out with Viola for the last two. Why don't you arrange a dinner with Win next door? I'm sure she'd welcome an evening out.'

'I don't want to see Winifred Roberts any more than I already do, thank you very much.'

Biting back a retort that she was sure their next-door neighbour tolerated her aunt in much the same way, Esther forced a smile. 'Well, anyway, it is only seven o'clock. Why don't we play some cards? I'll just make myself a quick sandwich and then we can play until you're tired.'

'I haven't got time to play cards. I need to get this blanket done so I can take it to the Salvation Army tomorrow. I've knitted a total of seven in the last two weeks. That will put Dorothea firmly in her place.

Lord only knows who she thought she impressed by knitting three in one week. I suspect the woman has blisters on her silly fingers.'

Esther left the room and walked along the hallway into the kitchen. Although she should be used to her aunt's abrasiveness by now, coming home to it every night took its toll. The house had never felt so claustrophobic. She looked at the bare brick walls, the black Aga and yellowing net curtain hanging at the window. The only dash of colour and brightness came from the copper pans hooked above the fireplace and the tea towels drying on the cupboards' steel handles. Sometimes, the only places she could breathe were at Pennington's or with her Society associates. Yet, tonight, it was more than Aunt Mary's curt words and poor attitude that riled Esther. She should've gone to the Circus and knocked on Lawrence's door.

Fear he might one day break her heart if she were to fall in love with him was what made her flee from his home that fateful, sensual night they'd been alone. Yet, she hadn't felt beautiful or worthy since.

She walked into the larder and extracted butter and cheese before closing the door and wandering to the table. She took a knife from one of the drawers beneath the tabletop.

'Esther?'

She hovered the knife above the block of cheese as her aunt's voice filtered along the hallway. 'Yes, Aunt?'

'Don't leave any mess in there. I specifically told Veronica I wanted it spotless. Time and again, the pair of you treat my home as a vagrant would a park bench.'

Tightening her grip on the knife, Esther gritted her teeth. 'Yes, Aunt.'

216

'And you might as well make me that cup of tea while you're there.' Esther counted to ten for the second time since she'd been home. 'Yes, Aunt.'

Waiting a beat to see if any more instructions were forthcoming, Esther only released her held breath once she was certain her aunt was spent. Putting down the knife, she took the kettle from the stove and filled it at the sink before staring into the small back garden.

How was she truly to gain independence when her savings were still low enough that she couldn't possibly leave her aunt and live somewhere halfway decent? The liberty she aspired to seemed forever locked away, as though only an unknown formula could free it. There had to be a way for her to break away from constraint and make her mark in the world.

Surely if she concentrated on her work at Pennington's and the Society, her liberty would come? Nowhere else had given her as much satisfaction. Until Lawrence. Her mind wandered to his idea of an auction and ball at his hotel. His eyes had gleamed with possibility as he'd proposed his ideas. She had been wrong to shut him down — shut him out — so conclusively.

She had to seek him out and apologise. Even ask him to the demonstration the following day if that would encourage his forgiveness. He'd already asked her if he could attend one of their rallies, after all. Fingers crossed, his desire to support her wouldn't have been quashed entirely. With the upcoming Coronation, it was really the last chance the Society had to make another public stand before the streets were inundated with royal well-wishers.

Esther returned the kettle to the stove and lit the

flame, before walking back to the table. She finished making her sandwich, put everything back neatly in the larder and wiped down the table. With thoughts of Lawrence tumbling through her mind, she mechanically pulled the teapot from a shelf, along with cups and saucers, and spooned leaves into the pot. She laid everything on a tray, adding a small jug of milk, sugar and teaspoons.

No matter how much she tried to deny it, she'd experienced infinite freedom every moment she'd been with Lawrence. Every moment she'd spent with his children. They made her feel so very unequivocally free and happy and, for the first time in her life, she sought the company of a man . . . a lover. Could this be the first step towards trusting a man again?

Everything about Lawrence spoke of kindness and care. He was a true gentleman. It had been her who'd taken the lead with their physical intimacy, but he had taken a far braver leap into emotional intimacy by sharing his like of her, even if he hadn't quite managed to tell her what so profoundly bothered him.

Walking to the stove, Esther took the boiling kettle from the heat and poured water into the teapot before adding it to the tray alongside her plated sandwich. Hefting the heavy tray from the table, Esther left the kitchen and walked along the hallway into the parlour. 'Tea is served.'

Her aunt stood and picked up her knitting basket. 'No, thank you. I think I'll go upstairs to read. Goodnight.'

Esther opened her mouth and then snapped it closed again. There was little point in starting an altercation.

Her aunt stopped. 'Oh, I almost forgot.' She delved into the pocket of her dress and extracted an envelope.

'This was delivered to you by a young man claiming to work at Pennington's. I've no idea why he should deliver a note for you at home when you work there. Senseless.'

'That *is* strange.' Esther took the letter and opened it.

Dearest Esther,
   I hoped to find you at the store, but, alas, I did not and can only assume you were busy —

'Well? What is it?' Her aunt's steely gaze burned with curiosity. 'Is it something so important it couldn't wait until morning?'

Esther fought to suppress her smile. 'It is.'

'Such as?'

'Miss Pennington would like me to pick something up for her on my way to the store on Monday.'

'Then you are little more than her lackey. Window designer, indeed. Thoughts above your station. Just as your stepmother often implies.'

Esther glared at her aunt's retreating back as she left the room, but even she couldn't dampen Esther's spirit. Once alone, she sat on the settee and quickly unfolded the letter again, happiness kicking at her heart.

*   Therefore, rather than have someone interrupt you, I am writing you this note in the hope it reaches you this evening. I long to see you. Have longed to make contact but have refrained in anticipation that you might come to me. As you have not, and I now have my sister and her children visiting awhile, would you possibly consider having lunch with me at my hotel*

tomorrow? I really would like to pursue my ideas in support of the Cause, regardless of any personal relationship that might, or might not, develop between us.

If you find such an invitation tempting, I will wait for you in the restaurant at one o'clock.

Sincere wishes,

Lawrence

Esther pressed the letter to her chest, her heart racing. He had his family staying with him. Would that change things between them? What might his sister think of Lawrence spending time with a working woman, unchaperoned?

Oh, what did it matter? She smiled. Tomorrow, she would see Lawrence again and her heart positively sang with joy. The living room had never seemed so alive, or its decor and atmosphere so bright. As it was Sunday tomorrow, she didn't have to work. Was it too much to hope that lunch would turn into an entire afternoon together? A thrill rippled through her at the thought of Lawrence's lips against hers, his hands on her body as they'd been before.

As Elizabeth had so passionately insisted, a person had to fight for their wishes. Resist and power through fears and constraints. Esther liked Lawrence, could possibly one day love him. That shouldn't be frightening, it should be empowering.

26

Lawrence glanced at his watch as he sat in The Phoenix restaurant, his foot incessantly tapping the stone floor tiles. What if Esther had not received his note? Or she had, and felt such disdain at his invitation, she'd shredded his words into pieces? He'd not received a returned acceptance or any other message and now sat alone avoiding the curious stares of his staff.

She would come. He was sure of it. Their connection was too instant, too intense for either of them to ignore. He had to believe she would have been pleased by his letter.

A young staff member caught his eye, her gaze concerned as she cleared the table beside him. Lawrence immediately smiled and purposefully relaxed back into his seat. She hesitantly returned his smile, although the line at her brow remained.

'How are you this morning, Freda?' Lawrence asked. 'Everything as it should be?'

The young girl nodded. 'Yes, sir.'

'Then we are both enjoying this sunny afternoon.'

She smiled again before lifting the plates she'd stacked on the table and moving away. As she retreated, Lawrence's smile dissolved and self-loathing unfurled inside him. How was he to convince Esther she could trust him when he continued to keep his shame and fears from her?

To pretend to himself, was to pretend to the universe. Nothing good would enter his life if he kept aloft his barriers of fictitious contentment.

What did it matter if he was in a state of nervous anticipation as he waited for the arrival of a particular woman? He did not need to feel guilty that he longed to spend time with Esther, see her laugh, look into her beautiful eyes and feel the softness of her hand in his. There was no shame in such things. Didn't he look at lovers in the hotel and on the street and secretly harbour envy for all they had and enjoyed?

The delicate tap of approaching footsteps snagged his attention and he turned.

Esther.

His heart kicked, and he slowly rose, his smile genuine. 'Hello.' She smiled, her cheeks flushed. 'How are you?'

'All the better for seeing you.' He waved towards the chair opposite him, the truth of his words making him realise just how miserable he'd been without her. 'Take a seat.'

She sat and laid her purse on the table.

Words stuck in his throat as he studied her hair, her eyes, her mouth. She was so beautiful and seemed completely unaware of it. His desire for her stirred once more and he quickly snapped his gaze to hers. 'I'm glad you came.'

'I was glad to receive your invitation.' She hesitated before turning to look about the restaurant. 'Are we alone? I wasn't certain if your sister and nephews would be joining us?'

'Cornelia and the boys are enjoying a jaunt in the park with Helen, Rose and Nathanial.'

'And Cornelia is your eldest sister? Is that right?'

'Yes. Harriet's the younger.'

She smiled softly and sighed, looking about the lounge again. 'This room is wonderful. It almost

222

competes with the luxury of Pennington's Butterfly restaurant.'

Lawrence relaxed his shoulders at the teasing in her voice. 'Almost?'

She smiled. 'Almost.'

He laughed. 'Are you hungry?'

She nodded, her gaze lingering on his. 'Famished.'

Lawrence stilled, his entire body frozen by the heat in her eyes. Teasing. Challenging. Nothing in her gaze or demeanour indicated she had a wish to eat food. Although, it was suddenly clear she was ravenous. For what, he dared not think, lest his thoughts illustrated his lust. Or was he a fool to think — to hope — that her desires mirrored his?

The atmosphere had irrevocably shifted. Attraction rose, tangible and arousing. Memories of her creamy, satin-smooth skin, the floral scent of her barely-there perfume surged through his body and mind. God, how he longed to touch her again, kiss her, love her . . . The hunger in her eyes could not be mistaken. They wanted one another, regardless of their circumstances. But he would not think about, or act upon, his physical yearnings until she understood how serious he was about helping with the Cause. Until she trusted that her thoughts and passions came above everything he might wish for himself.

He turned away and raised his hand to a nearby waitress. 'Could we each have a glass of champagne and the lunch menus, Jenny?'

'Of course, sir.'

She walked away, and Lawrence turned to Esther. 'So, as you're here, I hope you want to continue with my plan to host an event at the hotel?'

'I do.' She inhaled a shaky breath and grimaced as

the flirtation in her eyes diminished. 'But first I want to apologise for walking out on you the way I did. You want to help with the Cause and instead of being grateful, I thought only of my fears rather than the good of the Society.'

'We all have fears. There's no need to apologise.' He reached for her hand where it lay on the table and gently squeezed her fingers. 'But I think we can easily work through them together. What do you say?'

The light he loved to see in her eyes brightened. 'Yes, I think maybe we can.'

'Good.' He released her hand. 'Then once we've eaten, I'll take you to my office. I can't believe how hard Anna, Victoria and Ruth have worked. I want to show you what they have planned for the auction and even the ball. They are determined to organise events everybody and anybody wants to attend.'

'That's wonderful. If we're really going to do this, it has to be spectacular. I should never have doubted your sincerity to help.'

'If you doubted my sincerity, then the fault lies with me. Every part of me wants to share in this with you. These events and more.' *God willing, you'll want to be with me as I do you. Spend time with my family and friends. Let me court you as you deserve . . .*

She lowered her gaze to the table for a moment, before her eyes met his. 'Would you like to join me and my associates in a rally tomorrow? It will be our last chance to do something before the city is taken over by Coronation celebrations.'

He smiled, pleased she'd extended an invitation that showed she wanted to let him in. 'I'd love to.'

He sipped his water and glanced again at her hand, itching to curl his fingers around hers, but he refrained. Despite her flirtation when she'd arrived, self-preservation and control lingered in her words. No matter how long it took, he would wait to hold her again, wait to make love to her, but, one day, he was certain, she would open to him and let him witness her vulnerability as he vowed she would see his.

Today.

'I want you to trust me, Esther.' He stared deep into her eyes. 'I've made no secret that I'd like to spend more time with you, but I understand your reservations. I understand my children affect your feelings, your decision of whether to deepen things between us, and I respect that.'

Her eyes glistened beneath the lights and Lawrence's heart quickened.

Tears.

'Don't cry. To see your tears will undo me. The last thing I want is to upset you.'

'You misunderstand.' She shook her head and inhaled, her chest rising and then falling as she blew a soft breath. 'Part of me wishes I hadn't wanted to come here. That my heart hadn't leapt with joy when I read your letter.' A tear quivered on her lashes, and she quickly swiped at it with trembling fingers. 'Sometimes I wish I didn't have such a deep distrust that a man will threaten my need to make a difference, but I can't . . . I won't . . . give that up, Lawrence. Not even for you.'

Even for me? Was she telling him she was falling in love with him? Did she carry the same niggling certainty they were meant to be together? 'I would never ask you to stop being who you are. You must believe that.'

'But how can you promise such a thing? Neither of

225

us can predict the future.'

'But I can promise it. Abigail wanted a husband, a family and a home and I gave all of that to her. If you want to work and continue to support the Cause, I'd never stand in your way.'

Jenny returned to their table, carrying a tray bearing two flutes of champagne. 'Here we go, sir. Madam.' She placed down the drinks and offered them each a menu. 'I'll be back shortly for your orders.'

'Thank you.' Lawrence took his offered menu and nodded. As soon as the waitress walked away, he faced Esther once more. 'I want you to trust me, to explore where we can go together. Tell me you want that too, and I'll tell you who I really am. After that, if you wish to walk away and not look back, I promise to never bother you again.'

She frowned, wariness seeping into her eyes. 'What do you mean?'

'Things happened to me, Esther. Terrible things I fear I shall never fully recover from.'

'Things bad enough that you think I might want to walk away?'

He closed his eyes. Her tone was clipped, the warmth and desire of moments before replaced with distance. *Damn fool.* He'd frightened her, but he had to go forward with his truth. To do anything less, would mean he'd lose her anyway.

Opening his eyes, he forced a smile. 'We'll enjoy our food and then I'll tell you everything. If you decide to leave thereafter, it will be with a full stomach, if nothing else.'

'And if I don't walk away? If I'm stronger than you give me credit for?' Determination burned in the depth of her eyes, her shoulders high. 'What then?'

226

Passion twisted and turned inside him. 'Then I'm quite sure if you can find it in your heart to love me, love my children, we'll not part ever again.' *Please, God, let my every instinct about this wonderful woman be right . . .*

27

Esther laid down her knife and fork as their main course came to an end, her heart not yet quieted after Lawrence's confident assertion that, if she accepted what he had to say, their union would be permanent. The thought that they might be together warmed her rather than scared her, but she'd eaten very little. Instead, pushed the food around and around her plate, taking copious sips of her replenished champagne and water as her anticipation escalated. Whatever he told her would not dampen her feelings towards him.

When she looked into his beautiful blue eyes and admired the strong cut of his jaw, she fought the temptation to flee and, instead, stand firm in her decision to fight for what built so tenuously between them.

Although a maiden, she was not naïve to the ways of the world, but she couldn't help worrying the impulse and desire running through her was nothing more than the wish to be brazen. To grab a few moments, minutes or hours of happiness without any sacrifice to the building of her life on her own terms.

Lawrence had mentioned love. Not just for him, but for his children and, as much as she admired him more for making it clear Rose and Nathanial were a part of him, she had to guard her personal goals like a lioness over her young. Or else, risk hurting so many more people than herself.

The subtle knock of cutlery against porcelain cut through her thoughts.

Lawrence's gaze was dark with concern. 'What is

it?'

She shook her head and swallowed against the dryness in her throat. 'I was just thinking about the Coronation. The window is almost ready and — '

'You're worried by what I've said?'

She slumped her shoulders. 'Yes. Yes, I am.'

He exhaled a long breath. 'I promised to be entirely open with you and hope I might receive the same promise from you when you're ready.'

'I'm ready now, Lawrence.' She took a deep breath and slowly released it. 'My openness is that I'm afraid of the differences it will make to my life if I decide to be with you. Afraid of falling in love with you and your children. Afraid I'll become so immersed in your family that my passions will eventually snuff out and I'll find myself with nothing.'

He stared and, with each passing second, Esther's heart beat faster.

Just as she was about to fill the silence, he spoke. 'I understand and the only way I have of reassuring you is to say I promise I'll not let you lose yourself. Not for me, and not for Rose and Nathanial.'

Sincerity shone in his eyes, his jaw tight. What else did she want him to say? How could either of them be certain they wouldn't disappoint the other? Love was always a risk, was it not?

'Now . . . ' He blew out a breath as though gathering strength. 'I'm not sure how far I should go back with my story, so I'll start from the very beginning.' He sipped his champagne and lowered the glass to the table. 'My father was a successful landowner who built a farming business from next to nothing. He lived in a modest farmhouse when he married my mother and worked day and night to build their finances until he felt they had enough to support a family.

'I was born and then my two sisters. In between, we moved home twice. The third and final time was to a manor house in Oxfordshire. He named it Culford Manor in nineteen-hundred and died eight years later, leaving my mother extremely comfortable and in want of nothing. She lives there with Harriet, who has somehow become my mother's clone.' His jaw tightened, and his eyes glinted with a coldness she thought impossible of him. 'What I feel about my mother and how she's influenced Harriet goes beyond and above maddening.'

'If not maddened by it, then what do you feel?'

'Failure. Guilt. That I deserve none of this.' He waved his hand, encompassing the restaurant. 'Not the hotel. The fortune. The success and accolades.'

Burying her immediate wish to reassure him, compliment and bolster him as she wanted to, Esther sipped her champagne. There was so much she wanted to know about him in her need to be certain they had a chance of succeeding in everything they might do together. 'Because?'

'Because I left my sisters behind. I was twenty-five years old, married to Abigail who was pregnant with Rose. I had learned the business of farming, running the estate and looking after the tenants as my father wished when he struck me for the very last time.'

Shock stilled her glass at her lips. 'He struck you?'

'As he had for as long as I can remember. From his hand to a belt buckle or switch when I was a child and adolescent, to a fist as I grew older.'

Sickness rolled through her. 'But why?'

'Because, as he would remind me daily, he built his fortune from scratch. Working ten- to twelve-hour days until he could afford to employ help. Slowly, that help increased until he was able to buy more land, a bigger house. He felt that if he didn't make me of the same stock, then I would lose everything.'

Shock and care for him stilled her tongue. He had clearly endured so much for many years. It was a miracle he was the kind, considerate and loving man and father he was today. Anger and revulsion towards his father rose inside her at the same time as shame engulfed her that she'd wallowed in her father's treatment of her when Lawrence had suffered so much more. 'And he thought he could ensure your competence through violence?'

He smiled wryly, venom burning in his eyes. 'Ironically, he did. I have this hotel and I'm without financial worries. What I didn't want was Culford. On that particular day, he hadn't struck me for maybe a year, possibly longer. I thought the violence in our relationship was over, but when he raised his fist to me again, I hit back, determined that neither him nor any man would raise their hand to me again. Leaving him unconscious in the field, I walked into the house and asked Abigail to pack our bags. I wanted away from him, from my mother, from the entire estate. Could not bear the risk of becoming my father one day . . .'

Esther's helplessness to change his past tightened her hand around her glass. He stared across the room, seemingly lost in thought. 'Your mother was complicit in this abuse?'

'Yes. In fact, some part of me thinks she thrived on it. When I was in trouble, she looked positively gleeful about it. Almost as though my father's anger and ferocity added some sort of elation to their relationship. Dysfunctional is the word I'd use to describe

231

their marriage.'

Pain squeezed her heart. 'Oh, Lawrence.'

He shook his head and drained his champagne. 'Anyway, Abigail and I came to Bath to start again in a city where no one knew us. I found some rented rooms and we made ends meet as I worked with various chefs at different hotels. Rose was born and then two years later Abigail died giving birth to Nathanial. I have only returned to Oxfordshire once. For my father's funeral three years ago. I have fairly frequent correspondence and visits with my sisters here in Bath but vowed to never set foot on the Culford estate again.'

Her mouth dry, Esther took another sip of her drink. Never had she seen such blatant anger in Lawrence's eyes and it unnerved her. His fury was undoubtedly justified if he was so badly treated by a father who was meant to love him, but could Lawrence's temper flare like this again? With her? 'And your sisters and mother? Did your father hurt them, too?'

'No. With them, he found restraint. That's not to say he didn't verbally and mentally terrorise them.' He glared towards a spot over her shoulder as though battling for control. 'If he would have ever raised a hand to them, I'm sure the outcome would have been so much worse than it was.'

'Meaning?'

He faced her. 'I would've killed him.'

She swallowed. 'You cannot mean that.'

'I do.' His face had whitened, his gaze enraged. 'Which is why I needed to tell you my truth. The fury I feel when I look back at my life terrifies me and that's why I am careful to bury it deep inside. I love my children more than life itself and feel I could come to love you the same way. If anyone were to hurt or lay a finger on Rose or Nathanial, I'm not entirely certain what I would do about it.'

'And you've never . . . met anyone you've felt you could care for that way in all those years?' She looked to the table, feeling foolish but wanting to be sure Lawrence didn't fall in love easily or court women and then discard them. She had let him touch her so intimately . . . had let him into her heart. 'I mean, there must have been — '

'Dalliances, Esther. Nothing more. You're different. You must believe me.'

Esther studied him before reaching for his hand and holding it tightly. 'Feeling you would do anything to protect your children does not make you a monster, Lawrence. In fact, I would wager those instincts are perfectly natural. I have spoken to enough parents to know them all capable of murder when it concerns their children. It doesn't make them fiends, and I don't think you one, either.'

Slowly, the anger seeped from his gaze and his shoulders lowered. 'Do you mean that?'

'Yes.' She smiled softly, wanting to dissolve the fear and doubt in his beautiful eyes. 'You are nothing less than a father who passionately loves and cares for his children and doing all he can to ensure your family history is not repeated. Am I right?'

He squeezed her fingers. 'Yes. Yes, you are.'

Relieved that he smiled again, Esther released a breath. He had too much good in him to linger in his childhood. Too much care to give others to think badly of himself. The more time they spent together, the more she would do to make him see that. 'Good. Can I ask when you last saw your sisters before Cornelia arrived? I hope you've managed to at least maintain a relationship with them, even if you couldn't your parents.'

His gaze softened further. 'I saw Cornelia a couple of months ago, but it's longer since I've seen Harriet. I'm glad Cornelia has brought my nephews. They are growing up so fast.'

'And their father?'

'Is a different story. One I intend getting to the bottom of. I will be paying David a visit tomorrow. So . . .' His tone was soft, his gaze gentle on hers. 'Do we have a chance to make one another happy? Because I am the man my father made me, Esther. The anger is the part of me I hide. The side to which I never wish Rose or Nathanial, Charles, Helen or Mrs Jackson to bear witness. You say you're scared of losing your independence. I'm terrified of losing my pretence. But you . . . ' He inhaled. 'You have a way of lessening my anger and making me feel entirely human. When I'm with you I'm a better man than anyone has made me before. Because of that, I want to live authentically for what could quite possibly be the first time in my life.'

Esther closed her eyes against the hope in his. Responsibility weighed heavy on her heart. He bore a pain so much deeper, so much rawer, than hers. Since she'd left home, there had been times when she'd barely held herself together. The last thing Lawrence needed was for another person he loved to fail him.

She opened her eyes. 'You've had to live with so much more pain and heartache than I have, Lawrence. I just hope I have the strength to support you as I'd want to.'

'Your father's treatment of you was no less harsh.

I left my family home and made something of myself through sheer will and determination, but I'm not arrogant enough to deny being a man made that easier than if Cornelia or Harriet had left. You're wonderful and strong. A woman who wants to make a difference in the world and I want to be a part of that, right beside you. Let me show you, and you show me, that there's more to life than protecting yourself and those you care about.'

She ran her gaze over his dark hair and beautiful smile. Want and the tiniest flicker of daring ignited deep in her chest.

'Will you trust me, Esther?'

She stared into his eyes. How could she not? He had become so important to her. Had proven his strength and commitment to both her and his family. She wanted him and no longer wished to fight their possible happiness. She nodded. 'Yes, I think I will.'

He stood and walked around the table, offering her his hand. 'Then come with me.'

She glanced from his hand to his eyes. They burned with the hunger and desire she hadn't been able to resist the last time he'd looked at her that way. Her body heated and her centre pulled, as his honesty dissolved all the apprehension and concern she'd had when she'd left his house days before. She picked up her purse, slid her hand into his.

Anticipation thrummed through her as they left the restaurant and entered the lobby. He led her past the reception to the lifts and she tightened her fingers around his. His gaze burned into her cheek, but she couldn't look at him for fear he'd misinterpret her desire for nerves. She didn't doubt her eyes were wide with what he could mistakenly assume to be unease.

She didn't doubt her trembling would make him hesitate if she didn't get a hold of herself because she wanted their lovemaking to happen, if that was indeed what he intended. She suddenly wanted his hands on her skin. Him inside of her, deep and wanting.

Just the thought sent a pulsing between her legs and a tingling in her breasts. Never before had she desired a man this way. Never before had she felt more needed or beautiful. And never before had she thought of a man day and night or longed for him to be beside her.

Her passion, excitement and yearning for Lawrence pushed her to step into the lift. This was her decision. She was a modern woman. One in control of her choices and destiny.

His eyes met hers as the doors closed. He pressed a button and the lift shuddered to a stop. Alone and unwatched, he took her in his arms, pulling her firmly against his hard chest. The adoration and fire in his gaze melted the last of her anxiety and Esther softened in his embrace, lifting her mouth to his as he slowly closed his eyes and dipped his lips to hers.

The contact further fuelled her desire and she pressed closer, easing her tongue into his mouth. His grip tightened around her, pushing her breasts against his solidness, his erection rigid against her abdomen. She wanted to explore him. Touch and learn from his reactions.

Slowly, they parted and he brushed a stray curl from her brow. 'Are you sure you want this?'

She smiled, having never been so sure of her heart. 'Yes.'

'I don't want you to think I'm asking — '

'You're not.' She shook her head, her stomach

knotting. 'I am.'

He kissed her again before restarting the lift and, when it stopped, he gripped her hand and they walked into the corridor.

Closed bedroom door after closed bedroom door stretched in either direction and her heart thundered as he walked forward, seemingly entirely sure of his destination. Was this madness? If she laid with him, would he then abandon her, his hunger satisfied?

She glanced at him, hating that her insecurities rose again. As much as she wanted to think herself grown and ready for such a big step, she should not risk regretting her first time, no matter how wonderful and sensual the man.

She tugged on his hand. 'Lawrence, wait.'

He immediately halted. 'What is it? Have you changed —'

'Why do you have your own room here? You have a beautiful home. I see no need for you to have permanent access to a room unless — ' Heat crept into her cheeks as she glanced along the corridor. 'Am I one of many women you've brought here for . . . for this?'

He trailed his fingers along her jaw to gently lift her chin. 'I keep this room so I have somewhere to stay if I am hosting business late into the night. For when I hold parties for the staff at the end of each holiday. I keep this room . . . ' He brushed his lips over hers. 'For nights when I'm so exhausted, so miserable and down that I cannot bear for Rose and Nathanial to see me that way.'

She studied him before her heart was eased by the sincerity in his eyes and the honesty of his words, but still she needed to be certain. 'No women? Am I really to believe myself the first?'

'Would it matter if I said you're the first I'm petrified I'll fall woefully low of her expectations. If I told you I have brought two women here in the last four years, but neither of them has mattered to me as much as you from the first moment I laid eyes on you, would you stay with me? Trust me?'

A jolt of jealousy shot through her before she staunchly quelled it. Lawrence was a passionate, virile man. Why would he not seek company elsewhere when he'd been alone for so long? Her heart swelled with confidence and — dare she think it — love.

'Come.' She pulled on his hand. 'What is the room number?'

He smiled, and they walked along the cream and gold threaded carpet. Soft music drifted from one of the rooms they passed, from another came laughter and banter of what sounded to be a mid-afternoon party.

Excitement whispered through her as Esther contemplated whether there were others like her and Lawrence behind some of the closed doors. She couldn't imagine another woman feeling so risqué and wanton. Yet, she hoped someone, somewhere, experienced the same thrill and exhilaration.

He stopped in front of one of the rooms and released her hand to pull a key from his inside jacket pocket. Esther glanced either way along the empty corridor, thankful no one was around. He pushed open the door and waved her inside ahead of him.

She entered, unable to drag her gaze from the thick cream drapes, edged in gold, the plush ivory carpet an endless pillow beneath her feet. Slowly, she walked around the circumference of the room, running her fingers over the oak furniture, the delicate lamps and tiny bowls of perfumed buds on every surface. She strolled to the window and stared at the street below. She was so high, the people looked like insects darting back and forth, trams and horses like tiny playthings.

'Goodness.' She turned, her smile so wide her cheeks ached. 'It's beautiful.'

'So are you.'

He stole his hands onto her hips and Esther gripped his upper arms, her stomach pulling at the feel of hard muscle beneath her fingers. 'So, what happens next?'

'I make love to you.'

Happiness and anticipation whispered through her. Dropping her purse to the floor, she kissed him firmly and with every ounce of her desire.

With his mouth on hers, he gently guided her backwards until the bed bumped the back of her knees. She waited for the hesitation, the fear, but only delight and pleasure came.

Gently easing from his kiss, she lifted her hands and helped him to shrug out of his jacket. She then unknotted his tie and tossed it to the floor. Once she'd unbuttoned his shirt and hitched it from his trousers, raw craving pulsed through her, her nipples tightening as she pulled the shirt from his shoulders and moved her hands over his chest, scoring her fingers through a fine smattering of hair, lower over his ribs and hard stomach.

Silvery welts and scars shone at his upper arms and across his stomach and tears leapt into her eyes as she purposefully, gently, smoothed her fingers over them. Her heart ached for all he'd endured, yet he had fought back. Now, standing before her, was a decent and honourable man that she wanted with every part of her.

239

He quivered, releasing a low breath between clenched teeth.

Emboldened, Esther bent her head to his nipple and gently grazed it with her teeth. His fingers moved into her hair and he carefully plucked out the pins until the tresses fell heavy down her back.

She leaned back and he flipped the clasps on her jacket, revealing the silk blouse beneath. He kissed her, his thumb rubbing back and forth over her nipple until moisture gathered at her core. Insecurity threatened at the prospect she could be so easily malleable to his attentions, and she quickly pushed her doubts away and unbuttoned her blouse, drew it from her shoulders.

His gaze lingered over her brassiere. 'My God, look at you.'

With their eyes locked, Esther removed the rest of her clothes, until she stood in only her underwear, erotic sensations coursing through her.

He gently eased her to the bed and lay down beside her. Torturous seconds passed, as his gaze feasted on every part of her stockinged legs, her silk drawers and breasts spilling over the cups of her brassiere. He expertly flicked open the front fastenings and cupped her bosom as he trailed kisses over her shoulders and upper arms.

Esther closed her eyes and rejoiced in his caresses, her body heating to these new and welcome sensations. Slowly, he eased back, and the rustle of clothes filled the room before his warmth enveloped her again. She breathed in the musky scent of him and tugged on his arm, inviting him closer.

'Open your legs a little.'

She did as he bade even as her mouth drained dry.

What would happen next, she had no idea and her body tensed with erotic anticipation.

His tongue had been the last thing she'd expected or imagined.

She sucked in a breath as warm wetness trailed from the top of her stockings, higher until he gently eased the leg of her drawers to one side and then . . .

She gasped and squeezed her eyes shut, curling her fingers into the bedspread. 'Lawrence, you can't. Don't. I . . . '

Yet, she didn't move away. Instead, she writhed against the firm pressure of his tongue as sensations throbbed and pulsed through her. His finger eased inside of her and Esther snapped her eyes open, her mouth dropping, too.

Deeper and harder the sensations built and, still, she didn't move away from him. He slowly inched up her body, drowning her stomach and torso in nips and kisses.

She wanted more. *Needed* more.

A desperate moan escaped her, and she clamped her mouth closed for the shame and fear of it.

His fingers stopped their exquisite teasing, and he eased her drawers down her legs and over her feet. Her heart raced. There was only one thing left that could happen and her centre pulsed with wanting.

He entered her slowly and she closed her eyes, her body entirely ready.

This. This was what she wanted. Lawrence close. Closer than any man had been before.

Slowly, he inched inside her. A little more. A little more . . .

There was a shot of pain and then the brush of his pubic hair. He filled her completely. She released her breath as he moved within her and, after a few moments, she instinctively moved, too. He slipped his hands over her perspiring skin, cupped her breasts, pinching her nipples which amplified every sensation he awakened.

Harder, she pushed, and harder he thrust.

Until . . .

She gritted her teeth as she clenched around him.

A power like she'd never known rushed through her veins, causing a forceful climax that she'd never experienced alone.

His hands gripped her hips tighter, his fingers digging into the flesh.

'Esther.'

His breath whispered over her breasts as he shuddered again and again, until at last he was spent. He lowered his head to her shoulder, the rapid beat of his heart banging against hers. She had no idea how long they stayed that way, in each other's arms, their breaths fast and shallow.

Slowly, she regained her equilibrium and he slid gently away from her, grasping her hand tightly.

How was she to explain that she had just become entirely his? That — for her at least — they were joined. Possibly forever.

Tears threatened, and she fiercely blinked them back.

Now was not the time for doubt or to submit to the consummate fear that Lawrence would one day tire of her . . . Now was not the time to contemplate the risk of a babe being born in nine months' time.

For now, she would bask in the pleasure he'd given her and nothing else.

28

Lawrence studied Esther as she sat on the settee in his office, her brow furrowed and her clothes slightly rumpled as she flipped through his pages of plans for the auction in aid of women's suffrage. His heart had yet to slow since their lovemaking. His gaze yet to be sated as he watched her.

She had been a virgin and trusted him enough to give him the honour of her first sexual encounter. He would guard the privilege with passion. Stay with her for as long as she wanted him. Whatever happened next, he would let Esther set the pace and lay down her conditions.

He was hers.

Smiling, she met his gaze where he sat in the armchair beside her. 'These are wonderful, Lawrence. The Society will be absolutely thrilled.'

'You're pleased?'

'Very. In fact, I can't wait to get started. I wish I could do more to help right away, but with the Coronation looming and tomorrow night's rally, it will be impossible for me to be involved until the end of the month.'

He slid the papers from her hand and pushed them onto the coffee table in front of them. Taking her hand, he pressed his lips to her knuckles. 'Don't worry about that at all. The girls are working on it and loving every minute, as far as I can tell.' He inched closer and kissed her, relishing the soft warmth of her mouth and how her fingers lightly dug into his thigh.

'You're going to make me a changed man, Miss Stanbury.'

'Am I really, Mr Culford?' She eased back, her big hazel eyes twinkling. 'Well, that makes me very happy.'

The knock at the door made Esther jump and Lawrence stood. He smiled in a bid to reassure her. 'You have every right to be here. Remember that. Always.' He took a few steps to the door and stopped. 'Enter.'

William Moorebrook stepped into the room and visibly flinched when he saw Esther sitting on the settee. Lawrence bit back his smile as William's gaze darted between Lawrence and Esther, two spots of colour appearing high on his cheeks.

Lawrence lifted his eyebrows. 'What can I do for you, William? I didn't know you were working today.'

'I . . .' He looked at Esther again before snapping his gaze to Lawrence and lifting his chin. 'I wasn't aware you had company, sir. As your secretary isn't here and others saw you come in here, I assumed you to be alone.'

Lawrence turned to Esther and held out his hand as she slowly rose. 'This is Miss Esther Stanbury, William. Esther, this is my manager, William Moorebrook. Esther is the head dresser at Pennington's and a suffragist. If you'll remember, I told you I have plans to hold an auction in aid of the Cause at the hotel?'

'I do, sir.' William nodded at Esther. 'Miss Stanbury.'

Esther returned his nod, her wide gaze illustrating her nerves. 'Mr Moorebrooke.'

William faced Lawrence. 'I think it best I speak with you later, sir. Shall I come to your office around four o'clock?'

'Perfect. Clear your duties for an hour, if possible.

I'll bring you up to speed with mine and Miss Stanbury's plans and then I must get back home.'

William's cheeks darkened, his gaze shadowing with concern. 'You've already decided to definitely go ahead with the auction?'

'I have. Also, a ball near to Christmastime.'

'A ball? For the Cause?' William's eyes widened, and he flitted another glance at Esther. 'But, sir — '

'An auction and a ball, William. These two things will go ahead with or without your help.' Lawrence raised his eyebrows. Whatever his manager's reservations about the events or even the Cause, the fundraising would happen. 'Now, which is it to be?'

'Well, with, sir. Of course.'

'Good.' Lawrence smiled and clamped his hand to his manager's shoulder, steering him towards the door. 'I look forward to sitting down with you at four.'

'Yes, sir.' William slid another glance at Esther, his eyes ever so slightly narrowed. 'Four o'clock.'

He left the room and Lawrence firmly swung the door closed behind him. He turned to Esther and laughed. 'Oh, dear. Did you see the poor man's face? I wager he might take a little persuading to get on board with our plans, but I'll bring him around.'

Esther picked up her purse from the settee and slid it beneath her arm as she came closer. Her eyes were filled with doubt. 'Doesn't Mr Moorebrook support women's suffrage?'

'I'm sure he does. It will be the extra work involved that he'll be fretting over. Between us and the staff I'm bringing on board, he'll be enthusiastic soon enough.' Lawrence placed his hand on her waist, brushed his lips lightly across hers. 'These events *will* happen. I'll make sure of it. I hope you know by now that I'll do anything for you. Whatever it takes.'

She studied his mouth for a long moment before exhaling a soft breath. 'I trust you, but now I really should go. Will I see you tomorrow at the rally?'

'Of course.'

The pleasure in her eyes showed all too clearly how she had been worried their intimacy might have changed his interest in her. Didn't she realise it was her in the driving seat, not him?

'The things we do together, the things we say to one another, have only become more important to me, Esther. Side by side, remember? I'm looking forward to seeing the work you do and meeting some of your associates. The more suffragists I know, the more I can use their opinions and views to make the auction and ball a success. Where shall I meet you? Shall I come to your home?'

She quickly shook her head. 'No. I'm not ready for you to meet my aunt. She is a formidable woman, but one whiff of your success and she'll be putty in your hands. I need some time before I can bear witness to her transformation.'

Lawrence laughed. 'You clearly have her card marked.'

'Hers and my stepmother's elitism and snobbery are beyond me.' She sighed. 'But at least, in our own way, my aunt and I love one another. I pray she'll come around to my impulses, as she likes to call everything and anything I do.' She inhaled a long breath. 'But now I must go. Why don't you meet me outside the Abbey and I'll take you to our meeting place? It would be good for you to get acquainted with a few of the women before we walk to the rally.'

'I'll see you there at six o'clock.'

She nodded and then rose on her toes to press a

quick kiss to his lips. 'See you tomorrow.'

She stepped towards the door and Lawrence followed. 'Don't you want me to escort you downstairs?'

'No, you stay here. That way we'll avoid any tittle-tattle and Mr Moorebrooke might go some way to believing our meeting was purely business.'

Lawrence opened the door and stood on the threshold and as he watched Esther walk along the corridor to the lift, he couldn't remember the last time he'd felt so genuinely happy.

29

The next day, Esther strode into Pennington's with a smile on her face and a spring in her step. Ever since she'd left Lawrence's hotel yesterday, she'd waited for a wave of shame to overcome her, yet she had only experienced elation, excitement and a deep awareness that choosing to make love with him had been one of the best decisions of her life. Every now and then, the worry of pregnancy threatened her happiness, but she pushed it firmly away. The chances were slim that she might be with child after only making love a single time, although possible. But what good would it do to linger over what ifs and maybes?

Whenever she'd looked into his eyes during their conversations in his office, only admiration and desire had stared back at her. Her trepidation of whether she could live up to Lawrence's wonderful parental standards and fully embrace the responsibility of his life and his children's lives still lingered, but, somehow, the possibilities were no longer as frightening.

Waving to a few of the shop girls, Esther walked to the lift and smiled at Henry, Pennington's young lift attendant. 'Good morning, Henry. Fifth floor, please.'

'Are you seeing Miss Pennington?'

'I am.' She stepped into the lift and Henry pulled the doors shut with a clang. 'Would you happen to know if she's alone?'

'I think so. I've not dropped anyone to the fifth floor so far today. Not that it means no one has taken the stairs.'

248

They rode the rest of the way in silence until the lift shuddered to a halt at the fifth floor and Esther stepped onto the thick, plush carpet of Pennington's executive floor. 'See you soon, Henry.'

Esther strode past Joseph Carter's closed office door, past the assistant manager's and into Elizabeth's secretary's domain. Although a lot had changed since Elizabeth took over the running of Pennington's a year before, Mrs Chadwick, once Elizabeth's father's secretary, had not. No matter what Edward Pennington might have thought of Mrs Chadwick's loyalty to him, it was to Pennington's that her allegiance was truly stalwart. The store and whoever was in charge.

'Mrs Chadwick, good morning.' Esther approached the secretary's desk. 'Is it possible Miss Pennington is free to see me for a few moments?'

'She's just with Amelia Wakefield.' The older woman rose and nodded towards some chairs lining the wall. 'If you'd like to take a seat?'

Esther sat and pulled her purse into her lap, her fingers tightly clutching the soft leather. Why was Elizabeth meeting with Amelia first thing on a Monday morning? And without Esther, too. Had Amelia done something wrong that Esther had missed? She frowned as unwelcome nervousness whispered through her. Could Elizabeth be promoting Amelia? She was an exemplary dresser and had an idea for ladies' fashions that Esther considered second to none.

Silently admonishing her nerves, Esther relaxed her shoulders. Well, if it was a promotion, it was well deserved, and Esther wished one of her most favoured colleagues the best of luck . . . even if it did irk a little if Elizabeth hadn't felt the need to include Esther in the meeting. Amelia was proving herself an excellent addition to the Society and Pennington's.

Esther turned her mind to the reasons she wanted to speak to Elizabeth. She was excited to share news of the events at Lawrence's hotel but also wanted Elizabeth to consider Pennington's sponsoring a crowd-pleasing, crowd-pulling auction prize. For so long, Elizabeth had been adamant she would not show favour to one group of suffrage campaigners over another, but Esther was confident her friend would want to contribute something to the auction in support of women's progression, if not the suffrage bill itself.

If Elizabeth was willing to tie the Pennington's name to the fundraiser and advertise the event in-store, it would be a huge coup for donations, lots for the auction and, most importantly, buyers' and bidders' attendance.

Elizabeth's office door opened, and Amelia came out ahead of Elizabeth. Esther stood and studied Amelia's expression for a clue of what might have been said between her and Elizabeth. She looked extremely pleased with herself, standing straight-backed and proud.

Esther smiled. 'Good morning, Amelia, Elizabeth.'

'Good morning, Esther.' Amelia smiled before turning to Elizabeth. 'Can I tell Esther what we've discussed?'

'Of course. The dressers' department is headed by Esther, after all.'

Amelia blushed and faced Esther, who brimmed with curiosity. Amelia gripped Esther's arm. 'If it's all right with you, Miss Pennington would like me to head up the displays for the new summer lines in the ladies' and men's departments. I can't believe both of you have such faith in me.'

250

Esther immediately relaxed, hating that she'd been at all rattled by Amelia and Elizabeth talking. 'Well, of course, it's all right with me. I suggested it to Elizabeth just last week.' She smiled. 'Fashion is your forte without a doubt. I'm sure you'll come up with some spectacular displays.' She squeezed Amelia's hand. 'I'm really happy for you. It's a brilliant opportunity.'

'Thank you, Esther. That means a lot to me.'

Amelia smiled at Esther and Elizabeth before hurrying along the corridor towards the lift.

Esther turned to Elizabeth. 'I'm not sure I've seen her so happy.'

'Well, you were right, it would be good to give Amelia a chance to prove herself with a solo project. You don't mind that I called her to my office without you, do you?'

'Not at all.'

'I'm glad. Now, why don't you come through and tell me what I can help you with. Is this about the Coronation window? I've had so many customers and staff desperate to know what you have planned.'

Esther followed Elizabeth into her office and closed the door. Elizabeth strode to the seating area in the far corner of the vast room which showcased a splendid view across the city, the Abbey's tower displayed like a beacon in the distance. Esther sat on the settee and Elizabeth settled beside her.

'So,' Elizabeth smiled. 'What can I do for you?'

Esther put her purse on the table in front of them and pulled her hands into her lap. 'I'm hoping for your sponsorship with something.'

'Sponsorship?'

'Yes. Do you remember Lawrence Culford?'

'Of course.' Elizabeth's green eyes lit with undisguised triumph. 'Why? Are you stepping out with him now?'

Heat leapt into Esther's cheeks. She and Lawrence had somewhat bypassed *stepping out* . . . 'Yes, you could say that.'

'Well, that's wonderful.' Elizabeth squeezed her hand. 'Is he as truly charming as he seems?'

'Yes, he is.' She laughed, her cheeks warming. 'Probably too charming if my growing feelings for him are anything to go by.'

'Well, I'm pleased he's providing you with some fun. Too much work and no play isn't good for anyone. You included.'

'Maybe, but it's actually my work for the Cause that I want to talk to you about.'

'Oh?'

'Lawrence and I plan to host a fundraising auction at The Phoenix in aid of women's suffrage. I would love for Pennington's to sponsor a lot of some sort. If you were to donate a few items, I could come up with some poster designs to dot around the store. It really would help entice some interest.'

Elizabeth's gaze wandered slowly over Esther's face in obvious contemplation. 'Is the auction for a specific group of campaigners?'

'I planned to host the event for the suffragists rather than suffragettes, but I suppose the funds raised could be equally split if you would prefer it. That way, Pennington's won't be seen to be taking sides.'

'That's what I've stipulated before whenever Pennington's has been attached to any sort of campaigning but, as the suffragettes' actions grow more hostile, I can't help wondering if Pennington's should choose a side. However, it's difficult, as there's no way of knowing which customer favours which group of campaigners from the next; so we risk losing a sizable number if we misjudge.' She shook her head. 'No, the store must remain neutral in all but the fight itself. I want the public to know we are for the vote, but not which course of action we support.'

'So, if the fundraiser is for *all* women campaigners, Pennington's will add their sponsorship?'

Elizabeth smiled. 'Yes.'

'Oh, that's wonderful.' Esther squeezed Elizabeth's hand. 'Thank you. Do you think Joseph would be willing to compere? He's such a fabulous orator.'

Elizabeth's eyes shadowed and her shoulders slumped. 'I wouldn't approach him at the moment.'

Esther frowned, concerned that her friend seemed suddenly drained. 'Is this about the something you said you'd share with me when you could?'

Elizabeth nodded as her eyes glinted with what Esther was surprised to see were unshed tears.

'Elizabeth, please let me help you. You know I'll do anything I can.'

Her friend blinked, her gaze turning worryingly sombre. 'If I tell you something, can I trust you not to share it with anyone else? You must promise me, Esther.'

'Of course.' Esther inched closer and slid her arm around Elizabeth's shoulders. 'What is it?'

Elizabeth exhaled a heavy breath. 'As you know, Joseph was a widower before he married me.'

Esther frowned, the low, careful tone of Elizabeth's voice deepening her concern. 'Yes. That is true, isn't it?'

Elizabeth nodded, her chest rising as she inhaled a

long breath. 'Joseph's first wife was murdered.'

'Murdered?' Esther stilled. 'My God.'

'And Joseph continues to feel responsible.'

'Why on earth would he think the blame lies with him?'

'Because he hates that he chose to work the night Lillian was killed rather than accompany her on her mercy visits to feed the poor, as he usually did. She was attacked in an alleyway by the river.'

Esther's heart raced. Beatings and occasional killings around the poorer parts of the city were sometimes reported in the newspaper, but both were rare. Very rare. 'And her killer — '

'Has never been found. Joseph has done all he can with the police and by himself to find this man, without success. This past month, he's become obsessed with finding him once and for all. It's as though he suddenly feels that he must find his wife's murderer or his life will never move forward, no matter how much I promise to stand beside him for however long it takes to find this man.'

'To lose a loved one in any circumstances is terrible, but to murder? I cannot imagine living with such a thing.' Esther tightened her grip on Elizabeth's hand. Her friend's and Joseph's behaviour in recent weeks now made complete sense. They must be consumed by this horrible situation.

'Exactly, and the longer Lillian's killer walks free, the more it's tearing Joseph apart. I've done all I can to help him, but we're running out of ideas of how to even begin to look for someone without description. Her killer could still be in the city, but he could just as easily be abroad. Maybe even dead or incarcerated.'

'Oh, Elizabeth. I'm so sorry.'

Her friend shook her head, anguish burning in her dark green eyes. 'I just feel so selfish.' Her voice cracked.

'Selfish? This is not your doing. You must not blame yourself for Joseph's horrible pain.'

'But . . . I want us to start a family, Esther. To have a baby. But until Lillian's murderer is brought to justice, I fear Joseph will not even consider us moving on together. You see? I'm being unforgivably selfish.'

'No, you're not. Wanting a baby. Wanting to add to the love you and Joseph share does not equate to selfishness. You must talk to him. Tell him how you feel. Aren't there others who can help him? I'll certainly do anything either of you asks of me.'

'Joseph refuses to let me involve anyone else. It's as though it's his sole mission, *our* mission, to find the killer. I've tried persuading him to let a few trusted friends help us, but he always says no.'

'You must keep trying to reason with him. He'll soon see the responsibility of her death and finding her killer does not lie on his shoulders alone. That there will be people willing to help.'

Elizabeth nodded and swiped her fingers beneath her eyes. 'I know, and I'll find a way to get through to him. I love him so much. I can't go on watching him suffer this way.' She abruptly stood. 'You should go. I've kept you from your work. You have my promise of sponsorship if it's for the Cause rather than a specific group. Is that all right?'

Her mind whirled with what Elizabeth had told her, her heart breaking for her pain. She forced a smile. 'That's wonderful. Thank you.'

They embraced and walked to the door.

Esther pulled the door open and stopped. 'I'm

255

always here for you. If you ever need to talk — '

'I know where to find you.' Elizabeth smiled. 'I'll see you later.'

Esther nodded and walked past Mrs Chadwick's desk and along the corridor to the lift, her heart heavy with what Elizabeth and Joseph secretly struggled with. There had to be someone who could help them, but who?

There were so many problems in the world. So many people with silent despairs, both from the past and in the present. Pennington's employed hundreds of people, had thousands of customers. It was awful to think how much pain existed in Pennington's alone.

Esther pressed the button to call the lift and stepped back, her earlier happiness depleted. The work needed to brighten and better the world could not be done through love alone. Elizabeth and Joseph were deeply devoted to one another, their love showing through every look and touch, yet still they suffered. Who knew what might happen between her and Lawrence, but it would be foolish to think that because they had found one another they'd be entirely happy for the rest of their lives.

Which meant a person's life had to remain their own regardless of who they chose to share it with. It was the only way to fight for what they wanted. Fight for change and progression.

Simply . . . fight.

30

Lawrence walked through the door of Oxfordshire train station and onto the flagstone pavement outside. He smoothed his tie before putting on his hat and scanned the line of cabs ahead of him. He'd had sufficient time on the journey from Bath to formulate his plan of how to approach David, Cornelia's rat of a husband. Striding forward, Lawrence welcomed the pent-up anger that bubbled inside of him.

David Parker had always fancied himself a cut above other men in looks, intelligence and wit and, as much as Lawrence had been fond of the man, that vanished the moment Cornelia told him of David's adultery.

Pleased to see three or four horse and carriage cabs awaiting fares, he hurried forward and opened the door of the carriage in front.

'Afternoon, sir.' The driver turned in his seat. 'Where can I take you?'

'Harlington Place, if you will.'

'Straight away, sir.'

Lawrence settled back in his seat, his jaw tight. Not only had David been unfaithful, he'd chosen a lover who would inherit a pretty penny in due course. The man was, and always had been, Lawrence now realised, a social-climbing leech. When he'd married Cornelia, it had been a mutually beneficial match for both David's family and the Culfords.

From the Culford's point of view, the Parkers were wealthier, and from the Parker's point of view, the land

Lawrence's parents owned adjoined the Parker estate. It was their fathers' ambition for the two estates to eventually join.

With no siblings, David stood to be a very wealthy man one day.

Lawrence gripped the bar in front of him. He could not imagine for a moment that David's lovely mother and father had taken kindly to their son's infidelity and Lawrence hoped they disinherited him and left the estate to his and Cornelia's sons, Alfred and Francis. Justice would then most definitely be served.

Whether or not that happened, after Lawrence had seen David today, the cad would understand in no uncertain terms that Lawrence expected David to ensure his family were taken care of. According to Cornelia, it had been weeks since David had as much as telephoned or written to the boys, let alone seen them. That in itself was enough for Lawrence to see red. Their father had clearly moved on to a new life without as much as a backward glance.

'Here we are, sir. Which house would you like to be dropped at?'

Lawrence looked at the houses alongside him. Cornelia and David's home stood at the far end. 'Just here will be fine.'

The driver drew his horse to a stop. 'There you are then, sir. That will be — '

Lawrence passed the driver a note that more than surpassed the fare. 'Here. Keep the change.'

'Much obliged to you, sir. Have a good day now.'

Lawrence opened the door and stepped onto the pavement. He stared towards Cornelia's house, his heart beating a steady rhythm and his hand fisted at his side as the cab drew away, the horse's hooves clip-clopping against the packed earth of the quiet, suburban road.

He'd taken a risk not telephoning David first to make sure he was home, but an element of surprise was needed to knock his brother-in-law off-kilter.

Taking a deep breath, Lawrence strode along the pavement, his mind whirling with a hundred scenarios of what might happen when he came face-to-face with David.

Oxfordshire was picturesque any time of the year, but, in the summer, it became picture-postcard perfect. The quiet street was lined with stone houses, their terracotta roofs shining and their latticed windows glinting. He passed gardens filled with shrubbery and blooming flowers, their small grey-stoned pathways leading to the pristinely painted doors and spotless doorsteps. The scene was quintessentially English, and Lawrence could fathom no idea why David had been so ignorant in the beauty of his home and his family. The man was a buffoon. A buffoon who would soon be stepping up to his responsibilities.

Reaching the Parker home, Lawrence pushed open the wooden gate and walked purposefully to the front door. Lifting his knuckles, he sharply knocked before flexing and relaxing his fingers as he waited.

After a few seconds, footsteps sounded behind the door and then it was pulled open. Cornelia's housekeeper, Mrs Green, started, before her round face burst into a huge smile. 'Mr Culford. Well, I never. How are you, sir?'

Lawrence smiled, a little of his anger temporarily abating. 'I'm well, Mrs Green. How are you?'

'All the better for seeing you.' She glanced behind her and, when she faced Lawrence, her smile had vanished and her gentle gaze was darkened with disquiet. She lowered her voice. 'Is Mr Parker expecting you? Only, you do know Mrs Parker is not here at the moment?'

'Yes, I know. She, Alfred and Francis are staying with me and, no, David is not expecting me, but, if it's all the same to you, I'd like to come in anyway if he's here.'

'But —'

'I've come a long way; Mrs Green and I won't be leaving until I've spoken with him.'

Her cheeks flushed pink and she stood back, the anxiety in her blue eyes escalating. 'You'd better come in then. Mr Parker is in the garden, reading his newspaper.'

'Excellent.' Lawrence brushed past her. 'I know the way.'

'Would you . . . Shall I make coffee, sir?'

'That would be most welcome. Thank you.'

Lawrence removed his hat and walked along the narrow passageway, through the kitchen and into the back garden. As soon as he saw David lounging back in a cushioned seat, Lawrence's anger ignited once more. The man smiled at something he read in the paper, his posture relaxed and repulsively content.

Stepping onto the small terrace, Lawrence walked along the path to the outside seating area. 'Good afternoon, David.'

His brother-in-law jumped and lifted his head. The colour immediately drained from his face and he abruptly stood. 'What the devil are you doing here?'

'Surely you were expecting me at some point, David? I would've thought it quite obvious that I'd be paying you a visit once I discovered how appallingly you've been treating my sister.' Lawrence lowered himself into a chair opposite where David stood and waved towards his seat. 'Why don't you sit down? Mrs Green is just preparing coffee.'

David's face turned red as he glared. 'Get out.'

Lawrence smiled and crossed his arms. 'I don't think so. Sit down, David.'

His brother-in-law continued to glare, a pulse jumping in his jaw.

Lawrence continued to smile congenially even as his simmering anger burned ever closer to the surface.

Slowly, David resumed his seat and picked up his paper which had fallen to the grass when he'd leapt to his feet. He folded it and carefully placed it on the arm of his chair. 'I have nothing to say to you.'

'Good, because I have plenty to say to you. Ah, here's our coffee.'

Mrs Green came towards them carrying a tray laden with a silver coffee pot and cups. Her hands trembled ever so slightly as she placed the tray on the table in front of David and sympathy swelled in Lawrence's chest. Mrs Green had worked for Cornelia since she and David were first married and moved into Harlington Place. She was more of a mother to Lawrence's sister than their own had ever been and he imagined Mrs Green didn't enjoy her job nearly as much as she had when Cornelia and the boys were here. Hopefully, they would be able to return soon, and David would be gone.

Mrs Green laid out the cups and a plate of biscuits before nervously glancing between David and Lawrence. She executed a semi-curtsey and hurried back to the house without having uttered a word.

'I'll pour, shall I?' Lawrence picked up the coffee

261

pot without waiting for a response and filled a cup for each of them. 'Cream?'

'Black.'

Lifting their cups, Lawrence handed one to David and sat back. 'So, I'm happy to have found you here rather than at Middleton Park. I would've thought that as Sophie's father is urging you to divorce my sister, you are more than welcome there on such a fine summer's day.'

David studied Lawrence, his gaze full of venom. 'What do you want, Lawrence? Cornelia and I are over. Our marriage is an unhappy one and has been for a number of years.'

Barely resisting punching the man square on the nose for his imperiousness, Lawrence gripped his cup and took a long sip. 'And did that unhappiness start when you took Sophie Hughes as your lover or before?'

'I don't have to answer to you.'

'No? Then you will answer to my sister.'

'She's my wife and should conform to my wishes. I do not need to offer her any explanations.'

Lawrence huffed a laugh and shook his head. 'My God, you really are so damn self-righteous. You bed another woman while still married. You spend more time with your lover than your children and you sit here as though *Cornelia* is in the wrong. Clearly, part of your brain has fallen out.'

'How dare you — '

'Oh, I dare, David.' Lawrence banged his cup onto the table, his temper snapping. He shot forward so his face was inches from David's, satisfaction rippling through him when his brother-in-law flinched back. 'Let me make the reason for my visit very clear. I don't

262

want you to reconcile or even speak to my sister,' he growled. 'If she deems to take a call or reply to a letter from you that's her prerogative, but, as far as I'm concerned, she has no need of you. However, your sons are a different matter entirely. I understand it's been weeks since you've seen or spoken with them. Is that right?'

David glared. 'What I do, or don't do, is none of your damn business.'

'Is that so?' Lawrence smiled and leaned back. 'Well, then, how we proceed from here is simple. You will ensure a generous allowance is paid every month, without fail, into Cornelia's bank account, which she will be setting up shortly. If she decides to move back here, you will move out immediately. If, on the other hand, she chooses to stay in Bath, you will allow her to live and raise your sons as she sees fit.'

David smiled as he shook his head, his expression filled with unadulterated arrogance. 'We're still married. She will do as I say.'

'I think not, David,' Lawrence growled. 'I know my sister very well and I would think her instigating a divorce is imminent. So, again, you will pay her an allowance and ensure she is comfortably provided for. I've contacted a solicitor and, once Cornelia and I have met with him, I will instruct that a settlement is sent to you, which you will sign immediately. Not after the divorce. I want everything laid out neatly and cleanly before the judge when the time comes for your divorce hearing. I will not risk you crawling back to my sister if your farce of a relationship with Miss Hughes fails to become what is clearly a social-climbing effort on your part.'

David sat back, his eyes glinting with malice. 'And

how are you going to get me to sign such a thing? Hold me at knifepoint?'

'If I have to.'

'Don't be so absurd, Lawrence. It's beneath you.'

Lawrence curled his hand into a fist. 'That's the deal, David. If I were you, I'd take it while I'm still succeeding in keeping my temper under control.'

David studied Lawrence until he shook his head and raised his hands in surrender. 'Fine. Send me the settlement. Money is of no consequence.'

'Not once you marry Miss Hughes.'

David smiled. 'Exactly.'

Lawrence picked up his hat and stood. 'Good, then I'm glad you have seen reason. I'll expect you to return the signed settlement to my solicitor along with a commitment to how often you'd like to visit your sons. If you're considering never seeing Alfred and Francis again, I will personally see to it that those boys know just how much of a bastard their father is.'

David's eyes widened and his cheeks mottled. 'What did you call me?'

'You heard.' Lawrence put on his hat and strode towards the house.

31

By the time Lawrence returned home, his temper had cooled and, instead, concern filled him of what Cornelia would say when he told her he'd been to see David without her permission. As close as Lawrence and his sister were, he hoped she'd understand that he could not have stood back and allowed David to swan around as though he'd not a care in the world and had nothing to answer for.

He let himself into the house and followed the sound of murmured voices and clinking china. Entering the drawing room, he found Cornelia at tea with Francis.

Taking a deep breath, he forced a smile and entered the room. 'Well, what do we have here? Is there room for one more?'

Cornelia laughed, looking extraordinarily happy, relaxed and beautiful in a floral dress of light blues and pinks, pearls glinting at her neck and ears. 'Of course.'

Lawrence winked at his nephew and the little boy giggled before taking a mammoth bite of jam sponge.

'So . . . ' Cornelia poured Lawrence a cup of tea and pushed it towards him as he sat. 'Where have you been these past hours?'

Lawrence glanced at Francis, not wanting to discuss David in front of his son. 'I worked this morning and then paid a visit to someone this afternoon.'

'Oh? Anyone I might know?' She wet the corner of her napkin with her tongue and dabbed at a dot of jam on Francis' mouth. 'Lawrence?' She faced him

265

and something in his expression caused her to frown. 'What is it?'

He tilted his head towards Francis and raised his eyebrows. 'I'll tell you all about it later . . . once we're alone.'

Never one to stem her curiosity, Cornelia's frown deepened before she turned to Francis with a wide smile. 'Why don't you join your brother, Rose and Nathanial upstairs? I'm sure Helen will have something to keep you busy.'

'Yes, Mama.'

Francis clambered from the table, flashing a shy smile at Lawrence before running from the room. Lawrence faced Cornelia.

She frowned. 'Well? Who did you visit?'

He held her gaze. 'David.'

She immediately paled. 'What?'

'I was never going to wait around and do nothing after what he's done to you, Cornelia. You must have known that.'

'Yes, but so soon? Without talking to me first? Oh, Lawrence. Why would you do such a thing?'

'Because I will not risk that man hiding his money or not stepping up to his responsibilities. Once you instigate a divorce, he could've done anything to further hurt you.'

She stared at him before picking up her cup, her hand slightly trembling. She sipped her tea and slowly lowered the cup into its saucer. 'And what did you demand of him exactly?'

'I told him a settlement will be drawn up with my solicitor and I expect him to immediately sign it as well as stating when he'd like visits with the children.'

'I see. And what was his response?'

266

'He didn't take too kindly to begin with, but eventually he saw sense.'

Her shoulders slumped. 'Good. That's something, I suppose.'

'So, now I have his agreement, we'll make an appointment to see my solicitor as soon as possible.'

She offered him a small smile. 'Thank you.'

'You're welcome. Am I forgiven? I only want what's best for you. You do know that?'

'Of course.' She raised her eyebrows, her eyes glinting with mischief. 'Did you hit him?'

He laughed. 'What? Of course not.'

She grimaced. 'That's a shame.'

The tension evaporated and Lawrence took her hand, relieved his sister had taken his unauthorised excursion so well. 'Forget David for the time being. I have something to ask you.'

'Oh?'

'What are your plans for tomorrow evening?'

She frowned. 'Nothing at all. I planned on spending a quiet night with the boys. Why?'

'How would it be if I invited a friend for dinner?' His heart filled with anticipation of introducing Cornelia to Esther. 'I'm quite sure you'll like her.'

'Her?' Cornelia's brow creased before her eyes lit with understanding and she wiggled her eyebrows. 'Is this a *lady* friend, by any chance?'

Rare heat leapt into Lawrence's cheeks. 'Yes, as a matter of fact. Her name is Esther. Esther Stanbury.'

'And?'

'And, I like her very much. So much, I'd like you to meet her and have the children see her again.'

Surprise flitted through her gaze. 'Rose and Nathanial have already met her?'

267

'Yes.'

'My, then clearly things are quite serious by your standards. I've not known you bring anyone to meet the children since Abigail died.'

'I haven't. Esther is special, and I don't mind admitting it.'

Cornelia narrowed her eyes and he struggled not to squirm under her closer inspection. 'Hmm. Then I would most definitely like to meet her. It will take a special woman indeed for my brother to risk his heart. Is she of status? Did you meet her at one of the hotels?'

'She's a working woman and, as far as I'm concerned, that makes her of supreme status. I very much admire and respect her.'

Cornelia grinned and covered his hand where it lay on the table. She squeezed his fingers. 'And hearing you say that with such fervency is why I'm here and not with Mama. You, my dear brother, are a breath of fresh air and have no idea how happy it makes me to hear you refer to this woman as you have. It's that kind of respect I want for myself.' Her eyes brightened. 'I want a man to look at me and see what you see in Miss Stanbury. I want to be able to stand tall and proud.'

'And you will. I have no doubt of that.'

'You're right.' She gave a curt nod and picked up her teacup. 'Why should I beg David to come home or force him to see the beauty in his children's faces?' She hesitated. 'That's not to say I'm not terrified at the prospect of going home to Mama and telling her David and I are separated. She'll undoubtedly pick up where David left off, but I have renewed strength to ignore whatever words she chooses to throw at me.'

She smiled. 'I'm excited to embrace life as a divorcee. After all, I'll be free for the first time in years.'

Lawrence's concern deepened. 'As proud as you will undoubtedly make me, people can be incredibly unforgiving, Cornelia. Even in these changing times. Mother will no doubt have more than her fair share of opinion if you should divorce.'

'And it will be me, not her, who has to live with the consequences. I'd rather be a divorcee and a good mother to my boys than a woman who plays second fiddle to another woman and wife to a husband who barely looks at me. If I must live with only the boys for company, so be it. You've shown me what life can be like as a lone parent. I can do this. I know I can. Please . . . ' She took his hand again. 'Tell me you'll support me? Help me to speak with Mama?'

'You really want me to come home with you?' Dread unfurled inside him. 'Why don't you stay here for a few more weeks?'

'Mama is gravely ill. We *must* go home before her declining health worsens. At least for a while. Now . . . ' She stood and began to gather the condiments and cutlery. 'Tell me more about Miss Stanbury.'

She carried the breakfast things back and forth from the table to the sideboard, where she meticulously stacked everything ready to return to the kitchen. There was no mistaking the tremor in Cornelia's hands or the stiffness in her shoulders. Whatever the fervour of her words, she was hurting and afraid. Over his dead body would he allow their mother to berate Cornelia, or her plans. No matter how he abhorred the idea of seeing his mother again, he wouldn't force Cornelia to face her alone. He had no choice but to accompany her, even though he was suspicious about the true gravity of his mother's illness. There was every probability her ailment was little more than a ruse to get him back to the estate. It wouldn't be the first time she or Harriet had tried such a thing.

'Lawrence?'

He blinked and met Cornelia's concerned gaze. 'Yes?'

'What are you thinking about?'

'Nothing.' He forced a smile. 'Let me tell you about Esther.'

She returned his smile and took her seat beside him, her gaze expectant. 'Well?'

'She works as a window dresser at Pennington's. She —'

'Pennington's? She's responsible for their astounding window displays?' Something indiscernible appeared in her eyes. 'Has she been employed there long? I imagine it's a wonderful place to work.'

Lawrence studied her. Was she considering approaching Pennington's for employment? He could certainly think of worse places for her to work. 'She's worked there for a number of years and is very happy.' Pride twisted inside him. 'She has quite the talent, doesn't she?'

'And ambition and flair . . . ' Cornelia beamed, her gaze filled with admiration. 'And quite an insight for the future. I couldn't take my eyes off the displays when I was at the store a few days ago. I can't imagine what she has planned for the Coronation.'

'It's all very top secret. She's shared nothing of her designs with me. The buzz of the Coronation continues to escalate, so I'm happy you're here. I would have hated you and the boys to miss the procession the city will be hosting.'

'A procession? Oh, the boys will love that. And

Esther likes working at Pennington's? She's happy there?'

'Very.'

'And her other interests?'

'Women's suffrage. It's her passion and one I think will never lessen until women are rightfully given the vote.'

'Hear, hear.' Cornelia gave a curt nod before her eyes glazed, seemingly to look straight through Lawrence.

'Cornelia?'

A faint blush coloured her cheeks and she grinned. 'Oh, Lawrence, I can hardly wait to meet her. Will we dine here?'

'I thought so, yes.'

'With the children?'

'Yes.'

'That will be wonderful. I'm so happy she's fond of Rose and Nathanial.' She leapt to her feet and gathered their napkins. 'The idea of them having a kind and ambitious mother so different than our own is most exciting.'

She walked to the sideboard and put their napkins on top of the plates before picking them up and walking to the open dining room door. She threw him a smile over her shoulder and entered the hallway, disappearing in the direction of the stairs.

Lawrence drained his coffee cup. A kind and ambitious mother? Cornelia had just leapt several months, if not years, ahead. Usually, he'd find that kind of throwaway comment from his sister amusing, but instead, it turned his mind to the possibility of he and Esther one day marrying. He smiled. Nothing would make him happier.

32

At just before six o'clock the following evening, Esther stood a little taller as Lawrence approached her across the courtyard in front of the Abbey. His handsome face shone above a moving sea of bodies, his gaze on hers. Her stomach emitted a loop-the-loop as he neared, her hands turning clammy inside her gloves. Was she in the first throes of love? If yes, she prayed this feeling lasted for the rest of her life.

He stopped in front of her and took her hand, pressing a kiss to her gloved knuckles. 'You look lovely.'

She smiled. 'Thank you. How are you?'

'Surprisingly nervous.' He released her hand and glanced around the bustling courtyard. 'I've no idea what to expect when I meet your associates.'

She slipped her hand into the crook of his elbow, tugging him gently forward. 'There are a few you might need to charm with your knowledge of the suffrage bill, but I'm sure most will wholeheartedly welcome you. The only person you really need to be made aware of is Cecilia Reed.'

'Oh?'

'The woman is a force of nature when she's in the mood. Sometimes, I wonder why she's part of the group, at all.'

'Why is that?'

Esther lifted her shoulders. 'I just get the feeling she's not always entirely behind our endeavours. As though she's merely keeping watch. Throwing in negative comments and generally undermining anything

272

positive members might put forward.' She sighed. 'I've voiced my suspicions to Louise, my closest friend in the Society, but she thinks my reservations unnecessary.'

'Well, I hope my presence doesn't upset this woman. The last thing I want is to make things harder for you. Are you quite sure you want me here?'

'Positive.' Esther smiled. It was wonderful to have him beside her both in a suffrage capacity and personally. Her qualms they might not have a future together declined each and every time they were together. 'I'm so looking forward to introducing you to Louise and her husband.'

'So, there will be at least one other man joining us?'

'Oh, yes. More than one. In fact, I'm surprised with you being a member of the Men's League that I haven't seen you at a rally before.'

'I've always taken a behind-the-scenes role in the past. Now I've met you, everything's changed.'

Esther smiled, her heart giving a little kick of pleasure.

They walked past row upon row of shops and houses that lined the main streets of the city centre before entering a darkened alleyway where the Society often met before a rally. Esther drew her hand from Lawrence's arm and knocked out the top-secret code on the door.

Standing back, she glanced at him as he stared resolutely at the door. Footsteps sounded and then the door opened.

Louise grinned. 'Esther! It's lovely to see you and . . . ' She paused, a flash of surprise passing through her pretty dark eyes. 'And Mr Culford. Welcome.'

Esther stilled. Louise knew Lawrence?

273

Lawrence shook her hand. 'Have we met?'

Louise blushed. 'No, but I know you own The Phoenix hotel and have heard sentiments that you are a kind, fair and generous member of the Men's League.'

Lawrence smiled. 'Well, that's very nice of you. Thank you.'

'Come in, both of you.'

Esther stepped inside ahead of Lawrence, confident her decision to invite him today had been the right one. She felt immensely proud to have him beside her. They walked to the stairs and Louise led them to the second floor.

'Everyone's here, so I'll make the introductions and then we'll head to Laura Place.'

Esther turned to Lawrence. 'We've decided to demonstrate there again as we catch the attention of a lot of people coming in and out of town.'

'And who will be making the address?'

Esther inhaled a deep breath. 'Me. It's my very first time, but I can hardly wait. I am a little nervous but, with you here I know I can do this.'

He pressed a kiss to her cheek. 'Of course, you can.'

Louise opened a door to a cacophony of female and male voices, laughter and clinking china. The moment Esther's gaze landed on Cecilia's, protectiveness for Lawrence stole through her. The older woman narrowed her eyes as she blatantly assessed Lawrence, her mouth pinched into a thin line.

Determined to deflect any negativity, Esther clasped Lawrence's elbow and drew him to the centre of the room, flashing Amelia a quick smile where she sat at the back of the room, her hands tightly clasped in her lap and her eyes wide with expectation. She was clearly apprehensive but excited too for what would be her first rally.

Turning, Esther caught Louise's eye and nodded, silently indicating to her friend that she would like to address the group.

Louise returned her nod and clapped. 'Everyone, quiet down, please. We'll be leaving shortly, but first Esther would like to introduce a new friend to the Society. Esther?'

'Thank you.' Esther purposely kept her gaze on Cecilia's. If she could coax her into accepting Lawrence, she was quite sure there wouldn't be any worse naysayers. She had every intention of keeping a closer eye on Cecilia. There was something amiss about her and, sooner or later, Esther was determined to get to the bottom of it.

She raised her voice and spoke firmly. 'This is my good friend, Lawrence Culford. He's already a member of the Men's League but is joining us this evening for his very first suffragist rally. Lawrence is a long-time supporter of the Cause and agrees it is time for men and women to show solidarity and unity to the government.' She glanced at him and smiled, before facing the gathering once more. 'I'm sure you'll all make Lawrence welcome and help him to learn more about our objectives, methods and practices.'

A swift applause broke out as men and many of the women came forward, their hands outstretched to welcome Lawrence. She moved to the side and looked at Cecilia who remained seated.

The woman scowled, her cold gaze on Esther's before she gave a curt nod and stood.

Esther released her held breath. It was the closest she could expect to an acquiescence, for the time being, at least.

Once Lawrence had shaken hands with as many people as possible, the members gathered up their placards, pamphlets and banners. As they headed from the room and down the stairs into the street, Esther's confidence was buoyed by Lawrence's confident authority.

They soon emerged onto Laura Place along with the crowd who had gathered and followed them across Pulteney Bridge.

Esther studied the various faces for any signs of hostility, relief lowering her tense shoulders when she only saw expressions of interest or encouragement. The right for women to vote had steadily gathered supporters and members over the last twelve months and the atmosphere this evening held a simmering fever that was inspiring and intoxicating.

They congregated in front of the stone fountain in the centre of Laura Place and Esther laid the crate she carried on the cobblestones. Lawrence tipped her a wink and took his place behind her along with the other Society members.

Esther smoothed her skirt and pulled back her shoulders, battling the surge of nerves that took flight in her stomach. She stared at the people around them, revelling in the spectrum of high and low-class spectators, some dressed finely, others in ragged clothes and dirty, flattened hats. It cheered her to see them standing side by side, barely moving aside when horses, carriages and the occasional motorcar beeped its way around them.

With the sun shining brightly against a clear blue sky, a welcome breeze keeping the temperatures bearable, it was plain to see that these people wanted to be here for what promised to be a successful demonstration. Esther breathed deep hoping this evening would garner more support and, hopefully, more members.

The chattering quieted as the audience formed a semicircle in front of her. Esther looked to her side where Louise stood brandishing a huge placard bearing the words '*Women Demand The Vote – We Will Wait No More.*'

Esther nodded at her friend and turned to the crowd.

'We stand before you today as a united group of men and women determined to make the Government see women's suffrage is no longer something that people want to happen, but *will* happen.'

A smattering of applause sounded along with shouts of 'hear, hear!' and 'Yes, it will!'

'We are a suffragist group doing our utmost to hold peaceful campaigns. We write to Members of Parliament and our letters are ignored. How will our country ever prosper and grow under such blatant disregard for the voices of its people? Women are not the enemy but often the very people who keep our homes running, our children cared for and loved. Women are working in our shops, restaurants, factories and domestic service. How can we not have a view, opinion and passion for our workplaces, welfare and health services? We deserve a voice at the next election. We will continue in our endeavours, side by side with our husbands, friends and families. We *will* win!'

Rapturous applause thundered from the crowd and Esther lifted her banner high, her heart racing with euphoria as she started chanting. 'We will *win!*'

Joining their voices with hers, her associates walked

277

forward and thrust pamphlets into outstretched hands. The atmosphere was vehement with support. Women, young and old, cheered and waved, their expressions full of belief and tenacity. The tide was turning. The people had spoken and, one day soon, government would have no choice but to listen.

Esther glanced at the Coronation banners strung overhead between the black Victorian lamp posts either side of the street. They advertised the imminent events, stalls and games that would be displayed in Victoria Park and Pulteney Gardens on the day of the Coronation. The excitement of a new era loomed. There could be no doubt a definitive change was in the air.

She stepped from the crate and Lawrence immediately took her hand. He squeezed her fingers, his beautiful blue eyes gleaming with admiration. 'You were magnificent.'

'Thank you, but we still have so far to go.' She dragged her gaze from his to look around her. 'The spectators and support are growing, but still we get no further forward.'

'We will. You have to keep faith.'

Esther faced him, her earlier euphoria wavering. 'Sometimes I am so tempted to take drastic action. Do something like the suffragettes are doing. Those women aren't monsters, Lawrence. They're women who have reached the end of their patience.'

'I agree, but violence is not the answer and never will be.'

Esther studied his face, fearful of the anger swirling through her. Her tenacity for the vote, for a voice, sometimes consumed her to dangerous levels and it took every ounce of her strength to calm herself. Lawrence was right, violence wasn't the answer, but she could not accept more radical action was not needed.

'Esther?'

She blinked and forced a smile. 'Yes?'

'Would you have dinner with me tomorrow evening? I'd love for my sister and nephews to meet you.'

Her mouth dried, the noise around them fading. 'You want me to meet your family?'

'Yes.' His gaze softened as it grazed over her hair, then lower to her lips. 'Very much so.'

How was she to resist the tenderness in his eyes, the soft request on his tongue? She inhaled a shaky breath, slowly released it. 'Then I'd love to.'

'Good.' He lifted his gaze from hers and looked around the crowded area around them. 'But first we have people to talk to and recruit, do we not?'

'Yes. Yes, we do.'

Esther entered the fray with Lawrence at her side, suddenly feeling that maybe the breakthrough the Society wanted would happen soon . . . and she hoped Lawrence would be beside her to witness it.

279

33

The following evening, Esther snapped on her gloves as annoyance and trepidation whirled through her. Her aunt had not refrained from peeking through the parlour's net curtain looking for Lawrence's carriage for the last quarter of an hour. She really hoped it had not been a mistake deciding to tell Aunt Mary of her growing relationship with Lawrence. Esther had been finding it increasingly difficult to keep her happiness hidden and knew, before long, her aunt would guess something had changed in her niece's life.

Accepting Lawrence's offer of his personal transportation had been utilised to impress and, hopefully, appease her aunt. Although even Esther had to admit there had been a positive, if slight, shift in her aunt's attitude as the Coronation loomed. As a staunch royalist, Aunt Mary was in jitters of excitement over the upcoming events and that, in turn, had benefited Esther, due to her involvement in Pennington's Coronation window. An avid shopper at the store, her aunt was often astounded by the interior and had slowly begun to accept Esther played a big part in its execution.

Maybe, now, she could also hope for Aunt Mary's blessing to pursue a possible courtship with Lawrence . . . even if she'd never surrender to her aunt's snobbishness or her constant association with Viola.

She pressed her hand to the jumble of nerves in her stomach. The prospect of meeting Lawrence's sister and her children was far more disconcerting than

280

anything else that might bother her.

'Ooh, I say, this must be Mr Culford's carriage now. Yes, yes, it is. It's slowing to a stop.' Her aunt leapt away from the window and rushed to Esther, gripping her hands. She grinned, her eyes shining so brightly, ten years immediately vanished from her features. 'You have a lovely time, my dear. I'll wait up for you.'

'There's really no need to — '

'Nonsense. Nonsense. Now, don't keep the gentleman waiting.'

Esther opened her mouth to chastise her aunt's obvious social climbing but snapped her mouth closed. To say anything about Aunt Mary's misplaced rapture would only damage their fragile amicability.

She kissed her aunt's cheek. 'I won't be late.'

'Oh, my dear,' Aunt Mary laughed, pulling Esther into the hallway and towards the front door. 'Take all the time you need.'

Resisting the urge to roll her eyes, Esther exited the house and climbed into the carriage. The driver touched the brim of his hat to Esther and then Aunt Mary, who waved from the doorstep. Once Esther was settled inside, the carriage door closed with an expensive thud and the driver climbed aboard, emitting a sharp whistle to set off the single piebald horse.

Esther leaned back and gripped her purse.

The city passed by the windows. The evening was clear and warm as women strolled by beneath their decorative parasols, arm in arm with their beaux or husbands, all of whom were smartly dressed in dinner jackets and top hats. Bath was a riot of colour in the wealthier areas and a sea of brown and grey in the slums, but as the carriage passed the Abbey and

281

through the winding streets lined with shops and restaurants, Esther couldn't imagine ever wanting to live anywhere else.

Bath was where she belonged and, as they continued up the steep slope of Gay Street into the Circus, her gaze was automatically drawn to Lawrence's beautiful honey-coloured townhouse, and she hoped he felt the same. For, surely, her heart would be broken should he ever move away with Rose and Nathanial.

As the carriage drew to a stop, she inhaled a strengthening breath and took the driver's offered hand, before stepping onto the flagstone pavement. Smoothing her dress, Esther adjusted her hat and patted her hair with slightly trembling fingers before starting along the short pathway to Lawrence's door. Just as she reached for the knocker, the door was abruptly thrown open and Esther came face-to-face with one of the prettiest women she'd ever seen.

'Miss Stanbury! You're here. It's so lovely to meet you.' The woman beamed, her bright blue eyes warm and welcoming and almost identical to Lawrence's. She pressed her hand to her breast. 'I'm Cornelia, Lawrence's sister. Come in, come in.'

Although uncertain what to expect from her first meeting with Lawrence's sister, Esther certainly hadn't anticipated such an unadulterated salutation. Mystified, she somehow found her voice past the frantic thump of her pulse. 'Thank you. I'm glad to be here.'

'Might I take your shawl?'

'Cornelia, will you please give Esther a modicum of breathing space?' Lawrence's rich, deep voice came from behind his sister. 'You'll frighten her away.'

Esther glanced over Cornelia's shoulder and her

282

heart flipped when her gaze met Lawrence's. Dressed in a dark suit and snow-white shirt and tie, he looked positively edible. He slowly came towards her as Cornelia lifted Esther's shawl from her shoulders.

Without breaking his gaze from hers, Lawrence took Esther's hand and tugged her gently forwards and pressed a kiss to her cheek. 'You look wonderful,' he whispered against her ear.

An illicit thrill shot through her body as she turned to face him. 'As do you.'

'So, Miss Stanbury . . . ' Cornelia came between them, causing Lawrence to step back. She threaded her hand through Esther's elbow. 'Lawrence tells me you work at Pennington's?'

'I do and, please, call me Esther.'

'Well, Esther, I want to know everything. What it's like to work there. How you came to your position as head dresser. Everything. Let's go upstairs to the drawing room.' She propelled Esther towards the stairs. 'The children will join us shortly. Would you like some wine?'

Buoyed by Cornelia's infectious warmth, Esther smiled at Lawrence. He grinned back, his eyes soft with transparent love for his sister. Esther relaxed her shoulders, happy that Lawrence held so much affection for his eldest sibling. As an only child, Esther couldn't think of anything more delightful than to love a person she'd grown up with.

She stared around her at the wonderful opulence of the hallway. From the gorgeous silk wall coverings, to the gilded mirror above an ornate side table, to the beautiful Persian rug beneath her feet, Lawrence's home was welcoming, warm and perfect for raising his young family. They mounted the stairs and her gaze was drawn again to the portrait of Abigail. Yet something felt different from the last time she'd been here when she stared into Abigail's eyes. This time Abigail seemed to smile back at her, her gaze soft with welcome.

Esther smiled. Maybe it was entirely right she was here. In the home of a man she could come to love.

Their pre-dinner drinks passed in a flurry of excited questions from Cornelia about Pennington's, and Esther did her best to keep up. She offered Lawrence's sister titbits about the store's plans and how much she loved her work, adding a few discreet details about her plans for the Coronation.

Cornelia positively beamed with delight when Esther confessed that London had acquired one or two pieces from Pennington's for the less senior royals to wear during the King's procession from Buckingham Palace to Westminster Abbey.

'I must come by the store and see you before I leave for Mama's.' Cornelia's smile wavered. 'Our mother is gravely ill, you see. I must visit her and hope that Lawrence will join me.' She glanced at Lawrence who stood at the fireplace, his sombre gaze as often on his sister as Esther. 'Everything is changing in my life at the moment and not just our mother's illness. My husband and I are separated, Miss Stanbury. Even though Lawrence thought me happily married, nothing could be further from the truth.' She took a deep breath and smiled once more, her gaze happy. 'But now I want to experience more of the world as you have. I simply must visit Pennington's again while I'm in the city.'

Sad for Cornelia's unhappiness but pleased by her enthusiasm for the store, Esther nodded. 'And I'd be more than happy to show you around. Be sure to send word of when you'd like to visit and I'll do all I can to take a break from my work.'

Cornelia squeezed Esther's hand. 'Thank you. I'd love to learn more about your suffrage efforts, too. If there's nothing else I've learned through my estrangement from my husband, it's women *must* unite. Now, I can hear the children. Shall we go into the dining room?'

She swept from the room and Esther slowly rose from the settee. Lawrence drained his sherry, placed his empty glass on a small side table and offered her his elbow.

'You know . . . ' he sighed, as they left the drawing room, 'Cornelia isn't usually this animated about anything. You're having the most bizarre effect on her.'

'I can't imagine what you've said to her to make her think me such an exciting dinner guest.'

'All I've said . . . ' he leaned closer, his warm breath tickling her ear, 'is you are special, talented and incredibly beautiful.'

She shivered and leaned away from him, arching her eyebrow. 'Is that all? Well, I really thought I would be worthy of so much more.'

He gently placed his hand at the base of her spine. 'Into the dining room with you, Miss Stanbury. The evening is young. Who knows what else might be added to your list of attributes?'

Laughing, they walked downstairs and into the dining room.

The moment Rose and Nathanial turned from their chattering with Helen and saw Esther standing at the door, they clambered down from their seats at the table and ran forward, wrapping their arms about her waist. Esther squeezed them tight, tears of happiness burning behind her eyes as she sent up a silent prayer of gratitude to God for granting her such contented delight.

34

Lawrence settled more comfortably on his drawing room settee and swirled his brandy. The dinner had been an outstanding success. Not only had the dining room rung with constant conversation and laughter from both the adults and the children, but Esther had looked entirely relaxed throughout. The longer he knew her, the more he could read the telling nuances of her expression and body and, tonight, her smile, shining eyes, and shoulders, so often shaking with laughter, told him she was unequivocally happy.

Even now, as she sat on the carpet with the children and Cornelia, playing a rather raucous game of Snap! he wanted her for his own. Her pretty hazel eyes lifted to his and her cheeks flushed as though she could read his thoughts. She turned back to the game, but Lawrence couldn't drag his gaze away from her. She'd come into his life and made everything feel entirely right.

She fitted.

She mattered.

Yet, time and again, he was afraid there might come a time when he'd have to let her go if she found his life could not easily blend with hers. He had to prove differently. Had to demonstrate his commitment to the Cause and her independence. Had to show he respected her work at Pennington's and her love of design.

One way or another, he'd find a way to dissolve the uncertainty that flashed in her eyes whenever he inferred to them enjoying a long-term future together. He'd once thought finding a mother for Rose and Nathanial meant seeking someone full of love and willing to be at home with them day and night. Someone to be there each time they returned from school or a day out. Now he realised it wasn't these things that altogether made a good mother.

It was also a woman whose heart was full of love, passion and care for not just herself, but those around her. Someone who could inspire and empathise, love and cherish. Someone who had beliefs, principles and dreams . . . someone whose wisdom and history meant she had more to offer the world than he'd ever thought possible.

That woman, for him, Rose and Nathanial, was Esther. Of that, he was certain.

Cornelia clapped along with the children before collecting the cards she had won. She seemed equally as enchanted by Esther and Pennington's. He was entirely convinced his sister had it in mind to approach Bath's premier department store for work. Even though he was intent that David would provide Cornelia and the boys with a generous income, it would be good for Cornelia to find employment and live by her own means. His sister had fire and he would be damned if her cad of a husband would extinguish it.

Standing, Lawrence walked to the bureau to replenish his brandy, his mind whirling as he poured an inch of amber liquid into his glass before replacing the stopper into the decanter. He glanced at the clock. It neared nine o'clock. Already an hour past the children's bedtime. Although desperate to be alone with Esther, he was reluctant to spoil the children's play. He could not remember seeing Rose and Nathanial so content.

The parlour door opened, and Helen entered, her gaze instantly drawn to the game. She faced him and raised her eyebrows, her gaze teasing. He narrowed his eyes in response, but his smile traitorously broke.

'Children . . .' Helen raised her voice above the laughter. 'It's time to bid Miss Stanbury goodnight. You should be in bed by now. Come along. You have much to do in the morning.'

Amid the groans and protestations, Rose, Nathanial, Alfred and Francis reluctantly got to their feet, kissed each adult on the cheek and followed Helen from the room, leaving the adults alone.

Lawrence carried his glass to the settee and settled beside Esther as she collapsed back, grinning.

'Well, there is absolutely no doubt I'll sleep incredibly well tonight. The children have worn me out.'

'In a good way, I hope.' Cornelia laughed, as she collected the cards and returned them to the open games box on the floor beside her. 'They've thoroughly enjoyed you being with us this evening.'

Lawrence tightened his fingers around his glass as he waited for Esther's response, his focus on the brandy. So often he feared she wouldn't be ready to take on an entire family just yet.

'I enjoyed it very much, too.' She sighed. 'I hope they didn't notice my initial nerves. It's not very often I find myself in the wonderful position to enjoy the company of children.'

'Oh?' Cornelia sat back on her haunches, her gaze flitting to Lawrence and back to Esther. 'Do you mind if I ask — '

'Would you mind if Esther and I had some time alone, Cornelia?' Lawrence interrupted. No matter how surprised he was by Esther's easy admission, he would not allow Cornelia to further question Esther on her views about children. Whether the reason resided within his cowardice, or Cornelia's inappropriate questioning, he couldn't be certain. 'We've barely had a moment to talk since Esther arrived.'

Cornelia's cheeks reddened, and she quickly stood, the games box clutched to her hip. 'Of course. I'm so sorry to have monopolised you, Esther, when you came to be with my brother.'

'Not at all.' She smiled. 'I enjoyed everyone's company tonight. Including yours.'

Cornelia lifted her chin and gave Lawrence a curt and triumphant nod. 'See, brother? No need to get your trousers in a twist.' She walked to the sideboard and placed the games box inside one of the cupboards. 'I'll bid you both goodnight, then.' She walked to the door and opened it, pausing with her hand on the knob. 'But I'll be sure to let you know when I intend visiting the store, Esther.'

'I'll look forward to showing you around.'

The door closed behind Cornelia, and Lawrence released a long breath. 'I thought we'd never be alone. Would you like me to call for some tea? Chocolate?'

'No, thank you.' Esther inched a little closer to him on the settee, leaned her head back and gently rested her hand on his thigh. 'I'm no longer afraid, Lawrence.' She rolled her head to the side and met his gaze. 'Being here with you and your family feels . . . a little nerve-wracking but nice.'

He brushed a light kiss across her mouth. 'I'm glad.'

'It's as though you've opened me up. Shown me how to not be fearful of what might or might not be. I still want to do so much, earn my own living and make my own decisions, but . . . '

Hesitation showed in her gaze and concern tightened his stomach. *Please don't say you're not sure about the children.* 'But?'

'But I think I can have more in my life than independence.' Her eyes shone softly beneath the lamplight. 'I think I can have you, too. You *and* the children. Would that make you happy?'

'Happy?' He huffed a relieved breath. Could she be considering they marry at some point in the future as he had repeatedly? 'More than you could ever imagine.'

He kissed her again. This time pouring his growing love for her into the kiss, praying she sensed the passion she evoked in him.

She slid her fingers into the hair at the back of his neck and eased him closer, her tongue gently exploring his, igniting his arousal.

After a long, indulgent moment, Lawrence moved back and brushed a curl from her cheek. 'I'll never pressure you to do anything you don't want to do. We can bide our time until you are certain this is what you want. The children . . . ' He drew in a breath. 'I don't want them hurt or disappointed in any way. We have to be patient for them as much as ourselves.'

'I know.' She cupped her hand to his jaw. 'And I hope we have all the time in the world. I'll be busy at the store this week, but please know it's not because I'm avoiding you after tonight. I would hate for you to think that.'

'Not at all. The Coronation?'

She nodded. 'There's still so much to do and only four days in which to get everything ready. I imagine I'll be at Pennington's late into the night until Coronation day on Thursday. It's so very exciting . . . ' She smiled wryly. 'And exhausting. What with keeping Aunt Mary happy, too, I'm not sure I'll have any energy left for you, the children or anyone else.'

'I understand.' He frowned as his mind turned to his and Cornelia's looming departure and visit to their mother. 'After the Coronation, it might be I have to return to Oxfordshire to visit my mother. Despite no part of me wanting to go.'

She raised her eyebrows. 'Are you not obligated? I had the impression Cornelia really wants you with her at what must be a very difficult time.'

'She does, but you don't know my mother. Her illness could be little more than a ruse to pull me back to the one place on earth I'd be happy to never set foot in again.' Resentment pulsed through him and when he saw that his fist was clenched upon his knee, he relaxed his fingers and pushed some lightness into his voice. 'Anyway, I don't wish to bother you with my family problems. Everything will sort itself out soon enough, I'm sure.'

Her concerned gaze wandered over his face, lingered a moment at his lips, before she pushed to her feet. 'And with that thought, I should go.'

'Why don't you go upstairs and say goodbye to Cornelia and the children while I ask Charles to bring the carriage around?'

Her smile dissolved. 'Oh, no. It would be far too presumptuous for me to go into their bedrooms.'

'Of course it wouldn't.' He squeezed her hand and stood, leading her to the door. 'They'll be disappointed if you don't bid them farewell.'

When he pulled the door open, they were greeted by a torrent of childish giggling from Rose, Nathanial,

Alfred and Francis . . . and a very guilty- looking Cornelia. She pressed her hand to her chest, her cheeks red. 'Sorry. We . . . we were waiting to say goodbye to Esther.'

Lawrence feigned a glare. 'By the keyhole?'

She looked sheepishly at Esther. 'I'm sure Esther doesn't mind, do you?'

He turned. Esther stood behind him, her hand to her mouth and her eyes brimming with tears of laughter. She lowered her hand. 'I'm pleased you all waited up for me.'

Smiling, Lawrence left them to their goodbyes and rang for Charles. The butler appeared so quickly, Lawrence wouldn't have been surprised if Charles, too, had been waiting for Esther. 'Yes, sir?'

'Could you arrange for the carriage to be brought around for Miss Stanbury, please, Charles?'

'Yes, sir.'

As Charles retreated, Lawrence waited for Cornelia and the children to take the stairs to the upstairs rooms before he helped Esther with her shawl. Once the garment was in place, he pulled her gently into his arms and kissed her. 'I'll see you again soon.'

Her gaze settled softly on his. 'You'll come to Pennington's to watch the Coronation, won't you? A brass marching band and all other manner of street entertainment will pass right by the store. I'm sure I could arrange for a first-class view for you from one of the upper windows.'

'That would be wonderful. The children . . . ' Lawrence stopped, uncertain whether she meant for him to bring Rose and Nathanial. 'The children . . . '

'Will be enthralled.' She touched her fingers to his cheek. 'Bring them. Cornelia, too. Although, I must warn you, my aunt will be there. I have no choice but to invite her. She's a staunch royalist and will want to be a part of the day's festivities.'

He smiled and brushed a lock of hair from her brow. 'I'm sure I'll be able to look after myself.'

She laughed. 'I'm sure you will, too.'

With a wave, she hurried to the door and along the short walkway into the waiting carriage. Lawrence strolled outside and watched until it had disappeared out of sight. He breathed the cool night air deep into his lungs, his gaze on the thousands of stars above him.

How long could such happiness last? A moment? A lifetime?

One way or another, the fear that it might not last would not lessen its torment. How could he relax when fate had taken Abigail? When, sooner or later, he would have to return to Culford Manor and face his mother, no matter how little he wanted to?

35

Esther trembled with suppressed excitement as she stood behind the emerald green drapes that concealed Pennington's Coronation window. From outside came the sound of murmuring voices, whereas even a dropped pin would have been heard where she stood behind the glass. At exactly ten to nine, she would draw back the drapes and her team's window would be revealed to the waiting public. Shortly afterwards, the store's gilded double doors would open and customers would be admitted through the entrance as staff greeted them for what promised to be a truly exhilarating day.

She couldn't be sure what made her prouder; today or when she'd given her address at the rally.

Straightening her shoulders, she glanced at her watch.

Three minutes.

She turned to the papier-mâché Britannia standing centre stage. Her golden helmet gleamed and her shimmering, gold-edged toga glittered, her trident held high. Tall marble plinths stood on either side, one swathed with the Union Jack flag, the other in a scarlet cape, trimmed with fur and dotted with balls of black thread to give the illusion of ermine. A crown dazzling with paste diamonds and jewels had been placed on top.

The backdrop was a black and white montage of enlarged newspaper pictures and headlines of the King and his beautiful queen, Mary of Teck. The

295

floor, covered in a gold sheet and sprinkled with hundreds of sequins, would dazzle and delight the waiting crowds.

Esther breathed deep and silently applauded herself and her staff. The display could not have been more mesmerising or astounding for such a momentous event.

She glanced again at her watch.

Five seconds.

She stepped to the rope pull at the far side of the window and tightly gripped it, her heart thundering.

Three ... two ... one ...

Briefly closing her eyes, she eased downwards on the pull and slowly drew back the drapes.

A loud, unified gasp sounded outside and then an ear-splitting roar of applause and cheers. Esther's cheeks ached with the breadth of her grin as she walked to the side at the front of the window and held out her hand to encompass her team's achievement.

She laughed when she caught Elizabeth and Joseph's gazes as they applauded alongside the hundreds of passers-by surrounding them. She gave a semi-bow and, when she lifted her eyes again, she met Lawrence's proud gaze.

His eyes glittered with pleasure and possession, making her heart skip. She moved her focus to his side. Rose, Nathanial, Cornelia, Alfred and Francis clapped, their eyes shining. Even Aunt Mary looked fit to burst with awe and, maybe, a little familial pride, too.

Esther quickly waved and retreated to the window exit.

As soon as she stepped into the small corridor, Amelia came forward, her hands outstretched. 'Congratulations, Esther. They absolutely love it. All our hard-pressed time and energy was worth it to hear the public applaud so unreservedly.'

Esther gripped Amelia's hands, enjoying how their friendship and camaraderie continued to deepen since Amelia had joined the Society. She laughed. 'It isn't congratulations just for me. It's for you, too.' She looked around her assembled team as they filed into the corridor, smiling and clapping. 'I could not have done this without you. All of you. The long hours you've worked, the enthusiasm and commitment . . . ' She shook her head. 'Thank you so much.'

They gathered around and Esther accepted and gave embraces and congratulations. 'We really should go to the shop floor where the rest of the staff will be waiting for the doors to open. I'm sure Miss Pennington will have jobs for us, even if they've nothing to do with window design. It's all hands on deck today, regardless of our roles.'

Her staff dispersed and Esther followed, her blood pumping and her grin stubbornly refusing to dissolve.

She had just got into position, lined up with the rest of her team when the store's doors were opened, and the crowds filed in, their eyes and smiles wide with anticipation. She looked above their heads to where Elizabeth stood with Joseph, shaking hands and welcoming customers into the store.

Esther was cheered to see her friend and her husband smiling so sincerely when they had so much more serious things in their hearts and minds.

Pushing down her threatening sadness, Esther turned and smiled at a trio of well-dressed women, their huge hats swaying as they turned their heads this way and that. 'Please visit the ladies' department as well as the jewellery departments, ladies. We have much on offer as well as some special pieces commissioned in the spirit of the Coronation.'

They each tipped her a nod and smile before eagerly approaching the grand staircase leading to the upper floors.

'Esther?'

She turned to Lawrence's voice and her heart kicked. He stood before her with his family all around him. Tears pricked her eyes that they were there with her on this special day. She couldn't wait to surprise the children by taking them upstairs to watch the Coronation procession from the toy department windows.

Taking Lawrence's hand, she smiled around the group. 'Do you like the display? Was it everything you hoped it would be?'

Rose slipped her hand into Esther's and squeezed. 'It's magical, Esther. You are a fairy godmother.'

Esther laughed and hugged her close. 'And you are my princess.'

She met Lawrence's gaze and he blinked as he cleared his throat. 'It's astounding. Truly.'

'Thank you.'

'Esther?'

She turned to Aunt Mary, where she stood smiling, tears glistening in her eyes.

'It's magnificent. Truly magnificent. Come.'

She opened her arms and Esther glanced at Lawrence. He smiled. Did her aunt mean to embrace her?

Turning, she stepped forward and her aunt pulled Esther into her arms and squeezed.

'I am so proud of you.'

Touched and more than a little surprised, Esther squeezed her and then eased back to hold Aunt Mary at arm's length. 'And I'm glad you're here to share this special day with us.'

She nodded and released Esther's hands, dabbing at her eyes with a handkerchief.

Cornelia stepped forward and touched Esther's arm. 'I can't wait to see more of what you do here.' Her gaze darted over the glass counters filled with colour and light, to the huge stained-glass dome high in the ceiling, to the opulent grand staircase that wound higher and higher to each floor. 'Pennington's is like a kingdom of dreams. A palace of possibility.' She laughed, her blue eyes shining. 'A haven of hope.'

Lawrence laughed. 'Never one for melodrama, are you, sister?'

She shot him a glare and Esther eased her hand from Lawrence's and touched Cornelia's arm. 'Pennington's is all that and more. Come on, everyone. Miss Pennington promised me a reserved place at the toy department window to watch the procession.'

The children cheered and skipped ahead to the staircase, leaving Esther, Lawrence and Aunt Mary to follow behind as Cornelia hurried after them, seemingly as excited as the children. As Esther watched them go, her gaze was drawn to Elizabeth and Joseph once more as they talked in a discreet corner of the atrium. Their expressions were now sombre as Elizabeth gripped Joseph's hand. He looked down at her and curtly shook his head. Esther frowned as concern whispered through her. They looked to be in a hushed argument. Something Esther had never witnessed between them before, at the store or anywhere else. How was she to help if Joseph continued to battle his demons alone? Elizabeth was one of the strongest women Esther knew, but even her friend could not continue to carry such a heinous burden without the aid of others.

'Esther? Are you coming upstairs?'

She started and turned to her aunt, forcing a smile. 'You go with Cornelia and the children, Aunt Mary. I would hate for you to miss a good spot by the window.'

'Thank you, my dear.' Aunt Mary flashed a beaming smile to Esther and then Lawrence before following the others up the grand staircase.

Once her aunt was out of earshot, Esther turned to Lawrence. 'Thank you so much for being here with your family.' She tipped her head back to look into his eyes. 'It means the world to me.'

He ran his gaze over her face. 'As you do to me. I'm happy, Esther. Really, really happy.'

'Me, too.'

As they neared the staircase, a cloud of familiar perfume cloyed Esther's nostrils. She halted and closed her eyes.

No, please. Not today.

'Esther?' Lawrence's gaze burned into her temple. 'What is it?'

Opening her eyes, she slowly turned.

Her stepmother smiled, her green eyes glinting with malicious amusement. 'Hello, Esther.'

Esther slid her gaze to her father and her heart quickened painfully as she fought to keep her face impassive. It had been so very long since she'd seen him and despite her wanting to feel ill towards her father, a wave of inexorable love swept through her.

She swallowed. 'Father.'

He looked so much older and sadder than when she'd last seen him. His dark brown hair was streaked

300

with grey, his once bright eyes hooded and his skin drawn about his cheekbones.

Battling the worry squeezing her chest, she glanced past him. 'What are you doing here? Are Benedict and Peter with you?' she asked, suddenly wanting to see her young half-brothers more than anything.

'Our sons are none of your concern.' Viola sniffed. 'And we're here to see your window display, of course. Mary told us that posters and advertisements have been circulating all over town for days, so we thought we would come to see what all the fuss is about. We're staying at a darling hotel across town for the night.'

Esther glared. *Please don't let them be staying at The Phoenix.* 'Which hotel?'

'Again,' Viola sneered. 'None of your concern. Apparently, Pennington's was to give the whole of Bath a wonderful surprise.' She gave a thin smile. 'I have to say the fuss was entirely misplaced.'

Lawrence took a step closer to Viola. 'Excuse me — '

'That's enough, Viola.' Esther's father snapped. 'We are here to visit with my daughter, not make further trouble.'

Esther stared at her father. 'What do you want, Papa?'

'To see you, of course.'

A sadness seeped into his gaze and straight into Esther's bruised heart. She glanced at Viola who stared at her through narrowed eyes. Esther faced her father again, her defences firmly in place. 'And now you've seen me, I see no reason to delay you any further.' She smiled, the strain making her cheeks ache. 'The doors are just behind you.'

'Esther . . . ' Her father lifted his hand as if to touch her, hesitated and dropped his arm to his side. 'The window is splendid and we didn't bring the boys as they are too young for the crowds. We didn't want to risk losing them.'

Esther's eyes immediately burned with the threat of tears. Her father seemed to be inexplicably pleading with her. What had happened to bring him here? Why did he seem changed? Softer? She quickly tilted her chin to curtail her love for him. If he were to reject her a second time . . . 'I see. Well, thank you for your kind praise, but I really must get on.'

Lawrence coughed and put out his hand. 'Mr Stanbury, Lawrence Culford. How do you do?'

Esther stilled. Having Lawrence meet her father and Viola was as if he'd placed his neck beneath the blade of a guillotine. One wrong move and the blade would come crashing down, slicing through their new-found happiness and spraying a bloody despair over them that neither he, nor she, would be able to wash away.

Her father slowly extended his hand, studying Lawrence with undisguised curiosity as they shook and released. 'Mr Culford. You're the owner of The Phoenix hotel, are you not?'

'I am, sir.'

'Viola Stanbury, Mr Culford.' Viola tipped her hand as though expecting Lawrence to kiss it. 'How do you do?'

Lawrence merely nodded. 'Mrs Stanbury.'

Despite Esther's satisfaction of Lawrence rebuffing Viola's absurd invitation, it did not overshadow Esther's unease that her father knew Lawrence's name and his ownership of The Phoenix. Had her aunt told her father and Viola that Esther had been stepping out with Lawrence? She suspected she had, along with news that he owned not just a hotel, but a magnificent carriage and horses ... and was extremely wealthy. Why else would they choose to visit her now?

Viola's eyes flashed with fury and an unnatural smile curved her scarlet-painted lips as she addressed Lawrence a second time. 'Did I see your children and wife go upstairs ahead of you, Mr Culford?'

Protectiveness of Lawrence's family unfurled inside Esther and she touched Lawrence's arm to halt his response. She held Viola's stare. 'They were Lawrence's sister and her children, as well as Rose and Nathanial, Lawrence's children. All of whom are none of *your* concern.'

'So, you've found yourself a ready-made family? How wonderful.' Viola turned to Esther's father. 'There, you see, Wilfred. Esther is quite all right and clearly capable of wheedling her way into another man's affections. As I have said a hundred times, she has absolutely no need to bother us or our little family, my love.'

Esther curled her hand into a fist at her side, her nails biting into her palm. 'You really are quite amusing, Viola.'

'I am, aren't I?'

Esther faced her father. 'Take care of yourself and my brothers, Papa. Goodbye.'

Turning on her heel, Esther slipped her hand into Lawrence's offered elbow and they ascended the grand staircase. Her legs shook, and her pulse beat in her ears, but she kept walking despite the carpet moving beneath her feet and the lights blurring her vision.

She would not show weakness in front of her father or Viola. Ever again.

36

A few hours later, Lawrence glanced at Esther as the carriage slowed to a stop outside his house, worry for her continuing to harangue him.

The Coronation procession had been a glittering, wonderful sight, the crowds four-deep along the pavements either side of Milsom Street. Colourful banners and Union Jack flags had been clutched in the hands of excited children as they waved and flapped, their parents and guardians joining in with equal aplomb. A lengthy line of street performers with men on stilts, some blowing bubbles from a huge hoop, had marched by Pennington's, headed up by a brass band dressed in smart red and black military uniforms, their gold epaulettes and buttons glinting beneath the hazy sunshine.

Yet, throughout the entire spectacle, the sadness had not once dissolved from Esther's eyes. Although she smiled and lifted the children onto her hip in turn, so they had a better view, the tension in her shoulders never dissipated. After the procession, she'd asked him if they might walk her aunt home, her voice cold and detached. Lawrence had presumed Esther would stay at home, too, but once Aunt Mary was safely inside her house, Esther had asked Lawrence if she could come back to the house with him for a while. He had, of course, agreed.

So, Esther had made an excuse to her aunt and he and Esther returned to Pennington's to catch a cab with Cornelia and the boys, all the while Esther insisting she was fine and she'd not allow her father's visit with her stepmother to spoil the day. The truth was, it had. The line between her brows had remained clear, the colour in her face not returning.

Now they were outside his home and as Charles opened the carriage door, Lawrence forced a smile. He stepped from the carriage, helped Esther onto the pavement along with Rose, who seemed reluctant to let go of Esther's hand for a moment. Esther barely looked at him as they walked past him towards the house.

'Daddy, down please.'

Turning, Lawrence lifted Nathanial into his arms and swung him around in a circle before setting him on his feet on the pavement. 'Have you had a good day?'

Nathanial grinned. 'Yes. I loved everything.'

'Everything? Even when we had to watch Aunt Cornelia look at one hat after another? One pair of shoes after another?'

'Everything.' Nathanial giggled. 'You liked it, too.'

Lawrence winked. 'I did, but don't tell Aunt Cornelia or she'll take me shopping every day.'

Turning, he paid the driver for their carriage as well as the second one that had come to a stop behind it. As Cornelia and his nephews alighted, Lawrence slowly walked to the house. Esther turned and finally met his eyes. He took a single look at her smile and genuine delight in her eyes as she smoothed her hand over Rose's curls and fell a little deeper in love.

It was as though now she was away from the spectre of her father and stepmother's visit, away from her aunt and just with his family, she could relax. He prayed his hopes were true.

She sighed as he reached her. 'Hasn't today been wonderful?'

He touched her hand. 'You've no idea the pleasure it gives me to hear you say that. You looked so distracted throughout the procession.'

'I was. But now I'm here, my father and Viola seem a million miles away.' She slipped her hand into his elbow. 'I was mad with Aunt Mary for telling father and Viola about us so soon, but I was foolish to think she would keep our courtship to herself for any amount of time.'

Before he could respond, Alfred and Francis tore towards the house, barrelling straight past Esther and Lawrence towards the front door just as it opened. Helen stood on the threshold, her worried gaze fastening on Lawrence as the children rushed inside.

Frowning, he slowly eased his arm from Esther's. 'Helen? What is it?'

'It's Miss Harriet, sir. She's been waiting inside since eleven o'clock this morning.' She glanced over his shoulder towards Esther and Cornelia as they chatted a few steps behind him. 'She's here about your mother.'

Dread whispered through him and Lawrence briefly closed his eyes before facing Esther and Cornelia and the laughter immediately vanished from his sister's eyes. 'Lawrence?'

He took a long breath. 'Harriet's inside. She's been waiting for us.'

Cornelia glanced towards the door and back again. Her mouth dropped open as if to speak, before she promptly closed it and hurried past him into the house. Lawrence turned to Esther.

Concern darkened her eyes. 'Is everything all right?'

'If Harriet's here, it means my mother has taken a turn for the worse.' Unwelcome guilt whispered through him that he'd suspected her illness a ruse.

'I'm so sorry.' She gently touched her fingers to his cheek. 'I'll go and leave you to be with your family.'

'Would you stay? I want you to be a part of whatever happens in my life from now on. I hope you want that, too.'

She tilted her head, her gaze sympathetic. 'Lawrence, it's lovely you want me here, but if your mother is ill I'm not sure your sisters will want me — '

'They will.' He grasped her hand, aware of how selfish and domineering he behaved but unable to bear the thought of hearing whatever it was Harriet had to tell him without Esther beside him. He looked into her eyes. 'Please. Will you come inside with me?'

She studied his face, her gaze unreadable until she closed her eyes and nodded.

Shame twisted inside him that he thought more of his own feelings than Esther's. Whatever ailed his mother, it wasn't Esther's responsibility. He shook his head. 'I shouldn't make you come inside if you don't want to. I apologise. Why don't I ask Charles to drive you — '

She pressed her finger to his lips, her gaze soft. 'I'm here now and if you want me with you, I want to be here, too.'

Relief lowered his shoulders. When and how had it come to be that he wanted Esther beside him in good times and bad? Would there be other moments, countless moments, in his life when he wouldn't have the courage to face the inevitable without her? The possibility was terrifying, yet thinking of her away from him even more so.

Touching his hand to her back, he guided her into the house.

As they walked upstairs, his sisters' murmurs drifted from the open drawing room door, mixing with the childish shouts of Rose, Nathanial and his nephews as they played in the nursery upstairs.

Lawrence glanced at Esther and she nodded her encouragement. He inhaled a long breath and entered the drawing room.

Cornelia and Harriet abruptly halted their conversation and looked at him.

Obligation, culpability and resistance burned inside Lawrence as their expectancy bore down on him. Harriet looked older than he remembered. The sparkle that was once so prevalent in her eyes had vanished, leaving behind a hard, lacklustre shade of blue rather than sapphire. Her complexion was ashen, her jaw and cheekbones far too pronounced. Yet, the stiff lift of her chin showed her stout comportment. A trait no doubt enforced under their mother's tutelage.

She slowly rose to her feet, her eyes glistening with unshed tears. She held out her arms. 'Lawrence. You look so well.'

He stepped forward and pulled her into a tight embrace, pressing a firm kiss to her hair as though he might diminish the sharp angles of her body and soften her hard gaze. 'It's wonderful to see you.'

She pressed her head to his chest before sighing and holding him at arm's length. 'You seem to get broader and taller every time I see you.' She glanced behind him and dropped her hands from his to hastily swipe her fingers beneath her eyes. 'And you must be Esther. Cornelia has been singing your praises. It's nice to make your acquaintance.'

Esther nodded and gave a small smile. 'Thank you. It's lovely to meet you, too.'

Lawrence carefully studied his youngest sister and braced, waiting to see how the following moments would unfold.

Harriet's gaze slid slowly over Esther's face and hair, her smile tight. 'My sister tells me you work at Pennington's?'

'I do.'

'And you enjoy your work?'

'Very much.'

Harriet stared at Esther for another long moment before she abruptly turned to Lawrence. 'We need to talk privately. Maybe Esther could find Helen for some tea?'

He walked to the wing-backed chair in front of the fire, annoyance simmering inside him. 'Esther stays, Harriet. Anything you have to say, you can say in front of her.'

Her politeness vanished as she glared, her jaw tight. 'But this is about Mother. She would not approve — '

'Approve or not, you are in my home and Esther is very welcome here. Whatever the circumstances.' He glanced at Esther, who stared back, her colour high and her gaze reflecting her unease. 'Esther, please. Won't you sit?'

She slowly walked to an armchair opposite him, as Harriet, although clearly unhappy, resumed her seat on the settee beside Cornelia.

Lawrence leaned back. 'So, what is this all about, Harriet? I'm delighted to have you and Cornelia in the same room with me for the first time in what feels like forever, but you would not come here unannounced unless something serious had happened. Helen said it's Mother. Is that right?'

Harriet's blue eyes were dark with annoyance, her posture stiff. She'd been groomed by their mother to be forever ladylike. Or at least, what the great Ophelia Culford considered ladylike. Controlled, yet subservient to her spouse and elders. Polite, yet unbending and intolerant of company she considered of a lesser class than her own. In other words, a contradiction that changed and altered at will.

Harriet flicked her gaze to Esther, her lips pinched. Her disapproval of discussing family business in front of Esther was palpable.

Lawrence pushed out his legs and crossed them at the ankle. He raised his eyebrows. 'Well? You're wasting time staring at my guest when clearly something important brought you all this way.'

She snapped her attention to him, her gaze venomous. 'Fine. Mama is ill, Lawrence. Gravely so.'

Still reluctant to trust Harriet's visit wasn't a trick orchestrated by their mother, Lawrence leaned back, his posture purposefully relaxed. 'So Cornelia has told me.'

'Yet neither of you appear to be in a hurry to come home to see her. Do you have any intention at all to adhere to her wishes?'

'Our relationship with Mother in no way replicates yours with her. You know that.'

'And that means even in her gravest hour, you'll not leave Bath to give her some moments of contentment? To try to absolve your differences towards an amicable reunion?'

'Reunion?' He huffed a laugh. 'You've had a wasted journey if you thought there might be some sort of reconciliation between myself and that woman.' He shook his head, annoyance burning hot inside him that his mother could be using Harriet as a pawn in another of her spiteful games. 'Don't look at me like that. You know how things were between Mother and I when Father was alive. You know how they've been ever since. If she wishes to see me, there will be a reason far beyond reconciliation.'

'She's dying, Lawrence.' Harriet's voice cracked, and she pressed her hand to her chest. 'How can you be so unfeeling?'

Weakening as Harriet's gaze lost some of its fire and became increasingly pleading, Lawrence turned to Cornelia in the hope she might reinforce his point of view.

His eldest sister held his gaze before standing and walking to the fireplace. She stared into the grate and then abruptly turned, crossing her arms tightly. 'Does she ask for me, too? Or just Lawrence?'

Lawrence stilled. Cornelia had an admirable talent of identifying the core of a situation exceedingly well. She always needed the truth. Once she had that, she would debate the components and then make a decision, thus confirming if the person or persons involved deserved her loyalty. If they did, they'd have her allegiance until the bitter end.

How she'd told him about David and her knowledge of the duration of his extramarital affair had shown all too clearly that Cornelia hadn't only been aware of his infidelity but lived with it for as long as she could. It was David who wanted away from the family home, not Cornelia. The man was a fool to not understand what a precious entity he'd had in his wife's integrity.

Harriet glanced again at Esther, whose discomfort only showed in the straightness of her spine and the sombreness of her expression. Finally, Harriet faced Cornelia and pointedly tilted her chin. 'She just asked for Lawrence.'

Cornelia flinched, her cheeks reddening. 'I see. Do you know why?'

'No.' Harriet flicked her gaze to a spot above the fireplace. 'She just asked that I come to Bath and bring him home. I can only reassure you that as your relations with Mama aren't as awful as hers are with Lawrence, she just wants to make peace with him before she passes.'

Lawrence uncrossed his ankles and stood, everything suddenly abundantly clear. 'That's complete rubbish. She wants something from me before she dies. What is it, Harriet? Is the house in disrepair? Are you having to get by on half a dozen servants rather than a dozen? What does she want? Because I guarantee her summoning me is not about seeing her son a final time or making peace. She wants something from me. So, what is it?'

37

Esther's heart quickened at the severity in Lawrence's tone. His palpable anger tinged the air around them like a thundercloud. Coldness seeped along her spine. For all the hurt she'd suffered by her father's incomprehension over her passion for women's rights, Esther still loved him. Witnessing Lawrence's taciturn, unmoving expression and the piercing ice in his words told her that he might believe he felt no love for his mother, but he most definitely felt *something* for her.

Full detachment meant the heart had closed, but the depth of his anger towards his mother showed she continued to dwell deep inside him. Even if she'd been buried to the lowest levels of his affection.

When she saw him behave this way, Esther realised just how much healing he still had to do to move past the cruelty he'd been subjected to. He needed to seek within himself and find the strength to forgive his mother and turn his love and trust to his sisters and children.

She desperately wanted to help him. Desperately wanted to be there for him, but how could she when she felt so woefully inept in that moment? Could she convince him that seeing his mother a final time might be good for him? That when he saw her, it might not become the confrontation he anticipated?

Clearing her throat, Esther braced for his reaction. 'Lawrence?'

He snapped his gaze to hers, his beautiful blue eyes

alight with fury and his jaw a hard line. She glanced at his sisters and they stared back at her expectantly, tension etched on their faces.

Turning to Lawrence, Esther prayed he listened to his head rather than his heart. He might mistake her care for interference, but all she longed to do was calm his rage. 'Your mother is dying. If you don't visit her now, you risk regretting that decision for the rest of your life. If my father summoned me to his death-bed, I would be there in an instant, regardless of what has happened between us. Don't let her grasp on you continue forever. If you don't at least try to find some peace —'

'Peace?' He huffed a laugh. 'My mother wouldn't know peace if she were alone in a meadow with nothing more for company than tweeting birds and blooming flowers. The woman is poison, Esther. She not only allowed my father to treat me the way he did, but she actively encouraged it. Look at her daughters. Harriet becomes thinner every time I see her and Cornelia is dreading going home to the one place she should always have as a haven. This is who my mother is. She's our enemy, not our damn mother.'

Esther flinched and turned to Cornelia and Harriet. Their gazes had dropped to their laps, their expressions hidden but for the identical flush at their cheeks.

Everything pulled at Esther to flee this horrible situation and she would, once she'd made some way towards soothing a little of Lawrence's shock and pain. She met his penetrating gaze. 'My estrangement from my father and my dislike for Viola doesn't mean I love him any less, Lawrence. He is old and wanted a wife beside him who had no need or desire to rally, lead demonstrations and so forth. He is not necessarily weak in not standing up to Viola. As he nears his twilight years, he clearly wants something different from what he once had with my mother.'

He carefully watched her. 'Why are you telling me this?'

'Because . . . ' She glanced at his sisters. 'Because it could be your mother wants something different now, too. Your sisters have come to draw strength from you. That tells me more about you than anything could about your childhood. You're a good man, Lawrence. A strong man who still cares for his sisters despite how you were raised. Harriet has done nothing more than your mother's bidding. Why would you send her back to your family home, her mission failed, knowing your mother as you do?'

His gaze held a dangerous fire and Esther's face heated. She'd overstepped an invisible boundary. Barged in where she was neither wanted, nor needed. She briefly closed her eyes before opening them again and standing.

'I apologise. I shouldn't . . . ' She raised her hands in surrender. 'This has nothing to do with me. I'll leave.'

She picked up her purse and stepped towards the door, but, as soon as she brushed past Lawrence, he gently gripped her elbow. 'Wait.' He drew his gaze over her face. 'You have to understand what my mother is like. How she can say words that slice a person's soul. How just a single look from her can make a person wish to be anywhere else but in her presence.'

In his saddened eyes, Esther saw the true depth of how his childhood still affected his thoughts and actions. A prisoner held behind bars by severe and cruel parenting which only convinced her that now, more than ever, he needed to go home and face his mother a final time. How else would he heal and move on if he did not tackle one half of the parental duo that had caused him such misery?

She cupped her hand to his jaw. 'You *must* go. Not for your sisters or on your mother's command, but for you.'

The silence lingered, intensifying as Esther's pulse pounded in her ears, her heart aching for Lawrence and every ounce of the pain he suffered.

A light, feminine cough broke the stillness and she and Lawrence turned, her hand falling from his cheek.

Cornelia crossed her arms. 'We should go home, Lawrence. This may be the last time either of us sees Mama alive.' Her gaze was soft with pleading. 'Did you not say you'd accompany me, anyway? Papa might have given the estate to Mama over you until she died, and you've made it clear to her you don't want to inherit it, but she is bound to want you to. Why don't you at least come back and hear what she has to say?'

His jaw tightened. 'I don't want Culford, Cornelia.'

'I know and, God willing, she'll see that myself and Harriet are just as capable of inheriting it as you. If that's the case, this could be the last time you have to set foot on Culford land. I promise, neither myself nor Harriet will ask you to come there again.' She glanced at Harriet, who continued to study her lap. 'If you wish to visit sometime in the future, then we will welcome you, but it will not be demanded of you.'

'Visit you? Surely, you're not forgoing your plans to stay in Bath because of Mother? This is what she does, Cornelia. She manipulates and bends us to her

316

will.'

'I have no idea what my future holds, but going home now is the right thing to do. Deep down, I think you know that, too.'

Esther stood stock-still as realisation of Lawrence's legacy dawned. He was heir to a vast estate. Surely, with his mother dead, he would not turn his back on such an inheritance? Surely, he'd choose to stay at the house and run the estate as he saw fit? He might come back and forth to Bath for his business, but with his parents gone, he might easily decide to return to his rightful home in Oxfordshire.

Whatever her doubts about her strengths to support him, Lawrence had responsibilities beyond her and their growing feelings for one another. She could not be the person that made him turn his back on the people and tenants who needed him.

She wouldn't.

There was every possibility this could be the beginning of the end of their relationship, but she was willing to surrender all that grew between them. The thought of losing him, having only just found him, twisted at her heart and sadness pressed down on her. But if it meant Lawrence finally laid the demons that hovered over him to rest and resumed his duty at the helm of his family's estate, walking away was the right thing for her to do.

He walked to the window and stared towards the green outside. Esther glanced at Cornelia and she tilted her head towards Lawrence's back as though asking Esther to talk further with him.

She shook her head. Whatever happened next was Lawrence's decision. She might love him but . . . She stilled. She loved him. Her heart burned like an ember in her chest and icy-cold perspiration broke on her forehead as certainty of her feelings for him and of how she would suffer if she lost him bore down on her, but he had to be where he was most needed.

'Lawrence?' Harriet stood and approached him at the window, her face pale and the hand she touched to his back ever so slightly trembling. 'I can't do this alone. Mama . . .' She dipped her head, a tear rolling over her cheek. 'She is little changed. I need you.'

With potential loss squeezing her heart, Esther held her breath.

At last, Lawrence slowly turned and studied Harriet with a renewed affection in his gaze. He opened his arms and she stepped into his embrace. He closed his eyes and pressed a kiss to her hair. 'I'll come. Of course, I'll come. How can I not be there for you at a time like this after my desertion all those years ago? I will see Mother. I feel too duty-bound in my love for you and Cornelia to do otherwise.'

Cornelia's exhalation whispered beside Esther as she released her own breath.

It was done.

Lawrence would go home, and she prayed with all her heart he would find his healing.

Tears burned her eyes. But, oh, how she'd miss him.

38

When Lawrence's carriage entered through the stone gateway of Culford Manor, dusk fell as heavy and morose as his mood. Pitted stones crunched beneath the wheels as he and his sisters were jolted along the long avenue leading to the house. It neared nine o'clock, the hour purposely late and chosen by Lawrence with the forethought his mother might be abed for the night and he would have until morning to prepare himself to face her again.

It had been almost three years since he'd last set eyes on her as he'd bid her and his sisters farewell for a second time. Three years that had badgered his conscience as he'd fought against his familial duties.

He'd returned for his father's funeral and the memory of the day still lay like a sepia photograph in his memory. A grey and cold day in March, the Culford family, their staff and a few chosen tenants his mother had deemed of enough importance to attend. Lawrence had stood frozen throughout the service and burial at the local parish church, not so much as a twitch moving his statue-like state. His gaze had never shifted from his father's oak coffin, his heart impervious to his sisters' sniffles and his mother constantly dabbing her cheeks with a lace-edged handkerchief. For Lawrence, the funeral and wake afterwards had been the first steps towards forgetting the past and moving on. Now he was home to witness what could be the final death that would secure an end to his parents' torment.

The carriage slowed to a stop and his sisters gathered their purses and skirts, readying to alight, his nephews on either side of Lawrence peering through their respective side windows. A tinge of resentment pinched his heart that he'd left Rose and Nathanial behind for fear his mother's malice would touch them in even the smallest of ways. And, no matter how much he'd wanted her there, he'd left Esther behind too. There was no way on God's earth he would have subjected her to his mother and the person he would undoubtedly become now he was here.

He met his sisters' cautious gazes and forced a smile. 'Here we are, then. Let the games begin.'

A modicum of a smile curved Harriet's mouth, but Cornelia turned to the window and stared at the stone, slate-tiled manor house beyond, light glowing behind some of its many latticed windows. 'I wish I had your sense of humour, Lawrence. I feel nothing but dread.' She glanced at him, then Harriet. 'Promise me neither of you will breathe a word about David. I'll tell Mama about our separation in my own time. Do I have your agreement?'

Lawrence exhaled and ran his hands over the backs of Alfred's and Francis' heads. 'Of course. It might even be advisable to keep your counsel until we know just how long Mother has to live.'

Harriet took a sharp intake of breath. 'Lawrence, do not say such a thing!'

'Why not? Have you brought me here under false pretences and she's not at death's door, after all?'

'Of course, she is, but to mention her death so off-handedly . . . ' She glared. 'To positively wish it, is grotesque and beneath you.'

320

Lawrence matched her glare. 'Maybe, but provoking my anger is what she does. I've no love for her, Harriet. The sooner you accept that, the better. I hate that I've had to bid farewell to Esther with just the promise of a telephone call or letter once I know how the land lies. Whether you or Mama like it or not, Esther is important to me and I won't be happy if my return to this godforsaken place risks what we have between us.'

'How on earth could visiting Mama affect anything between you and Esther Stanbury?'

'Because I change when I'm here, that's why. Everything I despise about the place seeps inside me again like poison and I refuse to have any of it taint Esther's goodness.'

She flashed him a glare before snapping her gaze to Cornelia. 'You cannot keep the strife between you and David from Mama. It's not fair. I'm still upset that you chose to keep your troubles from me until yesterday. Mama has every right — '

'She has no rights as far as my family is concerned.' Cornelia's tone was firm, her determination clear. 'What interest has she shown in me or the boys since David whisked me away to a life she considered suitable? A life she told me time and again I should be profoundly and endlessly grateful for.' She faced Lawrence, her jaw set. 'I'll heed your advice and keep quiet about the separation until we are certain how things are. Come, McIntyre is approaching from the house. Lord only knows how he'll react to the children's presence, let alone how Mama will.'

Lawrence stood and stepped from the carriage, the hired driver holding open the door. With his back to the house and his mother's approaching butler, Lawrence helped the boys out and then his sisters.

321

Only when they were assembled as a unit did he face McIntyre.

The butler gave a discreet bow, his rheumy gaze running over the Manor's newly arrived visitors. He dipped his head first to Lawrence and then to Cornelia. 'Mr Culford, sir. Welcome home. And the same to you, Miss Cornelia.'

Harriet stepped forward. 'Is Mother awake, McIntyre? We will see her immediately, if she wishes it. Otherwise, we'll allow her to rest and see her at breakfast.'

Lawrence inwardly cursed. All he'd wanted was the time and space of a single night before being forced to face his mother in the morning. Harriet had put paid to that wish.

McIntyre dipped his head. 'She's awake, Miss Harriet.'

'Then I'll go —'

'She asked that only Mr Culford be admitted to her room this evening, I'm afraid.'

Annoyance burned through Lawrence's chest and he breathed deep. Why, in God's name, had he come back? He'd acted as little more than his mother's puppet. Something he'd stopped entertaining the moment he'd walked from the estate. Clenching his jaw, he glowered at McIntyre before striding towards the house, leaving the others to follow.

He was here now, and he'd see her right away. Like a razor-sharp cut through skin and flesh, if its impact was quick enough, he'd barely feel the incision. It was the aftermath that would linger with potent pain, but he'd have time to rebind the wound of dealing with his mother once he'd safely returned to Bath, Esther and the children.

The aged-oak front door stood open and Lawrence marched inside. Little had changed in the vast hall-way and the same musty, dark smells lingered in the air. Lawrence shivered and clenched his jaw against his father's ghost as it passed through him.

The ornate staircase that wound to the second and third floors stood to his right and two wing-backed chairs were placed before a low mahogany table to his left. Ahead of him, a long sideboard, polished to a high sheen, held an enormous floral bouquet in a crystal bowl, sepia photographs, that he had no desire to con-template, fanning either side in a variety of glass and silver picture frames. Two lamps with red and gold painted shades held sentry at the sideboard's edges, the lit sconces on the walls sending prisms of colour over the entire display.

He lifted his study to the walls, where his father's watercolours still held pride of place. Each painting depicted a season, a ball, a garden party or shoot-ing weekend that had taken place at the Manor. The pictures held none of the menace he associated with his father. Only happy times, laughter and good cheer resonated from the canvases.

Sickness churned inside Lawrence.

Was he the same chameleon his father had been? Hiding his true feelings like a great pretender, mas-querading through life so no one really knew him?

Except for Esther.

With her, he easily became the real him. The true him. The man he wanted her and his children to know for the rest of their lives.

Blood thundered in his ears, muting the sounds of his sisters and nephews entering the house behind him. Even when Cornelia rested her hand on his arm and Harriet's fingers closed around his, Lawrence couldn't look at them. To do so would chip away some of his anger that he needed to hold onto until he'd seen his mother.

Standing united with his sisters, he breathed deep. The acidic, poisonous stench of his childhood filtered into his nostrils, bile rising bitter in his throat. Digging into the many reserves that had got him through the last years, he reached for the tenacity that had made it possible for him to become a self-made man, a father, a hotelier and employer.

His mother could no longer affect his emotional state.

Abruptly, he drew away from Cornelia and Harriet and stepped back. 'Why don't you go to your bedrooms and unpack? As Mother has asked to see me alone, tomorrow is soon enough for you — '

'But, Lawrence — ' Harriet pleaded.

Cornelia shook her head. 'Lawrence, no. We'll — '

'This is what she wants. There is little point in aggravating her the moment we come here. Besides, it's for the best that I have this first conversation with her alone. I've no idea how I'll react to seeing her again. No idea what I'll think or feel. Please. Just allow me this time.' He took a breath and lowered his shoulders. 'I'll see you in the morning.'

Cornelia opened her mouth as if to protest further, before shaking her head and turning to her sons as they ran about the hallway, much to McIntyre's clear consternation. His aged face had the expression of a man chewing a particularly poor brand of tobacco, his eyes narrowed and his cheeks scarlet.

Harriet sighed and nodded. 'Tell Mama I'll come to bid her goodnight as soon as I hear you leave her room. She won't like for me to go straight to bed without speaking with her.'

Lawrence glanced towards the landing balustrade. 'You said she has her maid attending her.'

'She does, but that will hardly make her forget my absence. She knows I've returned, Lawrence. I must see her.'

'As you wish.' He turned to Cornelia. 'Take the boys upstairs or maybe even into the kitchen if they're hungry. I won't be long with Mother and then I think it best we all retire.'

Her steady, assessing gaze stayed locked on his and Lawrence returned her study.

She nodded curtly.

Clearly satisfied with whatever she'd read in his gaze, Cornelia gathered the children with a firm hand to each of their collars. 'Tomorrow will probably be here quicker than either of us would like.' She flashed him a small smile. 'Good luck.'

His sisters and nephews climbed the stairs to the landing, where Harriet disappeared one way and Cornelia and the boys, the other. When McIntyre sent him a sneer before heading along the hallway, Lawrence watched his retreating back until the butler had disappeared, too.

McIntyre had always bent to Lawrence's mother's every whim and demand. 'Yes, Ma'am.' 'No, Ma'am.' It had been nauseating as a child, even more so now. Culford's butler had been a silent spectator to Lawrence's treatment and abuse and Lawrence could not wait for the day when Harriet, or whomever their mother chose to bequeath the estate to, came to the decision McIntyre's services were no longer required.

Pulling back his shoulders, Lawrence inhaled a

strengthening breath and ascended the stairs, stopping outside his mother's room at the front of the house.

A montage of memories assaulted his mind and senses. Shouting, crying, the slap of his father's belt on bare skin, the slamming of his sisters' bedroom doors, his mother's reprimands joining his father's before she was urged away from the ugliness by the ever-present McIntyre.

Raising his knuckles, Lawrence tilted his chin, knocked and pushed open his mother's bedroom door.

Lawrence squinted through the semi-darkness. Candlelight flickered on the walls and canopy of the four-poster bed, the rich gold in the wall coverings shimmering. Although opulent, the space was drowned in the cloying, acrid scent of death and the fact this visit could be the last time he saw or spoke to his mother finally hit him. Before any amount of care could set in, Lawrence pummelled it back into the recesses of his stupid, weakening heart. Wheezing and a soft female voice reading aloud filled his ears as his strained vision fell on the shape propped against the bed pillows, a white nightgown shrouding his mother's emaciated form.

He flicked his focus to the woman sitting by the side of the bed, an open book in her lap.

Mae Townsend.

Trepidation skittered along the surface of his skin. What in God's name was she doing here? Where was the maid who was supposed to be tending his mother?

He hadn't seen Mae in years, a childhood friend who'd been another candidate on his parents' list of the local gentry's daughters they considered suitable for their son to marry.

Walking closer, Lawrence curled his hand around one of the bedposts. 'Good evening, Mae. It's somewhat of a surprise to find you here.'

'Lawrence.' She slowly stood, closing the book and clasping it in front of her. 'You're home.'

'Culford will never be my home.'

He looked at his mother. Her eyes were closed, her mouth slightly slackened. Anyone else might assume her asleep, but Lawrence knew differently. Her quivering eyelids and unearthly stillness illustrated that she feigned sleep in order to eavesdrop on his and Mae's conversation. Clearly, his mother was not quite at death's door if she still had the strength to perform. Well, if she wanted a show, she'd damn well have one.

Facing Mae, Lawrence crossed his arms. 'How long have you been tending Mother?'

She smiled softly, and gently touched his mother's knee through the blankets. 'She asked if I would look after her while Harriet went to Bath to fetch you home. You don't mind, do you?'

Lawrence carefully searched her expression for an indication of what part she had in an assured and mitigated plan fully orchestrated by his mother.

He shrugged. 'Not at all, I'm no longer a part of this household. What happens between these walls doesn't matter to me.' He dropped his crossed arms. 'I can see my mother is in good hands. I'll bid you good —'

'Lawrence? Is that you?' Ophelia Culford moved and tilted her head to the side on her pillow, her steel-grey eyes watery, yet as astute as ever. 'You came.'

He clenched his jaw. Her eyes were sunken and her cheekbones as sharp as blades beneath the thinness of her skin. Merely a shadow of the robust, unyielding

327

presence he'd known his entire life. When his mediocre concern treacherously rose once more, he clenched his jaw, shutting it down.

'I was sorry to hear you are so unwell, Mother.' He inhaled. 'But as I haven't had a message from you in months, I was surprised by your summons.'

'Nor have I received word from you.' She stared at him, her lips drawn into a thin line until she snapped her attention to Mae who'd resumed her bedside seat. She gently smiled. 'Mae has been wonderful while Harriet was away. Are you pleased to see Mae, Lawrence? Doesn't she look a picture?'

He turned to Mae. Her green eyes were gentle on his, her hands drawn perfectly together in her lap, her blonde hair swept into a pretty style, not a strand out of place. He nodded. 'You look quite lovely.'

'Thank you.' She dropped her gaze to her hands. 'It's been my pleasure to nurse your dear mama.'

He stared at her bowed head, his unease reigniting. He looked to his mother. 'Why am I here?'

'I'm dying, Lawrence. Can't I ask to see my only son once more? The physicians say I have days to live. I need you here.'

'Why?' He asked, hardening his heart to her imminent fate. 'If you asked for me on your deathbed, your motivation can only be money or the house. Which is it?'

Mae's sharp intake of breath sounded in the room.

Lawrence waited with only the crackle of a guttering candle and the painful wheeze of his mother's tortured breaths echoing around him. He straightened his spine. 'Well?'

Slowly, her gaze changed from gentle concentration to wariness . . . to anger.

328

Lawrence glared back as memories pummelled him. Her icy-cold scorn, her rushing to tell on him to his father, however slight the provocation. Her demanding that her son, time after time, be beaten, taught a lesson and reminded of the greatness that awaited him amongst Society. His ears filled with his father's yells, the whoosh of his belt through the loops of his trousers and the crack of leather on naked skin.

His mother glanced at Mae. 'Would you be kind enough to leave us alone, my dear? Please ask Cook to prepare my medicine and maybe some hot milk.'

'Of course, Mother.'

Her skirts rustled over the floorboards, softly muted by the rug before Mae left the room, quietly closing the door behind her.

Mother? Lawrence's patience snapped, and his body trembled with a suppressed aggression he hadn't felt for months. He was here on a command . . . a demand to marry Mae.

'Sit down, Lawrence.'

The frailty had disappeared from his mother's voice. The matriarch had returned.

Fury whirled inside him as he clenched his fists and purposefully remained standing.

He lifted his chin. 'I won't do it, Mother. Not again.'

'Pray, do what?'

'I am clearly here to pay court to Mae in preparation for a marriage proposal. It is never going to happen.' Lawrence held her gaze as Esther burned hot in his heart. 'I plan to marry for love next time or I'll never marry again.'

She emitted a sharp laugh, which quickly turned into a crackling cough. She held a handkerchief to her mouth and coughed again. Once spent, she faced him.

'You are needed to run the house and estate. You'll need a wife to oversee the staff and be a friend and guide to Harriet. The girl is weak. Goodness knows, I've tried my best with Harriet, but to no avail. No one of any stature will marry her while she lacks such backbone. Mae can teach and advise her. You've had your liberty away from your true duties for far too long. It's time to come home.'

'The Manor stopped being my home seven years ago. I have no wish to be here. My home is in Bath now. You are delusional if you think I'll return or even entertain the idea of marrying someone of your choosing. Abigail died without knowing true love. Do you think I'd ever doom another woman to such a fate?'

She glared. 'So, you mean to give up the estate in favour of your hotel? Your work? Don't be a fool, Lawrence. Thanks to your father, we are a moneyed family and you could soon be a wealthy man.'

'I have enough finance to keep myself and the children in everything we need for the rest of our lives. Maybe even my grandchildren's lives. I need nothing from you or this estate.'

Her cheeks darkened, and her eyes narrowed. 'You *will* carry out my dying wish. You will marry Mae and live here with Harriet. It is your duty to bring your children back to their true place. To teach Nathanial to be a landowner and Lord.'

'No.' Lawrence glared as Esther's strength and care seeped into his soul, giving him all the power and determination he needed to sever his mother's control once and for all. If Esther could fight to be all she was meant to be, he could, too. 'I'm truly happy for the first time in my life. I'll not surrender that for you, for Culford, not even for Harriet, if it means I have to

330

live in this house. My door will always be open to my sisters, but that door will not be to this manor.'

His pulse beat in his ears and his shoulders ached with tension.

His mother's cold gaze travelled over his face and person until she lifted her eyes to his. 'Then I'll instruct everything to be sold and bequeath every crown to charity.'

Lawrence stared, entrapment closing in on him. 'You can't do that. This is Harriet's home. We have tenants. People who rely on the land —'

'It is mine to do with as I will.' Her eyes burned with spite. 'If you have no care for —'

'I might not care for the house, but I do care for our tenants, the farmers who rely on our land to feed their families.'

'Then it is them you should think of now. It is nothing short of selfish that you left this house and never came back. Your father needed you to continue with his work when he became ill. He spent his entire life teaching you how —'

'Yes, with violence, torment and degradation. He wasn't a teacher, he was a tyrant.'

'Nonsense. If it wasn't for McIntyre, the groundsman and every other member of staff I've relied upon, the tenants you claim to care about would've been without their homes and work a long time ago. How dare you stand there and tell me of your worry for them after a seven-year absence.'

Shame and culpability wound tightly inside him. He could not deny his mother spoke the truth. Cornelia and Harriet had kept him informed of things at the Manor. David often visiting the estate to ensure his mother had all she needed so things ran smoothly.

Now David had gone to pursue a new life with a new woman. Who would pick up the reins? Claustrophobia gripped him. How could he leave and allow the men and women who relied on Culford to fear for their homes and livelihood? Men and women with families and young children to love and raise without fear of where their next meal might come from.

He glared at his mother, despising the quiet triumph in her eyes. 'Why not just give the house and estate to Cornelia and Harriet? They know more about the day-to-day running of the place than I do. They will be perfectly capable of overseeing everything with the support of the staff.'

'Harriet needs to marry well and bear children, as Cornelia has done. They were not raised to run Culford, and well you know it. You were raised to be here, sire heirs and continue the family name.'

Lawrence curled his hands into fists. The house, staff and land were the only things Harriet really loved. Their mother selling Culford would be a spiteful blow to her youngest daughter. One for which Lawrence was entirely convinced Harriet would forever hold him responsible.

The longer he studied his mother, the more he concluded her claims were intended to goad him into staying rather than her belief the estate was where he truly belonged. Could he call her bluff? Make out that he no longer cared at all about its demise? The tenants or his sisters?

Bitterness coated his throat as he pulled back his shoulders. 'So be it.'

His mother's eyes lit with satisfaction. 'You will stay?'

'No.'

She glared. 'No?'

'Every Culford stone, every acre of land and piece of furniture is steeped in a poison that has run in my veins for years. If you wish to hurt Harriet this way, then sell the estate because I couldn't give a damn.'

'Don't be a fool, Lawrence.' His mother's shaky voice rose. 'It is your duty to run — '

'I said no. I'll stay here until the time of your passing and then I will leave and never come back. Speak to your solicitor. Speak to your banker. I hope to God they convince you to pass everything to Cornelia and Harriet. Let them be rich, Mother. Over my dead body will I become your puppet in death as I was in life.'

He whirled towards the door, his steps heavy and assured.

'Don't you dare walk away from me. I am your mother and I demand you show me your respect.'

Throwing a final look over his shoulder, Lawrence stormed through the doorway and onto the landing.

'Lawrence! Come back here.' His mother's shout was overtaken with a bout of heart-rending wracks.

He pressed his spine to the wall then leaned forward, gripping his knees and trying to get his harried breathing under control. To break under the guilt and duty pressing down on him was not an option. How could he give up the life he'd built without help from his parents? How could he give up Esther when running an estate was so far from her life's vision? But what of his sisters? What of the tenants and staff?

'Lawrence?' Harriet's rapid footsteps padded across the landing. 'What on earth is happening?'

He exhaled and straightened. 'Go and see to her. I want nothing else to do with our mother.'

'What did she say to you? Are you to inherit the house? The estate?'

Lawrence briefly closed his eyes against the panic in Harriet's eyes. All she wanted was to stay here, in the place she'd been raised without violence. His mother was cruel to her core.

He touched his fingers to her cheek. 'She's threatening to sell everything.'

'But . . . ' She glanced towards his mother's door. 'Please, Lawrence, don't let her do that. What will I do? Where will I live?'

Resentment towards his mother burned in his chest. 'Don't let her have the final say, Harriet. Don't let her torment you with emotion or blackmail. If she chooses to sell, I'm sure the money will be bequeathed to you and Cornelia. You'll be wealthy and have choices. You can always live with me until you — '

'I don't want to live with you. I hate the city. I belong at Culford. This is my home. Where I feel the safest.'

The differences in their feelings towards the same place couldn't be compared, but Lawrence felt nothing but sympathy for his youngest sister. Harriet had done everything her parents had demanded and enforced. Now, there was a possibility she'd have no money and be ejected from the place she forever wanted to be her home.

How could he be the hand that severed all she'd ever known and loved? Praying his mother didn't hold true to her threat, Lawrence dropped Harriet's fingers. 'We'll work things out. Just take one day at a time.'

'But — '

'Go and see her. Let's get past her dying and then we'll face whatever comes next.'

Her worried gaze travelled over his face before she

334

nodded and turned, slowly approaching her mother's door.

Lawrence watched her enter his mother's room, before walking along the landing to the bedroom that had been his for many years. Anger and frustration poured through him and he slammed the door with such force a picture leapt from the wall onto the floor. He stared at the portrait that bore all his father's trademarks.

It was Lawrence as a boy, painted with rosy cheeks, bright eyes and smiling.

An image forced from his father's imagination. A fake. A misinterpretation of the life Lawrence once had here.

He slammed the heel of his boot into the glass, the crack and splinter finally breaking any hold his parents ever had over him.

39

Three days had passed since Esther had last seen Lawrence, and every hour she missed him more. Standing in the basement department at Pennington's, she stared at the mannequin in front of her. Rather than her focusing on her work or joining in the chatter of her colleagues as they sewed and pinned, her mind was filled with thoughts of the man she loved and how he fared with his mother in a place he despised.

She'd received a brief phone call from him the evening before unhappily telling her that he'd summoned for the children and Helen to join him at Culford. It seemed his plans to say his piece and return to Bath had been scuppered when he'd seen just how deathly ill his mother was. He could not find it in himself to walk away from his sisters a third time, leaving them to deal with their mother's death.

So, he would remain in Oxfordshire until his mother died.

Her heart ached with love for him, every hour he was gone was another hour she missed him more. Her selfishness was abhorrent. He could hardly be blamed for her falling in love with him, for growing to care for him as she did.

They'd parted on good terms and she appreciated his dying mother should be his only priority. Now was not the right time for them to further deepen their romance. He had responsibilities that did not include her or the Cause. He had a responsibility to a family who were in real crisis. Whenever he returned to

336

Bath, he should not feel he had to pursue the suffrage auction or ball in haste. The Cause could wait, if necessary.

No matter his feelings about his mother, Esther could not believe her death would not in some way affect him. She would do all she could to help him through this difficult time, but would it be enough when she rarely felt strong enough to care for her own heart? Lawrence came from a landed family and had duties to the estate, tenants and house she could only imagine.

Maybe she'd been foolish to spend the weeks contemplating what it would be like — *feel* like — to become a part of his wonderful family. To have daily time with Rose and Nathanial, to enjoy laughter and games as well as helping them through trying times.

Lawrence barely knew her, or she him.

Their hopes and declarations of a future together had often been said during their more intimate moments, when their responsibilities and commitments had felt a thousand miles away.

She'd surrendered her barriers and given him her heart, body and soul.

Pride for him swelled inside her. No matter what Lawrence felt about his mother, Rose and Nathanial would now have the opportunity of seeing where their father had been raised . . . albeit despicably. Was there a small chance that Lawrence might now consider that Culford was where he belonged?

She wouldn't blame him if he came to see that she, a lowly shop worker, one who gave her opinions freely and passionately, who wore her heart on her sleeve, for better or worse, an activist . . . would hardly make a suitable wife for so successful a man. And what of his children? Would he really be happy with her opinions, thoughts and desires being spoken or demonstrated in front of them?

She thought not.

But all she could do was remain strong and pray Lawrence returned to her.

A lump rose in Esther's throat and she snatched a pin from the cushion on her wrist to finish heightening the hem of the velvet skirt on the mannequin in front of her.

She stabbed the pin through the material and straight into her finger. 'Damnation.' She sucked at the glistening red blob that immediately broke and spread across her skin. 'Now, look what I've done.'

'Esther, are you all right?'

She straightened and took her finger from her mouth. 'I'm fine, Amelia. My mind is so distracted today, I just managed to stick myself with a pin.'

Her colleague frowned. 'Your distraction has been present for more than just today. You've been absent from Society meetings for over a week and even suggested to Miss Pennington I be given free rein for the new east window on top of the extra responsibilities I've already been given.'

Esther smiled. 'Because you are worthy of the task. Not because I'm out of sorts.'

Amelia frowned, her gaze uncertain. 'Are you sure there's nothing I can do for you?'

Hating that she'd allowed her emotions to hover so close to the surface her colleagues had cause to notice, Esther walked to a chest of drawers and pulled out a kit containing an array of bandages and tape. Dabbing at her throbbing finger with a tissue, she quickly covered it and tied off the small piece of gauze.

338

'I'm fine. I think I might leave a little early, though.' She faced Amelia and glanced around the room where her team worked dressing mannequins or at sewing machines. 'Some fresh air might help clear my head a little.'

'Good idea. We're only working on adjustments, rather than design or display work. If you can't escape early today, when could you?' Amelia smiled. 'Let us hold the fort for a while. If Miss Pennington asks after you, I'll say you left for an appointment.'

'Thank you.' Suddenly desperate to be away from the store and outside, Esther strode across the workroom and took her hat and purse from the wall hooks. 'I'll see you bright and early in the morning.'

She walked to the door and up the stairs until she entered the atrium. As usual, the shop floor teemed with people busy perusing and buying Pennington's sought-after merchandise. The store's signatory black and white bags were prevalent amongst the array of coloured outfits, sparkling counters, glittering perfume and jewellery. A soft violin concerto serenaded the floor as people meandered back and forth.

Satisfaction warmed her. No matter the doubts about her personal life, she hoped she'd always have Pennington's in which to take pride and pleasure.

Heading to the double doors, she nodded to the doorman and walked onto the busy street. The late June sky was a perfect blue, the sun shining, basking people in its soft warmth.

Esther breathed deep. A perfect time for a walk.

With nowhere in particular to go, she headed towards Victoria Park.

The sun beat pleasantly against her face as she passed shops, hotels and the music hall. She continued to walk until a poster pasted to a wall snagged her attention. She stopped short.

Votes For Women! Join the Society today!

Amelia was right. Not attending the Society meetings was completely uncharacteristic of Esther. She'd thought of little else but Lawrence and his family since he'd left. How could she have neglected her passion and purpose for Pennington's and the Society? These were the places where she was truly in her element. Where she spent time with like-minded men and women, who inspired and energised her very reason for being alive.

She turned, quickly sidestepping a horse and its rider as she hurried to the other side of the street. Ducking into the narrow alleyway that housed the Society's meeting place, Esther passed the tightly packed shops which lined either side, lingering in perpetual semi-darkness. With each step, the mouth-watering smells of spices, baking bread and sweet pastries filled her nostrils, the cobblestones beneath her feet baked dry under the summer's slowly rising temperatures.

Deeper and deeper, she ventured into the alleyway, until she came to a stop by the nondescript, darkly painted door between a haberdashery and an ironmonger, Esther glanced either way along the alleyway. Content she wasn't being observed, she curled her knuckles and knocked out the secret code, apprehensive it would most certainly have changed since the usual practice was to create a new one each week.

Footsteps sounded, before a small opening in the door was pulled back and Louise's deep brown eyes peered through. Her gaze immediately widened. 'Esther! It's so good to see you.'

Smiling, Esther waited for Louise to open the

340

door and then stepped into her friend's welcoming embrace. 'I'm sorry for being away this past week.'

'Don't be silly.' Louise released Esther and stood back. 'I'm sure you had good reason. Come in. Quickly.'

Silently admonishing herself for showing such a lack of subterfuge, Esther quickly stepped inside.

Louise closed the door. 'Come upstairs. You've arrived just in time.'

'For what?' Esther's curiosity ran wild with possible ideas the group of women had put into place since she'd been away. 'Have I missed a breakthrough?'

'Unfortunately, not.' Louise stopped outside a closed door and smiled sheepishly. 'But I've called an unscheduled meeting to discuss some new plans.'

'I can't apologise enough for being away. I've had — '

'Things going on.' Louise touched Esther's arm, her eyes kind. 'Don't be so hard on yourself. Obstacles and commitments are bound to come up for all of us, meaning we have to step away from time to time. The important thing is, you're back and, hopefully, ready for our next strategy.'

Louise led Esther upstairs into the meeting room, the noise levels high at the table of gesturing, chattering women. Their fiery energy seeped into Esther's stomach, and she embraced the excited tingling that followed.

It was here and at Pennington's where she truly belonged.

Lawrence had sped her heart with his wonderful gaze, erotic touch and scorching kisses, but it was in this room and at the store she could make changes in an unforgiving world. No matter how much she hoped Lawrence would return to her and find a way to heal, he bore the scars of his childhood so deeply, she feared he never would.

'Come and take a seat.' Louise waved Esther to the table. 'You have much to catch up with, but I hope you'll cast your vote tonight after hearing what we have planned.'

Quickly discarding her jacket and hat, Esther hung them on the stand by the door and walked to the table. She leaned over Louise's shoulder and eyed the detailed and meticulously drawn map laid out on its surface. Esther frowned. The road which led from The Circus, where Lawrence lived, to Royal Crescent had been drawn through with red pen.

The women's voices whirled around her.

Fire.

Explosives.

Paraffin.

Unease whispered through Esther, raising the hairs on her arms. What on earth were they contemplating? Was the group turning militant? Nausea rose in her throat. The possibility of something violent unfolded in front of her and, in that moment, Esther knew with absolute certainty she could not take part in anything that would endanger another human being, no matter the Society's struggles.

'So . . .' Cecilia Reed stood and pushed out her ample bosom, her eyes alight with an almost manic gleam. 'We need a volunteer to actually plant and light the explosive in the postbox and three or four volunteers willing to create distractions, if or when, they are needed.'

Esther stilled. 'Have we decided to turn suffragette?'

Louise gripped her arm, her cheeks flushed with

342

excitement. 'Yes. We've had enough, Esther. Our peaceful efforts aren't working. Last week, the post office was broken into and — '

'Wait. The post office?' Esther stared at her friend in horror. 'Were you or Wyatt hurt?'

'No. It was after hours and it seems whoever was behind the break-in knew that we spend Tuesday evenings with Wyatt's mother. Anyway, the post office wasn't their target. Our meeting room upstairs was.'

'What happened? Did they take something?'

'No, but they ripped all our plans and pamphlets to shreds and left some rather disturbing threats on our blackboard. Wyatt informed the police about the break-in, but they can do little with the perpetrator unknown. When he told the local MP, his appeal was dismissed out of hand.' Louise looked around the room, her jaw tight. 'So, instead of backing away after this challenge, we've decided to increase our presence and, if making a stand comes in the form of fire, so be it. No more peaceful campaigning. It's time to join the ways of so many in London.'

'But — '

'Everyone, could I have your attention, please?' Louise raised her voice above the cacophony bouncing from the walls. 'I'd like you all to welcome Esther back after her brief time away.'

Esther forced a smile even though some of the faces around the table — especially Cecilia's — were less than friendly, her absence clearly resented and suspected. Heat burned in the centre of her chest. If she made a stand against their plans, would she be ejected from the group permanently? The Cause still beat in her heart and burned in her blood.

She had to prove to herself that her passion could

be unwavering and strong in any circumstances. Or else she would be nothing more than the weak woman she vowed never to be. Maybe, with her input, they could ensure no casualties and certainly no fatalities.

'It's wonderful to be back and I hope to do all I can to support our fight. However,' she inhaled a shaky breath, slowly released it as she anticipated the backlash of her opinion, 'an explosive in a busy street will clearly put the innocent at risk. Would it not be better to start by smashing some windows after nightfall just as others have in Manchester, Liverpool and London? How about the town hall? We can ensure the building is empty before we strike, minimising the risk of anyone being hurt, but we would have made a solid statement.'

Cecilia crossed her arms. 'The decision to set fire to the postbox on Brock Street has already been made. You are either with us, Esther, or against. You cannot expect us to bend to your suggestions. The fight is continual. All of us have families. Some with jobs they are committed to also, but we are here. You need to prove your involvement or leave.'

Annoyance burned in Esther's cheeks. 'All I'm saying is, if we —'

'No. You have not been party to these plans and weren't even aware of the attack on the post office. Now, in order to prove your commitment to the Cause, shall I mark you down as the volunteer to plant the explosives?' Cecilia sneered in triumph and looked around the table. 'Ladies, any objections to Esther planting the explosive on Brock Street?'

A ripple of murmured agreements and nods circled the table.

Esther's stomach sank. How could she set fire to a

344

postbox so close to Lawrence's home? How could she set fire to anything knowing an innocent bystander could be hurt?

'Well?' Cecilia's hardened gaze bored into Esther's. 'Are you to be our volunteer?'

Esther looked around the table, trying her best to make eye contact with each woman. Slowly, the hostility lessened, and a few smiles of encouragement were sent her way. How else could she be accepted back into the fold? She had to concentrate on what was real.

She cleared her throat, her gaze locked on Cecilia's as once more Esther's suspicions rose that the woman's motives weren't always founded in obtaining the vote. It so often seemed Cecilia's goals lay somewhere else entirely. Esther's distrust lingered. 'As I was not part of the vote to turn militant, I won't plant the explosive, but I will be a lookout for bystanders or police to ensure no one is hurt.'

Louise tightened her grip on Esther's arm, her gaze relieved. 'Perfect.' She faced the group. 'We need a different volunteer to plant the explosive. Esther has her role at Pennington's to think about. If she's caught, she would most certainly lose her job. I believe public interest in Pennington's will be important to us in the future. It would be a mistake to jeopardise the advantage of having members working there.'

Esther's heart thundered. To lose her job at Pennington's was to lose half of herself, but the Cause was the more ardent half in that moment. She had to be a part of this plan. Maybe, if she was there on the day the explosive was planted, she could find a way to stop the plan from going ahead. She had Lawrence to think of, Rose and Nathanial and so many others.

She moved her hand to her stomach as it knotted with unwelcome trepidation . . . possibly another life, too.

She stood a little straighter and held Cecilia's gaze. Her stubbornness regarding militant action and the planting of explosives unnerved Esther to everything she suspected in Cecilia's personality. The woman was up to something. Something that most likely had less to do with the Cause, and everything to do with Cecilia's own needs.

Turning away, Esther took a deep breath. If Lawrence were to find out she had been involved in anything violent, she would lose him. But how could she not do this when these women were whom she relied upon? Women who would stand by her no matter her background, breeding or passions. Surely, she could find a way to make her mark without anyone being hurt? She had to follow through her mother's struggles and do all she could for Britain's women. She had no other choice.

40

Three days later, Esther's heart beat hard with trepidation as she entered the Circus. Having barely slept a wink for the guilt and fear of what was at risk today meant her mind was blurred and her entire being apprehensive.

At just past dawn, the sky was a pretty palette of grey and violet hues, the promise of another hot day evident in the gentle, slowly rising warmth. The early morning beauty should have filled her with a sense of peace and relaxation, but she felt entirely the opposite.

Lawrence had been absent for nearly a week and she'd only received a single letter from him, telling her his mother still clung to life, although barely. He'd then gone on to declare his love for Esther and her heart had almost burst with happiness. So much so, she had hurriedly written back to him asserting the same depth of feeling for him, Rose and Nathanial . . . despite today's plans sticking like condemnation in every scratch of her pen.

Shame pressed down on her as she reached his townhouse. She surreptitiously glanced at the windows, pitifully hoping for a glimpse of Helen, Cook or Charles. Surely, the sight of their innocent faces would be what she needed to forge forward and prevent her Society associate from firing the post box?

Lawrence's sand-coloured house blurred in her vision as tears burned fiercely in Esther's eyes. How had she become a part of this? Why had she once

347

considered that the suffragettes' practices were the way forward? Once upon a time, she'd been willing to do whatever it took to make the government sit up and take notice, but now . . . now she knew the suffragists way was *her* way. The only way.

The street was eerily quiet as though every bird and person waited for Esther to act, to prevent such a potentially dangerous undertaking from happening.

Although she hated that she'd become embroiled in anything so perilous, she still couldn't fully believe her future — Rose's future — would improve without some form of forceful action, even if she could never condone violence. More and more women languished in prison, a number being force-fed and, some said, even tortured and violated whilst under His Majesty's care.

The entire situation was a travesty.

An insult.

Women all over the country had been pushed into acting in a way they never would have considered if the government had come to their senses by now. Even though Esther's affection for Lawrence's family had grown, her fight for the Cause had not lessened. How was she to turn her back on her fellow associates when her belief in their goal still burned strong? Be that as it may, she *could* do something to prevent hurt or harm.

Lifting her chin against the nerves rolling through her stomach, Esther walked around the circular pavement of The Circus and into Brock Street. The houses and shops lining the street glowed softly under the luminosity of the emerging sun, their doors perfectly painted, and their brass knockers polished to a shine. Even the railings surrounding the lower floors with steps leading to the kitchens and servants' quarters bore nothing as much as a paint chip. Brock Street represented just another picture-perfect residential area of the wealthiest people who lived in Bath. All so very different compared to the shacks and slums lining the river. Injustice ran throughout the city. Rich versus poor. Men versus women. Family versus family.

On slightly trembling legs, Esther made her way along the street where the postbox stood at the other end. With every step, her heart thundered with fear of being observed from behind a curtain or falling under the wily gaze of a suspicious bystander.

Tension inched over her shoulders.

The street became increasingly occupied with each passing minute.

A young flower-seller with pretty blonde hair and delicate features was busy setting up her stall. Her age little more than sixteen. Esther's stomach dipped. How could the arson attack go ahead when such an irreproachable girl went about her business? Esther glanced across the street and further culpability pressed down on her. The young road sweeper could not possibly have been older than eleven or twelve.

Swallowing hard, she nodded hello to an early-morning walker and he nodded back, his gaze seeming to linger an unnecessarily long moment on her face. She snatched her gaze ahead. Could he be a constable in plain clothing?

Hurrying on, she dropped her chin, hoping the wide brim of her hat would go some way to concealing her face. From beneath lowered lashes, she recognised one of her fellow Society members assigned the duty of causing a distraction if the planter of the explosives was at risk of being intercepted.

Their gazes locked for a beat before the other woman strolled past Esther in the opposite direction. She glanced across the street and noticed Louise casually talking to a shopkeeper, her finger pointed along the pavement as though asking for directions.

All was in place. All was ready.

Esther's pulse beat erratically in her ears, her hands clammy as a group of three respectable-looking young men came towards her, their suits and starched collars impeccable. They looked no different than Lawrence would on his way to his hotel. Were they fathers? Sons or brothers?

Esther slowed as doubt and indecision whirled inside her, making her light-headed. Perspiration broke cold on her upper lip.

Another colleague entered the street from the opposite end and walked confidently towards the postbox, her hands wrapped firmly around the bulge in her overcoat.

Esther swallowed. This was it. It was about to begin. She had to do something . . . Now.

She snapped her gaze to the road sweeper. He was approaching the postbox, humming quietly to himself as he pushed his brush along the gutter, oblivious to the danger all around him.

She could not allow this to happen.

She wouldn't.

Just as her colleague reached into her coat, Esther launched into a run. 'Stop! You there, get away. Get away now!'

She ran at the young road sweeper as he stopped and stared, his dark eyes wide with surprise. Less than three metres away from the postbox, Esther grabbed him and sent them both tumbling to the cobblestones. Holding him tightly in her arms, she tried to shield him with her body as she flicked her gaze to the post-box, her arm throbbing with a warm wetness where her elbow had struck the cobblestones.

No! Somebody stop her! Please!

The words lodged in Esther's throat as her colleague whipped the package from beneath her coat and the flint from her pocket . . .

The entire street erupted into chaos.

Five or six tall, burly men hurtled towards Esther and her colleagues.

Ear-splitting shouts bounced from the houses as the woman who would've set fire to the box had her arms pulled behind her back, the flower-seller screaming as falling dustbins crashed to the stones, loud curses and shouting ringing out from every direction.

Before Esther could draw another breath, arms as thick as steel bands grabbed her from behind, pulling her upwards. She released the boy and her assailant's breath burned hot against her cheek. 'You're under arrest, Miss.'

Panic bolted through her before Esther blinked and her senses spiralled into fight mode. She turned and struggled against the man's broad, six feet tall stature, her fingers reaching for his face and arms. All around her, bedlam and disorder reigned as her associates' shouts joined hers, but no matter how hard she struggled, Esther could not gain leverage over the policeman who held her captive.

He painfully yanked her arms behind her back and Esther helplessly watched as Louise and the others were manhandled into the same position, their hats askew and faces etched with hateful anger.

351

Shock rippled through Esther as she witnessed such venom and loathing . . . such hatred. How had the Cause come to this?

Another man jumped in front of three of her colleagues and the bright flash of a photographic bulb caused lights to burst in front of Esther's eyes, momentarily blinding her. The constable restraining her shouted, ordering a spectator to take off after the photographer.

Guilt and shame gripped Esther at the sight of the tear-streaked face of the young road sweeper as he cowered in the arms of an older man and woman.

What did it matter that she'd been trying to save him? She was as guilty as any of her associates of terrorising these people. If her picture appeared in the morning papers, if she was named and shamed, it would be entirely just. Regardless of her intentions, she was now part of a group willing to risk the lives of others for their Cause.

'Let's be having you.' The policeman growled into her ear and dragged her towards a black carriage on the other side of the street. 'There are cells waiting for you and your friends at the station.'

Afraid and in a state of shock, Esther thrashed against him, but her efforts were futile as his fingers pinched painfully into her wrists. One by one, Esther and the others were dragged across the street, the passers-by growing in number, their expressions scornful as Esther was tumbled into the back of the carriage. Her back hit the side of the door and she sucked in a breath before she was shoved onto a long seat lining one side of the carriage. Warmth trickled onto her lips and she pressed her gloved finger to it. A smear of blood against grey.

A mark.

A stain.

Shame enveloped her.

All too soon Lawrence, her aunt and father would learn of her actions.

If there had been even the slightest hope she and Lawrence could be together, she had destroyed it. He had Rose and Nathanial to think of, his reputation and the patrons of his hotel. Any association with her would surely ruin everything he loved and worked for. Who could blame him for not wanting to be with her? Not trusting her, or wanting her in his children's lives?

'Don't you cry, Esther Stanbury.'

Esther looked to her associate sitting opposite her and swiped angrily at her cheek. 'I'm not.'

'Good.' The woman's expression filled with contempt. 'Because this is just the beginning. We will not give up and we will not surrender. Crying will do nothing. Action is what we need. You've ruined what could've been our biggest stand yet.'

Esther glared at her, anger burning in her stomach. 'Can you not take a moment to think how much hurt, pain and heartache our actions today might have meant for others?'

'Our only concern is the vote. Nothing more, nothing less.'

Esther trembled with suppressed resentment as she realised the fight was turning some women into people filled with anger and hatred. The venom in the woman's eyes was above and beyond passion, it gleamed with insanity.

She looked to Louise. 'We have to think of others. We must accept it isn't right for people to be harmed as we fight. Shouldn't it be that we can hold our heads high in front of family, friends, neighbours and loved ones? The Cause is about so much more than the vote. It's about women being part of the country's prosperity. For the government to see us as a cog in the machine of Great Britain. Just because I don't wish to see people hurt by our endeavours, does that make me any less committed to the Cause than you? I think not.'

Louise looked at her lap, her hands clasped together, her knuckles showing white. She met Esther's gaze, tears glazing her eyes. 'You're right. The planned explosive should not have happened and I'm ashamed I agreed to it. People could've been hurt or worse. Goodness knows what the police will see fit to do with us now. I don't think I've ever felt so ashamed.'

The air was heavy with tension. The confines of the rumbling, jolting carriage only adding to the unease and dissatisfaction unfurling inside Esther's heart and mind.

For years she'd fought to feel worthy, to count and be respected by men and women alike. Was the price of that fight to be arrested and cast in the same mould as anyone else who thought nothing of risking people's lives?

Esther looked at all the women in turn. 'Part of me is glad we are here. It is right that we've been arrested.'

Louise sighed. 'Maybe, but how did the police know to expect us?' She looked around the group. 'Could it be we have a spy in the group?'

Esther stared at her friend. Was Louise right? Esther's suspicions about Cecilia suddenly made very uncomfortable sense. 'If we do, then he or she will be exposed in time.'

The associate who'd reprimanded Esther earlier, gave an inelegant sniff. 'Hmm, and how is that *friend* of yours, Miss Stanbury?'

Esther frowned. 'Who do you mean?'

'Lawrence Culford, of course.'

Anger surged through Esther as she held the woman's gaze. 'Lawrence had nothing to do with this. He is in Oxfordshire and has been for days.'

The woman smiled, her gaze full of malice until, at last, she looked away. Esther exhaled. Enough was enough. Her worthiness came in her ability to love Lawrence, Rose and Nathanial. To excel at an occupation she loved and that made her feel valued as an integral part of Pennington's success. She would not forgo the Cause, but if the others chose to remain militant after today, Esther would set up a separate suffragist group of her own.

41

Lawrence sipped his coffee on the Manor's back terrace as he watched Rose and Nathanial play at the
fountain. The sun shone brightly and only wisps of
cloud marred an otherwise perfect blue sky. The
Manor's gardens were vast and credited as a fine
example of modern design and horticultural accom-
plishment throughout the county.

Yet his memories and feelings for Culford were
too painful for Lawrence to ever be able to appreciate
any aspect of the estate's beauty. From the numerous,
decades-old oak trees to the abundance of hybrids,
rhododendrons and clematis, the Culford estate
looked spectacular all year round.

To others. Not to him.

The six long days he'd been here had been tortuous,
and no amount of cajoling or encouragement from
Harriet had made Lawrence visit his mother more
than his obligatory daily appearance at eight o'clock
every evening to wish her goodnight.

Her sunken eyes, refusal of food and almost constant slumber indicated her imminent demise and with
that came the possibility that Lawrence might end his
constant contemplation of the past. He gripped his
coffee cup as Rose's delighted shriek carried across
the lawns.

His children had been absurdly happy here. Playing
with each other and their cousins had brought them
complete pleasure, evident in their delighted smiles
and happy eyes. Cornelia had stressed time and again

356

how happy Rose and Nathanial were at the Manor, but, no matter how vibrant her picture-painting, Lawrence could not see how he'd ever be able to raise his children here. He belonged in Bath. He belonged with Esther.

The life he might have had vanished the day he'd walked away from his father, and now, Lawrence embraced his self-made existence with eternal pride and pleasure. To return to the Manor and become its next Lord held no appeal whatsoever, but he was determined to do all he could for Harriet, the tenants and staff. The majority loved their lives in the country and would have no wish to work and live in the city. He'd considered offering them all positions at The Phoenix, but how were farmers who had been raised to love the land turn their hands to uniforms and service?

'Lawrence? Where are you?'

He hastily set down his cup and stood, shielding his eyes against the sun. His heart quickened as Cornelia hurried down the stone steps that zigzagged along the back of the house.

'It's Mama, Lawrence. It's time. Come quickly.'

A heavy numbness shrouded him. His brain and body shutting down and blocking out whatever the next minutes or hours might deliver. He would not falter in his detachment. He would not waiver in his resentment. If he did, he'd come back here, and his mother would've won. Again.

He turned to his children. 'Rose, Nathanial. Into the house. Find Cook. She'll have some biscuits and lemonade for you.'

Abandoning their game at the fountain, the children bounded across the expanse of emerald green grass, straight past Lawrence and Cornelia as she came to stand beside him.

She slipped her hand into his, her blue gaze afraid. 'You must see Mama straight away. Harriet is barely holding herself together and Mae is beside herself.'

Annoyance rippled through him. 'Why is Mae still here? I appreciate her looking after Mother while Harriet was away, but she's been back for almost a week and Mae is still coming here every day.'

'Because Mama insists upon it. She wants Mae to be your wife and, whether you like it or not, I think Mae wants that, too.'

'Well, she'll have a long wait because it's never going to happen.'

Cornelia inhaled and released a shuddering breath. 'Mama told me of her threat to you.'

'Well, she is out of her mind if she thinks I'll ever consider a second arranged marriage. I love Esther and, if she'll have me, I mean to ask her to marry me.'

'Oh, Lawrence.' Cornelia grinned and squeezed his arm. 'That's wonderful.'

Lawrence smiled and covered her hand with his. 'Let's get inside. We'll have plenty of time to consider what happens next. For now, we have to concentrate on Mother.'

She turned to the Manor and sighed, her shoulders lowering. 'Will this house ever be filled with happiness?'

'No, I don't believe it will.'

They walked towards the house, their steps quickening as they entered and mounted the vast oak staircase. Ignoring the paintings of his ancestors as they stared accusingly down on him, Lawrence stomped over the carpeted stairs and along the landing. Determination pulsed through him as he sought strength to face his mother's death and move forward with his life. The Culford estate would survive without him. If nothing else, he'd find a way for the new owner to ensure the jobs and homes of the tenants and staff.

Harriet would have little choice but to come to live with him and Cornelia in Bath. The thought of imposing such a thing on her reignited his resentment towards his parents but, in that moment, he couldn't think of any more agreeable or plausible course of action. If it came that Esther accepted his marriage proposal, he would find somewhere else for his sisters to live, if Esther should want that.

Not that he could imagine her agreeing to such a thing.

Once they reached their mother's room, Lawrence stopped and turned to Cornelia. 'If Mother's time has come, I'll return to Bath and make the funeral arrangements from there. You and Harriet can do what you will, but I'll not remain another day or night in this house. I need you to understand that.'

She ran her gaze over his face, her eyes full of empathy. She nodded. 'I do.'

Lawrence squeezed her hand and entered their mother's bedroom.

Mae and Harriet sat on either side of the bed close to his mother's pillows, alternating a wet cloth to her brow or a glass of water to her lips. His mother remained motionless despite their ministrations, water or spittle glistening over her chin and onto the cloth laid at the base of her throat.

Regret for the childhood he could have had enveloped Lawrence as he walked closer and he laid his hand on Harriet's shoulder, his heart icy-cold in his chest. Without looking at him, she lifted her hand and squeezed his fingers.

His mother lay so pale and still, it was as though she'd already gone.

If it hadn't been for the light lift and fall of her chest, Lawrence would've thought him and Cornelia too late to say their final goodbyes.

Mae gently cleared her throat. 'You could speak to her, Lawrence. She would love to hear your voice.'

He snapped his gaze to Mae's, irritation tightening his fingers on Harriet's shoulder. Why was she here? Although the blame entirely lay with his mother that Mae might expect a marriage proposal from him, Lawrence would make it perfectly clear he wouldn't marry her the moment they stepped from the room.

Turning to his mother, he released Harriet's shoulder and took his mother's hand where it lay on top of the blankets. Her tired bones were prominent through the thinness of her skin. He touched his thumb to her wrist where her pulse weakly beat. 'Mother? It's Lawrence.' *Please God, let this be the end.* 'It's . . . it's time to let go.'

Cornelia came to Mae's side and took her mother's other hand. 'Be at peace, Mama. Everything will be all right. We're here. Where you wanted us. Say goodbye now.'

Their mother's eyelids flickered open and she stared at Lawrence. Once a vibrant blue, her eyes were pale and milky, their vigour and passion, hatred and anger gone. She looked at him with gentle pleading and deep, deep sadness.

He drew in a sharp breath and forced a small smile. 'I'm here. Let go, Mama.'

She stared at him for a long moment, her gaze

unreadable.

Slowly, she turned her focus to Cornelia, and then Harriet.

His mother inhaled sharply, and then . . . silence.

She was gone.

The room filled with stifled sobs and mews as Harriet and Mae lifted their hands to their faces. Lawrence met Cornelia's gaze, his body trembling with relief that, at last, he was completely free. His coldness was hateful, but necessary, even as tears ran silver over Cornelia's cheeks.

Turning, he leaned over his mother and gently closed her eyes, his fingers hovering on her paper-thin lids as a new slice seared his already scarred heart.

'Thank you for all you've done for my mother, Mae, but you can go now. There is no further reason for you to stay.'

Her stifled sobs echoed in the room and Lawrence pressed his lips together against an apology. He would never marry her, and, unlike his mother, he would not hold people in bondage that he might one day change.

It would be better for Mae, for the family and him, if they all started a new life now his mother had finally given them liberty.

42

The clang of the station cell bolt being thrown back shook Esther from an exhausted, sleepy haze and she sat bolt upright on the thin mattress. A middle-aged and rather robust police officer entered the tiny room, accompanied by a younger male officer with bright orange hair who looked to be no older than nineteen, judging by the fluff about his chin.

Esther slowly rose, her stiff, cold bones screaming their indignation.

'Miss Stanbury, good morning.' The older constable languidly drew his gaze over her from head to toe. 'I trust you slept well.'

Esther pulled her lips together and held his gaze.

He gave a wry smile. 'Well, maybe not. I'm Sergeant Whitlock and this is Constable Godwin and we'll be conducting your interview today.' His jowls quivered as he tossed a notepad onto the bed and crossed his arms, his brown, silver-streaked hair sticking out in tufts above his ears. 'I hope an uncomfortable night has made you a little more reasonable in your behaviour and you find yourself ready to talk with us this morning.'

Esther glared, summoning every ounce of her strength. She might not have agreed with yesterday's plan, but she'd been a part of it nevertheless and had to think about the effects any adverse response could have on her associates. 'As I told the constable yesterday, I've nothing else to say.'

'Well, that is a shame, because, whether reasonably

362

or not, you will come to talk to me.' He turned to the younger officer. 'Take her to the interview room, Godwin.'

Godwin stepped forward and clamped one hand to Esther's elbow, the other to her shoulder. Although young, the officer was tall and broad, his iron grip surprising her as he manhandled her easily to the open doorway regardless of her attempts to resist.

As she was dragged unceremoniously along the grey bricked corridor, Esther's ears filled with shouts coming from the station's two additional holding cells.

'Don't give in to them, Esther!'

'Keep strong. Never forget the Cause!'

Her associates' encouragement gave Esther dual injections of courage and determination and she straightened, renewed energy to fight giving her strength to grapple her arm from the officer's grasp. 'Take your hands off me.'

Her triumph barely lasted a second or two before his fingers pinched into the flesh of her arm again and she was pushed into a room, made marginally lighter than her cell by two small windows high in the wall.

'Take a seat, Miss Stanbury.' Whitlock spoke with cold, calm authority.

After a moment's hesitation, Esther slumped into the single chair on one side of the table. What good would it do the Cause to fight the police on everything? Each campaigner needed to choose their battles carefully if they were ever to win.

Whitlock and Godwin lowered into the two chairs on the opposite side of the table, Godwin sneering, his eyes steely.

She flicked her gaze to Whitlock.

He leaned back, his lips pressed tightly together as

he stared at her with open curiosity, his brow lined. Exhaling, he crossed his arms. 'As much as your evasive action helped to prevent a tragedy yesterday, I have to be honest with you, Miss Stanbury. I'm finding it difficult to understand how a woman who works for Pennington's, a well-respected city department store, came to be involved with a group prepared to set fire to postboxes. I am completely baffled and bewildered that someone of your class and clear intelligence would be swayed by a group of women who have nothing better to do than cause trouble and considerable danger to the public.'

Esther said nothing, her heart beating fast despite her enforced and stoic expression.

Whitlock leaned forward. 'You and I both know there are peaceful campaigners for the vote. Why choose the militant route?'

His disbelieving tone and the way his eyes widened as though he studied a prehistoric creature rather than a woman fuelled Esther to defend herself. 'As much as I understand why militant action is frowned upon, many women feel they are beyond the freedom of choice, Sergeant. The peaceful route hasn't proved fruitful, so some campaigners feel they've no alternative but to try other tactics.'

'Some campaigners? Are you saying you weren't a willing participant in yesterday's events? That you were forced into Brock Street, forced to accompany a potential bomber and only inclined to intervene when innocent people were put at risk?'

'I . . .' Esther pressed her lips together. If she betrayed her colleagues, she'd be blacklisted, cast out and excluded. If she was to persuade Louise and the other women to execute only peaceful campaigns from now on, she had to remain part of the organisation for as long as possible. 'Now you've arrested me, isn't it my right to know what happens next? I am under no obligation to answer your questions.'

He smirked and glanced at Godwin who shook his head. Whitlock fixed his gaze on Esther once more and she shifted in her seat, her heart thumping and her shame burning like a white-hot ember in her stomach.

She swallowed. 'All we want is the vote, Sergeant. As members of society, of humanity, women deserve to have their wants, wishes and desires added to those of men whenever government are making decisions that affect us all. We are half of the human race, are we not? How can fifty per cent of people in this country be ignored as though they do not matter? Can't you see how ridiculous that is? Does the reality not sound as ludicrous to you as it does to me? By having no vote, we have no voice. We are merely standing up for what should be our legal right. Our daughters' legal right.'

'Daughters? You're an unmarried woman. Are you telling me you have a child born out of wedlock?'

Esther glared. 'Just because I'm not yet a mother does not mean I don't care for the frustrations of the women who are. The fight isn't solely about me, Sergeant, it's about every woman in the country.'

'So, everything you're doing is about women and their roles in society, correct? About a contribution they can make that men have yet to understand?'

Esther narrowed her eyes, his irony curling her hands into fists beneath the table. 'Yes.'

'Then answer me this.' He leaned his elbows on the table, his brown eyes darkening. 'How is acting with violence, endangering the lives of other women and their children, helping us to see you as calm, law-abiding and decent people who can make informed, intelligent, level-headed decisions? Behaving as you are makes you little more than a threat to others. If you'd succeeded in your attempt yesterday, you would've killed at least one innocent bystander, making you a participant in murder. Your methods are merely strengthening the logic preventing you from the vote.'

Esther stared, her resolve wavering. He was right. Yesterday would've painted them as little more than selfish. Even deranged. What could she say or do without risking herself and her fellow associates, languishing in cells along the corridor, having to face steeper charges? She didn't doubt her saving the road sweeper had helped her case, but what of Louise and the others?

She pulled back her shoulders. 'What will happen to my associates?'

'They will be interviewed and dealt with accordingly. They are not your concern, right now. You should be grateful we received a tip-off to yesterday's events and were there to prevent what could have been a catastrophe. Don't you agree?'

Esther stared, her heart beating fast as every one of her suspicions about Cecilia Reed rose. 'You received a tip-off? May I hazard a guess as to who that was?'

The sergeant narrowed his eyes. 'No, Miss Stanbury, you may not.'

'I'll say her name anyway. Cecilia Reed was behind your presence. I am willing to wager my liberty on it.' She lifted her chin. 'Well, am I right?'

He returned her stare, his cheeks flushing with

tell-tale guilt. 'Miss Stanbury — '

'Say no more.' Esther shook her head and huffed a laugh. 'I am glad to have my beliefs confirmed. You no doubt pay a fine reward for any information that might lead to the imprisonment of militant campaigners. Cecilia is not one to shy away from monetary gain, I'm sure. Yes, our actions yesterday ran the risk of endangering innocent people and I did all I could to save that young boy. No doubt my associates will be angry I put a stop to the wanted outcome, but, at the same time, I understand why women have been pushed to act by whatever means necessary. To stand their ground and find a way to be heard. Regardless of how that might be achieved.

'If government would only listen and take us seriously, campaigners wouldn't resort to violence and the destruction of property. I fear the campaigners' actions will only grow in fervour and aggression the longer we are ignored. The more desperate women are to be heard, the more they'll increase their efforts, and every time they fail, more blood will be on yours and the government's hands . . . ' She raised her eyes to the black and white picture of the King hung on the wall opposite her before meeting Whitlock's eyes once more. 'On the King's hands. If peaceful action continues to be ignored and only acts of supreme violence lead to a breakthrough, it will prove that is all men understand. I have absolutely no idea when or how we'll secure the vote, Sergeant, but mark my words, we *will* secure it.'

He studied her, colour mottling his cheeks as a vein rhythmically throbbed at his temple. 'You're making a grave mistake by remaining resolute in this, Miss Stanbury. I can easily keep you and your associates here for a second night. How would that be?'

Thoughts of Lawrence and the children seeped into her mind and a prickling burned behind her eyes. She had to stay strong. For herself. For her associates. For *all* women. She lifted her chin. 'I'll stay here for a second and a third, if that's what I must do. The fight has only just begun.'

'Then that is a shame.' He picked up his notebook and stood. 'A young, lovely-looking woman like yourself could have a bright future ahead of her. If you continue with this nonsense, you'll find yourself without friends, a job, no chance of marriage or the children you state you think of in your campaigning. Each time you're caught doing something you shouldn't, you'll be arrested, and your sentence lengthened. But if that's the life you choose, so be it.' He rose and turned to Godwin. 'Take her back to the cell, Constable. It seems Miss Stanbury is more than happy to stay another night with us.'

Esther trembled with suppressed frustration as she glared at his turned back before Whitlock opened the door and disappeared into the corridor. Tears pricked her eyes once more and she swallowed, grappling for a hold on her fragile emotions.

Godwin's huge hands clasped her arm and shoulder and she was marched from the room and along the corridor towards the cells.

Whitlock's words of warning reverberated in Esther's mind, muting the shouts of encouragement from Louise and the others as she walked past their cells. She entered her own cell and sat on the bed, defiantly glaring at Godwin until he'd shut and bolted the door.

The noise and shouting filtered through the walls, speeding her pulse as Esther leaned her back against the cold stone wall and closed her eyes.

Lawrence's handsome face blurred with Rose's and Nathanial's as tears slipped from beneath her closed lids.

How could she stop campaigning now? How could she turn away from the women she had stood side by side with for so long? Her belief in the Cause and the rights of women consumed her as much as her love for Lawrence. She felt the same exhilaration, power and commitment whenever she fought against the authorities as she had when she'd lain in Lawrence's arms. She could not be with him and stand with women who turned militant. She had to think of her family, Lawrence, Rose and Nathanial.

Her hand wandered to her stomach. An unborn child. One she prayed Lawrence would embrace rather than reject. And what of her job at Pennington's, Elizabeth, Joseph and Amelia?

Swiping at her damp cheeks, Esther stood and pulled back her shoulders. Whatever happened next, the fight for the vote had to go on. *She* had to go on.

43

Lawrence entered Pennington's and headed for the grand staircase. Excitement pulsed through him at the prospect of seeing Esther again after more than a week apart. A week that had been draining, challenging, but also incredibly enlightening.

It had taken his trip to Culford, and maybe even the death of his mother, to realise he had to take what he wanted — and who he loved — now or forever regret it. Once his mother's final Will and Testament had been read, he, Cornelia and Harriet would know whether Ophelia Culford had gone forward with her threat to sell the estate.

If she had, then her children would work things out together. If she hadn't and done as Lawrence had asked and passed the estate to his sisters, he would do everything in his power to support them in their plans and work.

The third option, the one that weighed the heaviest, was if his mother had named him her heir. If that turned out to be the case, he would somehow find a way to either make peace with himself and his childhood home or he would ask Harriet if she would like to live at Culford and manage it in his absence. Cornelia, too, if that was what she wanted. Yet he had a strong feeling his eldest sister's plans stretched beyond their past and far into the future.

As did his.

A person's experiences, whether they be joyous or heartbreaking, shaped who they became. He dreaded

370

to think what might have happened to his parents for them to become such bitter adults. Whatever had taken place, he was utterly convinced it had been bad enough for them to join forces in raising Lawrence with resentment, violence and cruelty. Now they'd gone, he had to take what they'd taught him to be better, live better and, most of all, love better. That started with Rose and Nathanial and ended, he hoped, with Esther.

He took the stairs, edging through the crowds coming in the opposite direction and past the women standing at the mahogany banister with an optimum vantage to observe the atrium. He smiled. Pennington's was indeed a place people longed to see and be seen. Since he'd got to know Esther, he'd come to fully understood her passion in her work for the Cause and Pennington's. If she should ever accept his hand, he would make it clear he understood her joy and need to work. It was part of what made her such an amazing woman. A woman with whom he wanted to share his life and his children's lives.

He'd hidden behind a false veneer, playacted happiness and satisfaction, and so often become uncertain and second-guessed his choices. Yes, he wore his success well and loved Rose and Nathanial more than life itself, but, until now, he'd never quite managed to shed the skin battered and scarred by his father's words and belt.

Now, for the very first time, he was free. Untethered and ready to live authentically with his family and the woman he loved. No more hiding. No more believing he wasn't as deserving of happiness as much as the next person. No more repressing his feelings of fear, rejection or ridicule. Instead, he'd wear his heart on his sleeve and give his love in a way that was strong and assured.

He was not his father. He was a man who wanted to share his life with the first and only woman he'd ever truly loved.

He reached the ladies' department and strode between the alabaster posts at its entrance, happiness and joy rippling through him. The space teemed with giggling, chattering women as young shop girls bustled left and right, their arms filled with bolts of satin and cotton, or draped with dresses and hats of every imaginable colour. He scoured the room for Esther, hoping she was here rather than hidden away in the basement department.

Spotting an older woman at the counter, her pen moving at lightning speed across a ledger, Lawrence removed his hat and approached. 'Excuse me. Might I interrupt you?'

She looked up, her grey eyes glazed in concentration. 'Hmm?' She blinked and her eyes cleared, her smile slipping into place. 'Oh, pardon me, sir. I was immersed in my work. How might I help you?' She offered him her hand. 'I'm Mrs Woolden, the head of the ladies' department here at Pennington's.'

Lawrence took her hand. 'Lawrence Culford. It's nice to meet you.'

'Oh, you're . . .' Her smile slipped, her eyes a little panicked. 'Mr Culford.'

'Yes.' He smiled. 'I was hoping to catch Miss Stanbury before she left for lunch. I've booked a table for us at The Pump Rooms as a surprise.'

The woman's cheeks had paled, and she glanced left and right before facing him again. 'You don't know, do you?'

'Know what?' Lawrence's concern deepened as he looked towards the department entrance. 'Esther is well, isn't she?' Her gaze flitted about the room and Lawrence stepped closer. 'Mrs Woolden?'

'It really isn't right that you should find out this way.'

'Find out what?'

Her shoulders slumped, and she sighed as she waved him to the edge of the counter.

Foreboding tip-tapped along Lawrence's spine as he followed her. 'Mrs Woolden, if something has happened to Esther —'

'She's . . .' She urged him closer with a swift flap of her hand, her voice lowered. 'She's been arrested.'

'Arrested?'

'Shh!'

Lawrence huffed a laugh as shock reverberated through him. He lowered his voice. 'That's impossible. Surely, you are mistaken? What on earth would Esther do to —'

'She was part of a group intent on setting fire to a postbox, that's what.' Mrs Woolden's gaze filled with disapproval as she shook her head. 'It's a disgrace. I wholeheartedly support the fight for the vote, but to resort to violence? No. It's just not the done thing by any man *or* woman and I'm thankful Miss Pennington and Mr Carter agree.'

Joseph stared. Esther had been arrested? He swallowed and squeezed his eyes shut before opening them again. 'What have they got to do with this?'

'They're her employers, Mr Culford. This has everything to do with them. However Miss Pennington or Mr Carter feel about the Cause, they cannot be seen to advocate violence. Too much is at stake for the store if the masses hear that they've supported Esther in her actions. She's taken a risk and is now suspended from her duties until Miss Pennington and Mr Carter have heard Esther's side of the story.'

'Suspended? But Esther would never be a part of anything that might harm others. Surely, there is some misunderstanding.'

'There is most definitely no misunderstanding, sir. If there were she wouldn't be held at the police station.'

Sickness rolled through him. Had he really got Esther so wrong? Had he mistaken her passion for change for something harder, colder? He had to speak with her.

'She's at the station now?'

'I believe so. Tonight will be the second night they've kept her there. Mr Carter visited this morning to see if he could do anything to persuade the police to release her.'

'And the police refused to let her go?'

'If what I overheard Mr Carter saying to Miss Pennington this morning is correct, they've set an astronomical amount of bail for Miss Stanbury. If she's to be home this evening, a sympathetic soul with very deep pockets will have to take pity on her.'

Anger surged through Lawrence and he clenched his fingers. 'For the love of God. Bail is meant for real criminals who are a threat to society, not women trying to be heard.'

'Mr Culford, you must keep your voice down.' Mrs Woolden shot her gaze around the department and pulled him deeper into the corner. 'If Esther had been successful in her mission, she would have been a bona fide threat to society. Can't you see that? The police are doing their job.'

What in God's name had pushed Esther into thinking she had no other choice but to resort to violence? Disappointment and anger unfurled inside him. Hadn't she thought of the innocent? How could he forgive her for this? How could he allow her to be around Rose and Nathanial? The smallest crack began to splinter across his heart. Had he been a fool to love and trust her?

He faced Mrs Woolden. 'Had she been herself before this? There was nothing out of the ordinary in her manner or words?'

'Not really.' Mrs Woolden frowned. 'I suppose she's been more down and withdrawn these past few days than usual. In fact, I've tried speaking with her, as has Miss Pennington, but to no avail.'

Lawrence slowly nodded. Was it because he'd left that Esther had felt pushed to such radical action? That made no sense. She had urged him to visit his mother. To try to reconnect with a woman from whom he'd been estranged for years. Yet, he could not think of any other reason for her to do such a thing other than feeling she'd been abandoned a second time. Or was this all about the Cause and she was now prepared to do anything she had to if it brought about a faster result?

Putting on his hat, he nodded to Mrs Woolden. 'I must go. Thank you for telling me.'

She touched his arm. 'Mr Carter asked the police if there was anything he could do to aid her comfort, but they sent him away. There's only so much Pennington's can do for their staff, Mr Culford. We're responsible for our decisions away from the store and should always be aware of how they'll affect Pennington's reputation.'

'I understand, but I have to do all I can to get her out of there. After that . . . ' He clenched his jaw. 'After that . . . '

'You'll be better off thinking of those lovely children I hear you have than your desires. I thought the world of Miss Stanbury, but this — '

'Could be a mistake. Let us consider her innocent until proven guilty.'

She studied him before her gaze slowly softened. 'You're right. Good luck, Mr Culford.'

With a curt nod, Lawrence hurried from the department, apologising as he knocked and bumped into staff and customers. He'd had little choice but to visit his mother on her deathbed. Esther had said if he neglected to do so, there was a chance regret would linger in the same place as his childhood beatings. She had understood he had to go and loved her all the more for persuading him to do so. Did her recent actions stem from her fear of being left alone? He suspected it could only be that which made her feel cornered to do anything that meant unity with others.

She would fight for what she felt was right, to be a part of something bigger than herself regardless of the consequences. A passionate woman. A potentially dangerous woman. Yet with a deep sense of equality and freedom that he loved so very much.

Lawrence rushed down the grand staircase and through the atrium. How could he have not seen something like this coming? He, of all people, knew how frustration and resentment festered and built until it exploded into physical and psychological fury. Sometimes, infinite amounts of pressure bore down on people until they lost complete control and did whatever was necessary to escape the bondage to which they were subjected.

But he would never condone what Esther had been a part of. He worried he would never find it in himself to forgive her either.

Jogging along the street, Lawrence dipped and ducked through the crowds, swaying between carts and prams, dogs on leads and parasols hovering so close to his head he risked losing an eye.

At last, he turned into the street housing Bath's police station.

He took the steps two at a time and burst through the double doors, heading straight to the wooden counter and the sergeant standing behind it.

The sergeant's brow creased, his gaze sombre. 'Might I help you, sir?'

Lawrence forced himself to take a step back, keep the volume of his voice to a minimum. 'Yes. I believe you're holding a Miss Esther Stanbury?'

'We are, sir. Is she a relation of yours?'

'I'm her . . . a family friend. I'd like to speak with her, if I may.'

'I'm sorry, sir, but that's not possible.' The sergeant looked to the papers in front of him. 'There might be a chance she'll be released tomorrow. If I were you, I'd come back in the morning.'

Lawrence clasped his hands to the countertop, his frustration bursting wide open. 'What is the amount of her bail? I'd like to pay it.'

The sergeant held his gaze before shaking his head. 'As far as I know, it will be a fine to be paid rather than bail, sir. But, either way, I don't think it would be wise for you to settle the amount due. These women are not meant for saving.'

'Saving her isn't my intention. Believe me, Miss

Stanbury is strong enough to save herself. All I want is to give her the chance to explain herself. Doesn't everyone deserve that?'

The sergeant stared for a long moment before exhaling a heavy breath. 'As you wish. If you insist on paying for her release despite her intended actions, you're clearly a commendable *friend*, sir.' The sergeant stood back from the counter. 'Take a seat. I'm sure Sergeant Whitlock will want to speak with you.'

'Sergeant Whitlock?'

'The officer in charge of Miss Stanbury and her associates, sir.' He pointed over Lawrence's shoulder. 'Have a seat.'

He walked away, and Lawrence slowly made his way to the five wooden chairs lined up against a far wall. He sat and stared blindly ahead as he waited, fury, confusion and hope that this was all a misunderstanding whirling through him on a terrifying wave.

44

As perspiration trickled down her back and between her breasts, Esther paced another circuit of the cell, the dank and musty smell of urine and stale heat further permeating her skin. In the hours since she'd spoken with the sergeant, she'd managed little sleep, even less food and no liberty from her thoughts.

Would she spend tomorrow night here, too? The night after?

Whitlock had spitefully told her that her fine had been set at ten pounds for her and each of her associates. More than a year's salary for the majority of people in Bath. The amount was clearly meant as a deterrent to others fighting for the Cause. Several women and men had come in offering a room to the women upon their release, but who had ten pounds to spare for the release of a family member, let alone a stranger?

Aunt Mary now knew of Esther's incarceration and had left a message at the station's front desk which Sergeant Whitlock had allowed Esther to read. Although her aunt was 'utterly appalled' at Esther's involvement, she said she would do her best to gather the money together.

Esther closed her eyes. She'd hardly blame her aunt if she entirely gave up on her wayward niece having only heard the police's side of the story.

Humiliation burned hot at her cheeks. It didn't bear thinking about approaching her father. Lord only knew what Viola would have to say once she learned of Esther's arrest.

The heavy thud of boots on the corridor's tiled floor sounded beyond her cell door and Esther stilled.

Closer and closer they came until they abruptly stopped outside.

The bolt on her cell door was eased back and Esther lifted her chin.

The door opened, and Sergeant Whitlock stepped inside, Constable Godwin, like an ever-present shadow, once again behind him. The sergeant looked her up and down before meeting her eyes. 'There's a gentleman in the lobby willing to pay your fine.'

Esther's heart thudded in her chest.

Lawrence.

It had to be him. Who else would come to her aid this way but him?

She would not take Lawrence's money. What on earth must he have felt when he returned to Bath and learned of her actions and ensuing imprisonment?

Good God, were hers and her associates' faces splashed across the papers? Nausea coated her throat. She'd lose her job at Pennington's, Louise would lose her customers at the post office . . .

Lawrence could only be offering to pay her fine out of duty or kindness, which she was no longer certain she deserved.

Feigning nonchalance, she crossed her arms over her hammering heart. 'I know no gentleman with that kind of money.'

'Well, he claims to know you. Do you want me to send him on his way?'

An ache started in the pit of her stomach and rose to her heart, but she nodded. 'Yes.'

'Was that a yes, Miss Stanbury?' He leaned towards

her, his hand at his ear. 'You'll have to speak up. Did you say yes?'

She nodded again, further verbal confirmation sticking like a spike in her throat.

'Then I would take a moment to think about this situation very carefully. You see, after tonight, we can't keep you at the station. You'll be transferred. To prison.'

Esther flinched. 'Prison?'

'Prison.' Whitlock raised his eyebrows. 'Do you want to know who this kind, clearly misguided gentleman is who wishes to come to your rescue?'

'If it's who I suspect, Lawrence Culford is anything but misguided.' Her temper snapped to hear Whitlock saying anything negative about the man she loved. 'He's loyal, strong, caring and the most resilient man I know. I'll thank you to keep your erroneous judgement to yourself.'

He smirked and glanced at Godwin. 'Looks like a certain gentleman can provoke Miss Stanbury's anger as much as her claim for the vote.' He met Esther's gaze, his eyes darkening with clear irritation. 'What's it to be, Miss Stanbury? Do you wish to leave here with a caution or enjoy another night at His Majesty's pleasure?'

Hopelessness swirled inside her as Esther looked between Whitlock and Godwin. What could she do locked in a cell? How could she explain to Lawrence the part she'd played in yesterday's events, or even comfort him after visiting his mother? Had his mother died? Was that why he'd come back to the city? Her heart ached.

She had to see him and prayed he listened to her. 'And what of my associates?'

'They're none of your concern. Are you leaving? Yes or no.'

Her heart heavy with guilt that she was to be freed and the others not, Esther nodded. 'Yes, I'd like to leave.' At least if she was free, she could do something to aid Louise's and the others' release and try to make them see that violence was not the way forward . . . once she'd thanked Lawrence and endured the disappointment he was certain to be feeling. 'Thank you, Sergeant.'

'That's more like it.' Whitlock held his hand out towards the door. 'After you, Miss Stanbury.'

Forcing her head high, Esther battled the urge to run through the corridors and straight into Lawrence's arms. She had no idea what had occurred during his return to his childhood home. No idea what his sisters might have said about Esther and her new and unexpected presence in Lawrence's and his children's lives. He would now presume her to be militant. A part of something more dangerous and controversial than she'd been when he'd left.

Whatever his motivation for paying her fine, it could not be love. He would never jeopardise his children's welfare or happiness by openly connecting himself to an activist determined to see through her most wanted desire by whatever means.

So, why was he here? Why had he walked into a police station and offered money for her release?

Whatever the reason, she had to guard her heart. Had to keep it from further splintering when she saw him. For her sake and the sake of their baby.

She walked ahead of Whitlock and Gibson to the front of the station and through a gap in the counter. The moment her gaze landed on Lawrence, her heart

382

betrayed her, tears leapt into her eyes and her legs trembled.

He turned and everything she'd warned herself against vanished. She loved this man with all her heart and, if the cold, steady way he stared at her was anything to hold measure by, she had entirely lost him.

'Mr Culford?' Whitlock's authoritative voice boomed across the station, causing several bystanders to look their way. 'Miss Stanbury, sir.'

Lawrence kept his gaze on Esther's as he came towards her, seemingly heedless to Whitlock, Gibson and every other officer and person around them. It was impossible for her to see anything but him, too.

Her heart quickened as his presence enveloped her. Even though his gaze was yet to soften, her shoulders relaxed and her heart swelled with tenderness, her fingers itching to touch him as though to reassure herself he was really there.

Stopping in front of her, he looked deep into her eyes and his face blurred through her tears. There was so much she had to say to him. So much to ask his forgiveness for. If he wanted her, she would do whatever she could to keep true to herself as well as being the woman he needed her to be for him, Rose and Nathanial. Wasn't that true love? To maintain your own ardent desires and dreams but also compromise to ensure the happiness of your loved ones, too? Wasn't that what she'd wanted from her father?

Slowly, Lawrence's gaze softened as though he'd read her thoughts and seen the apology, the promise to loosen the stranglehold on her independence to be with him.

Abruptly, he turned as though remembering where he stood. He faced Whitlock. 'Let's get this sorted out, shall we?'

'Yes, sir, but first I need to ensure Miss Stanbury understands the conditions of her release.'

Esther dragged her study from Lawrence and faced Whitlock.

'You are now under caution, Miss Stanbury. As you were not the one intending to set fire to the postbox, no further charges will be made. This time. However, if you commit another offence, resort to anything that could endanger others, you will be arrested again and charged with something that will most certainly mean imprisonment. Do you understand?'

Shame burned through her entire body as Esther held the sergeant's stare, Lawrence's study burrowing into her temple. She swallowed. 'I do.'

Whitlock nodded. 'Good. Then why don't you take a seat while I sort out the particulars with Mr Culford?'

With a final glance at Lawrence's hardened jaw, Esther walked to the line of chairs at the edge of the room and sat, her body trembling. What happened next? Where would she and Lawrence talk? Would he walk her as far as the station steps and then leave? She had no idea of his intentions.

The minutes passed like hours as Lawrence talked with Whitlock, handing over cash for the fine and signing his name to a piece of a paper.

At last, he came back to her and offered her his arm.

Tentatively, she slipped her hand into the crook of his elbow and stared at his turned cheek as he led her from the station into the street.

Once they had walked along the road and turned a corner, he steered her into a side alley.

Esther swallowed at his angry expression. 'Lawrence —'

'I think it only fair I speak first, don't you?'

She stilled, the disappointment in his eyes was palpable and she stepped back. 'I tried to change their minds, Lawrence.'

'So the sergeant told me. He told me the police have been following your suffrage group for a while, suspecting a jump to militancy. You were an unexpected surprise on the day as your name had not been linked to the bombing. They also colloborated that you saved a young lad and essentially spoiled the attack.' He stared at her before whirling away and whipping off his hat. He pushed his hand into his hair. 'But what in God's name happened, Esther? Why would you even contemplate getting involved in such a thing? People could have been killed. *You* could have been killed.'

'I know, and I'm sorry.' Tears burned her eyes that even through his anger and disappointment, he seemed concerned over her well-being. 'I needed to be a part of something real. I'd neglected my duties to the Cause and when I went back everything had changed and they'd decided to join the suffragettes. I was out of my depth but desperate to prove my fealty. What they had planned was wrong, but I couldn't dissuade them. Could not risk leaving them entirely to their own devices. If I was there, I could at least do something to prevent the explosion from happening.'

'And now?'

'Now?'

'What next, Esther?' His eyes burned with hurt and anger. 'Will you continue with the militants? I have a right to know.'

'No. That's over.' She shook her head, praying he

385

understood her. 'Not the fight, but I don't want to be a part of anything violent. It's not the way forward and I want to persuade others to see that, too.'

His gaze bored into hers, the passing traffic echoing around them as her heart pulsed in her ears.

Please, God, let him forgive me. Let him love me.

He stepped forward, before, second by excruciating second, his gaze softened as he looked over every inch of her face. He pulled her hard against his chest and covered her mouth with his. Roughly, possessively and, God help her, she returned his kiss with equal fervour, her fingers stealing into the hair at his collar. Their tongues tangled for supremacy as he ran his hands over her hips and waist, easing her closer until her breasts pressed painfully against his solid chest.

She pulled away to catch her breath.

He held her waist tightly, his gaze lingering at her mouth. 'My mother is dead.'

'Oh, Lawrence. I'm so sor — '

'That doesn't matter. What matters is the future. I have no idea what will happen to the estate until the Will is read. I may have to return to Culford again. I can't leave my sisters to clear up what could be a complicated and emotional legal battle. I want you to come with me. Do you think you'd be willing to do that? It won't be forever. Just until I know what to do best for Cornelia and Harriet. They're my family and I won't abandon them any more than I would Rose and Nathanial.' He brushed a curl from her cheek. 'Any more than I would you.'

She smiled, her heart full of love for this wonderful man. 'Of course. I'm sure Elizabeth would give me a little time off from the store if I begged for it. I want to be with you.'

His smile faltered. 'Your job . . .'

Dread seeped inside of her and Esther frowned. 'What of it?'

He inhaled a shaky breath. 'I went to Pennington's looking for you and spoke with Mrs Woolden.'

'And?' Esther's heart picked up speed. 'Lawrence, tell me.'

'She said Miss Pennington and Mr Carter have placed you on suspension until they hear your side of the story.'

'What?' Nausea rose bitter in Esther's throat and she pulled away from him, pressing a hand to her stomach. 'I have to speak with Elizabeth.' She stepped further away from him, tears burning her eyes. 'I need to see her. Right away.'

She moved to brush past him and he gripped her arm, his determined gaze boring into hers. 'And you will see her, but not like this. You need to calm yourself, show your strength and commitment lies with Pennington's above all else. If Miss Pennington sees you this way, she'll believe everything you want is about the Cause and little else.'

Esther ran her gaze over his face, her heart thundering. He was right. Elizabeth would think her devoid of her sensibilities.

She slumped her shoulders. 'Yes. I'll see her in the morning.'

'Good.' He shook his head and softly smiled. 'I love you and I want you, Esther, and if you want me, I'll do whatever it takes to make that happen.'

His words were like dewdrops on her tongue on the aridest of days. They were tiny lifts to her soul when she thought no one would ever earn her trust to allow her to love again. They were everything she wanted to hear and more, but still her fear showed in the hammering of her heart.

She cupped his jaw. 'And what of the children? I'm known to the police now and the fight will not stop. I won't expose Rose and Nathanial to — '

'To what?' He gripped her tighter. 'You have no criminal record and were instrumental in preventing an explosion. All Rose and Nathanial will learn is how hard a woman will fight for what should rightfully be hers. See what can be achieved when you join hands with others and show your passion and commitment for a future that knows no bounds. What it is for them to have a role model, both male and female, who stand side by side for what is right.'

Esther slipped her hand from his face, hope burning deep inside her, but still so very afraid. 'What are you saying?'

He brushed his lips over hers. 'I'm saying that you, too, must find peace with your past as you encouraged me to do. Marry me, Esther. Come and live with me. Help me raise Rose and Nathanial to be adults who aren't afraid to show their emotions and fight for everything they want in the world, for how they want this world to be. I can't do that alone. Not any more. But with you beside me . . . ' He smiled. 'Who knows what we can achieve? I want to be with you in this fight, Esther. I want my children to know they are worthy. That everyone is worthy.'

Happiness bubbled inside her, and she clasped his fingers and brought his arms around her, their hands joined at her back. 'Are you certain?'

'I've never been more certain of anything in my life.'

She leaned into him and pressed a long, lingering kiss to his mouth. 'Then, yes, Mr Culford. I'll marry

388

you.'

Esther smiled against his lips, knowing she had finally found her true home. Her true love. Her true life . . . with a new life waiting to be born.

Epilogue

Two months later . . .

Esther alighted from the beribboned carriage and stared at the façade of the town hall.

Nerves leapt in her stomach and her heart beat so fast she feared it would burst from her chest, but she had never been so happy.

She pressed her hand to her stomach. Lawrence was so absurdly exultant she carried his child that he'd insisted they marry as soon as possible. Tears pricked her eyes as she thought of the moment they had announced their intention to marry and that she was expecting. Not a single member of his household had held an iota of judgement about their premarital affair and Rose and Nathanial were elated about the upcoming arrival of a little brother or sister.

Even Elizabeth and Joseph, when they reinstated Esther to her position at Pennington's, had been overjoyed for her pregnancy. Elizabeth, who desperately wished to start a family of her own, had squeezed Esther tight wishing her all the happiness in the world. Even saying in jest that she'd had the foresight to bring Amelia forward as assistant head dresser in preparation for Esther leaving.

Aunt Mary came to stand beside her and ran her gaze over Esther from head to toe. 'You look lovely, my dear. I'm still not sure how you managed to win the hand of a gentleman like Mr Culford, but I applaud your tenacity.'

Even her aunt's disparagement couldn't affect her joy. Although initially dismayed by Esther's pregnancy, when she told her that Lawrence had proposed, Aunt Mary's congratulations had been positively gushing, followed by a speedy telephone call to her father and Viola. Apparently, it was all down to Aunt Mary that Esther and Lawrence had fallen in love.

Esther smiled. 'Tenacity is my middle name, Aunt. Surely, you know that much about me.' She glanced towards the grand double doors at the top of the stone steps. 'Shall we go in?'

Her aunt reached out and tucked a stray curl behind Esther's ear. 'You won't forget me, will you?' Tears glazed her eyes. 'I know I've been hard on you from time to time, but I would not have allowed you to stay with me if I had entirely agreed with your father's decision to send you away. You have a good heart and big ideas, but you're a wonderful woman all the same.' She sighed. 'I'm sure Viola will realise that, too, in time.'

Genuinely touched, Esther clasped her aunt's hand and brought it to her lips. 'Of course I won't forget you. Or everything you've done for me by welcoming me into your home. You are as much a part of my new family as I am. Lawrence has already said you're welcome at his home whenever you might wish it.'

Her aunt's smile slipped and her gaze sobered. '*Your* home, my dear. Not his home. Yours and Lawrence's home. Now that nasty postbox matter is over and your part in it exonerated, it's time to be happy and enjoy your new life.'

Esther smiled, offered her aunt her arm and they climbed the steps into the town hall.

The foyer windows were swathed in soft rose-pink

drapery and matching roses were displayed in intricate glass vases upon alabaster plinths. The wooden floor shone beneath the electric lamps and the sand-coloured walls were ornate with cornices carved with vines and cherubs. Everything looked beautiful and entirely fit for a wedding.

Childish chattering to the side of them turned Esther's head and her heart leapt to see Rose and Nathanial, her bridesmaid and page boy, standing with Cornelia.

Esther hurried towards them. 'You look adorable. Both of you.' She bent down and kissed each of their cheeks. 'So very pretty, Rose.' She turned to Nathanial. 'And I hardly recognised you. You look so grown-up.'

Nathanial grinned. 'I look the same as Daddy.'

Esther straightened and faced Cornelia. 'Is he here?'

She laughed. 'Of course. He's as jumpy as a dog running over hot coals, but he's most definitely here.' She turned to Esther's aunt. 'Hello again, Mary.'

Her aunt smiled. 'It's nice to see you again, Cornelia.'

Esther inhaled a shaky breath and looked at each face of her new family before walking to the side of the foyer to greet her other guests.

'Elizabeth.' Esther held out her hand, the other clutching her small posy. 'I'm so glad you're here.' The two friends embraced and kissed cheeks before Esther pulled back and looked past Elizabeth. 'Is Joseph not here?'

Elizabeth shook her head and squeezed Esther's hand. 'I've warned you how distracted he is these days. He was dressed and ready to come when his father called and said he might have found a lead on you know what.' The skin at her neck shifted as she swal-

392

lowed. 'I fear it will come to be worthless once again, which will only serve to send Joseph into another spiral of frustration.' She inhaled a deep breath and smiled. 'But today is not for lingering on my woes. Today is about you and Lawrence. Nothing else.'

Sympathy for her friend whispered through Esther but she forced a smile. 'All will be well. I'll see you after the ceremony.'

Esther walked a little further to the side and accepted kisses to her cheek from Charles, Helen and Mrs Jackson who dabbed at her eyes with a handkerchief. 'Thank you all so much for being here and making me so welcome in Mr Culford's home. Now Lawrence has inherited his mother's estate . . . ' She drew in a heavy breath. 'There may be some, or a lot, of upheaval ahead of us, but as long as we stick together, everything will be fine. I'm sure of it.'

They nodded and smiled, Charles clearly fighting to keep a stiff upper lip and Helen blushing with complete happiness.

Turning, Esther focused on the closed double doors ahead of her and tried not to linger on Lawrence's anger when he'd discovered his mother had every intention of leaving Culford Manor and the estate to him all along. The claims and threats she'd made on her deathbed were nothing more than a way of further tormenting Lawrence and his new life in Bath. Cornelia and Harriet were barely mentioned in her Will past the clothes, jewellery and trinkets they would inherit. Everything had been left to Lawrence with what felt like a last stab of spite.

Esther had no idea what he'd want to do next, but whatever he decided, she would be right alongside him, supporting and loving him. The only spate of satisfaction he'd had thus far was travelling to the Manor to sack his mother's long-time butler.

The guests all walked into the room ahead of her and once they were seated and the doors closed behind them, her stomach quivered. 'Well then, it's now or never.'

Her aunt offered her elbow and Father slipped her slightly trembling hand against her aunt's forearm, happy and ready to start her new life with the man and the family she loved deeply.

'Esther?'

She turned and looked towards the town hall's main entrance.

Her father walked alone as he slowly approached, uncertainty etched on his weathered features. Esther's heart quickened as he came ever closer, dressed in a suit the same dark blue as Lawrence's and Nathanial's . . . and wearing the same pink carnation in his buttonhole.

She swallowed. 'Papa. Did Lawrence invite — '

'Yes.' Her father's eyes glistened with what looked to be unshed tears as he stared into her eyes.

Esther's throat clogged with love for her soon-to-be husband. Her father looked so very old. So very, very sad.

'You look beautiful.' Her father stepped in front of her. 'So much like your mother at your age. Resplendent and happy.'

Esther hastily forced back her tears. 'Thank you, but — '

'Esther, please listen to me. I made a grave mistake sending you away how I did. I should've listened to you and your mother. Learned more about your passion for the Cause. I understand that now. I realise the fight you're prepared to take on and it's right and just that you do. I was ashamed of you for no reason and now it is I who is ashamed.' He lifted her hand to his chest. 'Let me start two years of apologies today, my love. Please. I want to meet Lawrence properly and share in your happiness.'

Hope rose inside her, but Esther could not deny the fear that swirled through her, too. She would not withstand his rejection a second time. Lawrence had made her stronger than she'd even made herself since she left home, but, if the ache in her heart was anything to hold measure by, her father still held the power to hurt her as deeply as he had before.

She slipped her hand from his and grasped her posy. 'And what of Viola? I don't believe she can be happy about you being here, telling me you want to be a part of my life again.'

'She'll come around.' His face turned sombre and his eyes burned with determination. 'She'll have to or leave. I won't be parted from you. Not any more. It's a sad day when a parent must learn from a child, but your aunt and Lawrence told me everything you've achieved and strive to achieve. I'm in awe of you and realise just how wrong I've been . . . about everything.'

She stared into his eyes, looking for signs of his insincerity, but only genuine grief and candour swirled in his hazel eyes. She inhaled a strengthening breath. 'One day at a time, Papa. No promises.'

His smile lit his eyes, making him immediately younger. 'One day at a time.'

He offered his arm.

Esther hesitated before pulling back her shoulders and sliding her hand into the crook of his arm. He clasped her fingers and they walked forwards, Aunt

Mary following silently behind.

As her father opened the doors, Esther caught her breath at the ivory and cream splendour encasing the room. Lush drapery fell at the windows, the gold chairs and their ivory upholstery glowing beneath the low lighting. Flowers decked the cornices and top table, sweetening the room with soft perfume.

She slowly continued to walk, her hand trembling on her father's arm and her heart swollen with love for the man waiting for her by the magistrate.

When Lawrence stepped in front of her, Esther's heart leapt with happiness. He looked so handsome, she could barely resist leaping into his arms in front of everyone and kissing him until she couldn't breathe.

As though reading her thoughts, he winked before turning to her father. Lawrence nodded and took her father's hand. 'It's a pleasure to see you here, Mr Stanbury.'

Her father nodded, his gaze intently studying Lawrence. 'I should have been with Esther all along.'

Lawrence nodded, released her father's hand and wrapped his fingers around Esther's. 'Yes, I believe you should.'

Turning, he led Esther to a spot in front of the magistrate.

The elderly man had kindly eyes and a soft smile as he lifted his hands. 'Welcome everyone. Can I ask that you remain standing throughout the ceremony and keep your congratulations until the very end? Thank you.' He faced Esther and Lawrence, his eyes cheerfully twinkling. 'Are we ready to begin?'

Esther lifted her gaze to Lawrence's and tightened her fingers. 'Yes. We're ready.'

Lawrence squeezed her fingers. 'Always.'

Acknowledgements

I'd like to first thank the wonderful team at Aria who helped to make writing this book another entirely enjoyable experience. Especially my wonderful editor, Caroline Ridding, who always provides such fabulous feedback, insight and patience with her revisions and suggestions.

Also, thank you to the Swindon and Wiltshire History Centre and the Bath Archive Centre for sharing some brilliant inspiration with their footage and stories from the real-life women who fought for the vote in and around the county of Wiltshire.

Finally, as always, much love and gratitude to my husband and two daughters who tolerate, with patience and grace, my changing moods throughout writing every novel. I love you.

We do hope that you have enjoyed
reading this large print book.

Did you know that all of our titles
are available for purchase?

We publish a wide range of high
quality large print books including:
Romances, Mysteries, Classics
General Fiction
Non Fiction and Westerns

Special interest titles available in
large print are:
The Little Oxford Dictionary
Music Book, Song Book
Hymn Book, Service Book

Also available from us courtesy of
Oxford University Press:
Young Readers' Dictionary
(large print edition)
Young Readers' Thesaurus
(large print edition)

For further information or a free
brochure, please contact us at:
Ulverscroft Large Print Books Ltd.,
The Green, Bradgate Road, Anstey,
Leicester, LE7 7FU, England.
Tel: (00 44) 0116 236 4325
Fax: (00 44) 0116 234 0205

A SHOP GIRL IN BATH

Rachel Brimble

Hardworking and whip-smart, Elizabeth Pennington is the rightful heir of Bath's premier department store — but her father, Edward Pennington, believes his daughter lacks the business acumen to run his empire. He is resolute that a man will succeed him.

Determined to break from her father's hold and prove she is worthy of inheriting Pennington's, Elizabeth forms an unlikely alliance with ambitious and charismatic master glove-maker Joseph Carter. They have the same goal: bring Pennington's into a new decade while embracing woman's equality and progression. But, despite their best intentions, it is almost impossible not to mix business and pleasure . . .

Can the two thwart Edward Pennington's plans for the store? Or will Edward prove himself an unshakeable force who will ultimately ruin both Elizabeth and Joseph?